SHERI S. TEPPER

The Family Tree

HarperCollins*Publishers*

Voyager
An Imprint of HarperCollins*Publishers*
77–85 Fulham Palace Road,
Hammersmith, London W6 8JB

The *Voyager* World Wide Web site address is
http://www.harpercollins.co.uk/voyager

This paperback edition 1998
1 3 5 7 9 8 6 4 2

First published in Great Britain by *Voyager* 1997

Copyright © Sheri S. Tepper 1997

The Author asserts the moral right to
be identified as the author of this work

ISBN 0 00 651016 5

Printed and bound in Great Britain by
Caledonian International Book Manufacturing Ltd, Glasgow

Dora Henry and the Weed

Midmorning, a Tuesday in July, Dora Henry went out the front door of Jared's place to get the paper that the paperboy had, as usual, dropped just over the picket fence. On her way back up the immaculately swept walk she glanced at the front stoop and stopped dead in her tracks. She quit breathing. The world became hot and still as she teetered dizzily like a tightrope walker, thinking it would be nice to faint, but as she'd never done that, she didn't really know how.

Instead, she squeezed her eyes shut and made herself breathe, one long slow breath while she counted ten: Grandma's prescription for fear or anger or anything unsettling, one long breath with eyes shut, not looking at whatever it was that was bothering. Sometimes it worked. When her eyes opened, however, it was still there: a sprig of green thrusting up from the hairline crack between the brick of the stoop and the wall of the house.

It's just a *weed*, she told herself, looking at her hands

with disbelief as they twitched and grasped toward the encroaching green. She heard her own voice yammering at her, "It can't stay there. It has no right to be there. Jared will be so angry...."

Jared would be so angry.

She clasped her hands together and tightened them until the knuckles turned white, biting her tongue until it hurt, willing herself to stop all this foolishness. "Weed," she said, invoking a label. It sounded right. Just a weed. Which, if Jared saw it, would bend him all out of shape, but that didn't mean she had to have a breakdown. Even if Jared had a major hissy, my Lord, she didn't need to go into some kind of hysterical spasm at the sight of a weed!

She cast a quick, almost furtive look around to see first if anyone had seen her having a cow on the sidewalk and then if any other strange growths might have sprouted during the night. Negative on both counts. The block was as vacant as a hatched egg, and Jared's place was as usual: three meticulously trimmed rose bushes still marched up each side of the front walk; one geometrically sheared blue spruce still held down the corner opposite the driveway; six junipers bulged smoothly and uniformly across the front of the house, neatly carved into convex mounds; two flowering crab apple trees (fruitless) still stood at attention, each on a hanky of lawn that had been weeded and clipped and fertilized until it looked like a square of Astroturf.

She didn't need to look at the rest of it; she knew it by heart. The fences on either side and across the front were as pristine as when freshly painted. The driveway to the garage was smooth, gray concrete, as unstained as when newly laid. Out behind the garage, the trash cans were doing close order drill, each one precisely helmeted. The arbor covering the patio was grown with tightly clipped Boston ivy, and the narrow strip between garage and patio was planted with a single row of absolutely uniform hostas, which, so Jared said, were the least troublesome of shade-tolerant ground covers.

The Tree that cast the shade belonged to the people next door south, or, since it was on the far property line, maybe the people beyond them. It was huge and old with limbs like buttresses. Each fall it turned flaming red and scattered the whole block with glittering confetti, an autumnal celebration that went on for weeks while Jared fumed and snarled. He couldn't wait until the last leaves came down so he could vacuum them up, restoring his place to its usual purity. Once Jared had arranged things to his satisfaction, he did not tolerate alterations.

Dora hadn't known that, not at first. Under the assumption—quite wrong, as it turned out—that Jared's place was now "their" place, she had suggested some pansies by the back steps, a lavender plant, maybe, and some tulip bulbs under the hostas. Even some violets along the edges.

"They make a mess," Jared told her. "Tulip foliage dies and turns an ugly yellow. Pansies aren't hardy. The bloom stalks on lavender drop their buds. Violets seed themselves." His tone of voice made it clear that seeding oneself was a perversion.

Still thinking she was allowed a voice in the matter, she had argued, "Hostas have bloom stalks."

"Not for long," he'd crowed. Which was true, of course. The minute one showed, he nipped it off. All Jared wanted to see was those nice, shiny, evenly spread green leaves. Every week, he used the carwasher gadget on them, floods of soapy water to get rid of the dust. Even the roses out front were allowed their rare blooms only for a day or two. First sign of blowsiness, first sign a petal might drop, off they came. Jared had always been neat, said his mother. No trouble bringing Jared up, not a bit.

Dora sometimes entertained brief visions of the baby Jared sitting in his crib, neatly organizing his Pampers, folding his blankets, plumping his little pillow. Or the schoolboy Jared, sharpening his pencils and laying his homework out with a ruler, even with the edge of his desk.

"I wasn't at all like that," Jared laughed, shaking his long, high-domed head in pretend modesty. Varnish-haired Jared, high-gloss Jared. "For heaven's sake, Dora, what an idea!"

"I know." She smiled her meaningless smile, one of several conciliatory expressions she had adopted during their two years together. "It's just, your mother makes you sound like such a . . . perfect child." She had been going to say, "unnatural," but had caught herself in time.

"Oh, no," he said comfortably. "I had my share of scrapes. I had friends down the street, the Dionne boys. We used to get into trouble regularly. I don't think Momma ever knew. At least, *I* never told her." And he laughed again, just one of the boys, patting Dora's shoulder. He often patted Dora's shoulder in an under-standing way, though that was all he patted. Lately she caught herself flinching even from that casual touch.

"Jared did hang around those Dionne boys," Jared's momma sniffed, when queried. "Ragamuffins. No more civilized than young billy goats! And that slut of a girl. And that mother! No better than she should be. Well, I soon put an end to that!"

Jared's momma, rigid with rectitude, whose very clothes seemed carved from some durable material, ran the boardinghouse two blocks down, on the corner facing the avenue. It was a huge, vaguely Queen Anne hulk that had started as a hotel in the twenties. When Dora had sold the farm after Grandma's death, she had taken a room in the boardinghouse, meaning it to be only tem-porary, while she sorted things out. She'd met Jared, instead, and things never had gotten sorted out.

"Where are they now?" Dora asked Jared's mother. "The Dionnes?"

"Who knows," said Momma, mouth shutting like a trap. "Who cares."

"Where did they live?" Dora asked Jared.

"The Dionnes? Oh, a couple of houses down from here. They weren't here long." He laughed. "We have a certain standard in this neighborhood, and Vorn Dionne wasn't interested in living up to it.''

"Standard?" she asked, doubtfully.

"You know. Keep your car put away and the garage door shut, keep your lawn mowed, no weeds, no burning trash, garbage in containers with tops. Just good neighborly behavior. Old Vorn came from a more individualistic time.''

"It's an odd name. He sounds like a character.''

"Probably a family name. But the real character was the mother. I'm afraid she and Momma got into it a time or two.''

"Mother? Not wife?''

Jared's face went blank. "Wife? Vorn didn't have a wife, at least not when I knew them. I suppose he had had a wife, at one time. He had four boys. No, I mean the girl's mother.'' His tone said, "This is my last word on this subject.''

Dora persisted. "Two doors down doesn't look big enough for that size family.''

Jared turned away, busying himself. Complacent as a cockroach, Jared. Ubiquitous about the house, but hard to pin down. He said stiffly, "That house is new. The Dionne house was a big old thing. It burned down.''

"That's why they moved?''

He spoke in the oh-so-patient tone he used when he lost all patience with her. "I think it burned around the time they moved. They moved because they didn't like the neighborhood. They were only here long enough for everyone concerned to know they'd be better off somewhere else. And that's enough about them, Dora!'' And off he scuttled, avoiding any further discussion.

It hardly seemed the Dionnes had been around long enough for Jared to get into scrapes with them, but what did she know. Dora came to herself with a start, surprised to find herself still out in front of the house, still lollygagging, still staring at the weed. It looked very determined for such a feathery little thing, almost as though it knew it had a fight on its hands. She thought maybe she should pull it up herself, so Jared wouldn't see it, but as she moved onto the stoop, she heard the phone ringing, and she forgot about the weed in favor of getting herself into the house before it stopped. Then, after all that hurry, it was a wrong number.

She forgot about the weed, but when Jared's car pool dropped him off that evening, he came up the front walk and saw the weed the minute he wiped his feet on the mat. He had it out in an instant, before he even opened the door.

"Little devil had quite a root on it," he snarled, displaying his triumph.

Dora took it from him, laying it across the palm of her hand. Poor pathetic thing. One feathery sprig of green, and then that long, pale shoot, much like the pallid shoots that bindweeds spring from. Pull them up by the quarter mile, and all you'd get is a long white link with a smooth end where it had broken cleanly from the real root, the way-down root, the root from hell. Then, when you turned your back, up it would come again, squirming and proliferating, covering itself with those innocent little blooms while it strangled everything but itself. She opened her mouth to tell Jared, but then decided not to. Root or not, the thing was out and he wouldn't care in the least about Dora's experience with bindweed.

Time was she'd spent hours and hours on her hands and knees, pulling out mallow and bull heads and bindweed from Grandma's garden because Grandma wouldn't use spray.

"You can't kill bindweed this way, Grandma!" That'd been her plea from the time she was thirteen until she was almost grown.

"Not tryin' to kill it," the old woman said, grinning on one side, the way she did (like a fox, said Grandpa). "Just tryin' to keep it in its place, teach it some manners."

Dora doubted very much that the bindweed learned anything, including manners. Grandma should have seen

Jared's place. Jared's place was so mannerly it almost begged your pardon. Jared's place was cowed.

"How come you always say 'Jared's place,' " her friend Loulee asked her. "You never say 'home.' You always say 'Jared's place.' "

"Well, because it is," Dora answered. "He had it before he ever met me, and he decides what goes in it, and I sort of . . . just live there." As in another boardinghouse, sort of, except in this one she cooked and did laundry for her keep.

"How come you two don't have kids?"

"I don't know," Dora had answered in a genial voice, lying through her teeth. "Not everybody has children, you know. With all this overpopulation, not having is probably better anyhow."

"Oh, so it's ethical with you."

"No." She laughed, showing how unimportant the subject was. "I just pretend it is when people get nosy. Children just never happened."

Loulee didn't take offense, unfortunately. "Dora, there are such things as doctors."

"I know." She frowned, then, distinctly uncomfortable, making herself say lightly, "I've got plenty of time, Loulee. Give it a rest."

Loulee never knew when to quit. "Jared got plenty of time, too?"

Jared was somewhat older than Dora, and though his age might be a factor, the real reason they didn't have children was that they had never had sex. Dora admitted to being an innocent in such matters, from an experiential point of view, but after eight brothers and sisters, she certainly knew where babies came from. On their wedding night, Jared had indicated that the front upstairs bedroom was to be hers, saying casually that he didn't care for physical sorts of things, and at his age, those sorts of things weren't necessary. Which was one way of putting it.

The real question in Dora's mind had less to do with children than with why she had stayed married to Jared when it would have been perfectly simple at that point, or at any time since, to get an annulment. Was she, herself, interested in that sort of thing? Had she realized subconsciously that Jared wasn't? Had she married him for that reason? She honestly couldn't say. During the first thirty-three years of her life she couldn't recall that she had ever had time to worry about it. There had been some men she'd thought were pleasant enough, but never any trumpets blowing. It might have been different if she'd been hungry for children, but being the eldest of nine almost guarantees a person won't be hungry for children. Especially remembering a mama like Dora's mama, who actively loved getting pregnant, who indolently loved being pregnant, who had no trouble producing them one right after the other, but wasn't up to taking care of them once they were born.

From the time Dora was five she'd been changing didies and warming bottles and dandling little howlers so they'd stop howling. She could handle it without breaking a sweat, if and when, but it wasn't something she was exactly pining for. She figured she'd already done her duty by the human race.

"Why did you marry Jared?" Loulee had asked. "Forgive me being real blunt, but you don't seem to care that much for him."

Why had she married Jared? "I grew up in a big family, and when my grandmother died and the last of the kids left home, I missed having people around. . . ."

That sounded logical enough. It might even be true. Or, she might have married him on the presumption that marriage would let her escape from herself. On the farm, she'd been too busy to worry about herself, but once the farm was gone, there was too much time alone, time to replay her life. The chances she'd missed, or muffed. The mistakes she'd made. The college she'd had a chance to go to if she'd been able to leave the kids dependent entirely on Grandma and Grandpa, which she felt wouldn't have been right. The plum of a job she'd turned down because she'd have had to move away. So, instead, when Michael graduated high school back in 1984, when it was clear all the brothers and sisters were going to grow up and have lives of their own, she'd gone to the police academy, right here in town, where she could work but still live on the farm and help out.

None of which she said as she wound up her explanation to Loulee, not that she owed Loulee an explanation. "Besides, Jared is . . . well, he's predictable. I feel like I always know what he's going to do next." God knows that was true.

"How exciting." Loulee flared a nostril.

Dora forced another sprinkle of light laughter. "My job is excitement enough. It keeps me busy."

"Well, of course it does," said Loulee. "I just can't imagine how you became a cop, though. You don't seem the type. Not at all."

"What type am I?"

"Oh, I don't know. You look sort of studious to me. Librarian, maybe, you read so much. Or astronomer, because you're a stargazer." She giggled. "But not a cop!"

Dora knew well enough how she became a cop. Settling things among eight siblings gave you a very good foundation for working with people, and finding out who was really to blame was itself a course in investigating crime. Most importantly, being a cop meant having rules for everything. If you studied the book and did it by the book, you had nothing to blame yourself for. Once you knew the rules, you could relax and be yourself. You didn't have to second-guess yourself.

"I like it," she said.

"Well, of course, dear, or you wouldn't do it," said Loulee. "And you've got plenty of time to have a family, don't you? You're not even thirty-five yet."

She was now. Since yesterday, a fact which everyone seemed to have overlooked, including Jared. Thirty-five years old, thirteen years on the job. Not that she'd ever made a big fuss over her birthday. At home, they'd had

three birthday parties a year. One on the fourth of July
for the three born in May, June and July; one on Hal-
loween for the four September through December kids;
and one on Valentine's day for the January and March
kids. Three sets of cakes and parties was all Dora and
Grandma had been able to manage.

The first of the younger kids, which is what Dora
always called the other eight, had been born when Dora
was five. That was Michael, and he'd been a howler,
and Mama hadn't felt well enough to walk him or rock
him or dandle him, and Daddy had to have his sleep, or,
so he said, he couldn't get anything done the next day
(not that he got anything done anyhow), so Dora had
done most of the baby tending. All the summer after he
was born, and most of the year after that, with only time
out for school.

"Take care of the baby, Dora. You're his big sister.
That's why babies have big sisters."

She remembered Daddy's voice saying that in his
slightly peevish voice. She recalled Little Dora feeling
the weight of those words, more burdensome than the
weight of Michael in her arms. He was a big baby, hard
for her to hold. It was hard becoming big sister. She had
to become an entirely different person.

Sometimes now, when the day had been long and she
lay drowsily in her bed with everything quiet, she remembered Little Dora as she might remember a story
she had heard. A little girl who had heard ecstatic music
in her head. A little girl whose every experience was
accompanied by complicated and fantastic sound: the
thunder of deep drums, the bray of trumpets or the so-
norous clamor of horns. In that child's remembered life
the sun rose to sensuous violins, noons were a stutter of
brass, evenings waned in wandering oboe melodies,
night faded into plush purple violas and bassoons. Every
Little Dora day had been joyous with music.

Of course, music was appropriate in paradise. She
hadn't called it paradise at the time; she hadn't called it
anything, it was simply her world. When she walked out

the front door of the house, she entered a forest of trees, was surrounded by flocks of birds, met all kinds of animals that she talked with, had conversations with. It was as vivid in her mind as if it had been yesterday.

Until Michael. From the moment Daddy called her "big sister," the music stopped and other living things became sparse and occasional. The forest became one gaunt tree out back by the ash pit. The flock of birds became one fat crow perched on the fence pecking at something dead held in his talons. The beasts were only the neighbor's cat, the grocery man's dog.

She missed the music most, for it stopped so suddenly she thought she had gone deaf, wished she had gone deaf so she couldn't hear Michael's fretful howling and Mama's petulant "Can't you quiet that baby?" and Daddy's "For heaven's sake, feed that child, Dora, you know where the bottle is." Michael didn't tolerate the formula very well. None of them ever tolerated the formula very well. Mama said she had tried to nurse Dora, but she didn't feel well enough, and besides, she didn't like it, all that chewing at her, so she wouldn't try with Michael.

There hadn't been another baby until Dora was seven—that was Kathleen—but after that it was like Mama finally got the hang of it, and there'd been Margaret, and Mark and Luke and Millicent for Dora to be big sister to. Then when Mama got pregnant with Polly—Polly was number eight—Grandma arrived out of nowhere like a cyclone of gray hair and starched skirts. She spun around, looking here, looking there, then took thirteen-year-old Dora by the hand and said enough was enough, what was Mama trying to do? Set a new record?

And Mama just smiled that slow way she had and said she didn't think using anything was nice. That Daddy wouldn't like it if she used anything.

"Well, the two of you *have* been using something! You've been using Dora!" said Grandma. "Look at her! She looks like a dishrag! This child deserves a child-

hood.'' And that was it, because Grandma took Dora
with her when she went back to her own house in Denver, and it was like going to heaven, even with all the
weeding.

Meantime, back at home in Omaha, everything went
from pillar to post, and two years after Jimbo was born
Mama died from something perfectly preventable, except they hadn't bothered to prevent, and then Daddy
fell apart, and Grandma asked him what the hell he expected, a medal?

That's when the younger kids had come to Grandma's
house, too. Michael was eleven, and Jimbo was only
two. And from then on it was Grandma and Grandpa
and Dora and the kids, then after Grandpa died,
Grandma and Dora and the kids, and finally just Dora
and the three left at home. Daddy was never part of the
equation.

''It hurts to say it about my own, but he always has
been useless,'' said Grandma. ''Takes after my dad.
Why my mother married that man, I'll never know.
Nothing in his head but maybe this, maybe that. Sit there
for half an hour looking at his shoes, wondering which
one to put on first! Both my brothers were just like him.
I did my best to compensate, Dora, I swear to God. I
picked a man with some gumption to him, but it seems
I carried the strain, like a curse in the blood. Your daddy
showed the tendency by the time he was two. Most kids,
they'll holler, they'll reach for things, but not your
daddy. Too much trouble. He always did what was least
trouble. I thought he'd never learn to walk; he couldn't
decide to stand up. And school, Lord, he'd do just what
he was told and not a bit more. If the teacher said pick
a topic for a paper, he was a goner. The only thing I
ever saw him hot and bothered over was your mama,
and I guess it was less trouble for him to marry her than
to say no to her mama, and God knows without her
supporting you all these years, you'd all have starved.''

She frowned, shaking her head, pinching her lips together.

"You never had any other kids, Grandma?"

"Nope. Not after I saw how your daddy had inherited the diddle gene. Diddle here, diddle there, never get anything done. The world's got enough fool diddlers. Doesn't need any more."

Grandma was right about Daddy. He was ineffectual. Dora would say we need shoes for Michael, he's got holes all the way through the sole, we have to have lunch money, school says we have to get immunizations; and Daddy would say, sure, have to pick those up, have to get some change, have to plan a visit to the doctor. Then nothing happened. Nobody ever picked up, nobody ever got, nobody ever remembered the plan. They were always running out of diapers, running out of milk, forgetting to pay the gas bill. There were always notes coming home from school—this child doesn't do his homework, this child needs polio vaccine, this child, this child . . .

Daddy and Mama just couldn't get around to doing anything on purpose. The two of them were like leaves before the wind, just skittering along from bedtime to bedtime until they wore out or there was nowhere else to blow. The diddle gene finally killed Daddy when he went to bed with the gas heater on even though he knew it didn't work right. Have to see to that, he'd said. Have to see to that, someday, sometime, when I get around to it.

Which was maybe reason enough right there for Dora to have married Jared. Jared never went anywhere or did anything without planning it right down to the molecular level. There was something almost inhumanly rigorous about Jared. With him, you always knew right where you stood.

Grandpa'd been gone about eight years: stroke. Grandma'd died four years ago: heart. Jimbo'd been only sixteen. Polly was seventeen, ready to start college on a full scholarship. Milly was eighteen, not starting anything, just moping around. Grandma left the house to the girls, and Dora had kept the household together for a year, until the last three had gone: Milly to a cult, Polly to college, Jimbo off God-knows-where.

The other kids were spread all over the map now, and except for Milly and maybe Jimbo, they'd escaped the worst of the family curse. Michael and Margaret had married, Kathleen had a job in advertising, Mark and Luke had joined the army. They were going to make a career of it and never get married. So they said.

Milly had inherited the diddle gene, and a cult was easier than thinking, and drugging was easier yet. She'd died of a drug overdose, though Dora had told the others it had been meningitis. Polly had graduated from college the past June with a degree in botany. She'd always been a little soldier, now she wanted to get a graduate degree.

And the baby, Jimbo . . . well, God knows what would become of Jimbo. Every now and then he lit on Dora's doorstep, like a confused migratory bird, not sure whether he was coming or going. He never stayed long, though. Jared didn't look kindly on people like Jimbo. Jared didn't look kindly, period.

Maybe seven out of nine wasn't that bad. In a family with the diddle gene, seven out of nine was damn near a miracle. Dora didn't call it the diddle gene now, of course. She knew the curse for what it was. Chronic depression, something you could be born with, something you couldn't do much about, something you passed from parent to child, begetting misery and suicides and endless dark days of hopelessness and despair. Dora had seen it, firsthand, and why would she want more babies to pass it on to? After all the years, she still missed the music. . . .

"Did you ever hear music in your head, Grandma?"

"Like a tune, child?"

"No. Like a huge orchestra, with all the instruments, and playing the most marvelous music. . . ." She had looked up to find tears in Grandma's eyes. "Grandma?"

"Just remembering, child. Oh, yes. I remember the music. The horns of elfland, that's what it was."

"Elfland?"

"That's what Tennyson called it. Oh, well, child. I've never heard it since I was . . . maybe ten. It's a childhood thing, I think. Once we're grown, all we can hear are what the poet described: the echoes, dying."

Dora shook herself. Enough. Here she was, rolling around in the surf again, letting the undertow take hold of her. Currents of memory. Sadnesses that could turn you upside down, rubbing your face in the sands of what-if. Get up on your hind legs, as Grandma used to say, and put one foot in front of the other!

She had three days off, and she wanted to wash all the blinds and take the drapes to be cleaned. They were such heavy fabric, stiff as a board. Dora would have preferred light curtains that stirred in the wind, graceful fabric, like the skirts of dancers, but Jared preferred things that remained rigidly in place, always the same. If he hadn't known the neighbors would laugh at him, he'd have bought plastic rose bushes and plastic hostas, unfading, unchanging, ungrowing.

She caught herself grinning ruefully. If he hadn't known the neighbors would laugh, he'd have bought himself a plastic wife.

Wednesday morning she went out to get the paper, and when she came back to the door, there was the weed again. This time there was no shock. The sight of the unfolding green was almost expected. That smooth root had been the clue. Jared hadn't even touched the way-down root; it was still there, still pushing up.

"That was fast," she commented, leaning against the door. "You'll duck down behind the stoop if you know what's good for you. Jared'll just pull you out again." He'd have to do it himself. She wasn't going to help him.

She was just letting herself through the front door when the phone rang, and it was her partner, Phil Dermont, asking her about some case notes.

"I've got them here, Phil. What's the problem?"

He couldn't read his notes. What was the name of the

woman who'd seen that stabbing victim just before he was killed?

"That's Manconi's case. Did he come up with something new on that?"

"Nah," he muttered. "I'm just cleaning up the reports."

She and Phil had done some interviews for Manconi when his partner had been out sick, but the reports should have been done months ago! On a scale of one to ten, however, Phil's clerical and note-taking skills were a minus six. Phil sometimes couldn't decipher his notes five minutes after he took them!

She harrumphed and put the phone down while she went to dig out her notebooks from her desk. The notes were two books back. The victim had been a doctor, a researcher of some kind. He'd been working late at the medical center; he'd gone down to the parking lot to get his car; somebody had killed him, for no apparent reason. The witness's name was Fentris, Gerry. She'd seen the victim leaving the building; her hearing was good, she'd heard the guy screaming and yelling at someone to get away and leave him alone. As Dora remembered, he wasn't robbed; his car wasn't stolen; his family was close; according to his colleagues, he had no enemies. He was just a clean-looking, small, kind of nerdy guy that somebody had killed, and they hadn't a clue as to why.

She read the notes to Phil, waiting while he tapped them into the computer. Actually, the two of them made a pretty good team because she could do what he hated, like type and spell and put words together, and he didn't mind doing stuff Dora hated, like changing tires if they had a flat or dealing with drunks.

Jared came in the back door that night, so he didn't see the weed. Next morning, when Dora stepped out to get the mail before leaving for work, it had grown a foot. The coiled green had uncurled into lacy fronds of leaflets, multiple pairs of them along wiry stems. The top of each frond swayed in the light breeze as though it was nodding to her.

"Good morning," she said, bowing a little. It was what Little Dora had done, talking to plants and trees and stray dogs. Even when they quit talking back, she'd kept up the habit. It embarrassed her when she got caught at it, so she'd mostly stopped whenever people were around. Phil was okay about it. He didn't mind her talking to animals or pigeons or flower gardens. He just thought she was nuts, but then a lot of cops were, one way or another.

The mailbox held a card from Jimbo. He'd found a job in California, running a cultivator in fruit orchards, lots of other stuff needed doing, so it could be permanent. He was teaching himself to play guitar. Happy Birthday. Good Lord, he sounded almost grown up. Maybe there was hope, after all!

Kathleen had also remembered her birthday with a funny card covered with dolphins. An all-porpoise birthday card. And there was a letter from Polly, saying she'd be dropping in on Dora Friday for a birthday visit, a couple of days, maybe, on her way to visit friends in Seattle. Dora had always shared the July Fourth birthday cake with Polly and Jimbo, so of course the two of them had remembered her birthday. Dora wished Polly had given her some notice of the impending visit. Jared hated surprises.

Dora leaned against the door jamb, rereading Polly's note while the weed went on flirting its tendrils in the wind. "My sister's coming," she told it. "She's a botanist. She'll understand you better than Jared will. If you want to be around to meet her, better duck. Jared won't let this go on."

As Jared didn't. The minute he drove in that night, he saw the weed. He went on into the garage with a grim look on his face and came out a few minutes later with the sprayer. Dora, who had seen him from the kitchen, went to the living room window to watch him drenching the weed in weed killer. Then he stood there, mouth working, white in the face, his eyes bulged out like some actor in a Kabuki drama, as though waiting for it to cough or utter last words or something. Finally he stomped back into the garage and the door went down.

Dora went back to her salad making in the kitchen, shredding carrots and cabbage for slaw, not allowing herself to react to what she'd just seen. From Jared's facial expression you'd think he'd been slaying a monster that had eaten his family.

Jared slammed into the kitchen, banging the door behind him. "That damn weed came back." He scowled his way past her. She heard water running, doors jerked open and slammed closed. The banging and hammering diminished, slowly, and he had a less unpleasant expression on his face when he came back to the kitchen. They always ate in the kitchen unless they had "company," that is, Jared's mother. Jared didn't like to mess up the dining room unless they had to.

"Supper ready?" he asked from the door. He always asked if supper was ready. Even when it was on the table, he asked, as though what was on the table might be leftovers from some other meal she had served to someone else.

"Just dishing up," she said, setting the bowl of slaw on the table. "Did you have a good day?"

"As good as could be expected," he said, plopping himself down in the chair and reaching for the bread and butter. It was what he always said. Never good. Never bad. Just as good as could be expected. She'd promised herself she wouldn't ask him, but she always forgot and the question popped out. As though he'd programmed her.

Maybe he had. Here she was, getting the meat loaf out of the oven, dishing up the attendant mushy potatoes and carrots, taking the lid off the saucepan of over-cooked green beans, foods she had never prepared before she married Jared. The too-sweet slaw was on the table with the required white bread and the real butter and the grape jelly. Jared looked it over, slowly, as though tallying each item, then helped himself and fell to. It was a typical Jared meal, all prepared in accordance with the rules for "feeding a working man," that had been communicated to Dora by Jared's mother. Meals were uniformly dull, uniformly high in calories and fat, and Jared didn't gain an ounce.

Dora took a helping of slaw, a small slice of meat loaf, and some carrots.

"You need more food than that," he said disapprovingly.

"I really don't, Jared. I've gained five pounds the last couple of months."

"Ummm. Not enough exercise."

"Probably." Though how she could get more exercise without disrupting Jared's mealtime schedule was a problem.

"Tastes good," said Jared, around a mouthful of meat loaf. "Mom's recipe?"

"Of course," said Dora. Personally, she thought the meat loaf tasted of bread crumbs and steak sauce, but not at all of meat. If she substituted soy-something or sawdust for the meat, the taste would be the same, a flavor she identified as vague tomato. But then, Jared liked vague tomato. He liked vegetables boiled into submission. He liked things deep fried or chicken fried or barbecued. He liked his eggs hard boiled or scrambled or fried crisp in bacon grease, with the yolks broken so they didn't run at all. Salad dressing was okay, but not mayonnaise. She couldn't imagine why he didn't gain weight. All the exercise he got most of the year was walking from the car to his office.

Of course, mental activity could burn up the calories, and Jared probably did a lot of that at Pacific-Alaskan. Jared worked in the research and development department, thinking up more ways to use wood pulp, or designing machines to cut down and chew up trees more easily. Jared not only designed the machines, but he made the models. Jared probably made quite a good salary, too. Though Dora had never been told, or asked, about Jared's financial position, she knew he could have lived a lot more luxuriously if he wanted to. A few times he'd mentioned a trip one of his colleagues was taking, or an event he'd like to see, but when she'd suggested he go ahead and do it, he'd always said no, he'd rather spend his money on tools he needed, on expensive equipment he couldn't do without. He was always building weird machines in the basement, but what they were for, God only knew, because Jared never said.

She waited until his eating had slowed. "My sister Polly wrote me," she said in a casual voice. "She's dropping in tomorrow for a couple of days."

He put his fork down and scowled. "Couple of days? Well, thank you for the notice!"

"I just got the letter this morning, Jared. If you don't feel like company, I can put her up in a motel."

"I don't feel like company, but you won't put her up in a motel. She's family." His mouth clamped into a thin, dissatisfied line, meaning she wasn't his family, no member of whom would ever, ever arrive without at least six months' notice. Come to think of it, Jared and Momma were all there were of Jared's family, so how the hell would he know how families acted!

She had the sop ready to throw him when he growled. "I thought I'd take her out to dinner tomorrow, just us sisters, for girl talk."

His brow cleared at this. "Fine. Okay. I'll eat with Momma." Jared hated girl talk. Come to that, Jared hated talk. And he would eat with Momma, just as he always did when Dora got home too late to fix supper. Dora had known he would.

"If you got the mail this morning, you probably saw that weed," said Jared. If she had seen it, his tone implied, she should have done something about it.

She regarded her plate in silence for a moment. "I'm sorry, Jared. I was reading Polly's letter, and I guess I didn't notice."

He fixed her with a suspicious glare. "You had to notice. The damn thing was three feet high!"

She opened her eyes very wide, giving him the willing but stupid look, another expression perfected since their marriage. "Was it really? My gracious. What do you suppose it was?"

He was successfully sidetracked by the look and the tone. He nodded. "It was some kind of vine. I sprayed it with weed killer. Enough to kill an elephant. That ought to follow it down underground and finish off the root." He came close to smacking his lips at the idea.

"I'm sure it will." Poor weed. Didn't have a chance. Why hadn't it picked somewhere other than Jared's place?

"Maybe it's a shoot from that damned tree," he muttered. "The roots are coming up under the garage! They're making huge cracks in the floor! I'm going to have to have it jackhammered out and relaid."

She didn't reply. Jared wouldn't expect her to. After all, construction was men's business, just as doing the supper dishes was women's. He didn't expect her to lay concrete; she shouldn't expect him to wash dishes. While she washed and put away, Jared went down to the basement and moved stuff around in his equipment room. Dora never went down there. She'd looked in, once, when they'd first been married, but Jared made it clear he'd do the cleaning down there himself, he'd prefer she just leave it alone. So, hell, she left it alone. Walls hung with glittering sets of blades and sockets and benches stacked with complicated contraptions didn't exactly make her salivate.

Dora was getting ready for work the following morning when she heard Jared yelling and ran to see what the matter was. He was standing on the stoop, his face pale and rigid with anger.

"Damn, stupid chemicals, damn directions were all wrong, they'll pay for this. . . ."

The rosebushes down either side of the front walk had turned a seared, ashen hue, and most of the leaves had dropped. The little round evergreens on either side of the stoop were a sick yellow. Most of the leaves had fallen from the crab apple trees, too. The kill was so total that it looked as though someone had purposely sprayed everything with acid. Only the hankies of lawn remained untouched, green as ever, like plastic.

The weed was still there.

"Maybe the wind was blowing, Jared. The mist blew over onto the other plants . . ."

He snarled, his teeth showing. "Don't be stupider than usual, Dora. There wasn't any wind. Not a breath. I wouldn't have sprayed it if there'd been any breeze at all." He reached for the offending weed, grasping it firmly, only to yelp in pain and drop it. "Damn thing has thorns!"

He brushed past her, almost knocking her down on his way to the first aid kit in the bathroom.

Dora stood rigid, suddenly burning with anger. "Watch out," Dora snarled to the weed. "He'll take the ax to you next. And then he'll probably start on me."

The leaf tips stirred, turning toward her. She looked up, startled, seeing nothing else moving. There was no wind. Still the leaf tips turned, following her until she shut the door behind her and leaned against it, giggling helplessly. She was living in Weirdsville. The world was off its pivot, and old Jared was really shaken up, and here was Dora, doing nothing about any of it except giggle. It had been a long time since she had felt any emotion over Jared, and if she'd had to guess, she wouldn't have guessed she could feel this half-hysterical disgust.

Jared stomped out of the bathroom, his hand bandaged, almost yelling at her, "Since you seem to be unable to do anything around here, I'll take care of the damn thing this evening. You said you were going out with your sister. How late will you be?"

She actually opened her mouth to scream back at him, then clashed her mental gears and managed to keep her voice utterly neutral. "Not late. We'll go to the Greek restaurant at the mall. We'll probably walk over, it's so close."

He turned on his heel and left, not saying good-bye, leaving her to let the rage seep away into her customary calm. For a moment there, she had almost told Jared what she really thought. That wouldn't do. She wasn't quite sure why it wouldn't do, but she was certain that telling Jared anything about how she felt was a very bad idea. It was a lesson you learned, being a cop. Telling people what you really think is often a very bad idea indeed. As Grandma used to say, sensible people pour oil on troubled waters, not nitroglycerine.

She and Polly did walk to the restaurant, leaving before Jared got home. They went out the front, where Dora explained the mostly dead landscaping and pointed out the weed, taller than ever. Polly looked at the weed with a good deal of interest and agreed that no matter what Jared had said, he had to have sprayed the trees and bushes to kill them like that.

The avenue was only a block and a half away, and the mall was only six long blocks west. It had cooled off quite a bit and they strolled, enjoying the evening, stopping to buy some stockings for Polly, a blouse for Dora. They spent twenty minutes looking at shoes before going on to the Athena, where they had egg lemon soup and stuffed grape leaves and moussaka loaded with cheese. They laughed a lot, and drank wine and cried a little over old memories.

"Milly killed herself, didn't she?" Polly asked, as they were gathering up their purses and shopping bags.

Dora's mouth dropped open. "I told you . . ."

"I know what you told us. But she did, didn't she?"

Dora sat back down. "Yes. I don't think she meant to, but she did. You knew she was on drugs?"

"We were only a year apart, Dory. When Grandma died, you were up to your neck being a cop all day and taking care of the house and us all night. Sure, I knew she was on drugs. I used to beg her to stop, but she said it made everything easier. It didn't, really. It just made everything disappear."

"You should have told me, Pol."

"You had a lot on your plate. I figured you'd done enough, all those years, and then after Gran died, staying there to take care of Milly and Jimbo and me."

Dora fretted. Polly should have told her. Maybe . . . if she'd known. Oh, if she'd known, what? Her mind squeezed tight, the way it sometimes did, shutting grief away. Shutting the pain out, refusing to let the emotions strangle her, making herself go on. Not unscathed, but capable.

"That's what the good Lord gave us repression for," Grandma had often said. "So we can put the grief and anger dogs in their kennels and go on with our lives. If we let the dogs run, they'll follow the trail until they drag us straight to destruction."

"Whenever I remember Milly, I think maybe some people are survivors and some aren't," Dora commented, holding herself very still. "Seeing the things I do every day, I think sometimes it's better if we just let the nonsurvivors go. They don't enjoy life. They suffer through it, being angry all the time, hating people, grieving over things, and everyone who loves them suffers right along. They're like a fish out of water, flapping the whole time, from this disaster to that disaster, and we flap with them, feeling the air burning our gills, getting drier and drier with the pain. Better if we let them go."

Polly frowned. "Oh, that's hard, Dory."

She nodded solemnly, spoke through her teeth. "I know it is, Pol. It's just a feeling I get. I know it doesn't sound nice, but if they were animals, suffering that way, we'd put them out of their misery."

"You may be right. Milly was never happy. She was like Daddy, from what Grandma used to say." Polly looked up and spoke, as though to no one in particular. "But you're not that happy either, Dora. And I don't think you will be if you stay married to Jared. Why did you marry him in the first place?"

My God. Everyone wanted to know why she married him. Including herself!

She half giggled, shaking her head. "Oh, Pol! You

kids were all gone, and I'd sold the farm. And during the day, on the job, I was okay, but at night, when I tried to sleep . . ." How to describe that feeling, finding herself caught in an undertow of memory, thrashing around, trying to get something solid under her feet? "Jared asked me to marry him and share his house down the street. He said we were mature adults, we'd be able to design ourselves a comfortable life. And I thought, well, why not?"

"You didn't love him!"

"No. I've . . . I've never loved a man, not like that."

"You were afraid it might be your only chance, weren't you?"

Dora flushed. "That's probably true."

"Okay. I can understand that. But why in hell have you stayed married to him?"

Well, why not be honest? "He's never pleased about anything, Pol, but he is easy to keep contented. He lives by rules; all I have to do is remember them. And I'm comfortable."

"But Dora, God, you deserve more than that! You must know there's something missing! What's the matter? Are you afraid if you admit it, you'll have to do something about it?"

"Like go look for it? Aren't half the women in the world looking for 'it,' whatever 'it' is? Good sex, real romance, love and lust and ecstacy, pink clouds in the skies and violins in the shrubbery. Trumpets, trumpets, madly blowing! Thumpety-thump on the bedsprings. Wasn't living with Mama and Daddy enough of that!"

Polly laughed, and flushed, and they let the matter go as they crossed the parking lot. Sprouting up around the light posts were clusters of feathery green, and Dora stopped to point them out to Polly, saying they looked like Jared's weed. They laughed about that, feeling a gossipy and sisterly camaraderie as they strolled along the avenue looking across toward the pale bulk of the boardinghouse.

"She's a funny woman," said Polly, nodding toward the house.

"Who? Jared's mother? You've only seen her once, haven't you?"

"Um. At your wedding reception. That was the strangest bunch of people!"

"Well," Dora laughed, "they were my fellow boarders. Since we had the reception at the boardinghouse, it didn't seem nice not to invite them."

"What was that woman's name? Michaelson?"

"The talker?"

"Talker! That's like calling Everest a little hill. And the guy with the fish . . ."

"Mr. Singley. Mr. Singley talks to his fish. He has names for each of them. He calls them woozums."

"And the fanny pincher. The one with the strange eyes."

"Mr. Calclough. And Mr. Fries who does martial arts. When he shouts 'Haieeee,' the whole house shivers."

"You somehow just didn't fit in with that bunch, sis."

"I was only going to be there temporarily."

"I wasn't too crazy about the questions Momma asked, either. Were you a reliable cook and housekeeper? That pissed me off a little, and I told her just how lucky Jared was to get you, and what a great sister you'd been. Here's where we turn."

Something clanged in Dora's mind, like a coin in a pay phone. She chased the idea around, whatever it was, like chasing a memory of a dream when one first wakes up, only to lose it entirely.

They crossed the avenue and started down the empty street. Everyone was home from work, cars were put away, doors were closed, everyone was inside having supper. The street was like a vacant movie set as they moved down one block, then past the first two houses on the next block, then the house with the Tree, or the two with the Tree between them. Dora looked up at it as she always did, nodding to it. The Tree seemed to nod back, as it always did.

The next place was Jared's. Dora saw two of her neighbors standing on the sidewalk with their mouths open, staring. She saw what they were staring at: a pile of laundry on the stoop. Then her mind sorted out what she was seeing, and she realized it wasn't a pile of laundry, it was a body, Jared's body, Jared lying on the stoop, a set of clippers fallen from his hand, one arm curled protectively around his head. Dora broke into a run.

He wasn't breathing. "Call for an ambulance," she cried, handing Polly the key that had been in her hand. "Quick!"

Polly went in, Dora rolled Jared off the stoop onto the grass, got him face up, started doing CPR, just the way they'd taught her, push push push push push, breath, breath; push push push push push, breath, breath. He was a funny color. He had little wounds all over his face and hands. Maybe other places, too, for his shirt and trousers looked as though he'd been through a barbed wire fence. Push push push push push. Breath. Breath. Push push push . . .

Polly ran out of the house. "They're on their way."

Dora just went on doing what she was doing. She heard the neighbors talking, then there were sirens coming, she heard the ambulance stop at the curb, shoes come running across the sidewalk, and she was suddenly thrust to one side of things, no longer responsible. She took a deep gasping breath, looking around for the neighbors. They were standing by the curb talking to a patrolman she knew, Ralph Gadden. He dismissed them, then came over to Dora to ask what the hell was going on. She told him what had happened.

"You had any killer bees around here?" one of the paramedics asked. "Hornets, wasps, anything like that?"

"No, I don't think so. Why?"

"This guy looks like he's stung all over, neck, chest, back, even his legs. The medics are running him to Memorial. You have any idea what caused this?" He gestured around himself at the dead trees and the dead roses and the dead junipers.

"No," she said, truly baffled. "That is, I'm not sure. Jared used some weed killer yesterday . . ."

"Anybody hanging around?" Ralph asked. "Any strangers?"

"I didn't see any. Maybe the people you talked to, those two by the fence . . ."

Ralph shook his head. "No. They saw him just before you did."

She turned away helplessly, seeing the weed lacily arranged against the front of the house, now almost six feet tall. As she watched, all the leaflets turned in her direction. She shook her head, telling herself she was seeing things, then got into the ambulance with Jared. Polly would bring the car, she said. The two raggedy persons watched them go.

Jared was put into intensive care at the hospital. Ralph was replaced by another cop, one she didn't know, and he had her tell the story at least five times while someone else queried Polly. Neither of them had anything worth telling, no matter how many times they told it. No, Jared hadn't yet come home when she and Polly went to the mall. Yes, they could prove they'd been to the mall, they had their sales slips, their dinner check stub. They'd walked home. They'd been together all evening until they found Jared. Neither of them could possibly be suspected of anything.

"She tried to kill him," said Jared's mother, from out in the hall, early the following morning. "She was responsible . . . that woman he married."

Dora, hearing this, felt anger again. She almost never got angry, and here lately it was getting to be a habit, overreacting to stuff.

The detective said, "Dora couldn't have, Mrs. Gerber. She and her sister were elsewhere, and we've checked the story. The waitress at the restaurant remembers them. It all checks out. Besides, we don't even know how he was hurt, yet."

Jared's mama made an exclamation of surprise. Dora didn't hear her say anything else.

The next day, when the medical tests came back, they led only to further confusion. Jared's heart had almost failed following the injection of an herbicidal compound. He had at least a hundred different puncture wounds on his arms, face and torso. Dora cried, "The weed by the front stoop! Jared sprayed it with weed killer. And when Jared grabbed it yesterday, he said it had thorns."

The lab sent someone to look at the weed, but as Polly pointed out to Dora, it had no thorns. "Jared must have been stuck by something else, Dora. Maybe there were bees on the plant when he grabbed it. The plant isn't thorny at all. It's just . . . just . . . well, I don't know what it is exactly. The leaves look like oak leaves, but they're in a frond like some kind of acacia. And look at the little seed heads."

"I didn't know it had seeds," said Dora. "It's only been there a few days."

"It must have bloomed some time ago," remarked Polly. "See the little puff balls? Like tiny dandelion heads."

There was a frothy bubble, no bigger than a pea, an assembly of mist or spiderweb or something equally tenuous. As they watched, the wind broke the tiny sphere to send its particles flying, silken shreds glinting with an almost metallic light as they spun and twisted, borne upward and outward on the soft breeze. Now that she was looking, Dora could see other seed heads all over the vine, and the next puff of wind surrounded them with glittering floss.

Dora sneezed. "Cut that out," she exclaimed.

The weed just flirted its tendrils and went on shedding seeds into the wind.

"I'd be glad to stay with you," said Polly, who had already extended her visit to be with Dora through all the fuss. "I don't want you to be alone here."

"I'm not going to be here for long," she said, surprising herself. "You've sort of focused my mind, Polly, and I'm thankful for that. Now that you've done it, I'm going to get a divorce."

Polly rubbed her head as though it hurt. "Well, I'm not going to talk you out of it. You deserve a lot more than this."

Dora shook her head, torn between annoyance at herself and irritation at Polly's taking it so calmly. "Everything dropped into place when you told me about Mrs. Gerber asking if I was a reliable cook and housekeeper. I've really known all along that's what Jared wanted, just someone to cook and keep house, so he could move into his own place without sacrificing any of the comforts of home. I've known it, but I haven't dealt with it. I've been acting as though I'd been hypnotized." She giggled helplessly. "Maybe he put some kind of spell on me."

"Be thankful it didn't last. I don't suppose there's any possibility you're pregnant? It could foul things up if you are."

She would never have confessed it to anyone but Polly. "Giving Jared CPR the other night was as close as I've ever come to kissing him. There's no possibility I'm pregnant. The very idea scares me. I don't want to end up like Mother."

Polly hugged her. "Well, for heaven's sake, Dora, nobody has to have nine children, one right after the other. Mother did that because it was easier than thinking, that's all. If Mama and Daddy had been able to think, they'd have known it was selfish and wrong and they wouldn't have done it!"

"I know that. Intellectually I know it. Emotionally, though, what I remember is the mess and the confusion and nothing ever getting done. The clothes piled on the floor because no one put them away. The messy beds. The dirt in the corners, the cobwebs. The dirty plates all over the house. The smell of rotten food in the refrigerator. The cat poop in the back hall. The lawn that died because nobody watered it. The dead houseplants. I used to try, when I was there, but I couldn't do it. I remember how Mama and Dad looked at each other, that steamy look. And then the noises from the bedroom...." She laughed, embarrassed. "And then afterward, all that lux-uriating, mindless lethargy." She shook her head, amazed at herself.

"So, when you leave Jared, where are you going? An apartment, maybe?"

She thought about it. "I don't want an apartment. I need more privacy than that. I think a house. I've worked since I was eighteen, and I've saved some every year. Then I've got my share of the money we got for the farm when we sold it. I've got almost enough for a house of my own."

"You want me to stay and help you look?"

Dora came back to herself and considered the offer. "Polly, sweetie, I think you've hung around here long enough. I think you ought to go on and have your va-cation; you've earned it. My friend Loulee's dying for a chance to be useful. And Charlene Dermot, Phil's wife, is a realtor. Between the two of them, they'll find me a place."

Polly said she'd leave the day after next, and while she was on the phone making reservations, Helen Gerber rang the doorbell. Dora asked her in, not too politely.

Jared's mother flushed, then fixed her eyes on the car-pet. "I know you were upset with me the other day. I didn't mean you, you know. When I said it was that woman's fault—"

"Well, who the hell else did you mean?" Dora wasn't in a mood to be forgiving. "You said the woman he married—"

"He was married before. To that Dionne girl, the slut."

Dora's mouth fell open. "Married? Jared?"

"She wasn't even old enough to get married, only fifteen, but he ran off with her. First I knew of it was when he called me and said he'd run off with her and gotten married. I had to tell her mother, and she cursed him up one side and down the other and me, too. She said Jared had interfered with the girl, that he'd have to pay for it someday. Then when I told her I was having the marriage annulled, she just laughed. She said what Jared had started you couldn't annul.'' She sniffed. ''Well, I got it annulled anyhow.''

''And you think she's responsible for poisoning Jared? We can sure find out, Momma Gerber. That's a police job, and if you suspect her . . .''

Momma Gerber shook her head slowly, mouth pinched. ''No. The words just popped out of my mouth before I thought. It was all a tempest in a teapot, even back then, what? Almost thirty years ago! A couple of days after he went off with her, Jared came back and told me the girl had run away from him. He didn't seem too broken up. Her mother went off looking for her, and I haven't seen either one of them since. It's just when I saw Jared there, so pale . . . the words just popped out.''

''I'm not really following this,'' Dora said. ''Who exactly are we talking about?''

The older woman looked momentarily confused. ''I'm talking about the mother of the girl Jared married.''

''Wasn't she Mrs. Dionne?''

''She and her girl were some kind of cousins who came to town that summer to visit the Dionnes. And all the boys in the neighborhood, including Jared, started trailing after the girl like dogs after a bitch in heat! And the Dionne boys told Jared to stay away from her, and I guess that made Jared mad, so he took her off and married her. Anyhow, the whole thing, fire and all, was over in a few weeks. That's water over the dam, long gone, but I wanted to apologize.''

Dora wasn't ready to discuss the fact she was leaving Jared, so she contented herself with saying, ''Thanks, Momma Gerber. I do appreciate your clarifying that.''

She had the day free. Jared was out of intensive care. She dithered for a while until Polly asked her why she was so antsy.

''I'm going to go tell Jared I'm leaving.''

''While he's in the hospital?''

She'd been thinking about it. Somehow she didn't like the idea of telling him later, after he was home, after they were alone in the house. "Yes," she blurted. "While he's there."

Polly asked, "You want me to come with you?"

Dora almost said yes, then decided against it. It wasn't Polly's problem.

Jared was alone in the room, propped up, staring at the wall. His eyes swiveled toward her when she came in, then went back to the wall, as though he were watching the denouement of some compelling television drama. She pulled the straight chair away from the wall and sat on it, waiting. Eventually he would get tired of ignoring her. If he didn't, she could always start making annoying sounds in her throat.

"Where've you been?" he asked at last, letting his eyes swivel in her direction once more.

"At your place, Jared. And at work."

"You haven't been here."

"Your mother's been here. And I've called, every day, to see how you're doing."

"I don't like the food."

"Hospital food is usually pretty bad," she admitted. "Do you need anything from your place?"

He made a face without saying anything.

"I came today to tell you something," she began. He showed no interest. "I'm getting a divorce."

His eyes swiveled again. His head actually turned. "What do you mean, divorce? You can't do that. I've given you no reason."

"Well, Jared, people don't need specific reasons these days. It's enough if you just aren't happy, and you know, I'm not."

"Well, if you're not happy, that's your own fault," he challenged her. "It's got nothing to do with me."

She blinked slowly, turtlelike, pulling her psychological shell around her ears. Oil, not nitro, she reminded herself. "Well, you're probably right, Jared. My happiness has nothing to do with you. And that being the case, we ought not to be married. The fact is I want a home of my own, but your home is so much yours, I don't feel like I belong there.''

No response.

''You don't really have room for some other person in your life, Jared. All you need is a cook-housekeeper, and I'm sure your momma can hire one for you. So, I'm going to be moved out when you come home.''

He stared at her, or right through her, such a cold stare it set up an icy shiver inside. ''But I'm used to you. You serve a purpose! I won't allow it.''

Words left her. Who or what did the man think he was? More important, who did he think she was?

''I'm sorry you feel that way, but I really feel it's best, for both of us.'' Bland, meaningless, nothing words.

He didn't say anything more, just turned back to his private vision on the blank wall, leaving her with a shiver in her gut that stayed with her all the way home. Polly took one look at her face and said she'd help her pack. They spent the evening and all the next day packing everything that belonged to Dora, searching out every little thing, going through every drawer, every shelf, even though almost everything she owned was in the bedroom she'd used. The way Dora felt, just gathering up her things wasn't enough! She cleaned every room in the house from ceiling to carpet; she scrubbed the bathroom; she changed the sheets on the bed and put the used ones through the washer. She emptied the lint trap in the drier and took the garbage out, then she vacuumed everything three times and threw out the vacuum bag.

''What are we doing this for?'' Polly asked. ''You think he'll conduct an inspection?''

Dora laughed, a little hysterically. ''I don't want anything of me left here, Pol. Does that sound crazy?''

''No hair? No toenail clippings?'' Polly laughed. ''You think he's going to make a little doll and stick pins in it?''

Dora sobered up. "Let's just not leave any evidence I was ever here. Right? No skin flakes. No glass with my lipstick or fingerprints. No . . . no nothing."

"You *do* think he'll put a hex on you!" Polly started to laugh, but stopped when she saw the look on Dora's face. "What, Dory?"

Dora shrugged. "Let's pretend it's symbolic, like a way of erasing the past."

Her expression said, don't ask; Polly didn't. They polished everything as they left each room, leaving the keys on the kitchen counter and going out by the kitchen door. As they were driving away, Dora remembered her secret key, the one she'd hidden in the trellis as a spare. Jared didn't know about it. Jared wouldn't approve. People who were properly organized didn't need spare keys.

Never mind. Let it stay there.

They took a motel housekeeping unit where they could spend the night, and where Dora could stay until she found a place of her own. All that night she turned and half wakened and turned again, trying to get comfortable. Thoughts of Jared were like cracker crumbs in her bed, itchy and annoying. At last, along toward dawn, she fell asleep, only to be wakened a couple of hours later to take Polly to the airport.

2

Opalears Tells a Tale

"The sultan wants you," said the eunuch.

I looked around to see who the eunuch meant. In the pool across the courtyard a clutch of concubines was playing a desultory game of ball. Half a dozen wives reclined on their royal divans in the high, screened balconies along the wall. A slave gang was scrubbing the tiled floor under the drowsy eyes of a slave-mistress, but I, myself, was the only person near the eunuch.

"Me?" I faltered, hearing the word come out as a squeak.

"Opalears, daughter of Halfnose." The eunuch didn't actually yawn from boredom, but he very nearly did, keeping his lips barely closed, so the longer teeth at the corners of his mouth showed, very white and sharp.

"Now?" I said, squeaking again.

"Now." He turned and slunk away, leaving me tottering behind him, not sure what to do next.

He looked over his shoulder. "Come on, girl. Don't dither."

"But, I'm not . . . not . . ." I gestured hopelessly at my untidy self, halfway between fixing snacks in the kitchens and sorting linens in the laundry.

"He doesn't want you for that!" His furry eyebrows went up in astonishment as he grinned fiercely. "Why would he?"

Which was a good question. Here in the Palace of Delights lived seventeen young wives of Sultan Tummyfat, all of them beautiful and voluptuous and politically useful. Here were also over two hundred young concubines, mostly nice looking, mostly politically useful, mostly selected to gain the support of this faction or that. Elsewhere, in the Autumn Garden, Sultan Tummyfat housed an unknown number of retired wives and concubines, his own or his father's or uncle's, and between the Autumn Garden and Palace of Delights, he had hundreds of female slaves, each attractive enough of her type, none of them heretics or members of an opposition family, and not particularly distinguishable one from another. I myself was a slave called Opalears, and I was among the youngest and least distinguishable. I was surprised that the eunuch even knew who I was.

Which, it seemed, he wasn't all that sure of himself.

"You're the storyteller, right?" the eunuch asked, looking me up and down as though tallying points against a description. So high, so thin, such and such color hair.

"I tell stories," I murmured. "But lots of us do." And what else was there to do, shut up the way we all were?

"You're the one they like, though. Sultana Eyebright. Sultana Ivory-arms. Sultana Winetongue. They say you tell good ones." He slitted his eyes at me, then turned and went on.

"Very kind of them," I murmured, trying to keep up with him. He was the one named Soaz. "Very kind."

"Got stories from your father, I suppose," he said, leaping four or five steps at a time up the long flight of marble stairs while I scrambled to keep up. "I remember old Halfnose. He was a good storyteller, and a good quartermaster. Better than the idiot we've got now.''

I didn't reply. I couldn't. I felt the tears start and couldn't stop them.

"Oh, mustard and growr," said the eunuch, turning with a horrid scowl that made me cry all the harder. "I shouldn't have mentioned him, should I. Stop here. We can't go up with you sniffling.''

I wiped my face on my sleeves, sniveling, "I was there," which brought on another blubber.

"At the execution? Yes, I suppose you were. Typical. The regent could be a cruel old bastard. Some of us tried to tell him Halfnose wouldn't steal anything, but he wouldn't listen. After the execution, then he listened. He always used to calm down after an execution. That's when he took you in, was it?''

I was wiping my face with my wadded up veil, trying to soak up the tears. "I don't think he had much to do with it. I think it was Bluethumb.''

"Well, whoever. You've had a home, at least.'' He wiped at my cheeks with the backs of his hands, gave me a close looking over and then continued the climb. "That's something.''

I suppose it was something. A ten-year-old commoner orphan has small chance of survival out on the streets, except through degradation, so palace slavery had its good points. It wasn't like being a mine slave or a field slave or a brickyard kiln slave or a sex slave in the brothels. I always had plenty to eat, good quality clothing to wear, even some amusements. And no one fooled with me. Add to that the fact the regent had died shortly after I came to the Palace of Delights, and my life wasn't all bad. When they burned the horrible beastly creature, I was there, watching, relishing the smell, for when father died, I'd made an oath to avenge him, though I'd probably have been caught at it because I had no idea how to kill anyone. Since then, of course, I'd become well versed in killing. Half the harim occupied itself either putting curses on the other half, or warding off the curses that were put in return. The wives and concubines were secretive with one another, but they'd say anything in our hearing, as though slaves weren't even people. I'd learned all about poisons, which many of the concubines preferred, and hired assassins, which only the sultanas had sufficient treasure to procure. Every female in the harim was constantly jockeying for position, if not for herself, then for her children or friends.

"Put your veil down," said the eunuch, as we turned a corner and went through the tall, fretted door that marked the beginning of the salamlek, strictly male territory.

None of us harim dwellers veiled ourselves, usually, not unless Sultan Tummyfat brought kinsmen in, but we all wore the veil, nonetheless, usually folded back over the tops of our heads. Mine was all wrinkled from crying in it, and it took some doing to get it straightened out and pull the two embroidered ribbons apart, one straight across my nose with a fall of filmy stuff below, the other high across my forehead, its fringe falling across my eyes. When it was in position, it fell to my waist, hiding my arms to the wrists.

"What does the sultan want with me?" I asked as we came to a halt outside another door.

"Let him tell you," he said. "Turn around."

I turned, feeling him tug at the veil, smoothing it out behind, brushing the fringe forward, combing it with his armored fingers until it fell evenly, tapping me on the lower backbone so I stood up straight.

"Now," he said. "You follow me with your head bowed. Watch my legs so you don't bump into me. When I stop, you stop. If the sultan asks you a question, answer it clearly, briefly, keep your head slightly bowed. Understand?"

I was suddenly conscious that my mouth was dry. If the sultan asked me a question, I wasn't sure I could answer him at all!

The eunuch opened the door, went through, then turned to close it again, which was confusing because I had to make a little circle in order to stay behind him. Someone laughed, and I felt my cheeks burning. I must have looked silly, like a baby guz following its mother. Soaz muttered under his breath as we crossed the huge room, carpet on carpet on carpet, like walking on mattresses. He prowled, I stumbled after. When he stopped, he put his hand on my shoulder to stop me mindlessly putting myself behind him again when he stepped to the side.

"I have brought the slave as the lord commanded."

"What is its name."

"Its palace name is Opalears, Lord."

"Show me its face."

Soaz lifted my veil, then put a calloused fingerpad under my chin and lifted my face. I closed my eyes.

"Open your silly eyes," muttered Soaz. "He won't eat you."

I felt them pop open, like pea pods. There were two males seated on the divan, young and old. I had seen Lord Tummyfat before, when he came to the harim, a round person, smoothish in the face, without much hair. He had never looked at me before, however, and the look was disconcerting.

"You're the storyteller?" he asked.

"I tell stories," I gasped. "Sometimes."

"You cook, also."

"Yes, I do. . . ."

"How did we get her?" Lord Tummyfat asked the eunuch.

"Her father was Halfnose Nazir, who was falsely accused of theft by the regent and executed; her mother was a suicide; her brother fled; this one was left alone. Seems to have been enslaved as an act of mercy," said Soaz.

"Ah." Long pause. "I often think of Nazir. A good servant. She doesn't look like much."

"No, Sultan. She is very skinny. Like a stick."

"How old is she?"

"How old are you, girl?" asked Soaz.

"Middle of my third age, sir." The first being baby-hood, then childhood, then adolescence, all of which were well understood. There was some controversy about when the fourth age, that of reason, started, and I didn't worry myself about it. I hadn't found life reasonable yet, and something told me I might never.

Soaz nodded heavily. "The family was originally from Estafan, Lord. There are many ponjic people there, and as the Lord knows, ponji are bony, like posts, as well as being slow growers who seldom reach full size until the end of their third age."

"Then she's still almost a child!"

"As Great Sultan says."

"Look at me, child."

I looked up, seeing his head cocked, his nostrils wide, his eyes actually interested, his mouth pursed, ready to make words. "My son has been ill," said Sultan Tummyfat. "My son, Prince Keen Nose."

I managed to make a tiny nod. The harim had talked of little else for days. Keen Nose was a favored son, Sultana Winetongue's child. The harim thought he had been poisoned. Sultana Winetongue had rivals for the king's affection, and her son was naturally the rival of every other woman's son. Actually, there were a dozen sultanas' sons competing for the king's favor, not to speak of the constant ferment among the concubines, who bet on this one or that one, as though it were a race.

Sultan Tummyfat continued. "My son will journey to the Hospice of St. Weel, to be cured. Someone must go with him, to attend to him, to amuse him. Obviously, we cannot risk any of our own . . . palace people. He has heard of you from his mother. He has asked for you."

"As . . . as the lord w-w-wills," I stammered. Didn't he know there were monsters out there, and strange trees that grabbed people in their viny hands and smothered them in leaves? Hadn't he heard how people got turned into *things* at the Hospice of St. Weel?

"Why is she shaking?" the sultan asked, slightly annoyed.

Soaz murmured, "I suppose she's frightened, Lord. The harim enjoys frightening the young ones with tales of afrits and jinni and the trees that walk, as well as the terrors of the strangers at the hospice."

The sultan nodded, caressing his chin with the back of his wrist, as though stroking a beard. "It is well known that all females are as gullible as the guz."

"Not all," purred the eunuch.

The sultan quirked his lips and replied, "Your people excepted, of course, Soaz. You pheledian folk—though orthodox in belief—are notoriously cynical." He smiled in my direction, saying loftily, "The strangers are not ogres, girl. They are merely a different sort of people, not even as strange as the onchiki or the armakfatidi, and you've worked with the armakfatidi. The trees are our dear friends, as the teachings of Korè make clear. Besides, there will be an armed escort and servants. You'll get to see something of the countryside."

Unable to speak, I bowed.

"This is my son," the sultan said.

I turned to meet the eyes of the pale youth half re-clining beside his father. He too was smooth faced, though he had two lines at the corners of his mouth, as though he gritted his teeth rather a lot. And he was thin. Perhaps he was in pain. He smiled, then laughed. It was the same laugh that had greeted my entry, a kind of malicious snorting. I felt myself turning red.

"Thank you, my Lord Father," said the young one. "She will do very well."

It was an indifferent voice. Neither kind nor unkind. Did he plan to laugh at me all the way to the hospice?

Tummyfat stroked his son's head, keeping his eyes on me. "Soaz, have her outfitted properly. Prepare a con-veyance, if necessary, or an umminha, if she can ride. Can you ride, girl?"

In the harim it was thought unfeminine, but it didn't occur to me to lie. "Yes, Lord. There were umminhi on my grandfather's farm. I had a filly of my own." She had been a lovely caramel color, with a silvery mane.

She had been very beautiful and very stupid and her name had been Honey. I wondered, as I did from time to time, what had happened to grandfather and the farm. I hadn't seen him since the summer before father died.

The sultan nodded. "Well, then. Good. Take her back, Soaz. See that she's ready by dawn tomorrow."

We went back, me stumbling over my own feet, totally at a loss; Soaz making rumbling noises in his throat, preoccupied about something. He opened the courtyard door and shooed me through it, shutting it behind me to go off on business of his own.

One of the personal servants was waiting, a squarely built, dark-haired person everyone called Frowsea. "Sultana Winetongue wants you," she said, without preamble, taking me by one wrist. "Come, quickly."

She hauled me up a dim half flight of marble stairs and down the elaborately tiled corridor behind the royal balconies, stopping outside the curtained arch of the largest one. Though the curtains were heavy, a good smell leaked out, roasted veeble and onions and raisins and spice, making my mouth water. The curtain was lifted from inside, and I was dragged in.

"There, there you are," said the sultana, fastening her black-rimmed, long-lashed eyes on me, a hungry look, as though she might like to eat me. Her limbs were beautifully round and plump, and she was dressed in a low-cut shazmi that showed her smoothly ample breasts. "Have you seen my son?"

"I saw Prince Keen Nose," I said. "With his father."

"How is he? Did he look well?"

I thought of lying and decided against it. Doubtless the sultana had spies among the servants outside, and if I lied, the sultana would learn of it.

"He looked very thin, Uplifted One. As from a wasting disease. He was in good spirits, however. He laughed, several times."

"At you, no doubt," said the servant. "Don't they feed you, girl? What a draggletail."

I hid my annoyance at this, for whatever one might

say about me, it was unfair to say I dragged my behind!

"Her appearance is not why we picked her," said the sultana. "Are you going with him?"

"So says his father, Great Sultana."

"There, didn't I tell you!" She pulled me farther into the balcony. Waist-high carved stone screens separated it from the courtyard beyond, with wooden sliding screens above to give privacy. The screens were closed and more of the sound-deadening draperies had been pulled shut inside them, making as private an enclosure as could be achieved in the harim. To one side an open arch gave upon a twisting staircase; one of only two ways to the sultana's own rooms, above. The other was a corridor opening in the sultan's quarters, to which he had the only key. This was common knowledge.

"When?" the sultana demanded softly. "When do you go?"

"Tomorrow morning."

"So soon," breathed the sultana, tears in her voice. "Well, then. It's good we were prepared. Were we correct in thinking you can ride? Or will my son need a palanquin?"

"I think we are to ride. The Great Sultan asked if I knew how."

"Then the boy can't be too ill," murmured the other woman. "Not if he's riding."

"Frowsea, that-bitch-Amberknees said he was like to die."

"That-bitch-Knees doesn't care what she says." The servant rummaged in a basket and began removing clothing. "Here, girl, try these on. We've been making preparations. Riding trousers. Shirts. A mantle. A cloak."

I took one look at the clothing and went rigid with shock. "Great Sultana, this is male clothing."

"And so it is! Did you think you'd be shut in like a lady, behind curtains? You'd be no good to him so. On the back of a beast, you'll draw no attention. You're a common person, and common persons are not slaved to tradition as we royals are. Because it is written that our remote ancestors wore veils and hid themselves in harims, so must we, to honor tradition, but commoners may wear whatever their malefolk allow. When you came here, you weren't wearing lady's clothes, were you? You're skinny as a fencepost, titless as any boy, so let you dress like a boy. The matter will go easier for it.''

She was right about how I'd been dressed when I came. It was true I'd had no flesh on me at all, and I'd been dressed in sandals, shirt and trousers that my half-brother had discarded long years before. I had no objection to wearing boy's clothing, though considering the rules in effect in the harim, I wondered if she might not be risking beheading for it.

''I have already spoken to Tummyfat,'' said the sultana, as though she knew what I was thinking. ''He will allow it. And I've spoken to my son. A caravan traveling with females or with treasure is a temptation to the angels and would lure bandits from as far as Isfoin. An armed troop, without females or treasure, travels safer than a caravan, though if someone important is along, seizure for ransom may be attempted. An armed troop following the banner of a minor, and thus unprofitable, official travels safer yet, which is the way you will go. I don't want my son leaving one danger merely to fall into another.''

I heard myself asking, ''Was he really poisoned, Great Sultana?''

Frowsea grasped my shoulder, lifting, and for a moment my feet left the ground.

''Put her down, Frowsea!'' said the sultana in a fervent whisper. ''She didn't mean to be impertinent; she's merely curious.''

Reluctantly, Frowsea set me down.

The sultana said, ''We don't know that he was poisoned, girl. We are not priers and pokers, like those at the hospice, able to peer into our bodies to see what is awry. He may have been poisoned. He may have been cursed. He may simply be ill, there are illnesses enough that have no known cause. Whichever, among the Strangers at St. Weel, he may be healed, and the Great Sultan has permitted me this favor, to send him thence.''

"He loves his son," said Frowsea.

"He loves his comforts," said the sultana, pouting. "And those who know how to provide them. He has enough sons to afford wasting a good many. Such wastage is traditional. It is the custom of great kings to sow their seed widely, begetting sons by half dozens to assure much rivalry, much connivance, many plots, from which the clever, the ruthless and the strong emerge as victors to ascend the throne. Of such struggle comes tutelage in both diplomacy and power, creating a lineage to brag of!''

She sighed. "Unfortunately, Keen Nose is not ruthless, as the king well knows. He is an intelligent lad, rather old-fashioned, cleverer than all his rivals! Also, he is my son, and the king favors me by permitting this journey. Now, girl, do you understand your place in this?''

"No, Uplifted One. Except I am to tell the prince stories?''

"We cannot send one of us! Obviously! So, we send you. You are to amuse him. Because you are still a virgin girl, shut in here since childhood, you are probably healthy and thus no threat to him should he require intimate services from you. No male has given you a disease, the stinking air of the markets has not tainted your lungs. Because you were well reared as a child and have been always well treated here, you have still a sweet and unwounded character that does not bite without warning. My embroiderers tell me you have skill with the needle. You cook well, so the armakfatidi say.''

The armakfatidi were the kitchen people. I helped in the kitchen from time to time, and I had learned much. The armakfatidian people could taste things others could not and smell things others could not, and their dishes were recognized throughout all Tavor as the highest form of cuisine. Armakfatidian dishes, however, were

not for commoners. Only the wealthy had sufficient treasure to hire armakfatidi and to afford the spices and flavorings they required, some of them from far, strange
outlands. In Tavor, the armakfatidi mostly ran restau-
rants, grew specialty fruits and vegetables, or involved
themselves in the perfume and spice trades.

"Well?" the sultana prompted, waiting for an answer.

"Yes, Great Sultana," I said.

"Yes, what?"

"Yes, I cook fairly well, Uplifted One. Well enough
to see your son does not go hungry or uncosseted." Cos-
seting a scuinic prince went without saying. Scuini liked
their food. "Yes, I can do ordinary stitchery, well
enough to see his laces stay on and his headscarf stays
hemmed and his stockings are darned. But I don't know
what you mean by intimate services...."

"Oh, for heaven's sake, child. He may need you to
scrub his back. Something of that sort. Surely you didn't
think I meant..." She snorted, not finishing the sentence, amused by the thought.

"No, Great Queen." I turned red again. Of course the
prince would not want sex with a ... a draggletail, as
Frowsea called me. Or one as untutored as I in the am-
orous arts.

"Do you know where the Strangers live?"

"I have heard they live afar. The Hospice of St. Weel
is on the back side of beyond."

The sultana's mouth twisted in amusement. "Not
quite. Say rather the near side of beyond, on the west
coast of the Crawling Sea. Pay great attention to everything on the way. Use your eyes well, and your ears.
When you return, we will want you to tell us all about
it."

As I tried on the various articles of clothing, I wondered why Sultana Winetongue had really picked me to
go with Keen Nose. None of the reasons given seemed
enough. And why not send a male? Males could scrub
backs and tell stories, too. There was nothing gender
specific about either! Perhaps Soaz would tell me the

real reason. He was unlikely to have me beaten for impertinence so close to the time of departure, as this would inconvenience the prince and Sultan Tummyfat. On the other hand, if I proved too curious and importunate, they might choose someone else, and I really, really wanted to go! All in all, best keep my questions locked inside. Perhaps Prince Keen Nose would tell me on the way. Seemingly we were to have much time for conversation.

I peeled off the last shirt. All the clothing in the pile would fit, more or less. None of it was too tight, though some was a trifle loose, as though made for a larger person.

"That's all right," said Frowsea. "I'll put the bigger ones in the bottom of the pack. It's a long journey and likely you'll grow into them."

The sultana directed me: "Pack your own shoes and underclothing and any small treasures you cannot bear to leave behind. Come up here before first light. Don't say anything about the prince to those, down there." The sultana gestured at the curtained wall, meaning the women in the courtyard. "Make up a tale, you're good at that, but don't tell them the truth. And here, girl. Put these in your shoes, or sew them into your underclothes. They are for my son's help and safety. You may need them on the way." And she spilled gems into my hands, cut rubies and emeralds and a shimmer of poinuid pearls, glowing blue as the depths of the sea. These pearls are fished up by the onchiki or the Onchik-Dau, all along the coast below Isfoin.

I had only time to bow my acquiescent thanks and to thrust the gems deep into a pocket before I was seized up by Frowsea, jostled back down the stairs, and turned out into the courtyard as though nothing had happened. Except that something had happened, which everyone within sight or hearing knew. People drifted in my direction, as though aimlessly. Questions were whispered from mouths hungry for happenings; eyes peered rapaciously. What? What was going on?

"The Great Sultan learned that my father had been falsely accused," I said, surprised at the firmness of my own voice. "He wished me to know that no stain attached to my family, that my brother is safe, that I may join him if I wish."

"Why did the sultana want to see you? Her. Winetongue? Why?"

"The sultana said a kind word. She gave me a gem for my years of service." And I showed one cupped in my hand, a very small one, not enough to incite envy. In the harim, envy was as dangerous as a carpet snake; as readily hidden, it too could kill without warning.

Disappointed, they went away. No one cared about my years of service, or my father who had been falsely accused or my brother. Truth to tell, by this time I didn't care about my brother. He was older than I by a good fifteen years, born to a different mother, and gone to the outskirts of the city to live in a house of his own by the time I was five. All that was long ago, but today was now, and tomorrow morning would come soon.

All of the day had been interesting, though some of it had been slightly scary and at least one thing had been annoying. Why did Sultana Winetongue assume that I would tell them stories about my adventures? Now that they were letting me out, did they really think I would return?

3

Dora Henry's New House

Finding a place of her own had sounded simple when Dora had said it. At the end of two weeks, spending every evening looking at houses and condos, she was sick of the idea. Every place she'd been shown was either filthy, or dilapidated, or badly located, or too expensive. Each place was either the size of a phone booth or the size of a barn. Then on Friday, three weeks after Jared was hurt, Phil's wife called saying she'd found the perfect place, she'd meet Dora there.

Dora told herself not to be hopeful. She'd been disappointed too many times. Still, when she found the address and parked out in front, just behind Charlene's car, the surroundings gave her a tiny thrill of excitement. Something was right about this place! When she got out of the car, however, she shook her head slowly. The three-story stone house was huge!

"This isn't it," said Charlene, who'd driven in behind her. "Follow me."

She stalked down the concrete driveway toward the

gable end of a wide, two-storied garage. Its overhead
doors were tightly shut; the two windows above were
shuttered. The stone wall of the big house was on their
left, and where it ended at the back corner, a high,
wooden fence took its place, running from house to garage, with a gate at the garage end. Charlene unlocked
the gate padlock to let them through into an area of
scattered paving stones and cracked, hard-packed clay.
The space was separated from the big house by a cross
fence that ended at the neighbor's garage wall and separated from the alley by a chain-link fence with a gate
giving access to the garbage cans. Across the alley
was . . . well, nothing much: a field of ragged grass with
sprays of white flowers blooming in it. Queen Anne's
lace? Whatever, it was more attractive than the enclosed
area.

"This little yard is a mess, but don't get your mind
set yet," Charlene cautioned. "Come on."

Beneath a dangling lantern, a door opened into the
side of the garage. Charlene unlocked it and fumbled
inside for a switch. The lantern came on as well as an
inside light, disclosing a closet-sized laundry room on
the right, an empty cavern of garage straight ahead, and
on the left a narrow flight of stairs which led up to a
peaked and skylighted space, airy and open, with one
wide window looking westward across the alley toward
miles of uninterrupted country. The stairs were separated
from the big room by a long, low bookcase. In the back
corner opposite the stairs, cupboards and appliances
made a U-shaped kitchen, and beside it a tiny hallway
opened into a roomy bedroom and a sizeable bath, each
with windows facing the driveway they had walked
along. Charlene went from window to window, opening
them and thrusting the shutters wide, letting in the evening.

"What was this?" Dora asked as she wandered about,
trying to stay cynical and practical despite her growing
elation.

"Chauffeur's quarters," Charlene crowed. "This used

to be a country estate, before the city swallowed it. The people who bought the big house are converting it into apartments. They want to sell this little piece outright to give them some remodeling capital. There's enough ground set aside to comply with the zoning, and everything goes with: washer-drier, kitchen appliances, everything. The bedroom has a huge closet under the eaves. The fenced-off part gives you a yard or garden. You can either come in from the street, or, if you want more privacy, you can move the garage doors around to the alley side. It's a three-car garage, so there's lots of storage room.''

''Where did all this vacant ground come from?'' Dora asked, staring out the west window.

''It's part of the old air base. They closed it back in ninety-five, and it's been zoned as greenbelt. You could have a dog and take him for walks over there.''

Charlene had three poodles that, according to Phil, ran Charlene's life for her, but Dora wasn't thinking about dogs. She moved slowly back to the kitchen. New built-in oven and stove top, compartment sink and dishwasher, decent-sized refrigerator-freezer, pine cabinets under a wide counter where she could put two or three stools. More than adequate. Not huge, but then, she'd only be cooking for one. The bathroom was nice, all newly tiled in white with bright Caribbean stripes of blue and pink and apricot. The place could have been designed with her furniture in mind. Everything she had would fit!

''How much?'' she asked.

Charlene mentioned a price and Dora said a silent prayer of thanks. She could handle it. She would even have enough left over to do something with that messy bit of yard down below. When Charlene left to go type up a contract, Dora stayed there, hugging the place to herself, as though it were a child. She could have a little garden, and the garage beneath the living space was perfect for her car, and for storage. And a place to paint! Before she married Jared, she used to get a kick out of painting, but he'd said it was too messy to do anywhere at his place. All her painting stuff was . . . Damn! It was still at Jared's place. In the garage! She hadn't remembered to clean out the garage!

Never mind. She'd do it right away. And she'd plant a tree and some evergreen shrubs in the little yard. And the lavender she'd wanted. And the pansies. And this fall she'd put in some bulbs. She was amazed to find herself a little weepy at the idea. A place of her own. It would be the first time she'd had a real, honest-to-God place of her own.

Closing was set for ten days away, but the people told her she could move in before closing if she wanted to. On Tuesday she moved. Her furniture came out of storage: her own bright rugs and comfortable rocker, Grandma's pine bedstead and dresser. A new sleeper sofa for when one of the younger kids came visiting, Grandma's honey pine table and chairs, the coffee table she'd had made from a fancy old door she'd found at a flea market, the two leather chairs she'd bought on time payments while she was still at the farm.

She found some ready-made curtains at Sears, ones that would blow in the wind, and at the nursery a big terra cotta pot for planting lavender in. She found pansies at the Wal-Mart to put by the stoop downstairs. The final step was to drive to the post office nearest Jared's place and turn in a change of address form. Then, on her way home, she went down the alley at Jared's place and used her spare key to get into the garage. Jared had been out of the hospital for a week now, but Jared's mother had called Dora at work to say he was staying at the boardinghouse, with her.

"Jared doesn't want you to leave," she had said in her firm, unemotional voice, as though her saying so might change Dora's mind.

"Jared doesn't need a wife," Dora had told her. "He needs a cook-housekeeper. And he's making enough to hire one." Still, she hadn't filed for divorce. Not yet. She had a feeling it would be like poking a snake that was coiled to strike. She could let the legal part wait while Jared got used to the idea.

All her painting things were in the garage, dusty but undisturbed, not even dried out. She stumbled on her way in, for the floor was as badly cracked as Jared had said, and she stumbled again coming out, but she didn't forget to relock the door. She drove down the alley and came back to park at the curb. She used the key in the front door so she could pick up the mail that had arrived in the past few weeks. No more would be delivered to her at this address.

The weed had evidently won the war with Jared, for it was still there, ten feet tall now, anchored to the front wall with tiny sucker tendrils, its lacy foliage completely covering half the front wall of the house.

"Good-bye, weed," she said, as she relocked the door.

All the leaflets turned in her direction.

"I'm moving over to Madera Street," she said. "Ten thirty-two and a half Madera." The leaflets trembled. Or maybe she only thought they did.

Crossing the bridge on the way back to her new home, she started to toss the spare key into the river, but then stopped. She wouldn't be needing it again, but still . . . she hadn't remembered the painting stuff. Maybe she'd forgotten something else as well. When she parked the car, she put the key to Jared's place in the little magnetic box where she kept her spare car key, up behind the steering column. No one was likely to find it who didn't know it was there.

That evening she served herself supper at her own table, laid with her own china. Later she sat in her own leather chair, looking out the window toward the sunset, watching the sun sink past all that lovely emptiness, no buildings in the way at all, the feathery clouds flushing pink and fading to violet. Then she went to bed in her own bed, with the windows open so the night air could come in.

The next morning she went out to get the paper, and

when she came back through the gate, she saw the weed thrusting up between the brick of the stoop and the wall of her house, tiny and green and indomitable.

"Hello, weed," she whispered.

4

Opalears: Beginning the Journey

My father, Halfnose Nazir (so called because the sultan's nose was the proper length for a nose, and anything less could be called only a half nose) owned our house near the palace. It stood on Peacock Alley, a twisting line of cobble too narrow for more than slender persons and very small beasts, a corridor that wound its way among houses and shops to the intersection with the wider avenue. The only part of our house that was visible was the grilled balcony that hung over the alley and the high wall set with a gate, its tiny window covered by a grill. Inside was a flowery courtyard, with a fountain and chicken coops and the kitchen and a flight of stairs leading up to the grilled balcony and the living rooms and then on up to the roof, which was hidden from other rooftops by vine-covered trellises. I was born there, and I lived there in considerable freedom, often accompanying my father to the marketplace when he went to procure produce for the sultan, or for the regent, Great-tooth the Mighty.

My mother, so my father said, liked to think of herself as highly bred. In Tavor, this meant that females did not risk encounters with lesser peoples by leaving their homes. My father was amused by it, I was usually irritated, because people had to do all the shopping for her and no matter what father and I bought at the market, she complained. Except for an occasional trip to grandfather's farm, mother stayed in the house, in the courtyard beside the fountain, or in the grilled balcony that overlooked the modest traffic of the alley, or on the roof sometimes, with the caged birds and the vines, where she had a view of the more crowded avenue. She slept a lot. Sometimes I thought she was just lazy.

I was not always angry with Mother, however, for she was very pretty and she told lovely stories. It was she who taught me to read, with me curled on her bed holding the book and she at her dressing table, taking the jewels from her ears and fingers, dropping them into a china dish with a soft clinking sound before beginning to brush her hair. The sound of that clinking and the soft wisp of the hairbrush brings her back to me, even now.

I remember her stories. I remember her voice. She told me once that words were mysteries, that each time she spoke they flew from her mouth like butterflies that had hatched beneath her tongue, leaving her with no idea how they came there. "Do you ever feel that, Nassifeh?" she asked me. "That our words are not our own, that they were given to us by someone . . . someone else?"

I told her of course they had, by our parents and they by their parents, but this was not what she meant. "Why should this be *hairbrush*?" she asked. "Why should it not be *amthrup*? It could as well be. Who decided upon *hairbrush*?"

I thought about it, then told her that if each of us decided on our own words for things, we would not be able to speak together.

"That's not what I meant," she said. "I meant that some words feel very strange in my mouth, as though they were not born there. As though my word would have been a different one.''

I never figured out what she meant.

My father enjoyed working for Sultan Tummyfat, so he always told us, but when the sultan went away for a while and Great-tooth took the regency, my father quit talking about his work. He said nothing either good or bad about the regent, except once I heard him muttering to himself, a growl in which he uttered the regent's name like a curse.

The worst day of my life was my tenth birthday. Mother gave me a new mantle, and father gave me a treasure box and invited me to go to the market with him. I put on the mantle, put the treasure box deep into the pocket, and off we went to the fruiterers lane, stopping at the booths run by various peoples from various lands, armakfatidi and pheledas and kasturi. The fruiterers market smelled of ocris and oranges, dawara and dates, mangoes and marvellos, and the vendors always gave me bits to taste while Father haggled over prices and qualities and arranged for baskets, sacks, and boxes to be delivered to the kitchens of the sultan. Father was chewing a dried apricot with an expression of concentration on his face when the pheled guards came out of nowhere, seized him up, then seized me up as well when I shouted and ran after Father. The guards took us to the palace. Great-tooth was seated beneath the canopy of justice, like a toad under a leaf, the crier beside him trumpeting words of accusation—so I learned later. At the time, I had no idea what was going on. The executioner was waiting beside the block, all his teeth showing in a ferocious grin, and Father had not even time to claim innocence before his head was off. I started to run to him, only to scramble frantically away again at the smell of the blood, the horror of the severed head, while all the time Great-tooth merely stared at me as though I had been a bug of some kind.

The guards caught me and took me to the harimlek,

the female part of the palace, where they turned me over to old Bluethumb.

"Where do you live, child?" she asked me.

Between sobs and screams, I told the old one where I lived, and Bluethumb, after some conversation with this one and that one, sent me home with a guard. When we got there, the house was torn all apart and Mama's body was lying in the courtyard, all broken from falling off the roof.

Later I was told that the news of Father's execution had come quickly, and Mama had feared death less than she'd feared the torturers. Great-tooth had been known to kill one member of a family and then torture the others to death to amuse himself. Guards had come to search the house, as well, but that had been after Mama was dead.

The guard who took me home was bored, but kind.

"Gather up what you want to take with you," he said. "You can't stay here alone. I'll take you back to Bluethumb."

What was there to take? What I had on my back; what I could find among the clutter of the looted house. My other clothing. My books. There had been other, more valuable things in the house, but someone had already stolen them, and it wasn't much of a bundle that I carried back to the harim.

"What did my father do?" I begged, the tears coursing down my cheeks.

"Great-tooth said something was stolen," said Bluethumb. "We don't know what. Something important, something secret."

"My house was all messed up," I cried. "Did they find whatever was taken?"

"Not that I know of, child. And that's all anyone knows."

And that was the only answer I ever got. They looked for my half brother in the neighborhood where he lived, but he had fled, with his wife and child. After a few days, Bluethumb told me I'd been purchased as a slave, by the harim-masters, the eunuchs Soaz and Barfor.

"Who sold me?" I asked. "I belonged to Mother and Father. They were dead, they couldn't sell me!"

Bluethumb didn't know who'd sold me, though she'd seen the paper right enough, in the eunuch's office. "Don't worry over it, child. If you are the property of the sultan, no one will fool with you. It'll keep you safe."

Which was more or less true. They put me to work in the kitchen at first, scrubbing vegetables—which were never clean enough for the armakfatidi. Furthermore, the armakfatidi bothered me, even after I got to the point I didn't tremble and squeak every time one of them grummeled at me. Eventually, I even learned to understand them, which, though I didn't know it, was a rare talent, indeed.

Then, when Bluethumb found I could sew—Mother had also taught me how to sew—they put me with the chattery seamstresses, hemming veils and learning embroidery, then, when some of the concubines heard me telling stories to the stitchers, they brought me into the harim itself as a fetcher and carrier, mender of mantles and cooker of snacks. The concubines were plump and lazy (as the sultan preferred), while I was stringy and active. Also, I knew how to read Tavorian, which most Tavorians did not. Though there were few books in the harim, songs and love poems and such sappy stuff, Bluethumb had a brother working in the salamlek, on the other side of the great metal gate, and he brought books from the sultan's library, books I wrapped in clean linen and read secretly and returned timely so no one even knew they were gone. I read everything! Even the great history of Tavor, the *Almost Three Years of Bedtimes,* where all our customs and costumes are set out, just as they have always been.

Everything I read or heard was grist for the story mill, tales and facts to be reworked and twisted and made to fit into the kind of romances the harim enjoyed: deathless love between male and female, one of each, unlikely though that was. And adventure stories, where the princess dressed up as a boy and traveled far away. And stories about lands where females ruled, and all the males were conquered and locked up in cages. Once after I told that kind of tale, the harim decided to act it out—theatricals being one of their chief amusements—and at Sultana Winetongue's bidding even a few of the eunuchs helped, playing the parts of the terrible males who got locked up forever.

I had just turned ten when I came. I was well past my fifteenth birthday when I was summoned by the sultan. Almost six years. There was little evidence of it when it came to pack. Anything I'd gained in the last six years was in my head, mystery and marvel and adventure from all those years of reading. My actual belongings made no larger a bundle than when I came.

The morning of departure came, sooner than I had thought possible early in the night when I'd lain sleepless, wondering how it would all happen, too excited and fearful to believe I would ever sleep. Still, sleep I had, and the birds nestled in the fretwork were just beginning their drowsy comments on the day when my eyes popped open like squeezed pea pods and I staggered to my feet trying dazedly to remember why I was getting up at all. The memory came quickly enough when I tripped over the bundle I'd packed the night before—after the other slaves in the room were asleep, as they still were.

The bundle made only a light burden for one hand. I pushed open the door with the other, shutting it softly behind me. Then was only a quick stop at the midden, a scuttle down a long corridor, past the kitchens, down a short side hall, up a full flight to the courtyard level, down another corridor, and there was the courtyard itself, with the pool and the fountain and some bent old person I had never seen before going from flowerpot to flowerpot with a watering bucket and ladle. Frowsea was waiting at the foot of the private stairs, and on the sultana's balcony a set of clothes was laid out: full trousers and flowing shirt of white cotton, leather boots, a much-pocketed sleeveless vest of thick blue cotton, embroidered all down the front, a brightly striped woven belt, and a full-length cotton coat vertically striped red and blue and black. In addition I was given a white muslin head scarf with black-braided, gold-mounted cord and a plain black woolen mantle, which could be fastened on the shoulder with a golden pin, the head of a kanna, baying.

The sultana was nowhere in evidence. It was Frowsea who instructed me: "You and I are ponjic, girl. So far as the sultan's folk are concerned, our tribe is a lesser people. Except for one or two of the animal handlers, you'll be the only free ponja traveling in a largely scuinic-pheledian troop. Be careful to behave suitably, with modesty. So long as you have on trousers, shirt and headdress, you're decently dressed. Never take off the shirt or the trousers, not unless you're in a room by yourself or are readying for sleep. Only slaves and lesser servants expose their bodies. Free males cover themselves, no matter what tribe they are from. Well, unless they're with a suitable female...."

"The prince knows who I am...."

"The others may not. And travelers meet up with other travelers. If you're going as a ponjic boy, sort of a companion for the prince, try to act like a boy. What did you bring with you?"

I opened my bundle to display the few small books and several treasures, including my father's last gift, the ebony treasure box with the hidden drawer under the false bottom. The box held sewing implements, and, in the hidden drawer, the gems the sultana had given me. Aside from these there was only my underwear, stockings and the pair of sandals I had on. Frowsea quickly added all the clothing that had been tried on the day before.

"That's all," said Frowsea, as she tightened the pack with great vigor. "Plus this letter, from the sultana to her son."

"Can't she write to him anytime?"

"Of course. Or see him, when he's well enough to come here. But she hasn't wanted him to come here, for fear someone here may be doing him harm. She hasn't wanted to send letters for fear the letter carrier might be part of the conspiracy. She feels he will be safer without any touch of the harim."

It seemed overly careful to me, though, to hear the females talk, it was perfectly possible to put a curse on a letter, or to kill with a glance. Curses were very powerful, if one had skill at it. Of course, some people could lay curses every day in the month and not raise a pimple.

I was given no time to consider the matter. Once I was dressed and the pack was strapped up, Soaz appeared like a jinni out of nothing, picked up the pack and told me to come along. We went down another way, rather than through the courtyard, and old Bluethumb was waiting by the last gate.

"Well, now," she said, taking me by the shoulders and looking me up and down. "Don't you look like a proper adventurer. All you need is a scimitar."

I shuddered. I'd only seen a scimitar used once, by the executioner who cut off Father's head, and I had no wish whatsoever to use one myself. Bluethumb was busy hugging me, however, and did not notice the shudder.

"You'll keep your mouth shut if you know what's good for you," Soaz growled at the old one.

"Don't be so puffed up, Soaz! I've kept it shut about more than this, I'll have you know. Besides, better there's someone to say she saw the girl go off to her brother. That way there'll be no talk. No one's interested in her brother, after all."

Soaz grunted, rather like a poked guz, and unlocked the final gate, not the one made of great wooden planks with iron studs all over it and hinges forged in the shape of curly spears, but the little one set in at the side, only big enough for one person. He cracked it just wide enough for us to edge through, as though he was afraid some harim air might escape, then shut and locked it behind us.

We stood in a sunlit and paved courtyard with passages leading outward, toward the smell of blossoms, toward the smell of cooking, toward the smell of stables and the challenging mutter of umminhi. Soaz went in the umminhic direction, and I trotted along behind, through the unlocked gate and into a cobbled yard that smelled like a stable, like grandfather's farm when I'd been there as a child, outside the city, a day's ride to the east. One thing about umminhi, they stank. If they couldn't run like the wind, nobody would keep umminhi, for no one would put up with the stench.

The prince was already mounted amid a troop of silent attendants and guards. A dozen smaller pack animals stood in a vacant-eyed chain, managed by two kapric handlers. Another handler held the reins of two tall riding umminhi, stallion and gelding, saddled, but without riders. These were racing creatures, taller than any I had ever seen, much less ridden upon, their glossy hides set off by their silver collars and green breeder's tags. The breeding of umminhi, so my father had told me, was a monopoly, and no animal could be bought or sold without the proper tags.

Without a word, Soaz tossed me high into the gelding's saddle, gave my pack to one of the handlers, and went up the slanting ladder to his own saddle, quick and agile despite his bulk. On the farm, I had ridden astride, holding on to the umminha's mane, but she had been a mare, smaller and better natured. Here I settled myself into the cushions of the comfortable scuinic style box-saddle and leaned against the padded arms and back. I lowered the saddle bar into place, took the blinker reins into my hands and placed them as the others had them, tightly through the center notch of the bar. In this position, the spring-mounted blinkers were open, allowing the umminha to see in any direction.

I hoped my mount was well disposed toward its rider. Sometimes umminhi were not at all well disposed. Stallions were said to attack riders, female riders particularly. Breeding mares were too heavy to make good riding animals, though some persons used older females for pack animals. Even the old ones could carry quite large burdens. Sometimes, however, a steed took an outright dislike to one person or one kind of person, and then there was war between them. So I had been told.

This umminha seemed inclined to ignore me, as did the assembled people. No one looked at me. No one said anything to me. The prince let his eyes slide across me with only a hint of a nod, then gave a signal to one of the older persons, evidently the way-master, who leaned forward and spoke to his umminha. The steed thought it over for a moment—if umminhi can be said to think—blinking its eyes and working its jaws methodically before ambling toward the long barrel-vaulted masonry tunnel that led to the gate. Its shod feet thudded on the hollow planking, like an ominous drum that fell silent when they emerged from the gate. None of the palace windows looked outward, so this emergence marked the first time in almost six years that I had seen the city. From this roadway, high on the side of palace hill, I could look down on a thousand red-tiled rooftops, smell the hazy smoke of several thousand cook fires, see gardens green with trees, the whole protected by high walls with pheledic guards walking upon them five abreast, calling out the hours. This was lovely Tavor, gem of the orchard lands.

It was a Tavor seen as a blur, for at a signal from the way-master the umminhi ran, faster than I had known any creature could run, the walls spinning by, the streets like whirling shadows, the people mere smears of color, the soft thuds of umminhi feet making one continuous sound, like rushing water, and themselves arrowing toward the city walls, aimed at the dark gullet of the city gate, where they plunged into shadow and were spat out again, onto the sunlit road and away.

There, after a moment, everything slowed down. I looked up to see the prince riding beside me and re-

garding me with an amused expression. "You can un-
clench your jaw," he said.

I tried, finding it somewhat difficult. "They went so
fast!"

"A bit of diversion," he remarked. "So no one could
see who exactly we were, or where exactly we'd come
from, or where exactly we were going. Though everyone
knew we came from the court—only the nobles can afford to buy or maintain umminhi like this—they don't
know who exactly we may be. The banner isn't the royal
banner. Father hopes most of them will think it's some
minor official, escorted by troops."

"You don't want anyone to know you're gone?"

"Some think it wisest."

"Sultan Tummyfat?"

He looked loftily amused. "We don't call him that
out here. That's a palace name. A pet name. Like your
own, or mine. Out here I am not Keen Nose. I'm the
Prince Sahir. And you are my companion, Nassif."

"Nassif?" I asked, wonderingly.

"Don't be stupid, girl. Your father and mother did
not call you Opalears."

It was true. They had not. "They called me Nassifeh.
How did you know?"

"It was in the records."

"It was Bluethumb who first called me Opalears."

"A palace habit. A leisurely, female-ish habit. Inside
the palace, we all have soft, affectionate names, regardless of our tribe, even people like your father who live
outside but work within. It lends a kind of informality
that erases our separate tribes and castes, making rela-
tionships seem less rigorous and more familial. But we
do not permit it out here, where convention reigns."

"What is your father called, out here?"

"The sultan. That is quite enough. There are those
who say 'His Effulgence' or 'His Mightiness,' but such
is unnecessary. When you speak to me, you say, my
prince. When you speak of me, you say, the Prince Sahir. Unless you are talking to strangers, in which case

you will call me simply Sahir, who is a not very important someone with the fruit-marketing bureau.

"When I speak to you, I say Nassif, remembering to leave off the little girl *eh* at the end. When I speak of you, I say, my faithful Nassif."

"And will I be faithful?" I asked, wonderingly.

"One hopes," he sneered. "One always hopes." He rode from my side to the head of the column and stayed there, ignoring me. Soaz dropped into the place he had vacated.

"Are we going outside Tavor?" I asked him.

"Of course." He looked surprised at the question. "We would have to, wouldn't we?"

"I didn't know."

"Then you don't know much about Tavor."

"Almost nothing," I admitted. "My father never told me very much about the world. We always talked of other things."

"Such as?"

"Oh, we talked about animals. I love animals. I used to love the farm, because there were so many. And we talked about people, too. People he had met in his work. But we never really talked about the world. I never have figured out all the different tribes and the places that they came from."

"I will remedy the lack," he said, proceeding to do so at some length.

"Long ago, before the great Farsaki War of Conquest (of which it is now generally conceded there will be no end until the world is conquered), and before the prophets of Korè were so widespread among us, guiding us to righteousness, the tribes lived mostly in isolation, one from the other. Some were forest people, dwelling in the tree lands north and west of Sworp, like the armakfatidi and the scuini and my own people, the pheledas. Some lived in the jungles south of Isfoin, like the sitidian people and your own ancestors. Some lived on the prairies, like the kannic and kapriel people, and some near the water, like the kasturi, the onchiki and the Onchik-Dau.

Among these people, some were settled town folk and
some were people living in family groups and some, like
the scuinic people of Tavor, roamed as nomads over a
mixed grass and woodland in the far west, among scattered tribes of kapriel folk. Unfortunately, this wide
stretch of country lay in the road of the ersuniel raiders
of Farsak.

"Though the scuinic tribes cherish many traditions
involving fierce personal combat among males, the race
as a whole is not bellicose, and it was soon overrun. At
that time the Farsakian raiders were cannibalistic, as ersuniel tribes sometimes are, or were, so the scuinic people of Tavor thought it prudent to flee.

"Moving swiftly, mostly by night, the Tavorians traveled eastward, up toward the glacial ice of the Sharbak
Mountains. Here, there were no Farsaki to pursue and
they could take time to provision themselves by collecting fruits and nutritious root vegetables in the fertile
passes of the high range. They then made a more leisurely way down into the desert provinces, past the western and southern side of what is now the Four Realms,
which edge upon the marshes of Palmia. Here they
rested for some years around the kasturic marsh-town of
Durbos, where they sought advice from travelers. Following the suggestions of several nomadic peoples, they
then swung to the east, surmounted the Big Stonies,
crossed the valley of Wycos by the almost hidden fords
of River Roq, then traveled over the Little Stonies, coming in time to this wide plain, this land well watered by
the tributaries of the Scurry, this land grown up in wild
fruit trees, root vegetables, and fields of grain. At that
time, it was virtually uninhabited. Farsak was nowhere
near, and here at the southern end of the great plain, the
survivors made their homes."

"And built Tavor?" I offered.

Soaz shook his head. "The scuinic tribes have always
been nomadic people. They are not skilled builders.
They lived in this valley, moving occasionally south toward Isfoin, for several generations. By that time the

various tribes had multiplied; their people had spread out; they began to encounter one another at the edges of their territories; they began to trade and mix and establish multitribal communities which expanded into city-states and then into the nations we know today.

"It was then that people began to wander down the Scurry and build settlements along the flow. After another few generations enough of them had accumulated to erect our city of New Tavor. It was named, as the people were, after a revered sultan, one of the Six Revered Ancestors of Tummyfat, from ages long gone."

My father had often remarked that scuinic people did not labor. They considered it beneath them, except for earthworks, which they did very well. "What people built the city?"

Soaz nodded judiciously. "Oh, people who filtered in over the years: pheledic herdsmen following their flocks, kasturic people who followed the Scurry up from the lower plains, ponjic and sitidian farmers seeking land, armakfatidian merchants and peddlers who came over this pass or down that river from Palmia or Isfoin or even from far Estafan, where your family once lived."

"I never heard my father mention Estafan," I said. "I never heard of it until you spoke of it."

"There's no particular reason your father would have referred to it at all," said Soaz. "It was your great-great-grandparents who came from there. They were welcome, for a sensible country needs the talents of a varied people in order to get all the things done that must be done. Your family's history is in the archives. Your father's and mother's sides both came from Estafan, which is a strange, weird country where the ponji walk upside down."

"Where is it?" I wanted to know.

"West of here. Over the Sharbak Range, near Sworp and Finial, on the shores of the Crawling Sea. Near our own line of travel, in fact."

"Will we see it? Will we see the people walk upside down?"

When he laughed, I knew he was teasing me, and I shut my mouth tightly, much annoyed.

"Oh, girl, Opalears . . . no, I must say, Nassif. You must let me tickle your naïveté a little. We will go through the country of Estafan, though it may no longer be a kingdom. Everything north of the mountains and along the sea has been taken over by the Farsakian Empire." He fell silent, brooding, his eyes fixed on the horizon.

Since he was in a talkative mood, I asked another question, which had been bothering me ever since St. Weel had been mentioned.

"Why are we really going, Soaz? Surely there are physicians nearer than St. Weel. It seems a dreadful long and dangerous way to go."

"The prince's health is only an excuse," he murmured to me, watching the prince from the corner of his eye. "We are actually going because of an old oracle the sultan met in his travels, years ago, when Great-tooth was minding the throne."

I put on a slightly interested look, just enough to encourage him.

"The sultan tells me he was in the desert, far east of Isfoin. He'd been traveling for days in that blinding heat before he came to an oasis which encircled the ruins of a vast, ancient caravansary. In the ruins, off in one dusty corner, an old gray female had built herself a little hut, quite snug and safe and protected from the desert winds. She wasn't of the sultan's race. She was ponjic, and, like all of you, she was clever with her hands. . . ."

"Which is why we make such good slaves and servants," I said in a snippy voice, quoting my father.

"True," said Soaz, raising his eyebrows. "But she was neither a slave nor a servant. She wore the garb of a free person, and she said she had come originally from Sworp by way of Palmia and the Wycos Valley. The sultan gave her some food and spices, less from charity than from surprise at finding anyone there, and in return, she gave him a reading of the bones. From the pattern the bones made in falling, she could read, so she said, the sultan's future, and the future of his people.''

"An interesting tale," I murmured in a casual way, though in fact I was avid to hear the rest.

Soaz nodded and went on. "When she had peered at the bones for a very long time, she said, 'I have an instruction and a talisman for you. You must keep the talisman safe, unopened. If you go into danger, put it in a place of safety. You must not look at it until time of need.' ''

"What did she give him?"

"He told me it was a fortune. One of those folded parchment ones the onchiki use for money. Then she said, 'Sultan, are you true to the faith of your ancestors?'

"The sultan told her he was Korèsan born and bred, a faithful son of that faith. 'I see Korè being threatened,' she said. 'I see darkness coming. I hear trumpets blaring war and the umminhi screaming beside the picket fires. I feel treachery and a death of peoples, worse than a death, an unbeing. When that day approaches, help may be found at St. Weel.'

"The sultan believed the old one. He said there was something about her that made him believe. Since he would be riding into some danger, he sent the talisman to me, back in Tavor, with instructions to put it in the lock box in my own rooms. I never got it. I learned from my palace spies that a message from the sultan had been intercepted by Great-tooth. I challenged him to produce it, and he, to cover his tail, accused Halfnose Nazir of taking it, then cut Nazir's head off so he couldn't say otherwise."

My eyes filled. "Poor Father. Did you get the thing back?"

"Great-tooth died, quite mysteriously, before the sultan returned"—he smiled a strange smile—"and though I searched the palace for the talisman, it has never been found."

"And what has all that to do with this journey?"

"The last thing the old woman said to the sultan. 'If

you do not go to St. Weel, then send your son. Well before the year of the vulture, send him, for if he goes not and learns not, then in the year of that uncouth bird, the tree of heaven falls.' '' He sighed, then frowned. "She did not tell him which son to send. It has taken the sultan quite a time to decide on Sahir."

I was busy telling over the calendar to myself. "But it's still four years until the year of the vulture."

"Four years is only a little time," said Soaz. "Oh, child, you have no idea. For such a journey, four years is a very short time."

"Will we meet cannibals?" I murmured in a frightened voice. "And monsters?"

He hummed in his throat, the way pheledian people sometimes did, like a kettle simmering. "The Farsaki were cannibals once, surely. But they have changed over time. Though they're still determined to conquer the world, they've softened greatly in the way they're going about it. Something mysterious in that, I'm told. Some exotic influence. Or, perhaps Korè spoke to them."

"Is that true?" I asked doubtfully. "Or is it only a story?"

"True enough that they've changed, though no one knows exactly why. A few decades ago the Farsaki took Palmia as a tributary province, but instead of eating the inhabitants, they allowed it to continue under its own governance. And among the north lands, Wycos and Tavor are yet free of them."

"What about the Strangers at the Hospice of St. Weel? Do they belong to the Farsaki?"

His voice dropped to a mere murmur. "There have been whispers about St. Weel for generations! I wouldn't speculate about it aloud." And that was all he had to say about anything for that day, at least.

Dora Deals with a Body

Dora knew it was silly to think the weed had followed her to her new home like a pet cat, but the idea itched at her for the next couple of weeks until she drove over to Jared's place to look, half expecting Jared's weed to be gone. One look served to reassure her that Jared's weed, the weed that had put Jared in the hospital (she knew the weed had done it, she just didn't know how) was still there at Jared's place, very lush and green, covering almost the whole front of the house and looking very satisfied with itself. Someone had pulled out the dead trees and the dead bushes and had planted some saplings in little clusters. The grass needed cutting, but except for that, the place looked really good. Since she was already in the neighborhood, she decided to stop in to see her former landlady-cum-mother-in-law, if Jared's car wasn't there.

Jared's car wasn't, and Mother Gerber told her about the house, right off. "Jared's decided to sell it. He's tired of fussing with it, and he says he'd rather just live here with me than go through getting used to a housekeeper. I told the real estate lady about that weed thing, and she said it looked all right, she'd just get rid of the dead stuff and leave it at that.''

''Did she plant the new trees?''

''I saw that! She didn't tell me she was going to do that! I think it looks messy.'' She lifted one nostril. ''People don't keep up the way they used to. It looks like a wilderness. These environmentalists, someone like that, they'll probably love it.''

Dora patted her shoulder and went on to work, feeling obscurely sorry for Momma Gerber while still being thankful to have left Jared. Phil, as usual, had left the reports for her to do, and she'd no sooner finished the stack than she and Phil caught a call from a maintenance man at Randall Pharmaceuticals who said he'd found a body. Randall's was clear out on the northeast edge of town toward the airport.

The caller had had sense enough not to inform anyone but the police and to have a coworker guard the body while he met them at the gate. The man who met them wore green overalls and a company logo on the back: a double helix and test tube. He introduced himself as Joe Penton, then climbed in the backseat and directed them around the side of the gatehouse and down a rutted drive past a long, low annex and then a maze of pens and sheds and feed bins. Farther down the hill, through sparse clumped grasses, they came to a grove of trees that was part of a narrow woods stretching in both directions along the almost dry creek bed.

The body was there, half hidden in the trees, with another overalled man squatted down not far from it. ''It's Dr. Winston,'' this one told them, looking up from where he was crouched. ''Dr. Edgar Winston.''

Dora gave the place a quick going over. No sign of a struggle. Nothing disturbed. Just the body, lying there, the long white lab coat stained with something down the front, the elderly victim's face drawn in an expression of concentration that might mean something and might not. There was grass all around him, no surface to take footprints. The series of pens and shelters ran from the annex almost all the way down the hill to where they were.

"What's the low building there?" she asked their guide. "And the pens?"

"Animal labs," he replied. "The company makes veterinary medicines." He indicated the nearest pens, where half a dozen pigs were lined up against the fence, staring in their direction.

"For pigs?" Phil asked, in his disbelieving voice.

"Sure, pigs," said Joe Penton. "And horses and cows and dogs and cats and anything else people keep for livestock or pets or in zoos."

Dora took her phone from her pocket and called for the medical examiner and the forensics team. If they'd hurry, they could get here before people started piling out of that building. Already she could see round pale blobs at third-floor windows. They were no doubt wondering what the hell the car was doing down here, light flashing.

She took out her notebook. "And your name is?" she asked of the kneeling man.

"Twenzel," he said. "Bill."

"We take care of the animals," said Penton. "Once or twice a week we walk the perimeter and check the fences. There's a cut in the fence, by the way." He pointed down to the tree line, toward leaning posts and sagging chain link. "Anyhow, that's how we found Dr. Winston."

"And you know him?" Dora asked.

"Well, sure. We work for the animal labs. There's six of us altogether, four for weekdays and a weekend crew. We clean pens and do the feeding, stuff like that, so we see . . . saw Dr. Winston almost every day. He was the head honcho. He headed up the improved breeds project."

"Improved breeds?"

"They're using DNA to make new breeds of livestock. You know, like hybrids. Cattle resistant to disease, or leaner pigs, like those guys over there.'' He gestured toward the pens, where the pigs were still lined up, noses to the wire.

Leaving Phil to continue the questioning, Dora began to inspect the area. Her primary task right now was to locate and protect anything that might be used as evidence and keep people from messing up the crime scene. If it was a crime scene. They wouldn't know whether it was or not until they had a cause of death. The guy might have dropped dead of a heart attack.

''Poor guy,'' said someone.

She turned, trying to find the source of the voice, but could not. The pigs had gone back to their food troughs, and the other pens seemed almost empty, though she spied a scurry of quick movement from one about halfway up the hill.

''What kind of animals have you got out here?'' she called.

Joe walked over, ready to be expansive. ''Oh, different kinds. Farm animals out here, plus dogs and cats. Some exotic animals, too. Monkeys are housed inside. Dr. Winston uses this set of genes from this one and that set of genes from that one. One time he got this pig with horns, honest to God.''

''Poor thing,'' said Dora, depressed.

''Oh, hell no,'' the other man put in. ''Pinky liked his horns. He became the terror of the pig yard. It was a mistake, though. The others had nothing to fight back with. Dr. Winston had to cut them off.''

''What about the doctor?'' she asked. ''What was he doing down here?''

Joe replied, ''Who knows? I saw him in the labs early this morning, when I was cleaning the cages inside. Bill says he saw him having a coffee break about ten, in the company cafeteria. Then around eleven thirty, we came down here on our regular fence check, and there he was. We didn't touch him except to make sure he was dead, then Bill waited while I went back up to the gate to call the police."

"You didn't tell the boss, or whoever here at the plant."

Joe and Bill exchanged glances. "Nope," said Joe. "We decided to let you do that."

Dora frowned. "So they don't even know?"

"Not unless one of them did it," snarled Bill.

Dora saw a car arrive at the gate, lights flashing. That'd be the forensics people. She took a last good look around. They were in an open floodplain, no buildings nearby, just the long narrow line of woods, the space between the larger trees growing up in saplings with low grassland everywhere else. Through the trees she could see the cut in the fence, a man-sized hole, from top to bottom. The fence evidently marked the edge of the company's property. Beyond it was an upsloping grassy meadow with a ball stop halfway up, and at the top, the backsides of a row of houses. All very peaceful.

It didn't stay that way. Things got complex. Dora and Phil strung up a crime tape just before the first people arrived from the Randall Building, which they did, by dozens. Some head honcho arrived full of orders and instructions, and Dora had to tell him to back off, they'd do fine, thank you. The photographer arrived and departed, then the body went. All available cops began a close search of the area.

The lieutenant beckoned. Nodding at the backs of the houses across the way, he said, "Medical examiner says it's a stabbing wound in the back, he'll know more after the autopsy, but he thinks it's a wide, doubled-edged blade of some kind. Somebody might've seen something. Dermot, you and Henry start with the houses over there, both sides of the street, get the names of any kids might've been out in that field. Here's the vitals on the guy: white, five nine, blue eyes, mostly bald, brown hair where he's got hair, sixty-nine years old, past retirement, you'd think, but they say he was irreplaceable so they kept him on. No scars or tattoos. You saw what he was wearing: khakis, blue knit shirt, long white coat.''

Dora spoke up. "Did the medical examiner say what the weapon might have been?''

"Stabbed, not slashed. The blade went in between the ribs. You're not looking for a machete or a stiletto, but that's about all we know yet.''

They spent the afternoon going from house to house talking to this one and that one, coming back to the ones who weren't home, getting names of kids who might have seen something, names of other people who might have seen something. Not many. The row of houses was occupied by mostly older people, working people, people who wouldn't be likely to have been playing ball where they could see anything on a weekday. End of the day, effort max, results nil. Phil was in a hurry.

"Anniversary,'' he said. "I forget, I get home late, I don't bring a present, all next year is down the drain.''

"Go on home, Phil. I'll type up the report.''

"I ever tell you you're a sweetheart, Dora Henry?''

"Don't let Charlene hear you say it. And tell her thank you again for my house.''

"Hey, how's that working out?''

"I love it. Just the right size and everything.''

"Well, good luck with it.'' And he was gone, out, leaving her in the noisy room to struggle with the computer.

Roger Manconi dropped into the chair next to her. Roger was a perennial dropper and hugger and fanny patter, but he did it with guys, too, or anything else that breathed air. Dora liked him.

"Funny one, huh,'' he said.

"What do you mean?'' she said, concentrating on her typing.

"That guy Winston. The lieutenant says he wasn't robbed. Wallet still on him, and an expensive watch. Wonder who had it in for the guy? You and Phil were out there?''

"Yeah. He was just lying there, peaceful as an oyster. He looked more thoughtful than dead, to tell you the truth. Phil and I spent the afternoon going up and down the street across the creek.''

"I didn't know there was a creek down there."

"It's not much. Sort of wide flat gully and a ... I guess you'd say a woods. Lots of saplings coming up, right down next to the water. There's a field on the other side, looks like somebody mowed it within the last week or so, maybe cut hay on it or something. There's a ball stop. I don't know why. Nobody in the neighborhood seems to use it."

"Did you have any luck at all?"

"Even if somebody'd been home, nobody could've seen him from over there. Too many trees. Only chance would have been if some kid had been right down in the woods, chasing a ball, maybe."

He thought a moment. "Did I hear right, this guy was doing research?"

"Yeah. They're doing genetic stuff with animals. Seeing if they can gene splice them."

"Gene splice?"

"You know. Mix them up." She laughed. "Make a rat with feathers. That kind of stuff."

"Why?"

"You got me. Why do scientists do anything?"

"He's the second one killed, just lately."

Dora frowned, suddenly reminded of the other guy. "The one Phil and I did some leg work on. About a month ago."

"He was stabbed, too," Manconi remarked. "And nobody robbed him, either." He saluted with a finger and wandered off, leaving her to draw her own conclusions. It itched at Dora. What about the guy in the parking lot? Phil had completed the file while she was out. Hadn't that victim been a geneticist, too? She should have made the connection right away!

Both guys had been interfering with nature. Like Jared, in a way. Jared goes out and sprays a plant, then he gets sick from weedspray. And this guy, Winston, he fools around mutating animals, and then he gets very dead. What had the other one been working on?

She went downstairs to Records and waited around until Lynn Beatty was free, then went over to her desk.

"Dora! Hey, sorry to hear about your husband. That was very strange."

"Yeah, it was." She didn't want to say he wasn't her husband, or wouldn't be for long, but she didn't want to lie, either. She reiterated a truth, hoping that would do. "It was all . . . very strange."

"What brings you down here?" Lynn gestured at the littered desks, the messy, memo-hung walls.

"That guy who was stabbed in the parking lot outside the medical school? Manconi's case. Can you pull that file?"

Lynn went tap-tapping at her keyboard, searching for the name, the case number. "June twelfth. Dr. Martin Chamberlain. He was a geneticist."

"Refresh my memory. What was the weapon?"

Lynn tapped at her keyboard once more. "Wide-bladed, double-edged something."

"How did I know you were going to say that? What was he working on?"

"All it says here is he was researching into the cause of genetic diseases."

"I wonder if there might be more. Do you remember any other homicide or assault cases lately where somebody was trying to fool Mother Nature?"

Lynn sat back, opened her eyes very wide. "Fool Mother Nature? How?"

"Any old how. Like somebody who was killing animals or plants, or maybe changing animals or plants?"

Lynn nodded. "Your mentioning plants reminds me of one about two months ago. Back in May. Woman worked for one of the big lumber companies. I guess you could say she was fooling with Mother Nature. She was working on trees, ways to make them resistant to disease and pollution. That one's sort of mysterious. She was stabbed, too, but nobody can figure why."

"Two months ago? You want to look up the weapon?"

"Right." She tapped intently, then looked up, eyes wide.

"Wide blade, double edge, right?" said Dora. "And you can add another one."

"When?"

"They found him this morning. He was working with animals, not trees, but it was the same MO."

They sat, staring at each other. "Some kind of serial killer?" Dora asked. "Some environmental nut?"

"Why do you think that?"

She explained about Winston and the animal research. "Can you give me the case number and name on the case in May?"

Lynn tapped and muttered, coming up with the requisite name. "Dr. Jennifer Williams, Ph.D. and all that. What are you going to do with it?"

Dora shrugged. "Mention to the medical examiners that we've got three stabbings, each a month apart, each involving scientists, possibly the same weapon. See if maybe we can connect them up."

"It sounds crazy, but I'll let you know if any others pop to the top."

Dora left it at that. Crazy or not, it would come down to asking questions and looking at answers, over and over. It was always interesting. Frustrating sometimes, but always interesting. Always something intriguing for the next day.

She yawned. Too many late nights lately, getting herself moved in. It would be good to go home, have a bath, maybe sit out in her clay patch for a while. Maybe pull a few dandelions.

When she got home, the first thing she saw was the weed, now all the way up beside her door, arching over it in a little hood, like a tiny porch roof.

"Hello, weed," she said.

All the leaflets turned in her direction. Among them she could see the tiny spheres of seed heads, like bubbles of silken floss. A few strands came loose as she watched, floating away, almost invisible.

She swallowed deeply and went in. The light was blinking on her answering machine, a message from Polly.

"Hey, Dora, welcome to your new home. I got to thinking about your weed, you know. Or, Jared's weed, I guess. The way it kind of turned toward people. Anyhow, I've been reading up, and I found a couple of examples of what they call irritomotility in plants. Mimosa is one, and there's a sensitive briar, genus Shrankia, of the Leguminosae family. Anyhow, they grow a lot like the weed, and they move when they're touched. I'm wondering if the weed is related to something like that, only it moves in response to sound, maybe, or odors. What do you think? Call me when you've got a minute."

Dora went down the stairs and opened the door softly. When she stepped out onto the stoop, the leaflets turned toward her. As long as she stood there, they remained turned in her direction. So, it wasn't motion. Or sound. Odor? Maybe. Or body heat. Or maybe it could see her.

Silly! She shook her head and went back inside to call Polly.

6

Izakar, Prince of Palmia

"When one tallies the talents needed in a progressive nation, one would be at a loss to fulfill them without the varied skills shown by the ponjic tribes. Whether it is in architecture or the manufacture of furnishings, whether in the production of woven goods or the casting of metals, the ponjic peoples are supreme. It is said that a ponji needs see a process only once to be able to improve upon it! They are known as a talkative people— perhaps because they have so much to talk about!—but their loquacity is surpassed by their charm. Every military establishment has its ponjic aide de camp; every embassy its ponjic attaché, without whose good offices nothing would be done as well or as gladly, and who has not delighted in the marvelous dramas staged by this talented people. . . ."

THE PEOPLES OF EARTH
HIS EXCELLENCY, EMPEROR FAROS VII

Across the Stony Mountains from Tavor was the land of Palmia, and in Palmia lived Izakar Poffit, Izakar the Indifferent, smart-ass Izakar, entering upon difficulty and danger as he approached adulthood; Schizy Izzy, Prince of Palmia, who try as he would could not claim ignorance of the prophecy that held his life in thrall.

His maternal grandfather had first told him of the prophecy when he was a mere child, barely able to babble the Marconite Obfuscations. Aunt Aggie and Cousin Clair-belle had mentioned the prophecy in passing and with utmost sarcasm at least once or twice a week from the time he was a toddler ("Oh, isn't he the big male person, all ready to fulfill his prophecy!"). That is, they had done so until just recently when it occurred to someone that the prophecy, instead of being an amusing anecdote, was in fact a sentence of death, not only for Izzy but for the rest of them as well.

At that point everyone stopped mentioning it altogether, as though silence on the subject would make it go away. Izakar's time and place was, in this respect, no different from other times and places where imminent danger is met by putting one's head beneath the blanket.

As for Prince Izakar himself, the prophecy had been so frequently and inconsequentially mentioned that he had become indifferent to the subject long before he'd come to terms with it. He tended to put it in the same category as other adult concerns one would prefer not to consider: the inevitability of death, the necessity of toil, the malevolence of Fate, and sex between one's parents. Besides, he was more interested in other things.

Magic, for instance. Magic was intriguing, some of it was great fun, useful for getting even with cousins and aunts, except when one was caught at it and had one's mouth washed out with soap for Malicious Utterance. Though he was taught only beneficent, defensive, or protective magics, he had to learn about the others. It was rather like being taught to train and ride horses and donkeys, but learning about umminhi on the side. The former were useful, the latter could be deadly dangerous, but if a person was to have a chance at survival, he had to know about danger. As Uncle Goffio often said, ignorance may be bliss, but it's damned poor life insurance.

In addition to magic, Izzy liked green things rather a lot. This interest was both inculcated and sustained by his Aunt Aggie, who, as a closet Korèsan, considered the biological world the only thing worth people's adoration. Izzy also enjoyed cooking. There was something very satisfying about making a good sauce as well as eating it. He liked girls, also, in an associative sense. He found them less wearing than the males about the place, all of whom seemed dedicated to the competitive use of arms and the equally competitive consumption of food, drink and females. Belching, puking, or undergoing painful but ineffectual treatment for battle wounds or sexual diseases did not seem fun to Izzy, though Cousin Tonio was always doing one or the other and didn't seem to mind.

Tonio was a noted ladies' man, and he had promised to initiate Izzy into the gentle game of the boudoir epée. Frolic fencing, as Tonio called it, though he also used rather blunter words for it. Aunt told him he was not to involve Izzy until Izzy was Old Enough. Izzy doubted he was Old Enough yet, as he was lightly built and slightly less than seventeen hands tall. His hair was rather red, and longer than average, and he brushed it back from his forehead into a kind of queue, gathered up at the neck. His eyes were brown. Unlike most males of his class, he was somewhat abstemious and abhorred violence, believing, accurately, that anyone his size with any sense at all should not only abhor violence but go to great lengths to avoid it.

For relaxation Izzy played the larbel, a wooden instrument with a rounded sound box and six strings, which could be either bowed or plucked. In talented hands it was said to soothe the spirits of the damned. Izzy doubted this, for though he was very talented, he had not noted any soothed spirits floating around in his general vicinity.

Formally, the people of Palmia, Izzy's people, were

Bubblians, worshippers of Great Ghoti, who eight hundred years ago had blown the bubble-world just as it was now, complete with apparently ancient ruins and trees in order to give people the illusion of time. Ghoti blows such bubbles, so the priests said, for his own amusement. Ghoti intends, so the priests declared, that this particular bubble be very, very small—obviating the need for exploration—with only a few simple things in it—obviating the need for science—all of which any child could understand—obviating the need for study. Things which seemed more complex were only illusions. Things which could not be understood at first glance were better ignored.

The bubble was to last a total of one thousand years, at the end of which time the Arch-child, Ghoti's son Bandercran, would pierce the bubble with the Conceptual Needle and everything would go pop. Everything, so the Ghotian bishops said, except for those disobedient persons who had insisted upon exploring, experimenting, and studying, whom Ghoti would select to occupy an adjacent bubble called hell.

Izzy, orphaned early, had learned all this from various relatives and servitors. He had been about eleven when he had asked the castle wizard—that magician/cum shaman/cum sorcerer assigned to keep the palace and its residents free of hexes, spites, and spooklice—about the death of Izzy's father. Izzy knew he had been beheaded, but he had never been told why.

The wizard, looking cautiously over his shoulder to be sure they were alone, had whispered that the former king came to grief through coveting a former time.

To Izzy, who woke up disputatious a dozen days out of a fortnight, longing for a former time did not seem to be a capital crime. Unwisely, he said as much.

"Hush," hissed the wizard, putting his fingers over Izzy's lips. "The Ghotian council of bishops said it was not a former time in *this* bubble your father longed for, but some other bubble altogether."

"Ah," said Izzy, astounded into indiscretion. "So you know about other bubbles."

"No, no," cried the wizard in a perfect frenzy of negation. "There are no other bubbles. Not for us! Your father longed for fiction, for fantasy, for a thing he called technology. He was found guilty of electrifying."

This crime, whispered the wizard, had something to do with machines. To be safe from heresy, the wizard gasped, one must accept that there are not and never have been any other bubbles for people. Izzy fumed, but despite knowing very well that there were jillions of other bubbles, he did not contradict! He had, after all, taken an oath not to reveal that knowledge.

His enlightenment on such subjects as space and time had begun on a memorable day during his sixth year when he had been astonished to see a group of dusty persons emerging from a seemingly solid wall in the corridor where he was, at the time, playing with his peepee. These persons first suggested that Izzy put his peepee away, then told him they had come to divulge the king's secret, a secret which the sudden execution of Izzy's father had prevented his passing on to any of his sons. These persons had seized Izzy up forthwith and taken him below, to a marvelous place that no one in the palace had any knowledge of whatsoever: the Great Library.

Izzy never grew really accustomed to the library. Even after years of frequenting the place, he still found it astonishing. There were shelves everywhere, most of them behind dusty glass doors that protected the books within from the fly and the moth and the worm. There were desks at which one might spell out, letter by letter, requests for information. There were ancient machines which still blinked to life and spoke in various of the speak-systems: from the early cycles Latyn and Frinch and Swajili and Inglitch—which was still spoken as a kind of trade language—from later cycles Armbun and Flok, and from the current time, Isfoinian and Finialese and Tavorian and Estafaner, the highly aspirated language of the sea peoples and the debased Uk-luk dialects of the Onchikian tribes who lived in the shore counties along the Crawling Sea. Though many of these languages were archaic, or even dead, one could make them out. With difficulty, with diligence, with dictionaries. With the help of the Linguists and the Librarians, people who traced their origins back to the very first cycle, almost back into the prelinguistic ooze.

Since that first day, Izzy had spent much of his time in the ancient and mysterious lairs below, being instructed in the many things Bubblians said people shouldn't enquire into. He had learned the ancient arts of alphabetizing and filing, the esoterica of reading and retrieving, the arcana of translation, the truth about the real age of life on earth.

Without doubt there had been, so Izzy was taught, an earthian history which had lasted some billions of years, during which time life had emerged and gone through five stages. Stage one—once the earth had cooled down sufficiently to allow it—involved a spontaneous aggregation of molecules in ever greater variety until self-replicating forms were achieved. Then came speciation and complication of self-replicating forms in every and all kinds until intelligence was achieved and began to ramify. Izzy identified this second stage as *gibbering and howling*. Then in stage three, language emerged, and with language, the seeds of eventual destruction: concepts, memes, ideas.

In stage four, memes multiplied, each two or three giving birth to dozens more. Also, they became self-perpetuating, using their biological carriers as copying machines. Vital concepts, deadly conceits, nonsense corruptions, all scrambled about in people's brains as they transformed themselves into more and more complicated structures that began to accumulate into systems of philosophy and belief and be arranged into canons, all of which led people about, getting them into trouble, often getting them killed! Thought, in brief, imitated life in its evolutionary strategies.

Oh, some societies saw the dangers inherent in thinking, but imposing thought control was like caulking a rotten boat, only a delaying tactic at best. The ideas would leak out. Or in. Censor though they might, people would learn to talk and repeat and dream. Or, as Izzy paraphrased his best friend among the Librarians: During the censorship phase, it is lethal to espouse free speech, and in the free speech phase, it is too late to espouse censorship. Unthinking things was, as Izzy had found out to his dismay, impossible.

The final stage of life on earth came in two parts. Part A was when language inevitably begot literacy, which liberated ideas from the mind onto the page. Part B was when technology liberated ideas from the page into the network. Once so liberated, control of ideas became only a pretence. They spread like wildfire, aggregating and mutually destructing at every turn, changing reality more than mere creatures ever had. Self-replication had gone on in stable fashion for some billions of years; gibbering and howling had existed for hundreds of millions while making few changes; but only a few thousand years of idea proliferation changed reality both for good and bad in quite irreversible ways. So far, Izzy learned, idea proliferation had resulted in enormous though temporary scientific advances interrupted by the destruction of several successive civilizations, the last great one having ended some three thousand years before.

This last cycle before the present, so Izzy read in the ancient machines, had ended in a "terrorist coup," a holy war waged by some no longer existent set of ideas against all other ideas and their carriers. A disease had been used to wipe out most of the people in the world, including, presumably, all those who started hostilities. The people had had different tribal names then, of course. As best Izzy could identify them by their tribal characteristics, the ponjic people had been called Mericans, or maybe Joosh; the scuinic people had perhaps been Ahraban; the pheledic peoples had been Zhapanees; the armakfatidi had undoubtedly been Frynch; and the onchiki had been Skandians, people from the north. There had also been Stralians and Ladinos and Talians. It was possible the ersuniel people of the Farakian Empire had been Cherman or Stralian, but Izzy had no idea who the Talians could have been. Regardless of who they had been, almost all of them had been killed off.

"Voilà, there we went," said Izzy, throwing up his hands. "Back to gibbering and howling again. Back to the Dark Ages."

Unfortunately, people didn't always go back far enough. Sometimes they ended up with the worst of both worlds, primitive enough to smell very bad but not quite herder-gatherer enough to walk away from the stink. Thus Izzy found himself living in a citified but sewerless Dark Age from which persons would, presumably, slowly slog their long way up again, through ignorance and heresy, back to science and self-destruction once more.

Currently, there was no science worthy of the name.

Among the Librarians and Linguists, which is what the dusty people who lived below called themselves, was one who had become a surrogate father to Izzy. His name was Old Mock, and it was he who had wiped Izzy's childish tears and encouraged him when he was unhappy, and discouraged him when he wanted to do something silly or stupid, usually because one of his cousins put him up to it. Thus, when the reality of the prophecy finally began to sink in, it was down below to Old Mock that Izzy went for advice.

Getting below was not difficult, once Izzy had evaded the notice of cousins, aunts and uncles, servitors, guards under arms, priests, shamans, keepers of this and stalwarts of that, official cranks and mutterers, kitchen people, scullery maids, serfs, herdsmen—the whole feudal bit, which Izzy felt all sensible peoples had no doubt gone through often enough to have down pat by now. Once he knew himself to be absolutely alone, he went to the nearest secret door—in this case, a large chest in the scullery (used to store firewood when used at all)—where he lifted the false bottom, crawled down a dusty tunnel into a spidery hallway, and trotted a lengthy distance across rotting floorboards to the creaking metal cage where, with the press of a timeworn button, he was lowered below. Once there, he went in search of Old Mock, finding him, as he often did, sitting in a vagrant ray of sunlight on a bench, drowsing over a book.

"Halloo," called Izzy, when he was still some distance away.

"Umph," replied Old Mock, coming to himself with a start. "If it isn't the Prince of Palmia, Lord of the Four Realms, Duke of Isher and Fan-Kyu Cyndly, Horselord of the Mellow Marches. How's your kingdom?"

"I'm not Lord of the Four Realms yet. I won't be until I reach my majority, assuming I ever do. As for Isher and Fan-Kyu and the Mellow Marches, Uncle Goffio is keeping track of them for me. I have no very clear idea how they're getting on."

"What are you doing here on such a fine morning?"

"I've come about my prophecy," said Izzy rather grumpily. "And how do you know it's a fine morning?"

Old Mock gestured at the ray of sun. "There's a hole up there. I think it comes out near the stables, as sometimes there's a very horsey smell when the wind's from the west. When it's raining, it drips. When it's snowing or hailing, it emits hydrometeors of various other sorts. When it's a fine morning, it gives me sunlight." He snuffled, digging into his pockets in search of a handkerchief. "And, of course, when I feel like it, I do go outside. We're not prisoners here, you know."

Izzy nodded, seating himself on the bench. "I know you go out scrivening," he said.

"Right. Anytime anything happens up there, there's bound to be a scrivener, making a record. Nobody pays any attention to scriveners."

Izzy thought about this in companionable silence, asking at last, "Did you scriven a record of my prophecy?"

"Oh, I should think so," said Old Mock, getting up

to go rummage in a tall armoire that stood against the stone wall. "I keep such things in here, once they've been put in the machines. Here we are . . . no. Wrong thing. That's an account of the twenty-year drought in Isfoin. Let's see. Fishery information on the Crawling Sea; list of succession of Farsakian emperors; reports of climatic anomalies in the shore counties . . . this one looks likely. It's on parchment, of course. I do wish someone would reinvent paper."

"You could do it yourself," suggested Izzy, taking the parchment scroll and unrolling it on his knees. "What language is this in?"

"Palmian, of course. You've got it upside down."

Flushing, Izzy reversed the scroll. " 'Theyn dyd the mydwyve speake to alle those asseymblet. . . . ' What mydwyve?"

"The midwife who delivered you. She carried you out onto the castle balcony, showed you to the crowd assembled below, and said, 'This is the prince of Palmia, who before his majority shall solve the Great Enigma or die with all posterity.' "

"I'll bet my parents loved that," said Izzy.

"Not really, no. They banished the old woman. We kept track of her, of course. She ended up down south of Isfoin somewhere, telling the bones for travelers."

"What business did she have prophesying, anyhow?"

"She was only a part-time midwife. By profession she was a seeress. One of the Sworpian Society of Seeresses. They used to be sorceresses, years ago, before Faros VII made sorcery illegal. When Faros VII conquered Sworp, all the sorceresses changed professions."

"That was sensible of them."

"Very." Old Mock stared up into his ray of sun, humming a little under his breath.

"It raises a question I've been interested in for some time," mused Izzy. "Now this prophecy is magic; you know it and I know it, and we both believe there's something to it. I've learned magic. I can do some of it rather well. Why is it that in every cycle, people start out able to do magic, and then as time progresses, they are unable to do it anymore?''

''Ah, well,'' answered old Mock, ''I've always supposed it had to do with the nature of miracles.''

''I don't follow.''

''Consider, Prince Izakar: in the universe of all things that could happen, there are some events with vanishingly small probability of happening. Still, occasionally, things do happen which have a very small probability, and these things are called miracles. Some of them are quite nice, like instantaneous cures for incurable diseases or escapes from certain death. Some are quite nasty, like rains of frogs.

''Obviously, since the probabilities are so limited, the supply of natural miracles is always small. Magic is a system for tapping into the miraculous, that is, of changing the probability that certain things will occur, of bending certain natural forces in order to influence probability itself.

''As time goes on, however, people learn that things they thought were impossible are, in fact, merely improbable and they learn to make improbable things happen through technology, until the time comes when no one believes in magic anymore because all the improbable things are being done by machines.''

Izzy kicked the bench with his heels, sending a small cataract of dust cascading to the floor. ''How probable is it I'm going to solve this Great Enigma thing? With or without magic?''

Old Mock hummed for a time. ''I really couldn't say. It has all the aspects of a standard hero test. Hero tests take the form of labors, or riddles, or quests, and this is probably a quest. There are many kinds of quests: people go hunting lost jewels or books or heirs to the throne or swords. . . .'' He cocked his head. ''The sword is a favorite thing to quest for. The very word is ancient. In the very ancient language of Avestan it was called *svart*, *swart*, *savord*. It's phallic, of course, which probably explains why it is so often sought after.''

"I see no reason whatsoever that my phallus would be either sought after or referred to as a Great Enigma," said Izzy somewhat stiffly. "A small enigma, to be sure, of interest only to myself. Why should we think a sword has anything at all to do with this quest?"

"No reason," said Old Mock, rubbing his chin. "I just thought the possibility was interesting."

"Another thing," said Izzy. "Why is it that quests always take place in feudal ages like this one, with horses and misty mountains and banners blowing across a sullen sky? Are there no quests undertaken in sunny meadows, among pretty girls, in conditions of high technology?"

"Obviously, a magical quest requires a setting like ours, in which magic itself has evolved into a nice complicated thing with lots of lore, but before technology makes magic unnecessary! Lore is interesting. Technology is merely complicated." Old Mock regarded Izzy's sullen face for a time. "You might read up on quests," he suggested at last. "Though you've left it rather late."

"I've already read up on them. Most of them take at least a three-book to recount, and some of them are called cycles and go on volume after volume. I don't have time to go on volume after volume, as you yourself just pointed out. I shall reach my majority soon, and I have to solve the Great Enigma before then."

"You have three or four years," soothed Old Mock.

Izzy sighed. "That may not be long enough. Look, if this is a quest, can we assume the standard quest conditions will prevail? Will I find companions for the trip? Will I receive coded clues and mysterious directions? Will I meet with various roadblocks and dangers? Will I inevitably triumph?"

Old Mock sighed deeply. "I don't think you can assume so, Prince Izakar. In the quest books, virtue almost always triumphs, or sometimes bravado does reasonably well, but in real life, as common sense will tell you, evil wins out a good deal of the time."

"That leaves bravado," said Izzy in a grumpy voice.

"Your cousins are living—or dead—proof that bravado often ends up with a broken head. All we know for sure is that a member of the Sworpian Society of Seers became aware of something she called the Great Enigma. Now, the seer may have found this thing, or she may have invented it, or discovered a reference to it, or seen it in a vision of the future. She may have taken this thing and hidden it, or left it where it was, or she, the seeress, may be as much in the dark about it as we are. Whatever is true about the Great Enigma, you are somehow connected to it."

"That's not very helpful."

"I have very little help to offer. It would seem to me, however, that since your midwife was a seeress, and since she came from Sworp, your quest might well begin in Sworp. It is perhaps no coincidence that your mother's people came from there, as well."

"The Gershons," said Izzy. "Yes."

"You might use that machine over there," said Old Mock in his kindliest voice. "The maintenance team has just been at it, and it's working quite well."

He went back to his book while Izzy seated himself at the console and summoned up whatever it was the library knew about Sworp. A country to the west of the Crawling Sea. Capital city: the town of Gulp on the River Guzzle. Ruled by the emperor's nephew, Fasal Grun. Fasal Grun was of the ersuniel tribe, but Sworp was home to a varied people, all of whom were described, none of whom were pictured. Not for the first time, Izzy wished for pictures of people. At the end of the last cycle there had been a great purge of the machines, in an effort, said Mock, to remove harmful knowledge, and though the machines still held many pictures of ancient places and things, it contained no pictures of people. Back three millennia ago, the various religions had forbidden graven images along with certain ideas, and the machines had been programmed to exclude them.

Still, one knew the people were not terribly unlike

people today. They lived in many of the same ways. Some ancient people had been very religious, building huge structures, some of them as tall aboveground as the library was deep below. These had been called cathedrals, and in most of them the level of craftsmanship was higher than anything Izzy's world had as yet reattained. Of course, Bubblism would not serve as a foundation for such elaborate structures. What point was there in beginning a building which might take 500 years to finish when everything was going pop before then?

Which was, said Old Mock, one of the chief attractions of eschatological religions. When one's world was impermanent, difficult endeavors, like procuring justice or balancing the ecology, need never be attempted. One need only make contributions to the ascendant hierarchy, cast one's eyes heavenward with an awed and anticipatory expression, while continuing to behave as selfishly as one liked. When everything is going to go pop, one needn't bother to provide for or preserve for the grandchildren.

"Finding anything?" asked Old Mock from his bench.

"Nothing useful," said Izzy. "I guess there's no help for it. I'm just going to have to start out."

"Find someone to go with you," said Old Mock. "It's always better traveling with companions. And to answer your earlier question, I think you should plan on using magic. Without it, your chance of success is probably short of miraculous. A little intuition might not be amiss, either."

Izzy nodded, gave the old man a dusty hug, and found his way back into the daily life of the castle above. It was too late in the day to start recruiting companions, so he had a bath, then a good night's sleep, and only on the morrow did he get himself onto a bald-tailed, ewe-necked, hammer-headed horse called Flinch and ride out of the castle gate. Izzy often rode Flinch because he ran very fast when frightened, and he frightened very easily.

He had determined to begin the search in Palmody,

the town that began just outside the castle walls and ended up at the wharves along the river. The nearest houses were occupied by those in daily contact with the castle: the armorers and the bishops and the nobility. Farther down the hill were the persons of lesser involvement, the wine merchants and the fabric importers, and in the town itself were the homes of the emerging middle class, the guilds and merchants, purveyors of leather and pots and grain and whatall. Izzy had been riding about in Palmody town since he was about seven; he knew the place well and got along with its inhabitants. He had the touch, said Uncle Goffio, just common enough to seem friendly but allowing no presumption. Noblesse oblige, but not too damned far.

The inn was at one side of the village square, and it was in that direction that Izzy urged his fidgety horse. He had barely entered the square when he caught the unmistakable chatter of umminhi, large and impressive animals, their breeders' tags gleaming, tied by their silver collars to a tree on the far side of the square amid a cluster of kapric handlers and pheledian guards. Nearer the tavern stood a group of riders, among them a large pheled with two VIPs, one greater and one lesser.

Smiling in friendly fashion, Izzy trotted forward to offer his services.

7

Opalears: Nassif Continues

We arrived in the town of Palmody, left the animals in the care of the handlers while Soaz, Sahir and I headed toward the tavern. We had barely crossed the square when we were accosted by a young person dressed in rather eccentric clothing and riding a very peculiar horse. He was ponjic, like myself. "Welcome, travelers," he said, offering his hand, which I took, though somewhat at a loss. I gave him our names as I had been instructed to do by Prince Sahir, leaving out any honorifics. He introduced himself as Prince Izakar of Palmia, though he looked most unlike a prince, and he offered us the hospitality of the nearby tavern in return, so he said, for news of the country we had ridden through.

We went in. The three of us sat down at a table near the window while Soaz joined our guardsmen at another table. I asked for tea. Sahir asked for wine, as did our host.

"Where are you headed?" Izakar asked.

After a glance at Sahir, I replied, "We are going to the Hospice at St. Weel."

"Ah," said Izakar. "May one inquire the reason for your travel, or is it confidential?"

Prince Sahir gave me a look, as though to say, "Who does this person think he is?" but he replied, nonetheless. "My health has not been good. We in Tavor have been told of remarkable cures at St. Weel."

"A long journey for a doubtful result," remarked Izakar, taking a deep swallow of wine.

"He's feeling much better already," I remarked testily.

"The fresh air, no doubt," said Izakar. "And escaping from the vexations of the court. If your court is like mine . . ."

"I cannot imagine that it is," said Sahir, in a lofty tone. "If I had a court, which I do not admit to having, I cannot imagine that it would allow me to ride, for example, such an exceedingly ugly horse."

"Flinch," said Izakar, unperturbed by Sahir's manner. "Who can run like the wind. Faster even than umminhi. Besides, umminhi do not breed well at this altitude."

It was not a word I had heard before. "Altitude?" I asked.

"This far up in the mountains. If you come from Tavor, you have climbed the Little Stonies, you have crossed the Wycos plateau and the River Roq—by the bridge, I should think, this time of year—and have then ascended the Big Stonies before coming down into Palmia. While we are lower than the surrounding lands, we are much higher than Tavor. Though you have traveled slowly enough to minimize the effects, you may notice a slight breathlessness."

"I have noticed," said Sahir. "But you say horses can be bred in these mountains."

"Ours can, certainly. They are of very old mountain stock," said Izzy. "From many cy—that is, generations in the past. We sell the larger breeds as mounts and the lighter as chariot horses to Farsak, as a matter of fact. Horses are among our more lucrative trade goods.''

''We will no doubt encounter Farsakian authorities on the way to St. Weel,'' said Sahir. ''Are we likely to have trouble?''

Izakar shrugged. ''Faros VII considers Palmia a tributary province, but we are allowed to keep our own religion and customs. You will go through our province of Isher, which is Bandercranian, a sect of Ghotianism, and through our province of Fan-Kyu, which is Halfish, a similar sect.''

''I do not know these religions,'' said Sahir.

Izzy settled himself comfortably, as though for a protracted lecture on the subject. ''The Bandercranians teach that Ghoti's son Bandercran cares for this particular bubble, that in year three hundred two he was hatched *inside* this bubble from an egg laid by a virgin trout—as, indeed, all trout are, so to speak—and has thereafter appeared off the coast of various cities in the guise of a merperson or hemi-ghoti to preach a doctrine of Good Thinking. Since even so early as the fourth century the Ghotian hierarchy did not approve of thinking, they executed Bandercran, first bodily, by netting him and whacking him to death, then intellectually, by denying that he was the real Bandercran, and finally spiritually, by consistently misrepresenting his teachings. Nonetheless, so the Bandercranians teach, the hemi-ghoti has reemerged into the ocean of light and rises each day as the sun in our sky to inspire persons with Good Thoughts. If there are sufficient Good Thoughts, Bandercran may convince Ghoti to forget hell.''

''And the Halfishers?'' I asked.

''Though the Bandercranians teach that Good Thoughts are all-important, the Halfishers teach that Bandercran does not care if people deviate from thinking good thoughts so long as they spend much of their waking time committing Correct Actions. Correct Actions, according to the Halfishers, include some sensible rules about personal hygiene along with extensive provisions concerning the uses of wheeled vehicles, allowable salad dressings, and a cuisine from which most flavors are relentlessly extirpated."

"And in Estafan?"

"In Estafan they worship Bandercran under another name, though the Silver Swimmer is far more beneficent than the hemi-ghoti revered in Isher. In Finial I am told they worship a goddess who appears as a clock-owl; and it is not until one reaches Sworp that one encounters Korèsanism untrammeled, though even there, it seems they have made an exception for the Society of Seers. I am told that travelers of other faiths must take an oath of noninterference, nonevangelism, and nonblasphemy but need not themselves adopt Korè. Also, one must not be overheard commenting adversely about Faros in his persona as high priest."

I thought he was extremely well informed. Since the peoples of Tavor were mostly Korèsan, it did not appear we would have any troubles of a religious nature.

Izzy turned his glass upon the tabletop, seeming deep in thought. "Would you be interested in letting me come with you?"

The prince seemed struck speechless, as though he had been attacked rather than merely asked a question. His eyes darted.

I put my hand on his wrist, calming him as I asked Prince Izakar, "Why would you want to?"

Izzy shrugged. "Your mentioning the Hospice of St. Weel. I am faced with a particular puzzle of my own, one I must solve as soon as possible. There may be an answer in Sworp, through which you will pass, and that failing, it is said all kinds of questions may be answered by the wizards at the Hospice. Even a clue to my puzzle would be a help."

The prince was again startled. He shifted in discomfort. "Surely your people would insist upon providing you with an escort. And we are already quite a large group. . . ."

Izzy nodded. "It was the size of your group, and their

attitude toward you, that convinced me you were of the nobility. Throughout the lands, a commoner might travel with a servant. A baron from the Four Realms might have half a dozen guards. Someone related to a royal house would have a dozen or more. You have that many." He smiled and shrugged again. "As for my people insisting upon providing an escort—they are Ghotians: they will insist upon nothing. Our religion lends us a certain resignation in the face of events. What will, will, we say. What won't, won't. Any effort to assure my safety would be pointless if I am doomed, equally pointless if I am not, and in any case, the world may go pop very shortly, so why worry?"

"A despicable faith," murmured Sahir. "In my opinion."

Izzy leaned forward and said as quietly, "Mine also. However, it would not do to say so loudly. There are three Ghotian Inquisitors, a Bandercranian Contemplative and a Halfish Exemplary sitting at the table by the far wall."

"So many?" I breathed.

"Palmody is currently host to an ecumenical conference on the subject of revelation."

"I should not think revelation would need conferences," I murmured. "Doesn't it come when and how it will?"

Prince Izakar smiled at me. "My father was beheaded for speaking of something called electrification. When the bishops asked where he had heard of this subject, he said it had been revealed to him in a vision sent by Bandercran. They told him this could not be true, for though Ghoti used to allow revelation, he does so no longer. During the time when Ghoti did allow it, everything was revealed that was worth revealing, and the bishops memorized it all and have passed it down unchanged by jot or tittle through the years. Thus there could be no purpose for further revelation and claiming revelation is strictly prohibited. The Ghotians want this prohibition included in the catechism for all Bubblians, Bandercranians and Halfishers.''

I thought about it. ''If people were to believe that Bandercran goes about delivering personal revelations, it would be very upsetting, for no one would know what was true and what wasn't.''

''Exactly the Ghotians' point,'' he agreed. ''The Bandercranians, however, who include among their number certain persons who receive revelations fairly regularly, are holding out for exceptions.''

''Do you speak Farakiel in addition to Tavorian?'' asked the prince with a sideways glance at the Inquisitors. ''If you do, it could come in useful.''

Izzy nodded. ''Farakiel, yes, both low and high. I speak the trade language, Inglitch. Also Sworpian, Finialese, Estafaner, and the debased Uk-luk tongue of the Onchikian tribes who occupy the shore counties between. I can make myself understood in certain other languages, as well, though we would be unlikely to encounter them on this trip.''

''Where did you learn all that?'' demanded Prince Sahir in a petulant voice. ''I had sufficient trouble merely learning to read!''

Izzy shrugged. ''I am very bright. All the Gershons are. It's a genetic thing, inherited from my foremothers, like red hair and brown eyes.''

''And dwarfism?'' jibed the prince.

''That's unkind,'' I admonished him. ''He's small, but he's no smaller than I am, and I'm no dwarf.''

The prince sighed in a put-upon fashion. ''My faithful Nassif is my conscience, Prince Izakar. Some days I lose patience with this journey, even though I'm already much improved, physically. You were probably correct when you attributed it to removing myself from the intrigue of the court. There was some idea I had been poisoned.''

''You are your father's heir?''

''Among many.''

''I am my father's heir, the sole surviving one, but

my uncles have not cared about the matter sufficiently to poison me. While all my half brothers were eager, their deaths were due more to heedlessness than to ambition. Bubblians are not given to glory, or to power overmuch. We tend toward sloth rather than avarice.''

Our talk went on, wandering here and there, with not much said of grave importance, yet by the end of the meal we had considered many things and the agreement had been struck. Izzy (the prince) would join Sahir (not called the prince) in his journey north and west up onto the great plateau where lay the silvery expanse of the Crawling Sea. Izzy would bring a few people to look after him, but would rely mostly upon the Tavorian guards to protect him as they protected Sahir.

When this agreement had been reached, Izzy went out, got upon his bald-tailed horse and rode up the hill toward the castle, leaving us staring through the open door as his small figure retreated up the cobbles toward the crenelated walls. If we had had any doubt he was who he represented himself to be, these were allayed when the distant figure received a salute from the guards as he cantered across the bridge and disappeared inside the castle.

"He never told us why he was going," I remarked.

"We never told him why we are," said Sahir.

"We did. It's your health."

"That's the reason father gave you, before," murmured Sahir. "It doesn't happen to be the only one."

I cocked my head at him. "No?" I respected Soaz's confidence and had not mentioned the oracle story to the prince.

"No, my faithful Nassif."

He said it with a sneer, as he often did. For the most part, I ignored his tone. He sounded as most scuinic males sounded, and there was no point being irritated about it.

He went on, rather sulkily. "Mother thought it was, of course. It wouldn't have done to have anyone know why I was really going. We left three layers of stories behind. One, that I was ill and was going to the Hospice of St. Weel. Two, that while either going or coming, I had gone on pilgrimage to the Temple-Garden of Korè, near the locks at Giber. Three, I had gone on north on a diplomatic mission from the sultan to Faros VII. My real destination is the hospice, which, since I have said I am going there, no one will believe.''

I longed to ask him about the oracle business, but I contented myself with less. ''I take it then that we are definitely headed to the Hospice of St. Weel, or that vicinity?''

''Faithful Nassif, we are going to the hospice, yes. If there is opportunity, we will probably seek an audience with Faros the Seventh of that name. The sultan believes it is important that I visit Faros, if only to express our congratulations at the length and power of his reign. And finally, if we can, I would sail on the great lake to Korè's Temple-Garden. I am a faithful son of Korè, a believer, a worshiper, and much merit accrues to the person who visits that place. I am told the hymns that are sung there are of extraordinary beauty.''

''That reminds me of a story,'' I mused.

''Everything does,'' sneered Prince Sahir. ''You will story me all the way to Zallyfro in the country of Estafan, and perhaps, heaven knows, to Sworp itself.''

He went to arrange for rooms. Annoyed by his slighting manner, I stayed where I was, staring up the roadway at the castle. Meeting Prince Izakar had been exciting, or at least jolly after a steady diet of Sahir's jeers and glooms. True, Izakar had said a number of things I had not at all understood, almost as though he lived in some other world. Or visited some other world, from time to time.

Nonetheless, I looked forward to his joining us. Soaz had become my good friend and Sahir was at least bearable most of the time, but neither of them were what I would call fun. I had caught Izzy looking at me several times in a very fellow-tribal way that made me think he might be a lot of fun.

Onchiki

"What mystery surrounds the Onchik-Dau! This ancient people of few words and dour aspect rules the seashores and off shore waters as they have since time immemorial. Harbors are their special provenance, and those high reefs which lie just out of sight and present a terror to mariners. There is scarcely a captain who cannot tell a tale of his ship's being saved by an Onchik-Dau, of a voice in the night, calling to the watchman to beware...."

THE PEOPLES OF EARTH
HIS EXCELLENCY, EMPEROR FAROS VII

The Biwot house hunkered up Chilliburn Creek, its threshold well above the reach of even the highest waves. Nigh two hundred winters of storm had not conquered it, but the slow rip of the seasons had taken their toll: the rafters that held the sod roof were rotten, and woodworms had made powdery tunnels through the lord and lady beams on either side of the door. During the mild weather of midsummer, wrack relaxed upon ruin and all seemed homely enough, but when the gales of early autumn came, a rampageous seawind tongued the roof off like the peel of a fruit and spit it into the outgoing waves while the Crawling Sea slithered up the creek bottom and onto the moor, where it lapped its wet tongue across the threshold of the house.

The Biwot family, fisherfolk who were accustomed enough to being wet but didn't like sleeping in it, scurried for the cover of the boat bed and huddled within it, at least one of them awaiting an end that the roaring wind declared to be imminent.

"Oh, Lord Wind, have pity," cried Sleekele, bumping her head on the bedframe. "Oh, Lord Wind, great Lord Wind . . ."

"Shut face, woman," her mate, Diver, rejoined. "Lord Wind is too full of his own noise to hear thee talking."

"Enough, both thee," growled Grandmama. "I'm glad it's happened, do you hear? We've worried over it long enough. Now the roof's gone, we can quit worrying and do something with ourselves." She laid her head back on the hastily flung pillow that had preceded her own stringy self into the boat bed and stared at sloping sides around her, as though taking count of the seams that might, or might not, hold out the flood. "Now we can do something."

"Oh, we'll do, all right," said Burrow, the oldest boy. "Crawling Sea will crawl in here and float us out the door and down the creek and onto the sea, where we'll sail away forever on the boat bed, to the land where the bombats live."

Grandmama snorted at him, waving her webbed fingers in front of his nose. "Why float, boy? Swimming's easier. Just because we're shore people doesn't mean we've forgot our heritage."

"Onchik-Dau would like to hear you say that!"

"Onchik-Dau has nothing to say about it. Our roof's gone. We're homeless, boy."

Legally, she was right, of course. Onchikiel people

followed the home laws: due regard for shore and pasture, due regard for roof and floor, due regard for hearth and kinfolk, not to leave them evermore. So long as onchiki had a roof over their heads, their movements were restricted to the three Fs, fishing, flocks, and folk, which meant just what it said. Fish was what they caught and dried, eating some and selling some; veeble flocks were what they sheared the wool from; folk were what they kept company with in festive seasons, visiting back and forth. With no roof, however, they became homeless, and a homeless onchik was a wild onchik, able to go places and work or not as he pleased. Some had even been known to change their names and leave lifemates and children to go off into the unknown by themselves. After the long boredom of homefast life, the attraction of venturing was so great that some had been accused of weakening their own roof pins, no matter how the Onchik-Dau fulminated against such behavior.

"What'll we do with the veebles, Grandmama?" This was Lucy Low, the oldest girl child. "We can't leave the veebles for the cowjers to eat."

Mince giggled from his place near the bottom of the bed:

"Was a veeble, very feeble; was a cowjer, large and fat;
Came a Lucy, very juicy; cowjer ate her stead of that."

"Shush, Mince," said Grandmama. "Do thy rhymes when the sun's up. In all this wind, I've no patience with it. Now see, thee've made her sorrow!" She stroked the girl's smooth head and wiped her bright brown eyes, saying, "There now, there now," until Lucy Low gave over being sorrowful. It was the idea of a cowjer eating the veebles that had done it, for she had best friends among the veebles: Chimary and Chock, Willigong and Gai.

"Shush, child," murmured Grandmama. "We'll see

to the veebles, bless you. Your friends are safe."

Lucy Low managed a gasp. "Will we open the box of fortunes, Grandmama?"

"Why, certain we will, child. When the roof goes, what else can a family do?"

Inside the boat bed, protected from the wind and mostly from the rain—for the bed had a canvas cover though it wasn't boat-tight as it should have been— snugged down they lay: Grandmama, and her son Diver, his wifemate Sleekele, the three girls: Ring, and Bright, and Lucy Low. And the two boys, Burrow (who was near enough a grown male to be all trouble and no sense, so said Grandmama), and Mince, (who might never make it to his growth, irritating as he was). The veebles were out in the shed, and Uncle Wash, Grandmama's stepson, was abed in the shed loft, had the shed still a roof, praise Lady Heaven, and that was the lot of the Chilliburn Biwots, though not for long, for with the loss of its roof, Biwot had become a no-place.

Even with a roof, it hadn't been much.

Chilliburn was a small stream, barely more than a trickle oozing down from the Sharbak Mountains to make murmurous meanders over mossy rocks and through bits of marshy moor, into peaty pools, dark as tea, and out once more, past the legs of the herons and the bellies of the frogs, thence whispering over a fall onto a pillow of ferns, finally transforming itself into a silver song that lilted among the smooth shore stones, across the pebbly beach to the high mirror of the Crawling Sea. The sea was green with algae, but Chilliburn was drinking water, washing water, water for the garden, water for the veebles, and thank the Cloud Ladies for that, all in their billowy dresses with their big hats, floating across the sky on their way to meet the sky king, somewhere over Gosland.

Chilliburn had only the one fishing croft. There'd been another, farther up, years ago in Grandmama's youth, but it'd been gone now a lifetime, eaten by the wind. Onchik-Dau had refused to rebuild it back then.

He'd said it wasn't worth it, so the crofters had gone.

"Couldn't we put the roof back on?" asked Burrow. He was deep in a bottom corner of the bed, and his voice came out of the darkness like a haunting. "Wouldn't that be the thing to do? Wouldn't the Onchik-Dau want that?"

"Whoosh, lad, and get on with this nonsense?" said Grandmama. "The Onchik-Dau? Why would he be so silly? What's the rent he gets from the croft? Nothing plus nothing, and that's only when we've had a good season. Sale price of fish that nobody's buying. Sale price of wool, likewise. Without us in the way here, he can rent the hills to guz herders, and besides, aren't you sick and all of it? Fish for breakfast and fish for lunch and fish for dinner, with an onion if we're lucky. Feast days there's a hen that's all muscle and no meat, and odd times maybe we take the throat out of a veeble that's about ready to drop dead anyhow. Whoosh, lad, you want to go on with it?"

"Never been noplace else," he said.

"Nor me," said Grandmama. "And I'd say it's about time."

"You're so brave," wept Sleekele. "You keep your spirits up so."

As somebody had to do, said Grandmama to herself, for if left to Sleekele, their spirits would all liquify and run down the Chilliburn into the sea to become weepy ghosts, lamenting ladies, blow-arounds for the Lord Wind, willow-wraiths to flow away down the Fraiburne into the distant ocean, way south, past Isfoin.

"Yes, Grandmama, you are brave," whispered Ring and Bright, as in one voice. They were twins, and Grandmama was of the opinion they had but one brain between them. Certainly it took both of them to do what one sensible person might manage.

"H'loo," came a voice from the wind. "H'loo. 'Nybody in there?"

"Wash, you fool," cried Grandmama. "Course we're in here. Where're you?"

"Shed roof blew away," he said, leaning down where he could peer in at them, his nose wrinkled back, his teeth showing white in the dim. "You got any room left in there?"

"How's the veebles, Uncle Wash?" Lucy Low asked. "Are they scared?"

"All curled up with their noses under their paws and the little ones snug in the middle. Veebles lived here on this poor moor long before folk, Lucy Low. They got their ways."

"There's room for half of you, Wash," said Diver. "Top half or bottom, it's up to you."

"Naw," he said. "I'm wet now. What I'll do is, I'll curl up under the washtub. Likely that'll do me until morning."

They heard him rumbling about and cursing for a time, with a rackety bang from the washtub, then quiet came and the wind settled and they heard only the *thunky-tunk* of raindrops on the bottom of the washtub as the storm drummed its fingers, trying to decide whether to start over or finish up. Evidently it chose to finish up, for it wasn't long before the rain ceased and then they could hear the sound of the sea crawling onto the shore, lisping to itself about all its secrets. The Crawling Sea was shallow and wind driven, and tonight it had crawled farther than any would have thought possible. Once the wind died, it began to hush itself away in little gravelly rushes. Lucy Low was between Grandmama and Diver with scarce room to breathe, but it was warm there, and before she knew it she'd drifted off to sleep to dream about waking in warm daylight and opening the fortune box.

Many families in the Shore Counties kept a fortune box. Fortunes were the acceptable coin of the place, the value placed upon them varying with the seer and the season. Fortunes not immediately needed to buy food or some such were put away against a rainy time, and seldom had one come as rainy as last night. Grandmama and her grandmama and even her grandmama had been saving sorts, always tucking a fortune away against future need.

"When a family can't eat something new or change a word from what's been said a thousand years," Grandmama often said, "it matters mightily to have a fortune box to open when luck gives out. People set in their ways as a root into stone can take hope from the time the root rots and the stone cracks."

The fortune box of the Biwots was at least five generations old, so it was bound to have a good many adventures in it. They didn't even wait for breakfast the morning after the roof went. Diver took up the flagstone from the floor, and Wash and Burrow dug up the black bog-oak box from where it had lain between diggings these long years. The last fortune had been put in the box ten years or more ago, by Grandmama herself, and it hadn't been dug up since.

They all sat in a circle on the floor. Grandmama was oldest, so she got to shuffle the fortunes, new with old, old with new, mixing them up, then putting them in a stack. She would pick from the stack, one at a time, and if the fortune didn't fit this one, why then, that one might take it. Some fortunes didn't fit any circumstances, and some fortunes were terribly dire, but direness and unsuitability were no bar. What was forecast, always passed, so said the Sworpian Society of Seers.

"All right," breathed Grandmama. "We don't want to open any more of these than need be, for we'll need some to spend on our way wherever we're going. I'll read out the one on top. I mind me this one. My mama won this at a fair when she was just a girl, kept it always, showed it to me time on time. It has a golden egg on the seal, that's how I remember."

She broke the seal, opened the flap, and took out the folded parchment. That took some time to be unfolded and laid down flat as Grandmama turned it this way and that, finding the right way up of it. Grandmama was a pretty good reader. There were hardly any words she couldn't make out if she took her time about it. " 'High ladies need sharp eyes to tend their geese,' " she read at last. "I think it's geese."

Lucy Low gave it a look. "It must be geese, Grandmama."

Diver sniffed. "No job for a man, goose tending. More a girl's job."

"Well, shall we give it to Lucy Low or to the twins?" asked Grandmama.

"We don't want it," said the twins in one voice.

"I do," said Lucy Low.

"Lucy Low's it is, then," Grandmama decided, handing over the parchment.

Lucy Low took it and smoothed it out, admiring the bright colors around the edges and the jiggery way it had been folded to make a long necked bird, and when she waggled the tail, the legs moved. Perhaps it was meant to be a goose. She'd never tended geese, but she'd seen them flying over, sometimes landing outside the reed beds and spending a day along the marshy shore, eating and gabbling to themselves. Goose tending would be fun, and it would keep her out of doors, as well. Lucy Low preferred the out of doors. Most onchiki did, truly, except for a few like Ring and Bright. The onchikiel heritage was an out-of-doors way of life, water and reed beds and fish and even the wild wind that pushed the sea. House living was nice when it was cold and drear, but out of doors was best most times.

Meantime Grandmama had unfolded the next one in the pile. "This says, 'Treasure on Hovermount.' Where's Hovermount?"

"In the Dire Mountains, past the Dread Marches," said Uncle Wash. "East of the Crawling Sea. I knew a peddler used to go back and forth through there. Wicked awful country, he said."

"Uk," said Sleekele. "I won't go there. Where do you suppose we got this fortune?"

Wash said, "Grandaddy got it, for some smoked fish he sold at market. See there, on the corner, there's his name and the year. Lord Wind, but that was a long time ago. I've always wanted an adventure, so can I have this one?''

Grandma gave it to him, with her blessing.

"A chimney needs mending in the sea town," said the next one. All the sea towns were west and north, past Isher and Fan Kyu Cyndly, all the way to Estafan, where Diver had often wanted to go. He perked up his ears. He was a good mender of most anything, and he thought it might be worth the trip.

And so it went, until they each had taken a fortune written on good official parchment and sealed with the signet of the Sworpian Society of Seers, certifying that the contents were true and binding, effective upon the breaking of the seal. There was an ale house fortune for the twins, and a fishing fleet destiny for Burrow, who said Mince could come along. Sleekele and Grandmama each had housekeeping fortunes, so it seemed likely they'd find their future in whatever sea town Diver found a chimney in. None of the family were holding any uncomfortable fortunes—though both Burrow's and Sleekele's were rather vague—and they were pretty well satisfied with the way things looked.

When Grandmama was putting the unopened ones back in the box, she came upon two little scrappy ones that didn't look official at all. They were in a curly faded hand that was hard for Grandmama to see, so Lucy Low read them.

"Well, what do they say on the outside, child?"

"One says . . . umm, it says, 'For Erntrude Biwot, A reward for service much welcome, give by Amalia Gershon.' And the other one says, 'For Erntrude Biwot, For thy kindness. Lady Amalia.' "

"Where'd we get those?" Burrow wanted to know. "They aren't even real. There's no seers' stamp!"

"Maybeso," said Grandmama, "and maybeso not. They're written on vellum, and it's expensive stuff, vellum. And there's gold around the lettering. Erntrude was my way-back grandmama, the one who came up the river from the sea. Both of these fortunes are in the same hand, and it's a lady's hand, and she signs it as a lady would. Amalia Gershon. I'd say she was a seer, right enough, though perhaps not one of the Society of Seers. Not just anybody's allowed to write a fortune, Burrow! That'd be forgery, and Onchik-Dau would chop off your hands for forgery."

Burrow said stubbornly, "Well, what good are they? You can't use 'em. Unless a fortune was give by a real Sworpian Seer, nobody'll give you a net sinker for it. What good are these two?"

"Well, now, who knows? Likely my grandmama knew this lady who wrote them and trusted them to be good. Likely she valued them for more than the redemption would have been, and it's even likely the fortunes inside were given for her, personal."

This made all their jaws drop. Fortunes were fortunes. They didn't go off until somebody broke the seal, and the only time somebody did that was when they had to. So long as the seal was intact, a fortune held itself in patience, just like coin, and when you paid someone with a fortune, they could look at the names and dates written on the outside and they'd know when that fortune was given and all the hands it had been through since. But a personal fortune! That was one given to a certain person, only for that person, and if these little scrappy ones were personal fortunes, then the person who received them was long gone.

"Well, fortunes work themselves out in the generations, so it's said." Diver nodded ponderously. "A fortune given your grandmama, Mama, should work out with your grandchild, don't you think?"

"I should think."

"Well, then. Lucy Low should take both these as well, just to have, in case. If they was give personal, like you say, doubtless only a descendant could profit by it. I imagine we'll find geese in the sea town where the chimney is that needs mending, and fishing boats going out from there, and an ale house there, and housekeeping needing done, and all our fortunes will be made in one place.''

In a bit they put their fortunes away, each in his or her own pocket. Grandmama put the leftover ones back in the box and gave the box to Diver for safekeeping. Then Sleekele and Grandmama pounded the dried fish and stewed it for breakfast. They started packing after breakfast. About noon Wash found a veeble that had been killed in the storm, so they roasted that, partly, leaving it underdone, though Onchik-Dau had told them they'd get worms if they didn't cook their meat. Onchik-Dau was a fuss budget. It was almost worth being roof-less just to get away from Onchik-Dau, always looking at them out of his watery eyes, always barking com-mands. Go here. Go there. Do this. Do that. Uttering directions at the top of his lungs, waving his arms, heav-ing his great fat body around. Well, worms or no, they ate heartily, putting the rest of the meat to dry in the smoke. Veeble jerky made good way-rations. By the time night fell, each of them had his or her belongings bundled up, and the household stuff—such as was moveable—was in the veeble packs. Uncle Wash took one pot, the littlest one, and a good veeble-hair blanket, for he was going east, around the Crawling Sea, to the Dread Marches, hunting the treasure that his fortune promised.

"Tomorrow morning," said Grandmama. "Tomor-row morning we load the pack veebles, turn the others loose, and away we go."

"Chimary and Chock and Willigong and Bai will like that," said Lucy Low. "They like to travel, even when it's only to market. So where will we go? What's the nearest sea town? Where are we headed to?"

"Down the coast of the Crawling Sea," said Diver, running his hands over his hair to smooth it down and scratching himself vigorously around the middle. "Through Isher and Fan-Kyu Cyndly, all the way to Zallyfro in the country of Estafan."

Several Saintly Ph.D.s

Dr. Winston, so Dora was told, could not possibly have been murdered for any personal reason. He was—depending upon whether Dora talked to his wife, his neighbor, his mistress, his boss or his coworkers—a jewel, a prince, a sweetheart, an irreplaceable project manager and a seminal thinker.

"What exactly is that?" Dora asked, with a straight face.

"Well, I mean," said the coworker, running his hands through his already disordered hair, "Winnie came up with stuff nobody else would ever think of. Like that pig. And the talking dog."

"Talking dog?"

"Well, yes, sort of. It could only manage about a dozen words, but you could tell the brain was there. When old Ralph—that was the dog's name—said 'food,' you knew he meant it."

"Do you still have this dog?"

"Poor thing got sick. Winnie took it home, but he said it died."

"What exactly does that have to do with improved breeds of livestock?"

"Well, the boss didn't think it had anything to do with anything," said the coworker. "Dr. Winston was always getting himself in trouble with the boss, but he used to say every time he isolated a particular combination of genetic instructions and saw what the effect was, he'd filled in a bit of knowledge. He said eventually we should be able to cure or prevent all genetic diseases. Eventually we should be able to tailor livestock to particular ecologies. Winnie really opened our eyes to the possibilities. He was working on clusters, you see. Discrete genetic items that added up to more than the sum of the parts. One change in skull structure plus one change in hormonal tissue, plus or minus some other odds and ends, gave us horns on a pig. Horns are useful for some animals, not for others, depending. We should be able to supply them either way, to order. Some brain modifications, another change in skull structure to make it curved instead of flat, and a change in throat and tongue structure should theoretically give us a sheepdog that could talk to the shepherd. You know, something along the lines of, 'Bring the gun, boss, there's a coyote over that ridge.' Actually, Winnie was still working on that."

"It sounds too simple," said Dora.

"I'm making it sound one hell of a lot simpler than it is," the man grated, almost resentfully. "The change in skull structure that makes it curved so it can accommodate a voice box might actually be sixty or seventy changes in DNA. No. It isn't simple at all! A lot of it seemed to be instinctive with him. Magical. There are only a few people in the country who can do even half what Winnie did, and I'm not one of them. He used to say, 'Bert, any fool can see so-and-so.' It would make me madder'n hell, because I couldn't see it. He was a genius, Winnie was."

"Would there have been any . . . oh, say, professional

jealousy? Any quarrels over who discovered what first?"

Absolute denial. No, and no. Winnie had been generally adored. Winnie was a prince, a jewel, one really nice guy.

"He really was an awfully nice man," said his widow. "I know all about his mistress, too, so don't go thinking nasty thoughts. He often had these little affairs because he was simply too nice to hurt women's feelings. I should have been jealous, I suppose, but I wasn't. It might have been different if we'd had children, a threat to the family and all that, but I have my own work. Having one's own work is a powerful anodyne against jealousy, don't you think?"

Though slightly shocked at this matter-of-fact attitude, Dora had to agree that having one's own work made a big difference. Sometimes all the difference.

The widow nodded. "He was such a good man, an ethical man! Do you know, he paid for all his animals himself, and for their food and upkeep. He owned them, and his contract with the lab specified so! He would not allow them to be taken away and used for some cruel experiment. He thought it unconscionable that men raised apes and taught them to talk, then when the grant was over, they let them be taken for medical experiments. Winnie wouldn't do it!"

"Remarkable," said Dora.

"We were so comfortable together. I'll miss him terribly," said Winnie's widow. And then the tears leaked down her cheeks, unregarded.

"We're getting nowhere with this," Dora told Phil, almost angrily, as they left Winston's home. "Lynn Beatty says there have been two other stabbings, one in June, one in May. Not our territory, but I think we ought to find out about it."

Phil demurred. "Hey, Dora, we got enough to do. . . ."

"Yeah, Phil. And I'd like to do it. I've got the names and case numbers. You mind?"

Phil, still feebly protesting, stopped with her by records, where Lynn Beatty furnished the file on Martin
Chamberlain, geneticist, and on Jennifer Williams, botanist who had worked for Pacific-Alaskan.

"Doesn't your ex work for Pacific-Alaskan?" Phil
asked.

Dora nodded mutely. He did indeed. She went
through the folder. All the recorded interviews seemed
to establish that Chamberlain had also been a prince, a
jewel.

"What is it with these scientists?" Dora grumbled.
"Three people stabbed, and two out of three were candidates for sainthood."

"I suppose you want to go out to Pacific-Alaskan and
ask some questions?"

She shook her head regretfully. "I don't, Phil. I don't
want to run into . . . Well, Jared. He's being rotten about
my moving out."

"Trouble?"

"I don't know. He hasn't . . . done anything except
make veiled threats. He says he won't let me do this or
that."

"Dora, if you need help . . ."

"I know, Phil. I know you'd help. God, there's half
a dozen of the guys I could ask to help if I needed it. I
don't know I need it. I want to know about Chamberlain,
though."

"Why don't I talk to Manconi, set up a lunch date,
maybe. Maybe we can solve both of them at the same
time."

The following morning, Dora read in the morning paper an account of what the reporter called "spontaneous
reforestation" of some badly eroded areas along creeks
that had been polluted by mining operations. Scientists
had found mineral-fixing weeds growing on the tailing
piles, weeds that pulled the heavy metals out of the soil
and concentrated them to a level that made recovery of
the metals economically feasible while also allowing re-
growth of native plants. Though metal-fixing plants in

general were not a new discovery, said the reporter, the very efficient ones on the tailings were a species new to science.

Elsewhere in the paper was a report on certain areas of northern Africa, where the U.N. had been attempting to restore native vegetation by reducing the flocks of goats and sheep which had denuded the land for centuries. Though starvation threatened the herds every year, the native peoples counted their wealth by heads of livestock and vehemently opposed reduction in their numbers. Recently a spontaneous mutation of the thorny growths native to the area had proved to be extremely palatable to the flocks. The new plant grew so freely and was so nourishing that the need for reducing herds was being questioned.

Dora read these accounts with a good deal of interest. On her way out, she remarked to the weed, "Morning paper has some stories about new plants. Maybe they're cousins of yours."

The weed nodded in the early summer breeze, unconcerned at the news. It had ramified itself above the door, creating a little half-domed sunshade before continuing up the side of the garage. One sprig had reached the eaves, where it had turned abruptly sideways and crawled along under the gutter, adding about three feet a day. A bird had chosen this runner for a nest location and the vine had obligingly ramified again at the nest site, forming an appropriate base for the collected twigs and fibers.

Dora shifted her trash can nearer the alley, where the garbage men could get at it. When she rolled it, she saw the area beneath it covered with fine, hairy roots that ripped away with a tearing sound. The fibers had actually perforated the bottom of the trash can and had evidently eaten the contents! Well, if they wanted garbage, what the hell. She went upstairs, got her kitchen garbage, brought it down and put it where the trash can had been, then went upstairs to get dressed for work. When she came down half an hour later, the garbage was gone.

That day, she had lunch with Loulee.

"I don't believe it," said Loulee. "All the garbage? What about egg shells? What about orange peels?"

"Gone," said Dora, chewing on a bit of tomato that had all the taste of cardboard. "The weed eats it."

"Can I have some seeds?"

"I haven't seen any seeds recently. How about a cutting?"

"You mean, like to put in moist dirt, to root?"

"It works with some things."

Loulee came over to Dora's place that evening. They went out on the stoop and Dora explained to the weed (Loulee giggling helplessly) that Loulee wanted a cutting, so she could feed her garbage to the plant. Dora then went in to get a knife. When she came back, Loulee was sitting on the stoop, very pale, with a chunk of weed in her lap.

"It gave it to me," she said. "It's got roots and everything. It dropped in my lap. It just gave it to me."

10

Opalears: The Journey North

"Traveling southwesterly down the length of the River Fraiburne, one comes eventually to the high dam at Barsifor. This marvelous structure, together with the outlying locks at Giber and the radiating canals which allow access to all the flat agricultural country beyond, inclines one toward true admiration of the kasturic peoples who not only designed but built the edifice. If it were not for kasturic talents in construction, the floods that once ravaged this pleasant plain would be with us once again. . . .

"This diligent and sturdy people, always productively occupied, has long been the inspiration of fabulists. . . ."

THE PEOPLES OF EARTH
HIS EXCELLENCY, EMPEROR FAROS VII

Prince Izakar's Palmia is split in halves, north and south, by the Fraiburne River. The river has as its source Pangloss Brook, which runs south from the Crawling Sea through that convenient chasm in the Sharbak Range

123

known as the Slash, the only easy access between the lands north and south of the great mountains. By the time the brook reaches Isher, it is much enlarged by tributary streams, and there it becomes even larger through confluence with the River Scruj—which drains the Mellow Marches—to which river was already added the fullness of River Roq, flowing northward from the Wycos Valley.

Thus the stream that comes down to the sea westerly through Palmia is wide and plenteous, a gathering of waters from many mountains, including all those south and east of the Crawling Sea. Much water traffic comes down this river into Lake Barsifor and farther down through the kasturic locks at Giber. Much land traffic goes up alongside the river, on roads well maintained for the sake of commerce. All this I learned from Prince Izakar, who was as well informed on the subject of ge-ography as he seemed to be on any other subject one might mention—or not. He was quite capable of lengthy disquisitions on subjects no one but he knew anything about.

After spending only one day in Palmody, our troop left the town to ride eastward along the Fraiburne, now accompanied by Izzy (which is what he asked to be called), two additional pack animals—burros, said Izzy—one additional body servant named Osvald Orbin, and two bodyguards, Oyk and Irk, who, after the manner of the kannic people, walked on foot at Flinch's heels. Both were large persons with sharp eyes and many battle scars, capable, so Izzy said, of taking care of him in any of the usual types of brawls.

"They do not bid fair to add intelligence to our dis-cussions of an evening, around the fire," I remarked with a sniff.

"No," Izzy replied. "The kannic people tend to be laconic and non-introspective. When some bully decides to take me apart for no discernable reason, however, I find that my usual preference for articulate speech gives way to admiration for mute muscle. Their scars speak for them.''

I knew what he meant. ''Some of the guards who worked for the sultan were of the other type, all thunder and no rain, full of the dullest bluster! In the stories I tell, I never include such simple bullies. In my tales, all love is true, all service is honorable, all nobles are faithful to their lord—as well as being handsome and well spoken. Except for great villains, of course, and they are much above mere bullying. I allow them to shine darkly as they seduce, entice, or play the traitor.''

''If there is one thing I have learned for sure,'' replied Izzy, ''it is that life is not a story.''

''I thought that's what Ghotians believe,'' said Sahir, cantering up and pulling his umminha—a tall white beast with a yellow mane and a ferocious expression—to a walk beside us. ''Isn't your world merely a story told by Ghoti to amuse himself?''

This was said in a purposefully nasty way, as though to provoke Izzy. Though Sahir was sometimes hospitable, at other times he seemed to relish being unpleasant to Prince Izakar, for some reason I did not understand.

Izzy refused to take offense. ''The bishops would not use that phraseology, though in essence you are correct. Personally, however, I've never accepted the doctrine. If a God is all imagining, as Ghoti is said to be, then why should he wish to imagine a place in which beauty and squalor are so inextricably mixed? If I were inventing a world for my pleasure, I would cover the trash bins and fence off the midden. In fact, I would probably make both trash bins and middens unnecessary. On the other hand, if the world is *real*, then one understands the necessity for squalor. One understands that though Ghoti, or some other god, may have created it, it is not an arbitrary fabrication but is susceptible to those inexorable natural laws which demand an up for every down.''

Prince Sahir said idly, ''What natural laws? Wouldn't the creator manufacture those as well?''

''I prefer to think of them as intrinsic to time and

space," said Izzy in his most serious voice. "In this universe, one and one always make two. Not two and a half. Not three. But two. In this universe, things fall . . . ah, down. Not up. Not sideways."

"You mean this world?" I asked, confused by all this talk of universes.

"Of course," said Izzy hastily. "That's what I mean. This is the nature of the stuff of which the . . . world is made."

I persisted, attempting to understand. "But if the deity had made the world of other stuff, then other things might happen."

"Possibly, but they would be consistent other things. As, for example, things would buoyantly fall up, and one and one would always, synergistically, make two and three-quarters. However a world is made, or whatever it is made of, each world must be consistent to its own laws. This, to my mind, is the main difficulty with Bubblism. The world is supposedly created only in the mind of Ghoti, where, presumably, anything may be imagined, but in fact, anything is not; only some things are, those which are consistent. One and one, do, in fact, always make two."

"Ghoti may have made up the laws first, as children make up the rules to games they play," I argued. "Allowing exceptions for himself, of course."

"Possible, but trifling if true. I prefer to think the laws are a consequence of materiality, which may itself be a consequence of the nature of space and time. An immaterial universe . . . ah, world . . . might have no laws. This one does, however, which leads me back to the point I made at first. This is not a story. Because it is not a story, it is unlikely to contain only honorable persons, and it is therefore entirely possible we will encounter at least a few unpleasant ones who will attempt to do away with us for any reason or for no reason other than a customary dislike of creatures other than themselves."

"We will protect you," said Sahir in his sneering tone. "Fear not."

Izzy smiled his thanks. He did it sweetly, quite sincerely, though I'm sure he thought Sahir himself did not look as though he were up to protecting much. The mounted guards, however, were another matter. They were a burly group who might well protect him, particularly Soaz, with his spiky whiskers and his almost amber eyes, who gave the impression of violence held barely beneath his skin. Even among a race that was known for bulk, Soaz would be considered large. And then there were the umminhi, which had been known to fight violently when attacked. And Oyk, of course. And Irk.

"This is very pretty country," I said, trying to change the subject. Though I liked Prince Izakar very much, he had a habit of going on and on about things that made no sense. He talked of Mathematics. He talked of Science. And he questioned everything, all the time, leaving a person no firm place to stand! Though we were little different in age, he made me feel very young and stupid. Far better not have learning if all it did was make things uncertain. Now I would have to worry about being attacked by some person who didn't like other kinds of people. Though, as I came to consider the matter, almost all the kinds of persons were already represented in the troop. Izzy and I were ponjic, and Prince Sahir was suinic. Most of the guardspersons were feledic, while Izzy's body servant was marsian and the handlers kapric. What type of person was left to attack us? Were we to be assaulted by kastori? Or armakfatidi?

Impossible! Armakfatidi were far too concerned about comfort and elegance to go about attacking persons!

Izzy had been watching my face. "I'm sorry," he murmured with a sympathetic smile. "I didn't mean to make you uncomfortable. Even though I don't believe in Bubblism, I've been affected by it. Ghotians tend to discuss the most outré possibilities without discomfort because they believe nothing can happen which has not already been ordained.''

"Well, talking about such possibilities in advance is just worrisome,'' I retorted. "If I'm going to be attacked tomorrow, I'd just as soon not think about it now.''

"When ignorance is bliss . . .'' said Izzy, then had to explain the saying, which neither Sahir nor I had heard before. We knew nothing of life insurance.

Thereafter we talked of the scenery. There were rafts of logs coming down the Fraiburne, each with its complement of forest tribesmen. The forest people provided wood for building and for fuel, as well as doing some construction. They were mostly kastori, known as a diligent, hardworking people, and they waved at us from atop their bobbing rafts, enjoying a rare opportunity for relaxation.

The farms along the way were mostly psitid. Some of the psitid peoples are less vocal than others, and those of larger size tend toward the agricultural arts. I saw numbers of them in the fields, tweaking out weeds as their long legs stalked along the rows.

"Look there,'' roared Soaz, as he galloped his steed from the head of the column to join us at the rear. "The joining of the rivers!''

We stared ahead, seeing a vast lake of disturbed water where the River Scruj met Pangloss Brook.

"The snows have melted,'' explained Izzy. "The rivers are bursting their banks. We must stay on this side until we reach Bannock Gorge, spanned by a high bridge across the flood. Then we will come back on the other side to Isher, which lies somewhere beyond all that water.''

"You are Lord of Isher?'' asked Sahir.

"Only in a manner of speaking,'' Izzy answered. "I may be, someday. Before leaving, I obtained letters of introduction from Uncle Goffio to the factotums in Isher and Fan-Kyu Cyndly, and I imagine we can depend upon their hospitality as we are traveling through.''

I thought privately that if the hospitality extended to

baths, preferably hot ones, it would be quite good enough. All this travel made one itchy, and the baths in Palmia had offered only cold water. "Beyond Fan-Kyu Cyndly we come to Estafan?"

"Fan-Kyu lies inland of the shore counties," Izzy replied. "The shore counties are high tundra, which is settled, where at all, by a water-loving people who dance in the flood as we would on floors. They are called the onchiki and they are ruled, if it can be called that, by the Onchik-Dau, an overseer caste of great antiquity. Basically, they are fisherfolk, though they also maintain flocks of veebles who graze on the downs along the sea."

"I did not know veebles could be herded!" I cried. Grandfather had had a pair of veebles on the farm, and they had lived in a pen.

"Only by the onchiki," Izzy averred. "They seem to understand the veebles as no other people do."

"Can these onchiki talk? Or are they like the armak-fatidi, always grummeling at one?"

Izzy shrugged. "Since I have been at some trouble to learn what is purported to be their language, I hope they do indeed talk."

We reached the confluence of the rivers and continued beyond it, upstream along the River Scruj. Far ahead on our right, we could see a great fall plunging from the broad height of the Wycos Valley, the River Roq that flowed between the Big and Little Stonies. Between ourselves and this cataract a high, arched bridge spanned the river from rocky pinnacle to rocky pinnacle, the riotous flood pouring beneath. On the near side of this bridge we espied an indistinct clutter which, as we rode closer, turned out to be a great number of wagons and persons and beasts, all waiting to cross.

We rode to and through the crowd, the umminhi snarling and striking out with their forelegs to make space, Oyk and Irk growling curses in their throats, Flinch nervously tip-tupping along in the rear. By the time we reached the bridge, a considerable path had been opened for our company.

Izzy rode forward. "Is the bridge closed?" he asked mildly.

The person in charge, while casting nervous glances at the umminhi, muttered, "Just warning the people, is all."

"Against what?" asked Sahir.

The guard jittered, shifting from foot to foot, jerking his head from side to side. "Them trees is all stirred up," he muttered, only to be replaced by another guard.

"Purpose of your travel," he demanded.

"I am Izakar, Prince of Palmia," said Izzy rather loftily. "I am traveling to Isher and Fan-Kyu Cyndly to familiarize myself with the needs of the inhabitants prior to ascending the throne."

The guard's jaw dropped. A mutter began among the crowd. "It's the prince. Izakar. Him, the ponji one. You know, Izzy. The one they cut his dah's head off! Lookit his hair. It's red."

The guard's mouth shut with a snap. "These are your . . . your people, Your Highness?" He gestured at our troop.

"Certainly they are my people," Izzy said loftily. "Would I travel with someone else's people?"

Sahir started to say something, then subsided with a glower. The guard opened the barricade and motioned us through, then approached within a handsbreadth of Flinch. "Watch out for them, Your Royal Highness, sir."

"Them who?"

"Them trees and the ones who've stirred them up."

Izzy told the guard we would indeed watch out for anyone stirring up the trees, but which trees had been stirred up?

"Them trees, you'll see 'em." He made a gesture that was half a bow, then stood scowling as we passed.

We heard the barrier clang behind us. The feet of horse, umminhi, Oyk and Irk drummed the bridge: *ca-*

*dop bawhop—shoof shoof (pit-pat), cadop bawhop
shoof shoof (pit-pat)*. The structure beneath us strummed
to the current boiling by, red as a brickmaker's bath-
water. Over the shivering arch we went, high above the
flood, staring ahead where the bridge sloped down into
the road. All along the road were trees in clusters and
clumps and copses, filling all the space between the road
and the river.

"The trees look quite all right to me," said Izzy to
no one in particular.

"I've been this way before," said Soaz, "though it's
been many, many years. I thought there were hayfields
along here. Of course, the woods could have grown up
since then. . . ."

We rode into the woods, into a comb of gold-green
light, a fluttering shade, a dazzle of molten gold seen
through a sieve of shadow. Blossoms of light burned in
the grass, vanished in shade, only to reappear once more
like sheaves of stars, twinkling. I took note. This was an
excellent story place. I could use it in a tale or two. The
road sloped downward, parallel with River Scruj, and
we had not gone a great distance before we saw the great
expanse of turbid water ahead of us, where the road
turned away to the north along the mere that was normally Pangloss Brook.

Beside the broad water an untidy encampment spread
itself, canvas and hide tents and a charred rock circle
surrounding a smoldering fire. At the shore, fishermen
plied their nets, while out on the water little boats
bobbed to and fro, struggling in the wind.

"I hear the broad accents of Isherian speech," said
Izzy, as he rode forward to engage someone in conversation. He returned shortly to report that the trees along
the road, though of fairly recent growth, were perfectly
nice trees who were not at all stirred up and to which
no one had any objection. *These* trees, said the fishermen, were very good trees indeed, if people minded their
manners. *Them* trees, said the fishermen, were another
thing altogether, but they were further north, and the

lords of Isher and Fan-Kyu Cyndly had barred the bridge as a kind of quarantine, to keep *them* trees from bringing their disturbance southward.

"He says we will know them when we see them," Izzy remarked.

We rode on, northward, up a long steady slope toward a break in the cliff wall, the canyon where the Pangloss, in some former incarnation, had either eaten a way through the Sharbak Range or had held place while that range moved up on either side. Or so Izzy said, at least, though I detected no movement in the mountains. The trees continued beside us, extending all the way from the stream to the feet of the cliffs and up the slopes of scree at their bottoms. Here and there on the high rock walls tufts of the same green sprouted from the stone, indomitably arrayed.

We stopped at noon to eat and refresh ourselves beside the waters. The ground was littered with dried branches. While the horse and the umminhi sucked at the stream, while Oyk and Irk lapped noisily beside the kneeling umminhi, Izzy's servant, Osvald, lit a fire and brewed a large pot of tea. Izzy sat idly on a stone, toying with several of the dry twigs with which the ground was strewn.

"These trees," said Izzy, "have a strange habit of growth. Have you noticed?"

We looked up, for a moment not seeing what he meant. He set his hand on the nearest trunk, where a tuft of leaves emerged from a round, smooth scar. Above the tuft, another branch had dried, and when Izzy seized it, it broke cleanly, leaving a round sapless scar on the tree. Izzy held a stick of firewood. "A firewood tree. I've read about them, but these are the first I've seen."

"Not all of them," I pointed out. "Look, some of them are all furry with leaves, all the way down."

Flinch had noticed the same habit of growth and was browsing on the leaves of the nearest tree, young, succulent leaves quite different from the glossy, almost black ones higher up.

"What happens if you try to break a green branch?" asked Sahir in an interested tone.

Izzy opened his mouth, but before he could get the words out, Soaz had risen and tried to break a green one, only to emit an agonized yelp. When he held out his hands, his fingers were bloody. "Thorns," he whispered, half to himself. "I didn't see any thorns. . . ."

"I didn't yell fast enough to warn you," said Izzy. "Is it very painful?"

"Enough that I won't do it again," he snarled, eyes slitted and teeth showing.

I went to Soaz's aid, finding ointment and bandages in one of the boxes. "Izzy says every world has its own rules, and evidently you broke one of them. If it's a firewood tree, we must take the firewood and let the tree alone. If it's a browsing tree, it's for the browsers!"

"Since when does a tree decide when we will or will not do with it as we please?" demanded Sahir. "If we were in Tavor, I would have it chopped down for presumption."

A little breeze swept the branches above us, followed by a hush so profound that we found ourselves holding our breaths. The silence continued, becoming wider and deeper with each passing moment, an abyss of silence.

"He didn't mean it," said Izzy, dropping a verbal pebble into the depths. "He was joking. I hadn't yet told him about firewood trees, so he was somewhat surprised. . . ."

The hush contined. Sahir cleared his throat. "Of course I was joking. A bad joke. I wouldn't . . . chop down a tree."

The breeze departed, leaving normal forest sounds behind it.

Silently, as though by agreement, we packed up our things and went back to the road, looking eagerly upward for a glimpse of sky. Sahir started to say something, and Soaz put a hand on his shoulder, shaking his head. Though Tavorians are historically a desert people, they have dwelt long enough among groves to know something about trees, and I thought Prince Sahir's comment had been pure petulance and arrogance, particularly for someone who claimed to be Korèsan.

None of us spoke until we had traveled several circums, at which point the road departed from the brook and ascended onto a high prominence from which we could look down into hilly Isher and beyond it toward the green water meadows of Fan-Kyu, the stream showing silver among them.

"I have traveled here," Soaz mused. "I have been here before. I have been through Isher and Finial and Sworp. I have even traveled into the Dire Marches, east of the sea. When I was a youth in Isfoin, I longed for travel, and when I was old enough, travel I did. I was not always eunuch to the sultan. I have been other things in other times! And when I was another thing, there were no trees like those that listened!"

Izzy remarked calmly, "So, their type must have come recently. Things do just come. Like a wind, or a great wave. We've always had fruit trees that bend down to be picked, and flowering trees that bend down to be smelled, and trees that get up and move if they're not getting enough water. From that to a tree that understands language isn't a huge step. These trees aren't that different, really."

"*These* may not be," snarled Soaz. "We haven't seen *them* yet!"

11

Countess Elianne Receives an Unwelcome Visitor

"When the great composer, Geelyflur, was completing his opera, Madama Missletoe, he was asked what singer he would cast in the role of Madama. "I care not," he cried, "so long as the audience is at least half scuinic." Thus the master gave credit for his success where credit was due. As appreciators and supporters of the arts, the scuinic people are without parallel. In government, they have long shown a talent for easing the burdens of the people. As citizens they tend toward cheerful compliance with the needs of civility...."
        THE PEOPLES OF EARTH
        HIS EXCELLENCY, EMPEROR FAROS VII

In Zallyfro, the Countess Elianne of Estafan was wakened early by her ladies of the bedchamber who reminded her, with squeals of mixed anxiety and amusement, that the Dire Duke Fasahd had announced his intention of lunching with the countess today, whether the countess would or no.

Elianne was annoyed. It wasn't funny. After a cup of hot tea and some thought, however, she decided to put a good face on the matter and lunch elegantly on the north terrace, among the lily ponds, surrounded by spice bush and roses, beside the bubbling fountains where the shade was deep and cool. The Dire Duke would see and smell nothing but tranquility and might thus be moved to peacefulness.

She, unlike her giggling ladies, knew what he wanted. He wanted an alliance against his brother, Fasal Grun. Antipathy was not inevitable among ersin brothers, this she knew, but this made no difference to Fasahd. A mere three minutes separated the birth of the Dire Duke from that of his so-slightly elder brother, and the Dire Duke was unwilling to accept the lifelong implications of such a brief delay. The Dire Duke saw no reason whatsoever that he should not be in command of Sworp now and of the empire later on.

A pity that Faros VII had no son and must rely upon these nephews. The Countess Elianne had met Fasal Grun on several occasions and had found him to be a sensible and even somewhat kindly person, all in all, a credit to his tribe. As for Faros VII, she heard many good things about him, more good than bad, at any rate.

"Plain muslin for now, Cerise," she directed a maid. "And I do mean plain. Also, that short wig. I want to go down to the kitchens to talk with Blanche and the new armakfatidian chef, what's his name?"

"Dzilobommo, Your Grace."

"Right. Dzilobommo. Did Kletter find out what the duke eats?"

"He eats most things, though he's allergic to cheese. He particularly enjoys fish or fowl."

"He would. We'll have to make sacrifice to the Silver Swimmer if we serve fish to a pagan, and Blanche will be upset if we serve fowl. The chickens are her friends, so she says. How about sweets? Ersuniel folk are known to be lovers of sweets."

"Kletter didn't find out."

"Well, we'll have a selection and let him choose."
She sat before her mirror and let Cerise fit the wig and
comb it over her ears, a simple style, taking little time.
All would have to be done over before she welcomed
the Dire Duke, who would try to get an agreement she
could ill afford to give him.

Thus far, Estafan and Finial had been allowed to re-
tain their own governance and religions and ways of
doing things. The countess and her people revered the
hemi-ghoti, the Silver Swimmer, who swam in the ocean
of light and brought that light to his people. Still, the
countess had agreed to accept Faros VII as the emperor
to whom loyalty was owed; she had agreed that no other
alliances or entanglements would take place, that no rebellion would be fomented, and that no anti-Korèsan
teachings would be promulgated. The estafani, said the
Emperor Faros VII, might continue believing in Sweet
Silver Swimmer so long as no disorder resulted.

The countess exemplified the pragmatism common
among her people. She felt there was no choice but to
comply. Estafan was small, lovely, and well cared for,
its people a multiethnic mix who were devoted to song
and dance and fertility, not warfare. They were not even
particularly interested in the theory or practice of government. They were quite willing to have the hereditary
rulers manage things, so long as they did so smoothly
and without corruption, remaining decorative, decorous
and diligent in the process. Elianne, when readied for
ceremonies of state, sometimes felt like a pet horse, ca-
parisoned for a parade and, like the horse, curried, cos-
seted and given an apple in thanks.

And now the Dire Duke Fasahd. Who did not care for
peace or the teachings of either Korè or Bandercran.
Who wanted power. Who thought Elianne might be a
help to him. Who had to be discouraged from that an-
ticipation without being insulted.

Muffling a sigh, trailing trotting ladies as a goose
trails down, she descended to the kitchens. Across that
vaulted room, in the shadows, her clerk Blanche perched

silently on a high stool, watching everything with her dark, beady eyes. Nothing escaped Blanche. She had an eye for trifles and an ear for nuance. Dzilobommo, dressed in ice blue apron and high pleated hat, bowed deeply. Elianne fought down the urge to chuckle which the armakfatidi always roused in her, assuming instead an expression of regal imperturbability.

"Dzilobommo, great culinary artist, I am faced with a most difficult time. I beg your assistance."

"Grummel grummel grummel," which translated, after a moment's consideration into, "How may I assist?"

"The Dire Duke who lunches with me today, Dzilobommo, is a difficult person. He is allergic to dairy products and is said to like fish." In deference to Blanche, she did not mention chicken.

"Grummel grummel," meaning, "No problem, religion aside."

"Ah, but this is only the surface, Dzilobommo. Beneath that surface lies another, and beneath that, another. Hath not the Sweet Silver Swimmer said, green depths lie beneath silver, and beneath the green lies blue, and beneath the blue, darkness?"

"Grummel." An assent.

"This man would threaten me into an agreement which would be bad for us all, including the armakfatidi. If I say yes, it will go ill for us. If I say no, it will perhaps be worse. He must feel kindly toward us when he leaves. He must think us charming small folk. Oh, Dzilobommo, he must believe we are both harmless and worthless. Of no help to him."

"Grummel!" Meaning, "I will serve you myself."

She bowed. "My thanks, Dzilobommo."

He touched his lean fingers to the edge of his folded hat and smoothed his apron over his substantial body, leaning back a little and nodding ponderously. "Grummel."

The countess turned and left the kitchens, walking quickly to be out of hearing before she giggled. It was an effect left over from childhood. The armakfatidi were not amusing. They had a dark nature hidden behind that amiable facade. So her father had told her over and over. "They are of a warrior race," he had said, more than once. Still, she found them amusing. Each *grummel* reached her humor as though she had been tickled.

Blanche came flying around the corner ahead of them to wait breathlessly at the cross corridor. She had come the back way to meet them. Elianne left Cerise and went to speak to her clerk. "What have you for me today, my friend?"

Blanche said in a whisper: "The armakfatidi talk of war, lady. There is a rebellion among the trees near Fan-Kyu."

"Among the trees? What is this?"

"They think it may be the Dire Duke who has stirred them up, lady."

"Odd. And the kitchen people still have no idea you can understand them?"

"None whatsoever. They believe I am deaf and mute."

"Thank you." She turned away from Blanche and went down the corridor at a furious rate, thinking madly.

"Countess . . ."

"Yes, Cerise."

"How can you and Blanche understand the armak-fatidi? All I hear is a kind of rumbling."

"It comes, Cerise, if one simply holds still and keeps the mind . . . quiet. They seem to speak . . . silently as well as vocally. My father taught me how to hear them, though I've never been able to understand their humor. Sometimes one of them will *grummel* and then they'll all bend over going *hnarf, hnarf, hnarf* until their hair stands out like a brush. I've seen it over and over, but I've never known what was funny. Blanche can't figure it out, either."

"Do you think they are laughing at us?"

"I don't get any sense that they are. I don't think we're sufficiently important for them to laugh at."

"Not important enough?"

"Not to the armakfatidi. They feed us, but it's the art they take pride in, not our perception of their art. Dzilobommo regards the effect of his food on diners as a painter regards the effect of his picture on an observer. The observer, or the diner, is only a recipient of an art which was accomplished without his, or her, help. By asking him to help me, I challenge his artistry. Dzilobommo rises to the challenge."

"How odd."

"No odder, however, than certain other creatures." She was thinking of the Dire Duke Fasahd, but the thought went nowhere. She was more comfortable when she did not think of him at all.

She turned to Cerise and held out her hand. "Come, lady. Let us get me up like a circus horse to glitter in the eyes of our guest. Perhaps the glitter will distract him. If not, pray the Silver Swimmer that Dzilobommo does."

It seemed a very short time until Countess Elianne was sitting across the table from the Dire Duke Fasahd, smiling with concentrated sweetness upon his dour and dreadful face, wondering, as she had before, how this one could be twin to the Prime Duke Fasal Grun when that one looked like a maiden's dream of naughty passion and this one looked like six weeks on short rations. "Do have more fish," she murmured. "Cerise, give our guest more fish."

"Excellent fish," he growled, the jowls at either side of his face jiggling, his teeth showing at the corners of his mouth, yellow and sharp as old thorns, dead and dried and evil even unto winter. "Though I did not come for the food."

Still Dzilobommo had prepared it, and Fasahd had eaten some of it. And if he could just hold himself in patience until some of it started to digest, he might find himself in quite another mood.

"Explain it to me again," murmured the countess in desperation.

He was not averse to explaining it as many times as need be.

"My brother is a fool," he began.

She could have recited his tale of woe. His brother was a fool who had accepted Faros VII's desire for peace and prosperity and for avoidance of armed conflict along tribal or social lines. The Dire Duke, on the other hand, was a realist who knew that conflict was coming. "The emperor's own seers tell him so. They say somewhere a dreadful conspiracy is taking place, one that will end our world and kill us all. But will the emperor act? He will not."

The countess murmured, "Perhaps it is difficult to know what to do."

"There is only one thing to do! Arm ourselves. Build up our armies. Whenever we find out who conspires against us, we will be ready! Therefore let all persons choose sides now, before the trouble starts."

Let the countess ally herself with the Dire Duke, he demanded, who already had made other such alliances, as, for example, with trees.

"Why have you made an alliance with . . . trees?" she asked in disbelief.

He gave her a sharp look. "The trees have learned of a conspiracy against them, as well, and they have reason to be outraged. If they will assist me in fighting my enemies, why should I not ally myself in their battle?"

"How have the trees learned of this conspiracy?" she asked.

"I have my sources, lady," he said, a shadow crossing his face as he answered, something bleak and horrid briefly looking out of his eyes. "My source knows much that the world is ignorant of. There are wheels moving within wheels, plots within plots. You would be wise to be on the winning side, so why should you not form part of this alliance, and with you all the people of Estafan?"

"Firstly, though you and your trees may be outraged, I am not, nor are my people. Secondly, I am not an absolute monarch. If I attempted such a thing, I would be deposed, and someone else would be appointed to rule.''

"But you would be backed by my armies!"

"Who would kill my people, and then you wouldn't have allies, you'd have a subject province. Do you want a subject province?"

He did, of course, but it wouldn't do to say so, yet. Though Faros was known to have forbidden cannibalism, the Dire Duke's followers were known to practice that filthy custom, and it was said they did it from appetite rather than in an attempt to terrorize. Though the ponji were too thin and stringy a people to tempt such creatures, many of the people of Estafan were of the countess's own more fleshy race. She felt his eyes undressing her, considering her in the light of various appetites, and she could almost see those appetites gain in strength.

His mouth watering, the Dire Duke helped himself to more fish, to more wine, to more fish yet again. When he left, he was in what for him might pass as an ebullient mood, by which the countess meant merely that he did not attempt to kill anyone during his departure. He had not obtained her promise of alliance, but he had not been directly refused. Perhaps that would hold him, for a time.

Blanche was waiting in her private chambers along with a very ruffled and breathless messenger who, though one of Blanche's kindred, did not share her usual calm.

"Countess," he gasped, bending forward until his beaky nose almost touched the floor.

"Get up," she said impatiently. "A slight bow would be quite enough. What's this you bring me . . . Dessur? That's your name, isn't it?"

"Your Grace is kind to notice." He fluttered his hands, cocking his head flirtatiously.

The countess was annoyed, though she knew the manner was simply a cultural artifact. Many of Blanche's people acted in that fluttery way, even the males. "My

Grace is not kind to notice. She wants to know who in Estafan is flitting about with messages. Who's this from?''

"It's from his Eminence, the Prime Duke Fasal Grun.''

Apprehensively, she opened it, finding inside enough to fulfil her fears. The Prime Duke had learned that Fasahd was paying her a visit. The Prime Duke wished to be informed for what reason the Dire Duke had left Finial and was agitating among the neighbor realms, and why he had been invited to Estafan.

She went to her desk in the moment, chewing the top of the pen as she drafted an answer. "Your Eminence knows that we are a weak nation, without protection, a nation which could not withstand an attack. Your brother came at his own invitation; he says the emperor knows from the seers that a conspiracy is taking place. Your brother has made an alliance with trees, which, so he says, are outraged. He has, so he says, a secret source of information. I have said we in Estafan are not outraged, but still he wishes to make a similar alliance with us, which I have so far dallied over. His eyes were hungry when he looked upon our peaceful land. Cannot the authority of Faros VII be brought to bear upon this unseemly appetite?''

She turned to the courier, who was preening himself with a sidelong look into the mirror. "I presume he expects an answer?''

He caught her glance and flushed. "Yes, Your Grace.''

"Well, give him this, and tell him to make all speed his sails will give him.''

When he had gone, she turned to Blanche, her face very pale. "Oh, Blanche. Sometimes I wish I had wings to take me far from my responsibilities.''

Blanche cocked her head and came as close as she ever did to a smile. "I think even wings cannot do that, Your Grace.''

12

A Certain Disposition of Garbage

Dora had breakfast at a fast food place, alone at a corner table, reading a paper someone had left, rubbing at her eyes. She'd had too little sleep. The divorce papers had been served on Jared two days ago, and he had started phoning her, three or four times during the night. She was to return to his place, at once, said he. No, no, said she, she was quite happy where she was. He persisted, in that totally egocentric way of his, not even answering her feelings or opinions, but only asserting his own. He threatened. He would make her return, in a way she would not like. Perhaps he would institute his own suit on the grounds she had abandoned him. Fine. That was all right. If he liked. He would make her sorry. She would regret.

At that point she had reminded him, "I'm a cop, Jared. You know I can file a report, saying you threatened me. I'll put a recorder on this phone so if you do it again, I'll have a tape of it. I can prove our marriage was never consummated, and you've often said you were perfectly

144

contented before we married. During our marriage, we only met over the dinner table. Our tastes are not alike. It was a mistake. Let it go.''

"It was not a mistake," he had growled. "It was exactly as I intended it should be."

She had found no answer to this outrageous statement. He would worry her less if she could figure out why he cared, if it could be called caring. Was it hurt pride? Was his mother chaffing at him? Despite everything, Dora thought Mrs. Gerber had rather liked her. Perhaps Jared didn't want to tell the men at the plant that he was single? Or he didn't want to tell his mother why she'd left him. Sighing, she shut the quandry away and concentrated on the paper.

A herd of cattle was reported lost, disappeared, there one day, gone the next. Hikers reported hearing noises in the woods during the night, a gigantic kind of gulping or blurping, they said, like a mud cauldron, which is what they thought it was. There were, however, no hot springs in the area.

"What do you think?" she asked Phil as they drove toward the pharmaceutical firm, where more questions were to be asked. "You think it's ETs?"

"I think it's greens, all right, but not little green men," he said. "Bet you the environmentalists have decided to fight fire with fire. They've given up trying to protect the land by law, so they're trying to make it expensive for people to let their cows graze up there."

"Could be," she admitted. "The thought crossed my mind. I suppose a few big trucks could carry a whole herd away. I should think it would be difficult, though, rounding up cattle in the dark. That's what baffles me."

"Ah, it's like those crop circles," he said. "Everybody says it's impossible, it must be ETs, and then some guy shows how he and his friends did it by flashlight, with their feet and a piece of old two by four."

She grinned. Phil was a cynic. He didn't believe anything unless he'd seen it at high noon when he was cold sober, and then only if it were repeated on several successive days.

He saw the grin. "You know, Dora, when you look like that, you're a hell of a good-looking woman."

"Hey . . . Phil. . . ." She flushed, embarrassed.

"You got pretty skin, like somebody twenty or so. I like your hair, like a shiny bell. Don't worry. I'm not making a move on you. I've got this friend, though. I'll bet you'd like him."

"Phil, for God's sake. I haven't been separated from Jared for even a month yet. . . ."

"Oh, shit, you never cared about Jared. I know you, Dora. You just married Jared because you thought it was time you married somebody."

She ducked her head angrily. "That's a hell of a thing to say."

He nodded, accepting that. "It is a hell of a thing, because it's true. I've watched you with Jared. You acted like you were his bored big sister. And he acted like you were the hired cook. So, let me introduce you to this guy. He used to be a neighbor of ours. He's a professor, at the college. He's got a terrific sense of humor. He's—"

To Dora's relief, the radio blared, a call to Bart's Used Cars. Phil said, "It's not our business, but tell them we'll take the call, it's only six blocks away."

He swung the car back the way they had come, turned right, and sped up, swiveling his head looking for cross traffic. "That's it." He jutted his chin. "On the corner of Thirteenth. Bart's."

An angry man approached them as soon as the car drew up, spluttering and waving his arms, making no sense.

"Hey," said Phil, "calm down. I didn't do it. Don't yell at me."

The man turned, still shouting, and led them across the lot to an area just outside the small salesroom. He pointed dramatically, stepping up the decibel level until he had to pause for breath, then he heard his phone ringing and ran for it.

"What?" asked Dora, looking at the ground. "What's he going on about?"

"The asphalt," Phil muttered. "Somebody tore it up."

The blacktop was disturbed, bumpy, as though heaved up from beneath. "It's got pimples," Dora offered. "It doesn't look like vandalism."

"Could be a water pipe, leaking under there," Phil offered. "Could be gas."

Dora backed away. "What? Call Public Service?"

"I'm not going to fool with it." He headed back to the car radio, to report, just as the angry man came plunging back out of the building.

"Well?" he demanded. "What're you going to do about it?"

"My partner thinks it could be a leak in a water pipe, or it could be gas," she said. "Just on the off chance it's gas, I'd move these cars away. You know, fire danger and all that."

Bart, if this was Bart, gaped at her, torn between argument and action. The economic imperative took over, and he ran for the nearest car. While he was shifting vehicles, Dora walked around the outside of the pimply area, a space about twenty by thirty feet. The second time around, she noticed something green emerging from the tip of one of the pimples. A bit of asphalt broke loose and slid; a tendril poked into the air; leaflets unfurled and turned to look at her.

"Fancy meeting you here," she said.

Phil spoke from just behind her. "What did you say?"

"Nothing, Phil. I don't think it's water or gas. It looks like something growing under there, is all."

"Under *asphalt*?"

"Mushrooms do it all the time. I've seen them push up blacktop along the edges of parking lots. What I think is, this guy should get himself a . . . botanist or somebody."

Between car shuffles, the man came at them again, red-faced. "What? Is it gas or not?"

She shrugged. "No, it's not gas. It's something growing. What you need is a . . . a scientist. Somebody to tell you what it is and how to—"

She had been going to say, how to kill it. The words had formed in her head, her mouth was ready to produce them, when she was overcome by a sense of imminent doom and bit her tongue instead. After a momentary pause, she gasped, "How to make room for it." She breathed deeply, her heart pounding, as though she'd almost stepped on a deadly snake. She recognized the feeling. She'd had that same sense of doom one time when she'd seen a suspect and the gun he was pointing in her direction and heard the shot, and felt the splatter of brick when the bullet hit the wall an inch from her head, all three perceptions in one instant, realizing in that moment that if it had been an inch closer she'd have been dead in the line of duty. *How to make room for it,* she repeated to herself. How to . . . get along with it. How to be a good . . . neighbor.

They left Bart when his complaints and annoyance ran down and went on to the pharmaceutical house. While Phil went to the men's room, Dora walked down to the streambed where they'd discovered the body. Something about it had nagged her memory, and she thought another look might clarify the thought, whatever it had been.

Just in the few days since she'd been there, the grasses had grown taller, and there were wildflowers blooming among them. She went slowly eastward along the dry streambed beside the line of pens. Animals came to the wire, watching her. A line of small pigs actually seemed to be in conversation with one another, mouths moving, heads shaking and nodding. And that was it, of course. She'd heard someone say something, that day when they'd been here. "Poor guy."

She strolled up the hill to the pens, along the wire, reaching fingers through it to entice the inhabitants. No takers. Before she reached them, the pigs, sleek and pink, left the wire and went back to their trough, still headshaking and nodding, making soft snorting noises. The next pen held a couple of sleepy dogs who opened their eyes but didn't move from their curled-up position in the sun. There was a pen of big, stumpy-tailed monkeys. They were Japanese, she recalled, the kind she'd seen on TV nature programs, sitting in hot pools while the snow fell around them. Another large pen held two young bears and a big stump they were pulling apart with their claws. Farther up the hill, two men were walking down a lane between two ranks of pens, wheeling a cart loaded with feed of various kinds. That's probably who it had been the other day, the guys doing the feeding. She strolled toward them, recognizing Joe and Bill, the two men who had found the body.

"Hi," she called, waving. They stopped and waited for her.

"Does anyone else work out here with the animals?" she asked. "The other day when I was here, I heard someone talking."

The two exchanged glances, their faces blank. "Usually just us this time of day," said Joe. "But there's other animal tenders, and sometimes the lab people wander down here during coffee break. That's probably who you heard."

She nodded, accepting this. She hadn't seen anyone. But every pen had some kind of shelter in it, a hutch or shed or mini barn. Whoever it had been could have been behind something.

"They find out who killed Dr. Winston?" asked the other man.

She shook her head. "So far we've got zip." She wandered along behind them, watching as they fed bobcats and otters and goats. "It's a zoo, isn't it?"

"Right now it is. The lab guys have been doing this study on how the same gene operates in different animals. They're writing a big paper about it for some national journal."

"Has that got anything to do with veterinary medicines?"

Bill snorted. "It's pure research. You never know what may turn up. Besides, it's good publicity for the company. Winston used to say it helped recruit good scientists. Guys who read those journals, maybe they'll decide this is a good place to work."

They went on with their feeding while Dora went back to join Phil. They repeated interviews with half a dozen associates of the victim, without learning anything new or helpful. Before they left, Dora asked if they had any written information about the research they were doing, and a harried lab assistant was sent off to get them. She returned with a dusty stack.

"Will I understand these?" Dora asked.

The lab assistant brushed dust from her clothing, muttering, "Honey, I sure as hell don't. You'll get a kind of rough idea, is all. Read the little summary paragraphs at the end or beginning. That'll tell you what's going on." She dumped the pile into Dora's arms, dust rising in a cloud around them both.

At the station, Dora went to the women's room to change her shirt. Tying a neat bow at the neck of the clean one, she considered herself in the mirror. So Phil liked how she looked. She herself had never paid much attention to how she looked. Clean, of course. And neat. Grandma had always insisted on that. The bell-shaped haircut was dictated by time and inclination—least possible expense, least possible fuss. The dark shiny hair was Grandma, too. The year before Grandma died, she'd still had dark, shiny hair. Who had bequeathed Dora the lean body and the good bones, GOK.

Wetting a paper towel to get the dust off her face, she continued the inventory. Good nose, nice and straight, not too big. The mouth was too big, but not unshapely. The only time she noticed it was when she put lipstick on, which was seldom if ever. If she had to claim a feature as best, it would be her eyes. Nice greeny brown eyes. And why in hell did she care?

Disgusted with herself, she brushed the last of the dust off her skirt and returned to her job, which proved to be a frustrating repetition for the rest of the day. Two out of every three calls were agitated people reporting stuff growing where it shouldn't. Around two, they went out for a late lunch at the deli around the corner, where Roger Manconi had agreed to meet them.

When he arrived, late and puffing a little, Dora laid out what they'd learned about Winston.

"It sounds like a carbon copy of the Chamberlain case," said Roger, running his finger down the menu. "Nice guy, smart scientist, everybody loved him to pieces, right? It's like him and Chamberlain was twins."

"Maybe they knew one another," Dora said. "I want to talk to Winston's wife again anyhow, so if you don't mind, I'll ask her. I don't want to step on your toes."

"Hell, you and Phil do what you want. I got nowhere with the thing. We put it down to murder during a robbery, only the perp got scared off. Maybe if it turns out they're related, it'll open up some new territory."

They had interviewed Mrs. Winston at the station previously. This time they went to the house, in the old country club area, once posh, still expensive, though with a kind of genteel shabbiness Dora rather liked. Nothing had been built here in forty years or more, and the trees had had a chance to grow tall.

"Looks like a forest," she commented.

"Shady," he agreed. "No place else in town has this many trees."

Melanie Winston was an appropriate woman, willowy, with flowing hair and an air of imperturbable calm. "Of course Edgar knew Martin Chamberlain," she said. "They were very close, professionally."

"As scientists," mused Dora. "Geneticists."

Melanie Winston nodded. "They worked on a number of research projects together."

"Your husband was stabbed."

Melanie pressed her lips together, eyes welling with tears. "Someone who would kill a man for his watch and his ring and his credit cards. And then not even take them!''

"Did you know Martin Chamberlain was also stabbed?''

Her mouth fell open, eyes glaring. "He was what?''

"Also stabbed. We've talked with the officer responsible for investigating his death. The weapon could be the same in both cases.''

"No one told me. . . .''

"It was in the papers.''

"I don't read . . . crime news. It's too upsetting.''

"Do you recognize the name Jennifer Williams?''

"I'm sorry. It sounds only vaguely familiar. Who is she?''

"She was another scientist who was stabbed. She was killed in May, Dr. Chamberlain in June, your husband in July.''

They stayed a while longer, asked a few more questions, but learned nothing else of help. By the time Dora got home, she was tired with that kind of weariness which had little or nothing to do with physical effort. Heart hunger, Grandma would have called it. "When your heart is hungry,'' she used to say. "That's when you feel so tired and down.''

Dora had recognized the symptoms. She'd had them every now and then since she was five. Before that, she wouldn't have had heart hunger. Now she did. "What do you do about it?'' she'd asked Grandma.

One of the nicest things about Grandma had been that she had taken such questions seriously. She'd made them cups of hot tea and sat down at the kitchen table beside her, and said, "Dora, child, you need to find out what you're hungry for. If you're in the city, maybe it's country you're hungry for. Maybe it's other people, if you're lonely, or no people if you've been rubbing up against too many. Maybe it's getting rid of something that's been giving you a brain blister every time you think of it.''

That's how she felt now. Jared was giving her a brain

blistei. Two long years married to him, as wasted as though she'd been unconscious the whole time. Thirty-five years of virginity and twenty-four months of marital coma, all of it so separated from reality that she was now unprepared to deal with it. Like an old nun, turned out of her convent onto the streets!

Why had she started worrying about that now? It was Phil's fault. He had started her thinking like this. Him touting his friend the professor. Professor of what? Probably something deadly, like economics. Or German literature.

She parked across her own driveway, telling herself she was too tired to cook, she'd leave the car out now then put it away after she'd had dinner somewhere. The Chinese place was closest. Or there was a Mexican place half a mile down the boulevard. The mailbox at the head of the drive held two sales announcements, three catalogues, and a postcard from Michael that she read as she walked down the drive toward her carriage house.

Preoccupied with Michael's news, she stepped through her gate unthinking, running on automatic, only to stop dead as the gate clanged shut behind her. This morning when she'd left, she had seen a board fence and the three little evergreens she'd planted plus about nine hundred square feet of ragged rock and weedy clay. If she had turned her head, she would have seen the chain-link fence, and through it, the alley, and past that, a stretch of vacant land.

What she saw tonight was forest.

In the corner before her a white-trunked copse of trees spilled leaflets in all directions, breaking the orange glare of the evening sun. A profusion of blue-flowered vines hid the board fence. Her little trees were there too, burgeoning. The hard-packed earth was grown up in something spongy, springy, like twiggy grass in all the cracks. She leaned down and picked a bit of it, the smell rising into her nostrils. She knew that smell. Chamomile. Grandma used to make it into tea.

To her right, where the fence and alley should be,

stood a grove of larger trees, about the height of the garage roof, as thick through as her arm. They had not been there that morning.

She found the alley gate by feeling for it through a cascade of leafy tendrils, swung it opened and stepped outside. More trees, taller ones, hid the alley—white and gray and green trunked, thrusting up through broken paving, wedges of asphalt still lying around, tarry and glistening. Among the trees was a rash of blacktop pimples, like the ones she had seen at the used car lot. Whatever was growing up from underground was still coming.

Bemusedly, she moved through the trees to what had been the edge of the vacant ground. Vacant no more. Trees and more trees. Bigger ones. Some quite big ones that reminded her of the Tree south of Jared's place. She walked among the trunks toward the cross street. As she went, the trees became sparser and shorter, until she emerged from the last of them about twenty feet from the sidewalk. She examined the blacktop under her feet, seeing nothing, wondering what the significance was of the trees being tallest at her house, which was halfway down the block. What the hell did that mean, if anything?

As she stood there, ruminating, a garbage truck approached the alley, started to turn in, then stopped. A burly man in stained jeans, his shirt sleeves rolled up to his shoulders, jumped down from the truck, nodded at her, and came to peer down the alley.

"When?" he asked, unsurprised.

"Today," she replied.

"Hey, Hal," shouted her interlocutor. "Back up! It's another one."

There was a mumble from the truck, a vast shifting of gears and hissing of brakes.

"You got garbage?" the man asked.

She shook her head, mutely. The weed had eaten all her garbage.

"Well, you got garbage, you bring it down to the end

of the alley here on pickup day. We can't get in there. This is about the twentieth one today is why we're running so late. Yesterday there was only two!'' Shaking his head, he returned to his truck, gripped a bar at the side and swung himself aboard. The ponderous vehicle turned left and groaned off down the street that ran along the vacant ground. The forest continued there, Dora noticed. Except for the street itself, everything was covered in trees.

A sound drew Dora's attention, a tiny shifting of gravel. She looked down. In the crack between the concrete sidewalk and the blacktopped alley, a sprig of green was pushing its way into the air. She saw it put its leafy little hands onto the surface, hunch up its green tendril shoulders and push, heave, push, up into the light. Disney couldn't have done it better. Now it rested, opening a leafy head to flirt with her while it summoned root strength from below.

Would it stop at the sidewalk? How about the street?

As she walked back the way she had come, she heard small crunching sounds as bits of paving let go, as wedges of blacktop fell back. If she intended to go to work tomorrow, it might be best to leave the car on the street, just in case the forest took over the driveway during the night.

13

Opalears: Meeting *Them* Trees

*"What world would be complete without the onchikian
tribes! As exemplars of vivacity, as practitioners of the
joyful, they cannot be matched by any other people.
Their laughter will enlighten any gloomy day; their music is a pleasure all too infrequently heard. Among all
the peoples of earth, surely the onchiki share the delight
of the divine. . . ."*

THE PEOPLES OF EARTH
HIS EXCELLENCY, EMPEROR FAROS VII

Sahir, Prince Izakar and I came along the trail into Isher,
riding close together, keeping an eye open for whatever greenery might prove threatening. We still hadn't
met *them* trees and were beginning to wonder if *them*
trees did, in fact, exist when, as we neared the crest of
a hill, we heard a thin screaming ahead, and voices
shouting in a strange language.

"Someone's yelling for help," cried Izzy, spurring
Flinch into a gallop, Oyk and Irk at his heels.

Soaz shouted and laid his crop onto his umminha's

side, yowling a war cry at the top of his lungs. I looked at Sahir, who looked back at me, very unsure what to do next. Our umminhi, however, who were accustomed to running in a herd, did not wait for instructions. We set off rapidly in pursuit of Soaz, with the pack animals and guards thumping along behind.

Just over the crest of the hill, we found half a dozen small persons being assaulted by trees, short but stout trees with long, flexible branches culminating in tufts of hard, bladelike leaves. The trees had the persons and their pack veebles surrounded and were swatting at them viciously with the sharp tasseled leaves, like a bee keeper who had encountered a ferocious hive. The vee-bles were crouched down together, their ears flat and their bodies trembling, while one young female person tried to shelter them all with her own slender body. Seeing this, Soaz immediately set to with his scimitar, lopping off branches right and left. Oyk and Irk grasped branch tips and pulled. Izzy, immediately, without a pause, grabbed something and shouted something. . . .

Them trees pulled back their branches and retreated, humping away on their lumpy roots until they had achieved a decent distance, where they quickly squirmed their roots into the earth and turned their leaves toward us.

"Oh, Lord Wind and all the Seven Natural Powers," cried the oldest one. "I thought we were goners, I really did."

"Thank you, thank you," cried a younger female, falling to the ground and bumping her forehead on the ground at Soaz's feet. "You saved our lives."

"Get up," he grouched at her. "No need for all this head bumping. What are you doing here?"

"Had a right," said the oldest male contentiously, responding to Soaz's tone rather than his words. "Got a perfect right. . . ."

Since Soaz was grumbling in Tavorian and the others were shrieking in—well, what were they shrieking in? I understood them, but I had no idea what language it was.

At any rate, neither understood the other. Diplomatically, Izzy intervened.

Izzy said, "Honored and elderly person, dear and sensitive female person, strong and virile father of this tribe, all offspring of whatever age and condition, this large and whiskered person means no disrespect. He is merely surprised to find onchiki in this place, so far from the sea."

"Our roof blew off," caroled the younger male, dancing about in post terror hysteria. "We're roofless, and that means we're free. So we set out—"

"Had a right to set out. Did all right about settin out," the older male interjected.

"We was going to Zallyfro," cried the old female, "but we come upon this nasty sort, great forests of 'em, all the way down to the shore, and they wouldn't let us through!"

"Shoulda turned back," mumbled the older male. "Shoulda stayed home. Shoulda known it wouldn't turn out right."

"You turned inland, looking for a way around the trees?" Izzy asked.

They confirmed that was the way it had happened, though this one had counseled otherwise, and that one had said something else, and none of them had specifically agreed to anything at all.

Izzy conveyed the sense of all this to the rest of us, who were, to a person, staring at him as though he had acquired another head.

"What?" he demanded.

"What was that thing you yelled? What did you do?" demanded Sahir.

Izzy shifted uncomfortably. "I made a gesture of Triple Admonition, pulled a vial of Arcana brand Re-Pel from my belt pouch, threw a pinch of it into the air and screamed an Imperative Estopal at the top of my lungs. To make the trees back off. Why do you ask?"

"You didn't tell us you were a sorcerer," said Sahir, stiffly.

"Any educated Palmian has some sorcery," Izzy said. "Anyone who can read and write, at least. How else could you get through life?"

"There are no sorcerers in Tavor," said Soaz, fingering his scimitar. "Magic has been illegal in Tavor since the founding."

"Magic is illegal a lot of places," Izzy said with some asperity. "Wherever the religious claim sole rights to it, they make it illegal for anybody but themselves, and they burn people for doing it, which makes the practice largely unappealing. No doubt in Tavor religious magic is holy and all other kinds are said to be superstition, but Bubblians don't see it that way. They think magic is just something else Ghoti thought up. So what? Do you want me to take off the spell and let the trees come back?" He raised his hands, obviously ready to allow just that.

Soaz shared a glance with Sahir, both somewhat troubled, then they stared for some time at the trees, which were obviously watching them and as obviously talking to one another, for the grove rippled with twig tipping and leaf flutter.

"Oh, don't let them come back," cried two younger female persons in one voice, correctly interpreting Izzy's motion. This plea was joined by those of the smallest male and female, who, up until that point, had been comforting the veebles.

"No," muttered Soaz. "Don't let them come back. No doubt our geographic separation from Tavor also separates us from its laws."

"A wise decision," said I, with a smile at Izzy. "Particularly inasmuch as we, too, will have to get through these trees if we are to reach Zallyfro."

"*Them* trees," corrected Soaz. "I think we've met them at last."

At this point the persons Izzy had rescued introduced themselves, and we met the Biwot family: Grandmama, Diver, Sleekele, Ring, Bright, Burrow, Lucy Low and Mince. Izzy suggested that they join the troop, and that in the interest of speed, they do so by perching on our larger pack creatures, who would not be greatly discomfited by this modest addition to their burdens.

"What about the veebles?" cried Lucy Low. "I can't leave the veebles. Not Chimary or Chock, not Willagong, not Gai!"

After a moment's conference, it was agreed that we would proceed at a walk, allowing the four veebles to keep up with the rest of the group for, as Lucy explained, though the pack creatures could move very quickly over short distances, they tired sooner than did the umminhi or the equines.

Though the road went up and down for the next several circums, Pangloss Brook climbed steadily in its bed, sometimes on a level with us, sometimes in a crevasse, but always ascending. We passed a sign bidding us farewell from Isher and another welcoming us to Fan-Kyu Cyndly. The mountains were some distance behind us, the brook had become a stream that meandered through water meadows where various animals grazed between fence rows made up largely of *those* trees. Afar, to east and west, we could see the chimneys and granaries of little towns, and scattered on the meadows between were stone houses at the end of narrow roads. Nowhere did we see a person, however, and to the north, in our direction of travel, the trees blocked our vision entirely.

Lucy Low regarded the growths with widened nostrils, and said to Izzy, "They wouldn't let us through. They swatted us."

Izzy asked, "Did you, by any chance, take an ax to any one of them?" I knew he was remembering the firewood tree.

"Only for a fire to make tea," she said innocently. "There was no dead wood about, so Burrow tried to cut some wood."

"And it was then they struck at you."

She admitted that was the case.

Izzy shared this with the rest of us. "If the firewood trees are, as you have thought, new to this area, there might be other types of tree with whose habits we are unfamiliar. Our encounter is a kind of culture shock. We must learn more about them.''

I said, ''I think they're trying to get along with us.''

Sahir grunted in amusement, twitching his nose.

''No, really,'' I persevered. ''Didn't you notice how they're growing, along the fence rows? They aren't taking up the meadows. They aren't threatening the stock. And they didn't bother the onchiki until they were threatened.''

''I'd love to know where they came from,'' said Izzy. ''Such trees have not been reported anywhere on earth before.''

''Listen to him,'' laughed Soaz. ''He knows everything that's been on earth before. You're only a pup, boy. You've never been out of Palmia! How would you know what may be across the sea, or over the Sharbaks west of the Four Realms? Besides, maybe Ghoti just thought them up!'' And he burst himself with chortles.

Izzy bared his teeth, momentarily annoyed, though I thought it was more at himself than at Soaz. He cleared his throat. ''Sahir,'' he said in his most ingratiating tone, ''have the people of Tavor heard any rumors of there being a wizard loose, or perhaps a journeyman magician trying to drum up trade?''

''The Hospice of St. Weel is said to be inhabited by wizards,'' said Sahir. ''Even Nassif has heard that.''

''I know about the hospice,'' Izzy remarked. ''But the wizards at St. Weel are not what I'd call loose. They stay at St. Weel and do their magic there, and do not, in general, intrude upon the affairs of the rest of the world.''

''You're thinking about the trees, aren't you?'' asked I. ''You think they may be magical.''

''Well, I wondered . . .''

''When I first saw them, that's what I thought. Lots of my stories have enchanted forests in them, living trees, talking trees, that sort of thing.''

Soaz made a troubled sound, deep in his throat. ''I

have always been told that to discuss such things is to summon them. Perhaps we'd be better off to talk of something else."

"Oh, speaker of many tongues, what are they saying?" Lucy Low called to Izzy. "Are they talking about the trees?"

"Small, helpful female person, they are."

"Why didn't the trees want us to get through to Estafan? Our fortunes say we need to go there."

"Did they actively block your way?"

"Well, we came upon them in the evening. And then Burrow tried to cut some wood. . . ."

"So, if you'd asked them instead of axed them . . ."

"That's what I think, too," she said, nodding with satisfaction. "Do you suppose they'd let us apologize?"

He shrugged. He had no idea.

"Is that a larbel case hanging from your saddle?" the sleek little person asked next.

"It is," he said stiffly,

"I love the larbel," she said. "I wish my hands were big enough to play one."

We both looked at her arms and hands, indeed very small, smaller than his or mine. Diver was a good deal bigger, about Izzy's own size. "There are no onchiki in Palmia," he said. "I've never met an onchik before, and I never thought about their being musical."

"Oh, we sing. We play the slide whistle and we pluck the harp. And drums. We love drums. At the midsummer fair, we have a band, slide whistles and drums and chimes of all kinds." She giggled. "It's lovely."

"Why are you going to Zallyfro?" he wondered.

She told him a long tale about a storm and a boat bed, and a box of fortunes. "I'm supposed to do something with geese. And Ring and Bright will work in an ale house, Grandmama and Sleekele will do housekeeping, and Diver will clean chimneys. Barbat and Mince will do something or other in the fishing fleet. It's all foretold."

"No surprises, eh?"

"Onchiki don't like surprises much, Grandmama says, nor do they in Estafan. Which means we should suit one another."

Soaz called from the head of our ragged column, "Town ahead. Do we want food and lodging?"

I most heartily did. Sahir and Izzy concurred. The onchiki demurred, explaining to Izzy about the fortunes, which served as money only in the shore counties. On being told of this difficulty, Sahir remarked they would be his guests. Since the onchiki had been rescued from the trees, he had been watching them every moment, finding them much more amusing than anyone else in the group, including myself. This pleased me. Being chief amuser for someone as sulky as the prince could be tiring.

We came to the edge of the town of Blander, finding there an inn called the Veebles's Hoof. The place seemed to cater to a wide variety of guests, having small rooms for small people and larger ones for large people, dormitories for servants and slaves, and various stables for horses and umminhi, as well as a capacious and sheltered pen that would do for veebles. Soaz obtained a suite for Izzy, himself, Sahir and me; he sent the guards and handlers off to the dormitories; he ordered food sent here and drink sent there, then collapsed in front of the fire, twirling his whiskers with one hand while yawning mightily.

Izzy and I, meantime, were making sure the onchiki were settled into a cozy room and provided with food, accepting their thanks with slight embarrassment. When we were assured of their comfort, we rejoined our comrades.

"Come, Prince Izakar," said Sahir. "We never finished our discussion about wizards. Do you think these trees are an enchantment of some kind?"

"I could find out," Izzy offered. He seated himself on the window seat, drawing up his knees and hugging them with his long arms. "It would probably be wise to do so. There are certain ways to see though enchantments, depending upon the strength of the magic. Someone of my limited ability is unlikely to learn the identity of the enchanter, but even a tyro could detect the resonance that magic always leaves.''

"There are none of *them* trees in the town," I said. "I looked, as we came in."

"Then I'd have to go out where they are," said Izzy.

"If not magic, what?" asked Soaz, yawning again, and rubbing his back against his chair to relieve sore muscles in his neck and shoulders. "All of a sudden, this way? If this had been natural, if these trees had grown from seed, wouldn't we have heard about them as saplings? As copses? Even as small forests? But this great number, this great woods, all at once! It boggles the mind."

Izzy nodded, resting his chin on his upbent knees. "The onchiki say they'd never seen such trees before they bumped into a thousand of them. However, they had never moved west before, either. None of us have traveled here, so it could be the trees have been here for some time."

"Whatever," Sahir muttered. "It still might be wizardry."

"Wizardry," said Soaz. "Or weaponry."

"Weaponry!" Sahir grunted, his eyes wide. "What do you mean, weaponry?"

Soaz got to his feet, stretched, turned around and sat back down again. "The Farsaki Empire, as we all know, is determined to rule the world. Suppose they invented these trees. Suppose they are sowing them all across the world. Suppose at a given signal, the trees will arise and march against the inhabitants!"

I gasped, and Izzy looked at me, frowning. Whenever he looked at me, he got a very peculiar expression on his face, as though he wanted to say something but could not. He brought himself to himself with a snap of his teeth and looked away, saying:

"It's as likely they were raised as a defense against Farsakian domination as it is they are part of the conquest." Izzy cleared his throat several times, as it seemed to have something stuck about halfway down. "They could make defensive walls against invaders."

"I don't think they're Farsaki," I said. "They don't feel Farsaki. The Farsaki are supposed to be dire and dreadful. They kill persons without even blinking. But the trees didn't even hurt the onchiki much, just whapped them, and that was after an onchik took an ax to them."

"How did you know that?" cried Izzy. "You don't speak Uk-Luk."

"No," I said in bewilderment. "You're quite right. I don't speak Uk-Luk, but I heard them saying it, nonetheless. The little one was telling you all about it. I wanted to put her on my lap and pet her, she's so sweet and quick and clever, and scarce bigger than a child."

"Lucy Low," said Izzy. "That's her name. Her father is Diver, her mother is Sleekele, her brothers are Burrow and Mince, her sisters are Ring and Bright. The old one they call Grandmama."

I nodded. "Well, I guess I understand them the same way I do the armakfatidi. You sort of hold your mind a certain way, and the words drop into it. Plunk. Like that."

"Nothing has ever dropped into my mind from the armakfatidi," growled Soaz. "Nor would I wish for such an intrusion. Does this talent allow you to speak to these people?"

I tried to make Uk-Luk words, but nothing came into my mouth of any purpose. "No. That is, I don't think so."

Izzy was looking at me with that expression again. "Perhaps Nassif's talent is magical," he said. "One of those wild talents I've read of, a survival from former times. In previous cycles, people were said to have had psychokinesis and clairvoyance and what all, though no one had ever explained them or been able to test them rigorously. In this era, such talents might have developed more recognizably and more reliably, since there was little technology to interfere. There is, after all, the Society of Seers in Sworp, a magical group that is officially recognized . . ." His voice waned as he saw us all looking at him in astonishment.

"What former times?" asked Soaz.

"What previous cycles?" asked Sahir.

"Nothing," he said in a quavering voice. "A fantasy of mine, that's all. Something I . . . amuse myself with."

We three were not about to let him off. We glared at him.

"What?" he snarled.

"We have been thinking about your being wizardly," said Sahir. "We are wondering if perhaps it is not time for you to tell us what brings you on this journey."

"Oh, that," said Izzy with obvious relief. "Of course, if you like. The midwife who delivered me, who was originally a Seeress from Sworp, prophesied that I must solve the Great Enigma by the time I've reached my majority, or I'll die with all posterity. Which could mean either my children or everyone's. Since the prophecy originated with a Sworpian Seeress, and we'll be going through Sworp on our way to the Hospice of St. Weel— where I hope the wizards may enlighten me about the Great Enigma—I thought I'd enquire on our way through. At any rate, it's better than sitting at home, wondering what I should be doing and waiting for everything to go pop centuries earlier than threatened."

"How exciting!" I cried, smiling at him warmly.

"Fool's errand," growled Soaz.

"And is that the only reason?" asked Sahir, his eyes slitted.

"So far as I am concerned, it is quite enough. And you?"

"Our family has misplaced a . . . talisman. We need to find it to assure continuation of . . . everything. Or so an old gray seeress told my father in the desert east of Isfoin."

"I'm told my midwife ended up in the desert east of Isfoin," mused Izzy. "I should not be surprised to find we are both on the same errand, sent by the same vision.''

''In your prophecy, do you think it's your life or the whole world that gets destroyed?'' Sahir asked curiously.

''The words could mean either,'' said Izzy.

''A Great Enigma,'' I said, tasting the words. ''It sounds very mysterious. Not very romantic, though. Not like rescuing a princess or finding the secret of immortal life or anything like that.'' I shook my head wonderingly. ''It would be more exciting if we knew what it was.''

''Much more exciting,'' said Izzy, seeming disheartened at this analysis. He turned to stare out the window. ''Quite frankly, I think this trip is quite exciting enough.''

I watched him. When he stood that way, looking slightly troubled, I thought him quite enchantingly handsome. His hair was as dark as his eyes, and as brightly gleaming. His fingers were long and graceful. His teeth shone between his lips, like stars. I sighed, a very small sigh. So long as I was supposed to be a boy, there was nothing I could do about it. Besides, we were both far too young. . . .

''What ails you, Izakar?'' asked Sahir.

''Nothing,'' he murmured with a sigh. ''Nothing at all.''

Soaz peered through slitted eyes, first at him, then at me, with a sly grin, his tongue in the corner of his mouth. I knew what he was thinking, and I turned quite pink. Soaz merely purred to himself as he dozed off.

We were all weary enough to sleep well, all healthy enough to benefit greatly from the rest. The troop that started out in the morning was an improvement on the rag-taggle that had straggled into Blander the night before. Izzy felt so much better that he uncased his larbel, set it upon his knees and began to strum a marching tune, despite Flinch's ears flicking at the music as though to drive away flies.

From atop the pack on one of the horses, Lucy Low began to warble a descant, and from another pack, Mince joined in with a slide whistle, which he had been carrying in a case hung from his belt. The umminhi, as was their habit when they heard music, made a harmonic bumbling in their throats, and I was just thinking how nice drums would be when I heard them thumping along. Diver was atop the baggage, *tumty-tumming* on a cooking pot.

"Your family is quite musical, madam," Izzy said to Grandmama, who was riding nearest him.

"Long winters, son," she replied. "Long winters and deep snow. That's what makes music sprout, ever'body gathered around the peat fire and all the doors tight shut."

"You don't fish in the winter, then?"

"Oh, we do, we do. Some fish are only catchable winter times, but when we've done it, we don't stay out in the cold. We get inside, where we can tend to our hides, be sure we're not frostbit."

We went tunefully along a considerable way, Izzy setting the melodies, and the others following. When he tired, he waved the larbel in thanks, then put it back in its case. Mince and Diver went on a few moments more, drum and whistle, a jiggety air, then they, too, put the instruments away.

"So far, we've seen no more of *them* trees," remarked Izzy to no one in particular. "Perhaps the whole thing was a tempest in a teapot."

We topped a slight rise as he spoke, and our mounts came to a rearing halt at the sight of the forest that blocked the wide road below.

14

A Babe in the Woods

The evening following Dora's discovery of a forest in her yard, she watched CNN, wondering if they had learned about trees growing where they shouldn't. Nothing appeared on national news. At ten, however, on the local news were pictures of a grove in an alley, a woodsy stretch at a cross street, a small forest in a park, grown up all at once, when no one was looking. A gray-haired, motherly botanist talked learnedly about the rapid growth records set by mushrooms and bamboo and some other plants, then speculated on mutation or the accidental escape of seeds treated with radiation. "We aren't that far," she said, "from the location of early atom bomb tests. These plants may have been reproducing for the last fifty years, but seeds hadn't blown into a populated area until now."

Dora shook her head as she turned off the TV. Even though it sounded logical, she didn't believe it. She pulled up her covers, resolved not to think about it, resolving to sleep, no matter what. She unplugged the phone but still roused at unfamiliar sounds, shifting restlessly, getting up at about seven, totally unrested. Nerves, she told herself. It had to be nerves.

There was no point fretting over it. She rose, took her usual shower, dressed in light trousers, shirt and the patchwork vest Kathleen had sent her as a late birthday gift. The curtains were drawn and she left them that way, a kind of superstitious awe; if she didn't see it, maybe it didn't exist. She indulged in a dab of lip gloss and a spritz of cologne, poured what was left of her morning coffee into a spill-proof sipper for drinking on the way to work, found a clean shirt to put in her locker for emergencies, and headed down the stairs.

During the night, the forest in the alley had grown taller. Some of the boughs overhung her apartment upstairs. A rain of petals fell around her, a scent of cinnamon and pinks, an old-fashioned smell, like a kitchen on Saturday morning when she and Grandma had baked for Sunday, making gingerbread and pineapple upsidedown cake to be served with big blobs of whipped cream. As she went through the gate, a bough drooped before her, blocking her way and bearing an apple at its tip.

Without even thinking about it, she said, "Thank you very much, tree," and picked the apple.

The bough went back up, out of her way.

She walked down the drive, now only a swerving footpath between two stretches of woods. The big house was invisible behind the leaves. Her car was parked where she had left it, but though the street had been two lanes wide plus parking lanes last night, now it was only one lane wide with trees everywhere else, including around her car and the few other cars that had been left on the street. She couldn't move the car from the space it was in. There were trees pressed solidly all the way around it.

Around her the leaves became still, waiting.

"I have a bicycle," she said.

The leaves rustled.

Biting into the apple, she went back to the garage, opened the big door, and burrowed through packing cases to the place she'd hung her bike. Lord, she hadn't ridden it in years. The tires were probably rotten.

She found the pump hanging nearby, brought both out into the air and inflated the tires. They held. Putting the pump back inside and the apple between her teeth, she shut the garage door and mounted the bike, wobbling desperately for the first few feet. By the time she maneuvered between several trees to reach the street, however, she thought she had the hang of it, though she needed both hands. She thought of spitting out the apple, then decided against it. If she had grown the apple, she wouldn't want it wasted. Instead, she dropped it into the basket.

At the wider avenues, there were more lanes of traffic, but very few cars. Most, she figured, had been trapped in their garages or on the street. Here and there walkers trudged or cyclists pedaled along, some looking confused, others angry, some muttering, some silent. A bus was just pulling into the stop when she arrived at the boulevard she usually drove along each day.

Moved by pure hunch, Dora wheeled her bike to the nearest tree. "This is mine. I'm Dora Henry. Will you take care of it for me, please, until I get back this evening?"

The leaves trembled, then turned to look at her as branches lowered protectively over the handlebars.

Did she believe this? Of course not. She was dreaming. Besides, it was an old bike. If it was there when she got back, fine. If not, she could walk home. Or, since it was a dream, she could fly. She retrieved her apple from the basket and ran for the almost empty bus without a backward glance. The driver glanced at her as he pulled away. "Didn't trap you, huh?"

"Are a lot of people trapped?"

He jerked his head at the passengers behind her. "Some of them said they was. One guy had to climb out a window. That old lady back there had to fight her way through branches and got all bruised. You don't look beat up."

"If you're nice to them, they're nice to you," she said. "One of them gave me this apple."

"I be damned," he remarked. "Is that the truth?"

Taking a crunchy bite, she dropped into a seat behind him. "The streets downtown, are they still there?"

"Far's I know. They was there when I drove out. Even out here, the big streets, the main ones, the trees haven't bothered much. Only the narrow ones, you know, residential areas and that. Must be a lot of people trapped. Most mornings, I'm full and people standing."

They drove down an asphalt lane through forest. The growth was not entirely uniform. Many streetlights were hidden, along with street signs, but only at intersections which were already closed to cross traffic by trees. On the larger cross streets, signs and lights were visible. Most of the lower buildings were obscured behind leafy barricades, and it was hard to determine their own location until they came to the hill that sloped down into the city and saw the urban center beneath them, largely unchanged. Even the side streets appeared to be open. They bumped unimpeded across railroad tracks, passed drive-in banks and parking lots, all blacktop and yellow lines with no growth in them at all. The wood behind them was a dreamscape, something they must have imagined.

The bus slowed, swerved, made a turn into a main thoroughfare. Half a dozen blocks farther on, Dora got off. The precinct was six blocks away. She was early. No hassle. She'd finished the apple, all but the core. That she dropped in a trash basket at the corner.

She had walked two blocks when Phil picked her up in his car. "How'd you get out?" she asked, before remembering that Phil lived close, out near the university, in a townhouse. "No trees at your place?"

"Trees everywhere," he snarled. His face was red, and he was obviously very angry. "My God, Dora, we've been invaded! Morning news says they're showing up in Philadelphia, too. And Boston and Cleveland and Charleston.''

''New York?''

''No. Not yet. At least, not Manhattan. According to the guy on TV this morning, they can't get across the bridges. At least, that's his theory. Queens's got trees though, and Staten Island, and all over New Jersey . . .'' He gritted his teeth, making a grinding noise.

The parking lot behind the precinct house was two-thirds empty, but a tangle of bicycles filled the spaces nearest the door.

''I started out on my bike this morning,'' said Dora. ''Then I caught the bus.''

''What'd you do with your bike?''

''Asked a tree to take care of it for me.'' She giggled.

He looked at her as though she'd gone insane, brows drawn together. ''Dora! This is bad enough without you talking crazy.''

''Well, crazy things have been happening, Phil. Jared tried to kill a weed, and he got punished for it. And we've got two, maybe three cases of people fooling with Mother Nature who got stabbed, and there's those bushes up in the mountains, pulling heavy metals out of mine tailings. And some herds of cows have disappeared or died. I mean, don't you think that's all part of one thing?''

''What one thing?'' he demanded harshly.

She shrugged, suddenly wary. Phil wasn't just making conversation; he was really furious.

''I don't know,'' she said placatingly. ''Maybe nothing.''

His mouth worked angrily. ''If it was some kind of . . . conspiracy, you ought to be upset! But you're sounding like it's all right with you!''

''No, that's not what I meant. It's just, I was in at the beginning, so to speak. The weed that poisoned Jared grew up the front of the house. It was the first one, as far as I know. I kind of got to know it.''

He got out, face red, words spewing, ''You're losing

it, Dora. You've gone over the line." He stalked away from her, back rigid.

"Come on, Phil." She averted her eyes from his shuddering form. The expression in his eyes had been fear, no matter what his mouth said. Phil didn't often get huffy with her. Usually he put up with her pretty well, but this thing seemed to have gotten to him. She forbore saying anything more. No point upsetting him more than he already was.

The day went on being weird. Hysterical people phoned about vines invading their bathrooms, trees sprouting through their sidewalks. Every available person worked the phones, making reassuring noises. "Yes, ma'am, it's happening everywhere. . . . No, ma'am, they don't seem to be dangerous. . . . Yes, sir, we'll let the public know just as soon as we do."

An hour or two later, after getting reports from the street and the hospitals, they were saying, "Not dangerous unless you try to cut them down, ma'am. Don't try to cut them down." Halfway through the morning, the captain came out into the room, looked around with a frustrated expression on his face, then beckoned to Dora.

"There's some kind of briefing at the statehouse. I'm sending you as liaison."

"Why me?"

"Because you get along with people, Dora! Most people, anyhow. Because I haven't got anybody else."

"I'm only a sergeant. . . ."

"You're a person with eyes and ears! You can observe, can't you? You can listen!"

She said yessir, took a car and went. The statehouse was downtown, the streets were passable; she got there to find the same confusion and conjecture she'd left behind. The briefing was equally confused. Some high muckety-muck botanists were supposed to be flying in from some high-powered university—different people mentioned three different ones—and a team of chemists was expected.

Into the silence that followed this remark, Dora blurted, "Chemists? Why chemists?"

"Experts in working with defoliants, weed killer," said the chairman impatiently.

"That would be a mistake," Dora remarked. "A very bad mistake. My husband tried weed killer on one of them. He ended up in the hospital. We've had reports of multiple injuries this morning. They fight back, you know."

Twenty pairs of eyes fastened on her. Twenty jaws went lax.

"Surely you're joking," said a pale, plump man in his sixties with an M.D. name tag. "Surely . . ."

"No." She shook her head firmly. "My husband tried to kill one of these new plants, and he would have died if we hadn't got him to emergency care fast. And he wasn't the only case. We've had calls all morning about similar things happening."

"Get her out of here," the man snarled.

Dora felt her face reddening. "Before you go on gratuitously asserting your authority Dr. . . ." She craned, getting a look at his name tag. "Dr. Jonas, wouldn't it be smart to check out what I'm telling you? All it'll take is a call to any hospital."

There were snarls and grumbles, someone recessed the meeting for twenty minutes, someone else went off somewhere to speak on the phone, returned, whispered. Meantime Dora sat, staring at the doctor and his henchmen, bureaucrats to the teeth. They had no idea what was going on. They had even less idea than Dora herself. They were scared, as Phil was, and when people were scared, all they wanted to do was kill something.

In the end, nothing happened. The doctor had a whispered conference with the man who'd been on the phone and then grudgingly agreed to inform the chemists and scientists and who all about the local cases of poisoning. It was almost five, and Dora had some questions she wanted to ask her former mother-in-law, so she drove over to the boardinghouse. From the corner, Dora peered toward Jared's place down the side street, which had also been narrowed to one lane. Curiosity got the best of her. She turned the car down that way, slowly swerving from side to side as the single lane curved one way and the other. The forest didn't like straight lines. The street was now a sinuous trail, like a snake track.

If it hadn't been for the Tree, she'd have gone right past Jared's place, for nothing showed of the house at all. Even the *For Sale* sign was overgrown. The driveway had vanished, the stoop was a green mound, the house a tangle of vines, the windows mere slits between heavy branches of liana. The Tree, two houses down, still towered above everything else, but it no longer seemed a strange presence. Now it was only part of the general jungle.

She drove around the block and returned to the boardinghouse, where she parked in the one empty space and got out, closing the door loudly enough that Mrs. Gerber could hear her. From where she stood, she could see the parking lot of the mall where she and Polly had had dinner. The lacy weeds around the bottoms of the light posts had grown into stout vines by now. Each light post had a growth reaching high around it, and each one looked suspiciously like Jared's weed.

"Dora." Jared's mother stood in the doorway, behind the screen. "Come in." She held the screen ajar, then led Dora down the immaculate hallway to her own private sitting room. The room looked as though it had been cleaned only moments before, everything shining, ruler straight, no clutter, no little ornaments or plants or doilies. Momma Gerber sat stiffly down on a straight-backed chair, gesturing to Dora to take the upholstered one. Through a closed door Dora could hear the clatter of pans and cutlery. Supper was being prepared for the boarders.

"Jared's firm is having a meeting tonight," Mrs. Gerber said. "He won't be home until later."

Dora had forgotten all about Jared. "I came to see you, not Jared."

The older woman sighed. "Well, I'm sorry to hear that, Dora, especially since Jared says he thinks he can change your mind. He says he would have done it sooner, only you cleaned the house too thoroughly. Now, what does he mean by that? It's nice you came to see me, through all this mess. Isn't this awful? What's the world coming to?"

"I don't know," Dora confessed. "But I thought you might be able to help figure it out. It's possible this started at Jared's place."

Mrs. Gerber didn't reply for a moment. She sat very still, finally saying, "Why would you think that?"

"I think it started with that weed that grew up in the stoop. It went to seed. I saw it. The little seeds were so tiny and light, they just blew away on the wind. But it started there. I'm sure of it."

"It couldn't have anything to do with her," the older woman mused, her face pallid in the evening light, slab-like, as though carved from marble. "That woman. Not after all this time. I'm sure. Could it?"

"Who do you mean?"

"That woman Jared married. And the older one."

Dora settled herself into her chair. "Why don't you tell me about that again."

"I don't like talking about it."

"I know. But I think you need to tell me. It may be very important."

The older woman sighed, got up and moved about the room, touching one thing and another, stopping at her desk to stroke a picture of Jared, taken when he was no more than seventeen. "He was always such a . . . stiff little boy. I suppose he got this stiffness from his dad and me. I'm that way. It's hard for me to warm up to people. I feel somehow they don't like me, really, and I mustn't impose on their good nature. And I got that from my pa, God knows."

"That sounds like a kind of shyness," said Dora.

"I suppose. With the mister it wasn't shyness, though.

He just never figured anybody was worth his wasting words on.''

"So, Jared's father died. . . .''

"And I used the insurance money to buy this house. Women didn't have as many choices then as they do now. Not so many ways to make a living. We lived here right along, just the way we do now. Nothing much out of the ordinary ever happened, except for Jared's accident and that girl.''

"Accident? What accident?''

"When he was hit by lightning. He was sixteen. He went on a field trip, a kind of scout trip, out where the airfield used to be, and he got hit by lightning. We thought he was gone. They had him in the hospital, and they told me he was dead, you know, in the brain. And then, all of a sudden, he woke up. He said, Mother, here I am, and he was. Just like nothing had happened. The doctors didn't believe it. So I brought him home.''

"He never told me about that.''

"Well, Jared doesn't talk about himself much.''

Which was true, so far as it went. "So, tell me about the girl.''

"Well, that was the year after the accident. Jared was in his last year at high school. Then that girl and her mother came to visit the Dionnes, down the block. . . .''

Words seemed to fail her, for she stared at the floor, mouth working, trying this phrase and that without uttering any of them.

"Yes,'' urged Dora.

"Vorn Dionne looked like a goat,'' she blurted. "All his kids looked like goats. They had hair all over theirselves. Once I saw them when they were out washing the car in the driveway, just with trousers on, and my God, Dora, they looked like animals. You could of skinned them and made a fur coat.

"Well, this girl and her mother came to visit. It was hard to tell which was which. The girl looked too old to be fifteen, and the woman looked too young to be her mother, more like her sister. Anyhow, the neighborhood boys trailed after either one of them like dogs after a bitch in heat. All the menfolks in the neighborhood did, including men old enough to be her granddaddy. And the next thing I knew, there was my Jared going after her, too, and before I could take a deep breath, he called me on the phone from long distance and told me he'd married her.''

"He must have been what? Eighteen?'' asked Dora.

"Well, he wasn't, not yet. He talked like somebody crazy, like he didn't know who he was. Neither one of them was old enough by state law, and they didn't have my permission, so I said they couldn't be married, that I'd get it annulled.

"And here came the mother, like a crazy woman, hair out to here and painted eyes, telling me the girl needed to marry somebody right away. Well, you know what that means! I said to her, like hell! I wasn't going to support Jared and any fifteen-year-old wife and then babies. I wasn't going to do it.'' She fell silent, chewing her lip.

"What happened?''

The older woman looked away, uncomfortably. "Well, she . . . she threatened some. I told her to match the girl—Cory, her name was—up with one of her cousins; they were two of a kind. But then Jared showed up, alone.''

"Alone?''

"He said the girl . . . well, he said she'd run off. I called her mother and told her that's what happened.''

"And then the Dionnes moved away?''

Long silence. She sighed. "She went off, looking for her daughter. Then the Dionne house burned down, so the Dionnes moved. And that was the end of that. Jared got through high school all right, and he went to college, worked his way through. He got his degree, and he went to work for the paper company, in their research department. And none of that would've happened if he'd gotten married to that Cory girl.''

"Cory. Was that short for Cornelia?''

"I don't know. It might have been. The mother cursed me up one side and down the other. . . ."

"Why you? You weren't responsible."

"Well, I was responsible for Jared, and the girl had run away from him, according to her mother. The way the woman acted, you'd think I'd been the one got her daughter pregnant! If she was pregnant. Well, that's why she popped into my head when Jared got poisoned that way."

"Do you know where she moved?"

A quick negation, a shake of the head that was almost a spasm. "No!"

"How about the Dionnes?"

"Somewhere out of town, that's all I know. Some junkyard, probably. That's what their place looked like when they lived here. Junk everywhere. And stuff growing every which way. Like a jungle."

"Like now?"

She looked surprised at the question. "Well, yes. I suppose like now."

"That big old tree down the block, was it on the Dionne property?"

Mother Gerber's mouth shut like a trap. "I suppose it was. Acted just like the Dionnes, too. Pushy! Roots comin' up everywhere, in people's gardens and sewer lines. When Jared was digging the foundation for the garage over at his place, he said there was roots every which way. And that's every bit I can tell you, Dora. It's long gone and over and they're all long gone and over, and now this jungle growing up like to cover us up, like to bury us. I don't know. I just don't know."

Dora patted her shoulder and went to the kitchen for coffee for both of them, and commiserated until supper was ready and Mrs. Gerber had to go oversee the dining room. "Pigs," she whispered. "Some of my boarders are just pigs. I got to keep an eye on them. If they had their way, they'd eat it all and nobody else would get any. . . ."

Dora smiled behind her hand. "How's Mr. Cal-clough?"

"Still pinching bottoms," Mrs. Gerber said with a sniff. "You'd think a man that age would let up. And Mr. Fries is still as messy as he ever was. I never saw so much underwear so many places it didn't belong."

"Does he still rattle the house doing judo?"

"He says it isn't judo, but it still rattles. I told him the chandelier comes down, he pays for it."

"How's Mrs. Sohn?"

"Poor thing. Her canary died. You'd think she lost a child."

"Well, it's all she had, Momma Gerber."

"That's true, Dora. Just like Jared's all I have."

Dora dropped the borrowed car back at the precinct and took the bus. Buses were still running, though the particular driver looked more than a little stressed and not quite sure who or where he was. Dora watched their progress out the side window and got off at the corner where she saw her bike. It was against the tree where she'd left it, two branches holding it fast.

"Thank you," she said to the tree as the branches came loose with a friendly rustle. "Very kind of you."

The tree reached down and dropped a handful of cherries into the bicycle basket. Dora ate them on the way home. Not quite as sweet as Bing cherries, but definitely not sour ones. And since when had cherries and apples ripened at the same time? It was late for cherries and way too early for apples.

She would have gone past the house if a tree hadn't rustled at her. She almost heard her name, *Doradora-dora*, like a whisper. They'd left her a bicycle lane back to the garage and enough space to open the door. Inside the gate, the copses and vines were taller than the night before, and outside the fence . . . or, rather, where the fence had been, the trees stood well above the second story of the garage. She went out into the woods, dropped the handful of cherry seeds on the soil and pushed them under with the toe of her shoe.

Upstairs, she turned on the TV before opening the curtains. Her living room window looked out on the woods, down a grassy swale with trees on either side and wild flowers peeking up at the sides through a litter of dead leaves or dropped twigs. There were stones she hadn't noticed before, complete with moss. The bedroom window, the one toward the front, was totally overgrown by a fine screen of rootlets. The air came through, but insects could not.

The newsman's voice brought her back to the living room. ". . . United Nations calls for all member nations to investigate the possibility of biological mutations unleashed by some dissident state. The Department of Agriculture reports no sizeable incursions onto cropland, though fallow land is growing up in woods while crop land is being surrounded by hedgerows. In the meantime, cities are reeling under the assault. Though gas, electric and phone lines have not been disturbed, street traffic is at a standstill in many neighborhoods. Police and rescue workers have been forced to work on foot or from horseback. . . ."

There were pictures of various cities on the eastern seaboard from Georgia to New Hampshire. Thus far, it had not yet reached the city of St. Louis, though trees were springing up along the highways of Illinois. The trees had reached Nashville. Another growth was centered on Denver, and others on Los Angeles and Portland. Hospitals were full of people who had tried to chop them down and had received stinging rebukes from the trees themselves. Trees. And more trees.

She went to the phone book and looked for an entry under V. Dionne. Nothing. There was a Harry Dionne. She called the number, hearing it ring and ring and ring before a far-off voice answered in an insect chirp: "Dionnes."

Dora introduced herself and asked about Vorn Dionne.

"That's Harry's father. He's doesn't live here in

town. Would you like Harry to call you?''

Dora thanked her and said yes, she'd like to talk to Harry. After she'd hung up, she wondered who else she could talk to. The people who'd bought the house where the Dionnes used to be? The firemen who'd fought the fire? Jared was forty-six, forty-seven. So the fire had been what, twenty-eight, twenty-nine years ago? Somebody who'd been a rookie then might remember.

She looked up the firehouses and called the one nearest to Jared's place. Sure, said the fireman, he'd been around that long, and he kept a kind of journal. Give him a day or two, he'd look it up for her. Don't mention it, glad to help the police. Brothers and sisters in arms, so to speak.

After a supper of leftovers, she had a hot bath and stretched out on her bed, intending to read. The air coming through the root-netted window was sweet and soft. The sound of the leaves outside was hypnotic—her name again, *Doradoradora*. Before she knew it, the book had fallen onto the bed beside her and she was asleep.

15

Opalears: Sorcerous Associations

I zzy led us down the road, Oyk and Irk just behind, with me close behind them, driven partly by curiosity and partly by the desire that he shouldn't have to face the trees alone. The rest of our group seemed inclined to let him handle matters. Certainly force of arms would not serve us against such a forest. When he arrived a few arm lengths from the first of the trees, he pulled Flinch to a halt and alit, scuffing the dust of the roadway into little clouds as he went still closer.

An ominous rustle among the leaves.

"What is it you want?" asked Izzy, in the Uk-Luk speech of the shore counties. I understood him, just as I had before.

A rustle, a yammer of branches scraped across one another, a shiver of leaves, nothing I could understand, though he evidently thought it to be a problem which magic might solve. He took his kit from Flinch's saddle-bag, set it upon a convenient stone, then went looking for something to build a fire with, finding some branches cast aside along the roadway. These he shaved into kindling, building a little tented shape of small sticks above them and dousing the whole liberally with a powder from a jar labeled *Sorc-a-Powr*.

Izzy saw me watching him and remarked, "For generalized ensorcelment, the castle wizard always swears by Sorc-a-Powr. It comes from Isfoin and its cost is twice that of any other enabling agent, but our wizard considered it well worth it."

"Um," I said, unhelpfully.

"Skimping on ingredients is an infallible sign of mediocre, minor-league magic," Izzy said firmly.

"What are you going to do?"

He mumbled, partly to himself, partly to me. "One tree, at least, has to have a mouth and vocal cords. Either that, or I would have to modify myself to understand them as they speak."

"Would that be easier?"

"No," he said firmly. "I was brought up on stories of sorcerers who enchanted themselves for some reason or other and then found themselves unable to perform the disenchantment. Many of them are, presumably, still wandering the world in the guise of enchanted swans or white deer or frogs."

I shivered. I had never much liked frogs. So cold, and rather slippery.

When all was in readiness, he lit the fire with a snap of his fingers and spoke commandingly into the smoke. He had phrased the spell in Uk-Luk, and now uttered it three times, dipping his staff into the fire and then pointing it at the foremost tree. Green lightning darted from fire to tree; the tree writhed, its trunk erupting into blotches and swellings that shortly resolved themselves into features, including a wide, angry mouth.

"Oh, woe," howled the tree in trade language, lashing its branches belligerently.

Flinch reared, whinnied, put his ears back and fled at top speed up the hill, where Soaz caught him with some difficulty. Izzy picked himself up out of the dust where

Flinch had knocked him. I helped him brush himself off as he swore mildly.

"We want to help," he said to the frantic tree, also speaking in trade language. "But we have no idea what you're going on about!"

"End of forest! End of tree! Death to saplings! Death to seedlings! All that is as never was, so all is woe! If it doesn't unhappen we won't happen."

"Who?" demanded Izzy, after sorting out this last outcry. "Who is ending the forest?"

"The traveler, the fixer, the season walker, the changeling. The evil creature. The being with the ax. The walker on fire feet."

"Who is he? Where is he?"

The forest heaved, branches lashing. The talking tree mumbled and bleated. "Everywhere, nowhere. He goes to kill everything. Forest. Creatures. People! All to die. All their roots to be cut."

"Everything is to die?"

Long silence ending in an agitated rustle. "Carrots may live, maybe," offered the tree sadly. "Maybe parsnips, maybe hay."

I didn't like the sound of that. Izzy crouched on his heels, shaking his head.

"Where did you learn of this?" he asked.

A windy sound, a troubled lashing of leaves, as though a question were asked in one place then passed from tree to tree, the wave of agitation moving from here to there, somewhere, then back again.

"Trees say north, near the sea."

"At St. Weel?"

Another lengthy conference, from which we gathered that the trees didn't have names for places. There were river places and sea places and high and low, rocky and deep soiled, and the place where they heard this particular thing was a high rocky place facing east beside a river that ran into the sea where the gervatch flower bloomed.

"Listen," Izzy cried, having no more notion than I of what a gervatch flower might be. "I was given a prophecy. I was told I must solve the Great Enigma or the world would end. Are we talking about the same event, here?"

"Who knows," cried the tree, while a shiver of anxiety ran through the grove surrounding it. A short distance to Izzy's left, one tree bashed another, who bashed back. The mouthy tree stopped speaking and turned toward this disorder, bumping another in the process. The bumpee lashed out with a large branch, hitting another tree. The disagreement spread, degenerating almost at once into a branch-flailing, trunk-butting battle between and among various factions. Izzy packed up his things, took me by the hand and trudged up the hill where the others sat watching. When we arrived and looked back, we saw that the fray had degenerated into numerous small battles that had broken the solid phalanx. The road lay open.

"Very clever," said Soaz.

"I didn't do it," mused Izzy. "Though I suggest we take advantage of the confusion before they settle down and start saying woe is me again."

The which we accomplished, Izzy stopping only long enough to scatter the fire, thus putting an end to the spell. We put off any discussion of what troubled the trees until we had gone some distance beyond them.

"And they didn't say who?" asked Sahir for the third or fourth time.

"They don't know who," replied Izzy. "Someone. Some entity. I guess that could be one person or a whole collection. And some of the trees think my puzzle may be part of what's happening. I mean, this Enigma thing."

"And some of them don't believe that," said Lucy Low.

"But they've agreed it's happening," I remarked.

"And you're headed in the right direction," commented Soaz rather lazily.

"As to that, yes," Izzy said, patting Flinch on his neck. "It is happening, and I, at least, am headed in the right direction."

16

Dora and the Family Tree

"Today, lunch, we got a date," Phil said to Dora.

He had scarcely spoken to Dora the last couple of days, and this announcement bewildered her. "You and I have a date?"

"You and me and this friend of mine. I told him what you said. He wants to meet you."

"What friend?"

"My professor friend. He's a biologist."

"I told you—"

"This's got nothing to do with you, Dora. I mean, it's got nothing to do with man-woman stuff. This is just about the trees, that's all." He frowned, a little shamefaced. "I got to thinking about what you said, about the trees being . . . intelligent, like."

"Well, they are."

Phil made a face. "That's what he wants to talk about. What you saw. Where it started. This whole business. I think you're crazy, I think he's crazy, but like I told you, he's a good friend, he was a neighbor of mine. His

189

wife died, he sold the house, moved over to the university, but we stay in touch. Way I figure it, stuff doesn't get solved by people not telling other people stuff, even if other people think they belong in a loony bin.''

She didn't try to sort this out. She got the drift.

The city center was still tree-free. Buses still ran to and from, though fewer and fewer cars were able to get out of the suburbs. Highways were clear. Railways were clear. Airport runways were clear. People could still travel, they could still make dates for lunch. If they chose to live in residential areas, including the suburbs, however, they would have to make a twice a day trek by rail, foot, bicycle, or horseback. The few stubbornly angry men who were still trying to clear their land with chain saws were still being killed. Autopsies established that the trees were the possessors of lethal stinging cells, nematocysts, previously thought to belong only to creatures such as sea anemones and jellyfish.

Phil and Dora went to a downtown restaurant which was doing a good business, considering everything. There Dora was introduced to Abilene McCord.

"Phil's told me about you," he said, offering his hand. He was a slender man with a narrow, foxish face, pointed nose and chin, curly mouth, and long-lashed watchful eyes. His teeth were likewise narrow, and very white, though his skin and hair were foxish also, reddish and tawny, freckled and curly haired.

"You're a biologist," she said flatly.

"Um," he said, staring at her.

"Could we, like, sit down," suggested Phil.

"Oh, sure," said Abilene, still staring.

"Did I hear right? Your name's Abilene?" asked Dora, feeling a little nervous. The way the guy was looking at her, maybe she had a spot on her nose or something.

"My mother's idea," he said, finally looking elsewhere. "It's where she and Dad went on honeymoon, for some reason I've never been able to fathom. I've just been glad they didn't go to Niagara Falls. You can call me Abby, if you like. A lot of people do.''

He grinned at her, and Dora gulped. It was a very foxish grin. Knowing, in a wild kind of way.

They sat. They ordered. Dora drank half a glass of iced tea all at once, trying to put out a sudden warmth in the pit of her stomach. Abby watched her curiously. When she set her glass down, he asked:

''Tell me about the weed where you used to live.''

So she told him, baldly, in few words, making it sound like nothing. He nodded, as though satisfied.

''It was more . . . eerie than that,'' she confessed.

''It had to be, yes,'' he said, moving his napkin out of the way of the waiter, who had showed up with their lunches. ''The fact you don't try to make it sound dramatic is impressive, however. If you were inventing or imagining—which is what my friend Phil here thinks— you'd probably make a better story out of it.''

''I don't tell things very well,'' she said, glaring at Phil.

''The hell,'' said Phil. ''She writes great reports.''

''You told it very well.'' Abby smiled. ''So then, you moved. And the weed moved with you.''

''Part of it. Or another one,'' she confessed.

''Why do you think that is?''

''Maybe it likcs to be talked to,'' she hazarded. ''At least, that's all I've ever done for it.''

''No little sips of fertilizer? No polishing its leaves? No playing music to it?''

''I never thought of that,'' she said, astonished. ''The way it looks, so healthy, I never thought about it needing fertilizer. And with all the birds singing to it, why would it need music?''

''She says it gave her an apple,'' said Phil, in a skeptical tone.

''Did it?'' Abby asked.

''Yeah,'' she confessed. ''And some cherries.''

''Your weed?''

''No.'' She stopped, confused. ''No, two different trees. One outside my house and one where I left my bicycle. Oh, and they'll take care of your bicycle for you, too, if you ask them to. And if you ask for some seedlings, it'll give you a little one. A sapling or whatever. My friend Loulee wanted one because it eats garbage."

And that was another story. And the garden was another one yet. "Yesterday, these two trees grew me a hammock," she said. "Two nice strong vines, one down each side, and this lacy little mat of shoots across the middle. You can lie on it, just like a hammock. There's a leaf pillow, and it swings by itself."

Abby put down his fork, chewing and swallowing a mouthful of lasagna before he spoke. "Did you hear about the new flora that's growing around the Mediterranean?"

"Something on TV. The flocks are doing real well on it."

"They are. Or were. It seems the plant is a first-rate fertility control agent. There have been no pregnancies among the sheep and goats since they started eating the stuff."

Phil said belligerently, "Now that's rotten. Those poor people probably need their animals."

"No," said Abby. "They need far fewer of them. It was the unrestricted breeding of sheep and goats that deforested the entire area. As may be happening here, as well." He turned to Dora once more. "Phil said you mentioned the missing herds of cows. I suppose you've figured out if it could eat garbage, it could eat a herd of cows."

She stopped chewing, eyes unfocused. "I never thought of that."

"But then, if it killed the cows and ate them, why didn't it eat the people it killed?"

"I don't know." She shook her head slowly. "They were left right there, where other people could see them."

"Do you think it could be because people learn by example, but cows presumably do not?"

Phil grunted, shaking his head. "You're both nuts."

Dora nodded, however. "It could be that. But then, you got to remember Jared's all right. I mean, it hasn't come after him or anything."

Abby grinned at her. "Then the plant could be said to be defensive but not vengeful. Can we take a look at his place?"

Dora forbid herself from returning his grin. What was this? She felt like . . . well, like she'd swallowed something buoyant. Something that wanted to soar! Unwillingly, she said, "I'm not sure it is his place anymore. Someone might have bought it by now."

Abby lined up his silverware thoughtfully, watching her from the corners of his eyes. "Not many people buying property these days. Things are too uncertain."

She shrugged, giving up. "I don't have a key with me, but you're welcome to look at the outside."

When they finished lunch, Phil went back on duty, saying he'd cover for her until two, when she could meet him outside the deli where they usually had lunch. Dora went with Abby in his little convertible, the warm air lashing her hair into tangles. They drove to the avenue, then down the swervy side street, stopping at last in front of Jared's place.

"What kind of tree is that?" Abby asked, pointing upward at the looming bulk of the Tree.

Dora confessed she didn't know what kind of tree it was.

They got out and walked through what had been a yard and was now a little forest, between two green mounds that had been houses, to the foot of the huge tree. In Dora's eyes, it seemed to have grown another twenty or thirty feet since she'd seen it last, and it had been huge then. "The roots go all the way across the next lot. Last time I was in the garage, I saw the roots were breaking up the floor."

"The roots of a tree this size could reach that far, though I don't know what kind of tree it is either," he said with a puzzled smile. "Which is rather interesting.

Trees being my specialty, I ought to recognize it." He pulled down a branch and looked at the leaves. He started to pick one.

"No," said Dora. "Don't take it. Ask it."

He stared at her a long, inscrutable moment, then turned back to the tree.

"May I have a few leaves, please?"

A tremble of foliage, a sound, as of wind through the boughs, and then a plop. The sprig lay on the ground next to his feet, an emerald spray drooping gracefully from a green stem.

He said in a very soft voice, "I live in a townhouse near the university. I've looked at the trees, but I haven't had any close contact with them. I didn't believe you." He drew a deep breath and fixed her with his eyes. "I honest to God didn't."

He picked up the sprig, and they went back to the car. He opened the trunk and stored the sprig in a specimen case before rejoining Dora. "I still don't recognize it," he said. "Leaves rather like an oak, but oak leaves aren't arranged like that."

"I always thought of it as an oak," said Dora. "It's been there forever. The nearest house is where the Dionnes lived. Before the fire."

Which led to her telling him all about the Dionnes, and her attempt to locate them.

"When Harry Dionne calls you back, will you call me?" he asked, giving her his card. "Please."

"You think they know something?"

"Not necessarily. One thing leads to another, though. You know that." He smiled at her and something inside her took fire once more. "You have beautiful eyes. In fact, you're an exceptionally lovely woman," he said with a laugh. "Especially for a cop."

She flushed, not knowing what to say to that, hoping he wouldn't say anything else like it, then hoping he would.

He didn't say anything at all, just dropped her off where she was to meet Phil, lifting his hand in farewell.

His card was in her pocket. She could feel it there, like a little sun, making a heat all its own.

"Nice guy, huh?" asked Phil.

"Very nice," she said primly, keeping her face straight.

"Think he believed all that stuff?"

She shrugged. "I don't know, Phil. I think after the tree handed him the leaves he wanted, he probably did."

Phil clenched his jaw and refused to ask. Dora, barely able to suppress laughter, pretended she hadn't noticed.

17

The Countess Elianne Welcomes Travelers

"Though the armakfatidi are a tribe which is unique in being unable to communicate with other tribes in speech, through a standardized combination of grunts and gestures, many armakfatidian peoples are perfectly capable of making themselves understood and thus taking part in the agriculture and commerce of the realm. They are a strong and ancient people, and their contributions to the arts of cookery and perfumery have never been surpassed."

THE PEOPLES OF EARTH
HIS EXCELLENCY, EMPEROR FAROS VII

Blanche went in search of the countess. She found her mistress on the west terrace having a midafternoon snack from the greenhouses, peaches so ripe that Elianne's hands and face were smeared with juice. The countess looked up from her enjoyment, slightly annoyed at the interruption.

"The guards have intercepted a party of travelers on the high road, Your Grace."

The countess started to lick the juice from her hands as a younger Elianne would have done, then, seeing Blanche's unwavering gaze, wiped them delicately on a napkin instead. "I imagine the guards intercept travelers several times an hour," she remarked loftily. "And what is that to me?"

"It's the assortment of the group," said Blanche in her harsh voice. "Pheled, ponji, scuinan, onchiki. . . ."

"Pheled? And onchiki?"

"Yes. A family of them. Plus guards and handlers and some very impressive umminhi. Expensive animals. Royal livery, or I miss my guess."

"Ah." Blanche seldom missed her guess. She was well informed on most matters, and when information was lacking, her intuition could be relied upon.

The secretary cocked her head. "Perhaps you'd like to enquire?"

"By all means, Blanche. Let us enquire. Let us invite them to tea."

"It looks like you've had tea." Blanche stared pointedly at the countess's still sticky hands.

"Not really. Just a little fruit."

"You'll be letting out your seams, next."

The countess snorted. "Kindly remember who is the countess here. Tell Dzilobommo to prepare confections and tea, something relaxing and mind expanding. Something to make the visitors talkative. I'll be along in a moment."

Blanche went away without a word. The countess rose, dipped her still sticky hands into the fountain, washed her face thoroughly, dried hands and face on a napkin, then smoothed her gown down over her ample hips. Dieting might make her unattractive to cannibals, which is no doubt what Blanche had in mind, but it would be boring, nonetheless. After allowing sufficient time to elapse to indicate that she was untroubled by anything Blanche had said or implied, she strolled toward the public chambers, intercepting a bevy of serving people laden with teapots and covered plates. Through the open door of the small audience room, she could hear the babble of onchiki speech. How very strange. Onchiki almost never came to Zallyfro.

"Her Grace, the Countess Elianne of Estafan!" intoned a servitor, thumping his baton against a hollow floor tile as she entered. Every room had such drumlike hollow tiles, built in for annunciatory occasions.

She drew herself regally erect and cast a smiling glance across the company assembled. One pheled, a sizeable fellow. A scuinic VIP, and a ponjic one. Plus a trio of onchiki. Evidently the handlers and guards were being fed outside in the courtyard.

"Good day," she murmured in Estafani.

"Our eyes are delighted to look upon your effulgence," murmured the ponjic VIP in flawless Estafani, with a bow so low that he all but brushed the floor with his auburn hair. This one was a play actor.

"Our senses are thrilled by your presence," said the scuina in a clumsy accent, bowing not so deeply. This one took himself more seriously than the other. When he straightened up, however, his dark eyes caught hers, and she felt herself flushing. He was a handsome devil. Lean, with a look of mystical intensity.

"Prince Sahir of Tavor," he said, as taken with her appearance as she was with his.

She nodded, indicating interest.

"Prince Izakar of Palmia," said the previous speaker, bowing even lower than before.

"Lucy Low, of the Shore Counties," said the littlest onchik, in trade language, with a bow so low that the others were left speechless. "With her brothers, Mince and Burrow."

The countess burst out laughing, and after a moment's discomfiture, so did Sahir and Izzy, as they settled around the tea table in a mood of general good nature. Sahir kept his eyes on the countess. Izzy kept his eyes on Sahir. As scuinic females went, the countess was a fine-looking specimen. If one liked that sort of thing, she was very much the sort of thing one would like.

The room was much ornamented with carved plaster; tall open windows striped the walls with views of the orange and lemon trees in the garden. The scent of roses wafted in, along with the subtle music of fountains, all conveying a sense of tranquility.

"Are you three all your family?" the countess asked Lucy Low in trade language.

"Sleekele and Diver and Grandmama and my two sisters are outside in the courtyard," said Lucy Low. "They didn't want to come in, and Nassif stayed with them, to keep them company."

"Nassif is my companion," said Sahir, to no one in particular.

"Are your family shy?" the countess asked the onchiki.

"We don't hold with buildings much," said Mince, around a mouthful of smoked salmon sandwich. "Makes us uncomfortable like. Specially places that stand so high from the ground."

"Is that true?" the countess asked Burrow, who merely nodded, mouth open.

"Little houses are all right," offered Lucy Low. "Little houses and little rooms. With not so much space all around. Big empty rooms with echoes in, well, those are a bit frightening."

The countess looked at the walls, which were some distance away, and up at the ceiling, which was lofty. No doubt the onchiki's feelings had to do with predators. It was sensible to fear things with teeth coming out of the night. One would want one's back to a wall and limited space for the enemy to maneuver in. If the countess's own people had built this palace, it might have been less lofty, but it had been built long ago, no one knew by whom, though it had been much elaborated since that time. She nodded, understanding.

"Thank you for coming," she told them. "I hope you are not too overawed to enjoy your tea."

They said the place wasn't all that awesome, which they proved by consuming a good deal of whatever was on the table. Dzilobommo had provided several sorts of tea, to suit various tastes. Soaz grew pleasantly drowsy, the onchiki became even more cheerful, while the rest of them conversed comfortably about their journey. Izzy and Sahir even unbuttoned themselves sufficiently to tell the countess about the Great Enigma and the sultan's lost fortune. She, in turn, mentioned the Dire Duke and the quandary he had placed her in.

Said Lucy Low, "These folk say there is help to be had at St. Weel, and perhaps you should seek help there, too. Oh, I would like to go to St. Weel. I would like to see the world."

"Well, then," said the countess, surprising herself, "why don't you?"

The little onchik shook her head and wrinkled her nose. "We have nothing to pay our way, lady. It is only the shore counties that will take our fortunes, and the little sea towns so far as Sworp. But these people will go beyond Sworp, and perhaps inland from the sea."

"What fortunes do you have?" asked the countess.

"Grandmama is keeping most of them, but I have two," she said, fishing them out of her pocket. "They were given to my long-back Grandmama Erntrude Biwot by the lady Amalia Gershon."

"Gershon!" exclaimed Izzy. "That was my mother's name. She was from Sworp!"

"Well, well," said the countess. "And have you opened these fortunes, child?"

"No, ma'am. Since they were given personal like, Grandmama thought maybe I'd profit from them, but then, maybe not, as who can tell."

"I think she should open them now," said Blanche from her position behind the countess's left shoulder. "I feel a tingle coming on." She gave a premonitory shudder as she fixed her eyes upon the onchik.

"What a good idea," Elianne remarked. "And if they lose value by being opened prematurely, I will compensate you, child. You and your brothers."

Looking around rather doubtfully at the company,

Lucy Low put the fortunes upon the tea table, cut the gold seals and slowly unfolded them. They were written upon fine vellum that remained unyellowed by time and were folded in the likeness of strange animals. When the first one was smoothed, she took it up and spelled it out, letter by letter. "It's not writ in Sworpian, ma'am. Nor Uk-Luk, neither."

"May I?" asked Izzy, taking the sheet from her. "Actually, it is in Sworpian, but it's an archaic form. 'I, Amalia Gershon, guided by fate and the Sorceresses, of whom I am one in all but name, send this message to my future grandson, whomever he may be, whenever he may appear. If Doom approacheth, get ye to St. Weel.'"

"By all the bans of Bandercran," said Izzy, almost reverently. "How can this be?"

"You're the magician," said Soaz, roused from his drowsy state. "You figure it out."

"And the other fortune?" asked Elianne, in a hushed voice.

Lucy Low handed him the second fortune, and he read, "'I, Amalia Gershon, guided by Fate and the Sorceresses of Sworp, send this message into a future time. Ye rulers and leaders of peoples, beware. Turn not to arms but get ye to St. Weel, for there I have seen the Door stand open.'"

"Not worth nothing, now," said Mince, staring regretfully at the fortunes. "She opened 'em, and they're not worth nothing."

"Not so," said the countess. "Simply because your sister is not the one directed by the fortune does not mean she cannot profit from it. She has done precisely what she should; she has brought them here and made them available to the people they were intended for. Both a grandson and a ruler were present at the opening, just as the seeress knew we would be. We have been warned, as was intended, and I will pay Lucy Low well for telling us of this geas, and—"

"Telling you of what?" cried Lucy Low.

"This geas, child. This warning, this weird. . . ."

"Well, and then maybe it was geas my fortune was about, and I would indeed rather travel the weird world than tend your geese, ma'am."

"What geese?" the countess demanded, taken aback.

It was Mince who explained about the geese, and the chimneys and the alehouse and all the rest of it.

"Do you have your fortune with you, Lucy Low?" the countess asked.

She brought it from her pocket and unfolded it upon the tea table, spelling it out letter by letter. The word could have been either *geese* or *geas*, as they all could see. The little onchik explained again how it had all happened, and how it was indeed her sharp eyes which had read it out, so that all was true.

"Blanche," said the countess when this account was done. "See to it, please. Appropriate jobs in the palace for Lucy's mama and grandmama and father. We have rooms to clean and chimneys to mend, enough to keep them busy, I should think. The sisters . . . well, if it is to be an ale house, at least let it be a reputable one. Perhaps the Eel and Anchor, or the Glamorous Clam. See to that as well."

"What about me?" asked Mince irrepressibly.

"I will ask my uncle, the admiral," said the countess. "He will find shipboard jobs for you and your brother, if that is what you desire."

"Rather not," said Burrow, suddenly articulate. "Rather go see the world. But it's said them as ignores fate, fate don't ignore. An' we got fortunes say fishing boats."

"Do you have them with you?" asked Blanche.

Burrow dug it from a pocket, much the worse for wadding.

Blanche smoothed it upon the back of the chair where the countess sat. "It says you will find a future on a fishing boat, but it does not say when. What about your brother?"

Mince came up with his fortune as well, in somewhat better shape, for he had kept it folded in his wallet.

" 'He who stays with his brother strengthens himself,' " Blanche read. "So, if your brother travels the world, you may keep your fortune by going with him, both deferring your piscatorial preoccupations until later in your lives."

Mince nodded. "Guess I'd got to, don I?"

"How wonderful," cried the countess. "What fun! We shall make a sizeable party, shall we not?"

"We . . ." murmured Sahir.

"Surely." She smiled sweetly upon him.

"What have you in mind, madam?" asked Soaz, still drowsy.

"I am going with you, gentle sirs. With the Dire Duke breathing down my neck, I would be a fool not to take this chance to escape him while at the same time seeking a solution to the problem he affords."

"Oh, my lady. . . ." cried Blanche in considerable agitation.

"Don't get all ruffled, dear Blanche. I couldn't do without you, now could I? You must come along as well."

This invitation merely increased the secretary's agitation, putting her in such a state that she went fluttering out of the room to engage in a fit of anxiety in the corridor outside.

Looking after her, Sahir said, "The journey may be difficult."

The countess nodded. "Don't worry about Blanche. Though she greets each new experience with trepidation, she is rocklike in her perceptions. I spoke only the truth in saying I could not manage without her."

18

Opalears: Upon the Crawling Sea

"Pheledas are well known as a proud and warrior peo-
ple. Even the females among them, nay, even the chil-
dren, show an exemplary ability to defend themselves
from attack or misuse. Pheleds have formed the bulk of
our armies for generations, and no person of wealth
would think of traveling without pheledian guards. The
ships that ply the Crawling Sea are largely crewed by
pheledian folk. To their fierce and independent nature
is allied an appreciation for certain arts, particularly
those of the table and of the dance. . . ."

THE PEOPLES OF EARTH
HIS EXCELLENCY, EMPEROR FAROS VII

When Mince, Burrow and Lucy Low returned to
their family, they were shown to rooms near the
stables and I rejoined Prince Sahir and Izzy, who told
me of the countess's plans, and I heard more about these
plans when they were discussed in greater detail over
the dinner table. For purposes of communication, we all
spoke trade language, based on the very ancient lan-

guage of Inglitch, said Prince Izakar, and long used to facilitate understanding among the people of various tribes.

I knew trade language, of course. My father had spoken it in the marketplaces of Tavor, and many slaves in the harim spoke it, since their own native tongues were often not understood.

The secretary, Blanche, said, "At all costs, we must avoid Finial. The Dire Duke has the province in his grasp, and we could not hope to get through the land without being certainly stopped, probably recognized, possibly eaten." She shivered dramatically.

"So Fasahd has indeed relinquished the ethical standards set by Faros VII," remarked Izzy. "How does he hope to endear himself to the emperor by eating the emperor's subjects?"

The countess agreed. "When I met him, I saw a person moved by envy, emboldened by rivalry, thinking no farther than the next acquisition, intending to prevail over his brother by pure force of terror, unmitigated by reason. He wants what Fasal Grun has, and what the emperor has, but not what the emperor wants."

"The emperor wants peace," said Soaz. "So I have often been told."

"The Dire Duke does not want peace," said Elianne. "The Dire Duke wants power. He wants it for itself; no other dream attracts him, though he would accept riches and fame, perhaps. His greatest joy is to see people bowing before him."

"So," yawned Izzy. "We won't go through Finial. How will we go?"

"We can go around," said Blanche. "On a boat."

"A boat?" Soaz frowned. "A ship?"

"A fishing boat. It was the fortunes of the two young onchiki that gave me the idea. The fishing fleet owes allegiance to no particular province. The little boats sail up and down the coast of the Crawling Sea, from Estafan to Sworp and back again, sometimes easterly along the shore counties and sometimes, though rarely, around the north coast even so far as the Temple of the Eye. Since they are crewed by pheledas, who can well defend themselves, since they carry no riches but do provide a good portion of the food of the shore peoples, they have attraction neither for privateers nor for the pressmen of the Dire Duke. We can hire a fishing boat to take us to Sworp.''

"What about our umminhi?" asked Soaz, his brow wrinkled.

"Several fishing boats?" suggested the countess. "If Prince Sahir takes the umminhi, we would need several.''

"Actually, it would be better to leave the umminhi here," Blanche said, fixing Sahir with her black-eyed stare. "Sell them or put them in stable awaiting your return. We can rent others in Sworp. Or,'' and she looked pointedly up and down the countess's voluptuous figure, "we can walk, which would probably benefit us all.''

I hid a smile. The countess chose to ignore this insolence. The conversation went on for a time in rather desultory fashion, and at last the countess excused herself with a yawn and was escorted from the chamber by Prince Sahir. Since I was sleepy, also, I followed them out.

"They'll sort it out," Sahir was telling her. "Soaz is good at that sort of thing. I'm afraid we scuinan people are less practical, Countess.'' He smiled warmly at the countess, and I stepped behind an arras, wanting to see what happened next.

"Let us say rather we enjoy our pleasures," she murmured, glancing flirtatiously from under her lashes. "I bid you good night, Prince Sahir.''

"I shall await a morrow already blessed since the Countess Elianne will be in it," he said, leaning forward to press her cheek with his own. He turned then and went down the stairs to the guest wing, leaving her to appreciate his retreating form, his robe swirling elegantly around him as he moved, almost at a trot.

She sighed.

I had not seen Blanche arrive, but she was suddenly there, beside the countess. "A fine picture he makes. A suitable person, as well. It is time you wed."

The countess stamped her foot. "No one is speaking of wedding, Blanche! Surely I may indulge myself in a few romantic thoughts."

"Only with care, Countess. The Dire Duke is no romantic. Given the chance, he would eat your lover as lief as he would eat you."

The countess's expression told me she did not find this a happy thought on which to end the day. "It will not keep me from sleeping, Blanche. I learned long ago that one must sleep when one has the chance."

A good lesson, I thought, going quietly away to my own room, full of wonderings about the prince and the countess and whether they would indeed have a romance, or even a marriage. I wondered what the sultan would think about that, if and when it happened. I wondered myself asleep.

When morning came, our entourage took measures to reduce itself both in numbers and bulk. One of the countess's hostlers took the umminhi and their handlers to be boarded at a stable in the southern fringes of Zallyfro. From among Prince Sahir's guards, Soaz selected four and put the rest on board wages at the palace, awaiting our return. Prince Izzy insisted on taking Oyk and Irk, though he left his body servant at the palace under the supervision of one of Elianne's under-butlers. All of us went through our baggage, removing bulky items which were not actually necessary, reducing the whole to a volume that could be handled by porters hired in Sworp, or put into a light wagon, perhaps, depending upon the roads.

I asked Izzy if I could help him, and he shook his head at me, saying that he'd gone through his sorcerer's kit half a dozen times and had quit trying to select from it. Since he had no idea what we would encounter on our way, he had no way to select from among the rather scanty supplies he had brought with him.

The countess and Blanche decided they could, as Blanche put it, "live on the country," so they would do without ladies' maids. Lucy Low, Burrow and Mince would take their veebles, mostly because the countess found herself enchanted by them. They had such lovely ears, she said, such soft muzzles, such sensuous fur.

When we were ready to go, the party included three principals: Izzy, Elianne, Sahir; four ancillaries: Soaz, Blanche, me, and at the last moment, Dzilobommo, who announced he would accompany us for reasons of his own having to do with the survival of his people. Whether this placed him among the principals or the supporters, I did not trouble myself to define. Also along were the three younger onchiki, four guards, plus Oyk and Irk and the four veebles: a total of twenty persons and creatures. A propitious number, said Blanche, to which Dzilobommo replied with a lengthy *grummel* which I understood to be a commentary upon fortune, fate or destiny, as it pertained to the armakfatidi.

Even so reduced in size and numbers, our group was too large for the little coastal boats, Blanche felt, so the countess's agents chose a deep-water schooner, the *Elegant Eel*, and workers from the palace were sent to remove the accretion of scales, guts and old fish heads with which it was ordinarily bedaubed. This cleaning took some time, so it was calm evening into which we travelers embarked, with the sun glinting low across the waters as we sailed due north, pressed forward by mild airs. The shoreline receded into dusk. Darkness oozed along the eastern mountains until the moon rose, bulging up like a leprous lantern from behind the Dreadful Mountains.

"If we could see far enough," said Mince, "We'd see Uncle Wash over there, climbing onto Hovermount."

"If he got through the Dire Marches," said Lucy

Low. "His fortune only said there was treasure there; it didn't say he'd find it."

"Uncle Wash is lucky," said Burrow, though with some doubt in his voice. "He's always said so."

"A man who wants little will be happily surprised at most anything," quoted Lucy Low. "Uncle Wash never wanted much."

"I don't imagine there was much to want, was there?" asked Izzy, who had come up behind us where we stood at the rail of the boat, looking out over the moon-spangled waters. "Chiliburn Creek sounds like a place with small wants."

"True," said Lucy Low, looking up at him. "There was always food, but it was always the same. There was always drink, but it was always water. There was always warmth, though it had to be huddled for. Such a life leads to small wants. Traveling, now, that's something else. I can feel my wants getting bigger every minute!"

"I hope you fulfil them all," I responded. The little onchik's cheer was infectious. It made me smile just to look at her.

The countess came from the cramped cabin onto the deck and joined the rest of us at the rail. "We will be past Finial by morning," I told her. "Then, so the captain says, we will run west with the dawn wind, into the harbor of Gulp, which lies at the mouth of the River Guzzle."

"All of which sounds very greedy and impetuous," said Izzy.

"They are so named for the sound the seas make when they are blown into the gaping caves ashore," said the countess. "I have been there, and indeed, they make a voracious sound, but only when the river is low. Now, with the snows melting on the Sharbaks, the river will be in flood."

"We must enter the harbor against the flow," I said, quoting the captain. "Or, we may anchor along the breakwater, which is some easier."

"Hoooh," came a voice from above, a whisper of

sound falling onto us like chilly water. "Hoh, sail-hoooh."

Soaz came out onto the deck, his face set into a frown, as the pheledian captain cried to his lookout, "What mark?"

"The Skull and Ax of Finial," called the lookout from his place atop the mast, where he clung by the tips of his fingers, as though glued to his post. "I think, though it's too dark to be sure. I'm sure it's no fishing boat."

"By the tonsils of Taskywheem," muttered Soaz. "How did the Dire Duke know we left Estafan?" He regarded the countess with a look that was almost accusatory.

"It was not my doing," she said. "May I borrow your glass, Captain?" Taking the proffered article with a somewhat quavery smile, she put the glass to her eye and spent a long moment searching the dusky horizon for the approaching ship, as though hoping it was not what it appeared to be. The distant ship changed course, heading more directly toward us.

"It is indeed the Dire Duke," the countess whispered, taking the glass from her eyes. "He has seen us. Somehow he has learned we would be here, upon the sea. Oh, I fear me he means us harm." She shivered, and Prince Sahir pressed against her so she could lean on him, though he too turned pale at the threat of the dark ship.

Izzy looked up to see our several pairs of eyes fixed on him. "What?" he demanded.

"It would be better if he didn't find us," rumbled Soaz. "The captain is a good fighter, and his crew is likewise, but this ship is small and we are not numerous. That black ship is large; it contains a good number of warriors, I have no doubt. This confounded moon will light us like a beacon."

Izzy shook his head doubtfully. "I could summon a fog. That is, it is theoretically possible for me to do so."

"He is a sorcerer?" the countess asked Sahir in a low voice.

"Of sorts," said Sahir "Not much practiced, it seems, though he saved us from a rather nasty battering by trees on the way here."

"By trees?"

"Hush. He will do better with us quiet."

Indeed, Izzy needed all his power of concentration. As he confessed to me later, the spells for calling up natural forces are complex in the extreme. He had learned them, of course, just as he had learned so much else, but he had never used them. Now, under pressure of that black-sailed ship in the east, he had to remember not only the words but also the gestures and the materials.

He handed me this and that to hold, ordering me to stand beside him as he worked. "I didn't bring some of the most effective antireflexives since they are expensive and I foresaw no use for them," he muttered. "I hope I have enough all-purpose cataphractics and anathematics to keep an elemental at bay. Fog is the least dangerous element to call. A storm at sea could become reflexive without warning, as could a firestorm among forests. Earthquake, volcano or tornado would be summoned only by a fanatic in the last stages of nihilism. The same for hurricane. No, fog will do. Fog will have to do."

Though this made little sense to me, I stood ready to help as he lit a fire in the iron pan the fishermen used for boiling their kettles.

"What summoning name?" he asked himself. "I have no idea! What language should we use, Nassif?"

I thought frantically, knowing nothing of magic, why did he ask me? "If it's to be a local fog, shouldn't it be the local language?" I asked.

He snapped his fingers. "Of course. I'll call upon it in three languages, Estafani, Finialese and Sworpian, thereby more or less confining it to this corresponding geographic area. Find my ampli-fire; it's at the bottom of the pack."

I dug into his pack, finding a stubby jar labeled *Jo-*

rush's All-Purpose Ampli-fire. I set it beside him as he ringed the fire with a circle of white powder.

"What's that?" I whispered.

"Cataphractic powder, to protect the ship and ourselves," he said under his breath.

"And what is that stuff?" breathed the countess, peering at the long-necked bottle he was holding aloft.

"Elias's Element-all," said Izzy. "Containing only the purest ingredients in ideal proportions. Elias has his shop on the square in Palmody. He has supplied our family wizards for generations."

"I thought wizards made up their own . . . stuff," commented Sahir.

"You may be glad that is not always true," muttered Izzy. "It would have taken me the better part of two days to make this up, even if I'd had all the ingredients to start with. Now if you'll all forego asking questions, I'll try to remember how to do this. . . ."

We kept silent as he began the invocation:

"I call upon you, child of sky and sea, great fog . . ." he began, ending with a string of imperatives. His voice faded as we all felt the clammy grip of the fog seize upon us, but then he gathered himself and finished the spell while the mists swirled up from the waves like a steam of rising ghosts, thickening as they rose, becoming milky and opaque, blanketing the *Elegant Eel* as if with batting.

Izzy trembled, wrapping his arms around himself. I took off my cloak and wrapped it around him. "There's an icy space in my chest," he whispered to me. "It came as I summoned the fog. I feel sick."

"What is it, Izzy?" I whispered. "What can I do?"

"Nothing," he murmured. "It's the effect of doing deep magic. They warned me it would happen. The deeper the sorcery, the deeper this sickness at the center of oneself. Summoning an elemental is a very deep sorcery, and only practice and time can cure this feeling, so the palace wizard told me."

He did indeed look very green. I wrapped my arms

around him to warm him, and he shuddered in the circle of my cloak.

The countess murmured to the captain, and he to his sailors. They tugged at ropes, the ship heeled as it veered to port, though only briefly, for soon the sailors scurried up the ratlines on both foremast and mainmast, drawing up the sails and bundling them upon the spars. The water ceased to boil along the sides of the ship, the planks stopped creaking. Within moments we were at rest, silent, lost amid heavy veils of mist, rocking only a little to and fro, as the sailors slunk about the vessel, tying up lines and blocks and bits of equipment so they could not rattle or clink. A long, quiet time went by before we heard voices off the starboard bow, people calling to one another as they came nearer and nearer yet. We on the *Elegant Eel* heard the creak of planks as the Dire Duke's ship passed our starboard side and then continued southward. Voices called again, and yet again, fading as they went.

The captain muttered to his sailors. In a few moments our sails were set once more, and we were on our way through the fog, steering by compass into the north. The captain came to us where we stood by the rail and murmured to Izzy:

"How long will it last?"

Izzy shook his head. He didn't know. "How long a run is it to Sworp?"

"We will be outside the bay by morning, but it takes clear weather to achieve the harbor, as we must make way against the flow of the Guzzle. There are big rocks and shoals, and it is not a mooring to attempt under adverse conditions."

We had not gone much farther before we heard ship sounds once more, this time behind us, crossing our track. While we heard the sounds, we were ourselves quiet, uttering not a peep, barely breathing. The noises faded as the pursuing ship went out toward the depths of the Crawling Sea. As the hours wore on, we heard the ship—or some ship—twice more, though the last time was only the barely audible chime of a bell, far to the south.

As the hours wore on, Izzy regained his strength. I reclaimed my cloak and moved away from him, though he remained crouched beside the rail, where he was joined by the countess.

"It is a good thing the Dire Duke has no sorcery," he said to the countess. "A lack which amazes me, quite frankly."

"Faros VII has forbidden sorcery in his realms," the countess murmured. "Thus far, at least, the Dire Duke has complied with that taboo though he disobeys many others of the emperor's decrees. When we arrive in Sworp, I would suggest we all keep silence about your skill. Fasal Grun is the emperor's favorite, and he will not hesitate to enforce the emperor's commands."

"Why is sorcery forbidden?" asked Izzy, almost whispering. "Have you any idea?"

She shook her head. She had none. She knew only that such a declaration had reached her, some years before, and that since that time there had been a notable dearth of wizards.

This brief conversation evidently exhausted Izzy's strength, for he staggered into the cabin and threw himself down on a narrow bunk. When I went to see if he was all right a few moments later, he was sound asleep and he did not rouse until morning, a dim and doubtful morning which found us still surrounded in impenetrable fog.

"We can run west a bit," the captain advised us, "until we hear the sound of waves on the rocks. But if this fog is still with us then, we won't be able to reach the anchorage."

"Can you dismiss it?" the countess asked Izzy.

"If I can remember how at this early hour," he said sullenly. "My stomach feels slightly better, but I've not had my tea, nor have I had any practice with this business. Until this journey, my studies were entirely theoretical."

While he collected himself, I fetched him a mug of dark tea, telling him it was burned bitter but better than nothing.

"It's hot," he said. "That's something."

"Thus far you've done very well," the countess assured him.

He yawned gapingly. "At least nothing has gone terribly wrong. I'm an amateur, way over my head, and I keep having the feeling I'm going to do something dangerous or stupid."

"I can understand that," she said soothingly. "I felt the same when I ascended to the throne of Estafan. My father had often talked to me about ruling the country, but the subject was, as you say, theoretical. Only recently have I begun to feel halfway comfortable about making decisions that affect my people. I'm sure it will be the same for you. You'll gain confidence as you go on practicing."

"I hope not to have to practice," he muttered. "It would suit me nicely if this were the last time I had to be responsible for any of the magical arts."

Still, when the ship came within sound of breakers, and when a bucket dropped over the side brought up brackish water, Izzy did not complain as he set about dismissing the fog. Again he mumbled half aloud to himself as he worked, and thus I learned he had to make several substitutions in the ritual. Perhaps this accounted for the fact that the veils of mist did not entirely dissipate. They thinned, however, gradually becoming transparent, until we could all see the pier and the breakwater—and the huge black ship of the Dire Duke anchored across the only channel, its sails set, its anchor chains straining to hold the ship against the offshore current of the plunging river.

A shout went up from the black ship, the combined voices of many. The sailors began to haul at the anchor chains.

"Do we retreat?" yowled Soaz, showing his teeth. "Or do we fight?"

"If we retreat, he'll catch us," said the captain. "What's left of the fog won't hide us."

"Can you thicken it up again?" Sahir demanded of Izzy.

"No," he snarled. "Elementals don't like being called up and dismissed and called up again, like servants. They get touchy and vindictive."

"Looky there," cried Lucy Low. "There's boats coming out from the land!"

And there were, a dozen or so sizeable boats with oarsmen at both sides, light reflecting dully from the armor of those gathered in the prows. A long, red banner flickered above the lead boat.

"The banner of Fasal Grun," cried the countess, adding in a low voice, "Prince Izakar, best hide those sorcerous materials."

Izzy scrambled to repack his kit. As he did so we heard an infuriated howl from someone aboard the black ship. Instead of coming toward the *Elegant Eel*, it swung wide upon its anchor chain and slipped southward along the breakwater, back toward Finial. The boats kept coming, however, the foremost very shortly pulling itself against the *Eel*. The captain dropped a ladder. A huge person came up over the side, seemingly unhampered by the steely claws extending from his armored gloves, to stand upon the deck, staring around himself, as though surprised at the company he found there.

"We welcome His Eminence, the Prime Duke Fasal Grun," announced the countess in a ringing voice. Everyone bowed deeply, several among us breathlessly.

"Countess Elianne?" the Prime Duke asked in a barely civilized growl.

"Your Eminence is kind to remember," she murmured.

"I had no idea you were aboard. I thought perhaps you were pirates or slavers being intercepted by my brother. That was my brother's ship, was it not?"

"It was." She sighed. "We intended to come ashore in Sworp on our way to St. Weel, but the Dire Duke did not want us to make the journey. He attempted to capture us on our way here.''

"Why?" demanded the duke. "Why would he care if you came here or not?"

The countess grew pink with annoyance. "Your Grace knows why! We have corresponded on this subject. Fasahd desires an alliance with Estafan. While he pursues this goal, he certainly would not want me talking with you! If he had an alliance with Estafan, it would give him a mask of legitimacy to hide his real desires."

"Ah," murmured the duke with a grimace. "I thought I had dissuaded him! Well, it is fortunate you were concealed by the fog." He raised his eyebrows and sniffed, as though to detect any odor of sorcery that might be about. "Particularly when fog is so rare at this time of year."

"It was fortunate," bubbled the countess. "Fate was very kind in not allowing us to fall into the hands of . . ." Her voice trailed into silence. She flushed, then turned and laid her hand upon Sahir's sleeve. "Your Eminence, may I present my friends and fellow travelers. . . ."

She introduced all of us, the duke bowing slightly as he heard each name, while keeping a watchful eye upon the countess. When the introductions had been made, he growled:

"I can only apologize for my brother. Fasahd has been informed that the emperor will not tolerate this behavior, and yet he continues. It's hard for me to understand what he thinks he's doing. You say you have not encouraged him."

The countess replied, "Your Grace knows I have not! And if anyone knows why he behaves this way, you must. Who knows him better than his brother?"

Fasal Grun sighed deeply. "Fasahd has it in his head to inherit the throne of Farsak."

"Very ambitious," murmured Izzy.

The Prime Duke shrugged. "Faros VII is my mother's much younger brother, reared by her after our parents died, and he is very little older than Fasahd and I. He is also in rude good health, so it is unlikely that either Fasahd or myself will ever inherit the throne of Farsak, no matter who outdoes the other. We are not in competition, but Fasahd will not believe that! The fact that I was born first so irritates him that he will do anything to cause me embarrassment.''

He turned and called over the side, telling his boat to put back to shore. ''I will go in with you,'' he said. ''Unless your captain would rather moor along the breakwater.''

Pheledas are all too eager to demonstrate their skill, which in this case took some time. I thought we could have moored and walked into the town several times over by the time the ship was maneuvered among the rocks and into the harbor. By the time we reached the cobbled street that gave upon the piers, Fasal Grun had learned of our reasons for travel, including the fortunes given to Lucy Low, though the subject of magic had been carefully avoided.

The duke took the countess's hand and placed it upon his arm, pointing up a slightly wider street toward the Imperial Residence. Townspeople cleared the way, bowing. As we walked, the duke spoke loudly enough that all of us could hear him clearly: ''Since this quest was laid upon you by the Seers of Sworp, I need take no action against you. I am gratified you have not been guilty of dabbling in sorcery.''

''Weren't there sorcerers in Sworp?'' Izzy asked, being very casual about it. ''It seems to me I've heard—''

''There was a tribe of sorcerers here in Sworp, but when faced with the edicts of Faros, they consented to become seers, instead.''

''Would they have included members of the Gershon family?'' asked Izzy.

''They would indeed,'' said the duke. ''Many of the Society of Seers were members of that family.''

''We are no doubt related,'' said Izzy, still casually.

"I thought your family name was Poffit," said the Duke.

"It's a long story." Izzy sighed, adding irrepressibly, "What's the difference between a seer and a sorcerer? Don't both use magic?"

The duke regarded him thoughtfully. "Prince Izakar, Faros VII feels there is a great difference between people seeing the future and people influencing it. He doesn't care who sees what will occur, but he himself intends to decide what will occur. He wants peace! He wants an end to invasions and battles. As did his forebears. As will his heirs. He wants the world unified under one government and an end to all intertribal strife. When he acts to influence the future, he comes to the seers to see if his acts have been effective. He uses the seers as a kind of monitor on his own plans."

"Is Faros VII aware of this message we have been given, this threat to the future of all people?" Izzy persisted.

"I don't know. Since he's even now here in Sworp to consult the seers, perhaps you can ask him."

"Here?" cried Sahir. "How fortunate. May I have audience with him?"

"If he is so disposed, of course. I would not presume to promise anything, but I will see he is informed of your wish to meet with him. In the interest of peace, of course."

"Of course," Izzy agreed, Prince Sahir concurring with a regal nod.

"If Faros is so set upon tranquility," said the countess with some asperity, "then why does he let the Dire Duke run about behaving like a cannibal."

His Eminence sighed. "When my mother lay dying, Faros, her brother, swore an oath to care for her own twin children, my brother and me, to advance us and let us achieve great things. Faros and our mother were close, almost as mother and son. He had not the presence of mind in that tragic moment to put conditions upon his oath."

"Then why don't you—"

"Because Fasal Grun and Fasahd were once Fass and Grunny, children and brothers," he said sadly. "And when we were children, we were friends. Thus far I have chosen merely to keep track of him and mitigate the harm he does, always hoping he will improve his behavior."

"I urge you to keep close track, Your Eminence, for he has threatened to eat my people," said the countess. "And there is the possibility he has made common cause with the trees. . . ."

"Trees?" The duke was astonished. "What trees?"

"A new sort," said Izzy. "A belligerent sort, who believe themselves threatened with extinction."

The duke stared at him, his amber eyes intent. "Now how would you have gathered that information?"

Soaz said smoothly, "Their belligerence could be determined from their actions, Your Eminence. And it was the talk of Blander that the reason for it was a fear of extinction. What else would move trees to attack people with axes?"

"Remarkable."

Ahead of us a line of pheled guards snapped to attention, maintaining their rigid stance while the duke and his guests paraded before a gleaming line of pikes to an iron-bound door that swung soundlessly open as we approached. In the courtyard, the veebles and our guards were put in the care of the stablemaster while the rest of us proceeded to the door of the residence. The High Duke bowed us in, muttering orders to an obsequious butler, who darted off at once in several directions.

"How did he do that?" I whispered to Izzy.

"Spontaneous disassembly," muttered Izzy. "The butler seems to be a communal entity."

"What in hell is a communal entity?" growled Soaz under his breath. "I've never heard of—"

"Just . . . something other than the usual," Izzy replied. "I'm trying to remember what I've read about communal entities. I thought they were imaginary."

Whether imaginary or not, the butler, or another similar one, met us at the end of the corridor and ushered us into a pleasant reception room overlooking the gardens.

"Breakfast will be served promptly," said the High Duke. "I have an enormous appetite this morning, no doubt stimulated by all that sea air. And you, Countess, are you the least little bit hungry?"

She dimpled at him, fluttering her eyelashes. "You are too kind, Your Eminence. I know we of Estafan have been a trouble to you. You are generous to overlook it."

"I overlook nothing," he said firmly, striking a determined pose before the empty fireplace. "The emperor, my uncle, would be disappointed in me if I were not vigilant. But being aware of a problem does not mean I, we, the Farsakian Empire, should respond with viciousness or evil. The emperor is interested in peace, in the welfare of the earth, in peoples living together with a minimum of conflict. He believes that in order to achieve this balance, he must bring all provinces and princedoms under one government and, gradually, to a shared language and culture. Nonetheless, within that government he intends to maintain room for many customs and kinds of people."

"I hope we will be able to meet the emperor, your uncle," Izzy murmured. "Perhaps he can cast light upon the puzzles we are trying to solve."

"Where's Dzilobommo?" asked the countess suddenly.

"He asked our leave to go to the kitchens," murmured the Duke. "He has some kindred there, lady, and he wished to spend some time with them."

"Kind of you," she murmured.

The Prime Duke bowed in acknowledgment. Servitors arrived with food—steak and eggs for Soaz, the duke, Oyk, Irk and the onchiki; fish, fruit and oatmeal for the rest of us—and our party, made hungrier by the danger we had so narrowly avoided, sat down to breakfast.

19

Dora Meets a Dionne

One evening, a few days after meeting Abilene McCord, Dora received two phone calls.

The first was from the fireman she had talked to. The Dionne house, he said, had been arson. The place had burned to the ground, the arson squad had investigated, but they'd never had any good leads.

The second call was from Harry Dionne. She introduced herself as a police officer who was investigating this phenomenon and thought it might have started in the neighborhood where the Dionnes had lived.

"Why would you think that?" he asked calmly, with a strange degree of uninterest.

"Well . . ." She didn't want to mention Jared. "I was living a few doors down from your old home site. I think I may have seen the first . . . ah, one of these new trees. And it may be related to that huge tree that was in your backyard."

"What an odd idea." His voice sounded removed and far away, like a bad long-distance connection.

She swallowed deeply and persevered. Well, it wasn't certain and this and that, but could he meet with her and tell her about the people who had lived there, his brothers, his father, their cousins from out of town? Mrs. Gerber had mentioned their cousins from out of town.

Long pause. "I was twelve years old when Demmy and Cory came visiting. If you want to know about them, you should talk to my brothers. Or my father. I was a little too young."

"Are your brothers or father here in town?"

"No. They aren't."

"Then, won't you talk to me, please? Just give me your impressions. Were, ah . . . the women attractive?"

"Of course. Considering who they were, are, they're attractive. That's part of it, isn't it? Though I was too young to understand what all the fuss was about, all the men in the neighborhood were prancing around like buck goats."

Goats again. "Your brother . . . brothers are older?"

"Yes, I'm the youngest. I have four brothers, but they're widely scattered by now."

"So, you were twelve years old. . . ."

"Tom and Dick were in high school, seventeen and eighteen, or thereabouts. Charlie and Roger were in their twenties, just graduating college."

Somehow, from Mrs. Gerber's satyric description, Dora had expected hooves and horns, people who peed on the ground and spit through their teeth, not a tribe of college graduates.

"If I met you for breakfast, could you tell me about that summer?" she asked.

He tried to put her off, half-heartedly, then agreed, still in that toneless and relaxed voice. Dora picked a hotel, one near the precinct. They'd try to be there at eight, they agreed, leaving it flexible, both of them realizing it might take longer to get there, depending on what the trees decided to do. She planned to leave a little early in the morning, which was no problem because she'd found herself waking earlier and going to sleep earlier. Somehow, the forest around her place seemed to settle when the sun went down, a kind of drowsiness descending that was very hard to fight off, even with the TV on. The corollary of this was that the forest woke when the sun came up, announcing itself through a good deal of bird chatter that Dora couldn't remember ever hearing before there had been trees.

Harry Dionne was six or eight years older than she, forty-two or three, maybe. He shook her hand and sat down across from her. He had an eponymous name, for as Mrs. Gerber had said, he was hairy, with a fine pelt on the backs of his hands and a blue shadow extending down his neck into the collar of his spotless button-down shirt. He wore a neatly trimmed beard and mustache, however, and the hairs of his neck were neatly shaved. Dora, trying to be reasonably subtle about it, sniffed the air for the smell of goat. An aroma was detectable, strong but not at all unpleasant. So much for Mother Gerber's characterization.

"Now," he said, when they had received coffee and ordered orange juice, omelettes and toast. "Though I doubt my ability to do so, how may I try to help you?"

"That huge old tree behind your old house . . . or, where your old house was, seems to be something very rare. People are interested in knowing about it, who planted it, how long it's been there, that kind of thing."

Long silence. He looked around the room, his face rather troubled. "You mean, because of what's happening."

She fidgeted, uncertain how much to say. "I wondered if it might not have started there, in your old backyard, where that tree is. It's the center, so to speak."

He fixed her with his gaze, and she found herself unable to look aside. "It's a family tree, Sergeant Henry. We've planted cuttings of that kind of tree everywhere we've ever been. We're an old family, very old, with old traditions."

They were interrupted by the waitperson bringing their orders and refilling their cups.

When she had gone, Dora asked, "Do your traditions include early marriage?"

"Why do you ask?"

"The mother evidently wanted your girl cousin to be married. According to Jared's mother, anyhow."

Another long silence. "She did, yes." Harry Dionne picked up his coffee cup and regarded her over it as he drank. "Tom was supposed to marry Cory. My brother, Tom. They were much of an age. That's the way it's done in our family, though I must admit that Tom felt quite rebellious about the whole thing."

"But she wanted to run off with Jared, instead?"

"For some reason I've never been able to understand, that is evidently what she did, but how would you have learned about that?"

She spoke without thinking. "I was married to Jared, Mr. Dionne."

He stared at her, forehead slightly furrowed, eyes intent. "You were married to him?"

"For a couple of years, yes."

"But you didn't stay married to him." It was a statement, not a question.

She flushed, at which he nodded, as though she had replied.

He said, "People who become associated with our family in that way don't marry someone else. Jared's mother forbade the marriage, said she'd have it annulled, but that was only a legal matter. It couldn't change what I assume had already happened."

"But Jared did marry me," she said.

He smiled at her. "You're quite a lovely woman, Ms. Henry, but I don't think Jared cared about that, did he? If our religion has truth in it, at best, your marriage would have been . . . let us say, companionate?"

She concentrated upon her orange juice, feeling again that wariness, that edginess, that almost fear. Was she wearing a label? Did everyone in the world know she was a virgin?

"My father would say that no one married to Cory

could ever again marry anyone else. I believe that's true, and it has nothing to do with you.''

Long silence.

"You asked about the tree," he said. "That particular tree, the one you're referring to, was planted by my father's father's father, back in the 1800s. There was a big farmhouse built there at the same time. The place subsequently changed hands several times. The farmhouse was still there when my family came back to it the summer I was eleven.

"The year we came back, my brother Dick nailed a ladder up the trunk of the tree, and he and Tom built a tree house in it. We used to hide out up there and spy on all the neighbors, not that we were in the neighborhood all that long. The house burned and Father made no effort to rebuild. After what happened with Jared and Cory . . . well, Father felt the neighborhood was rather too small town. Too many people minding everyone else's business. It was that kind of block.''

"Enforced conformity?'' she asked, forking a mouthful of eggs.

"Um.'' He nodded, buttering a piece of toast. "Yes. Mrs. Gerber, down on the corner, seemed to know everything about everybody and have an opinion on everything.''

"Especially your cousins?''

"As I said, I was too young to be emotionally involved, but I do remember Dad's surprise when he learned Demmy and Cory were coming that summer. He'd known they might arrive eventually, of course, but he hadn't realized it would be that summer. The place was a mess. It usually was with five boys, and none of us were housekeepers. We boys just couldn't be bothered, and of course Dad was very busy with the church—''

"Church?''

"I say church because it's conventional. Actually, we don't have *a* church, as in edifice, but my father is a leader of our religion.''

"What is your religion?"

"Sergeant Henry, I didn't want to get into this. I'm always explaining my family *and* my religion. Since I was six years old, kindergarten age, I've been explaining my family. When I fell in love with a non-family member, you have no idea what I went through, explaining my family. I get very tired of explanations! However! We are a family and we have a religion. I don't mean just my brothers and father, but all our family, everywhere around the world. There are thousands of Dionnes, though not all of us bear that surname, and we have a religion that maintains our traditions and performs our ceremonies. Think of us as being rather like . . . well, say gypsies, though we're rather better educated and acculturated than the Rom. We're more like the Diasporic Jews, separated but faithful to their heritage. No matter where we live, we're still family members. We still learn to speak the old tongue, at least for ritual occasions, and we cherish the old ways.

"Father is one of the Vorn, which is the priesthood. Vorn can be used as either a title or a name. You could say he is a Vorn, or he is Vorn Dionne. Demmy is one of our priestesses. The arranged marriage between a son of the priestly line and a daughter of the priestess's line is a periodic religious rite that takes place roughly once a generation, say three or four times a century. It is meant to be a binding between ourselves, our family, and the world in which we live." His tone was bland, as though he'd said it so often it had lost its meaning.

She thought about this for a moment. "Your brother, he was the human side of it, right? And Cory . . . she would have symbolized what? Nature?"

His eyes met hers with sudden surprise. "In a way, yes. Are you interested in religions?"

"In hearing about them? Learning about them? Yes. Very."

He nodded slowly, making up his mind. "Well, all right, since you're genuinely interested. Our religion teaches us that the maiden selected for the rite—and to be sure she is a maiden, she is selected at about age four or five—is the current receptacle of the divine. Think of it as similar to the selection of a little boy to be the Dalai Lama or the Panchen Lama. That child is widely sought, then identified, then reared to be the next Lama. This always seems to 'work,' which is quite miraculous, at least to outsiders. Is it in the rearing? Or is it in the inclination? Or is the child really an incarnation? Or is it some combination of these factors?

"What I personally believe about all this varies from time to time, depending upon who I've been talking with or what I've been reading lately, but my father sincerely believes the girl selected by the priestess is an incarnation. As a priest, one of the high priests, in fact, he could hardly believe otherwise, and the fact I can't always believe it causes some strain between us." He sipped his coffee, shaking his head with a rueful expression.

"The selected maiden becomes a 'daughter' of the high priestesses. She is *very* carefully reared and protected. Every few years, a boy is selected, too, from among the priestly lines of descent, so that when the female avatar comes of age, there will be a man of roughly her own age to mate with. My brother Tom was selected when he was about eleven, I think. The high priestesses meet each of the selected men or boys. It is up to them to arrange the mating."

She worried this for a moment, then set it aside. "What did you think of your cousin?"

"Well, she was gorgeous, of course. Even a twelve-year-old could see that. Wild, wonderful hair, eyes you could drown in, and a body like a wonderful cat, all muscle and sleek skin and lean bone."

"She must have caused a stir."

He smiled. "Among the neighbors she did. I remember thinking it odd that my brothers weren't affected, except for Tom, of course. Tom took one look at her and decided marriage couldn't be all bad. All my brothers were furious when they found out Jared Gerber had gone off with her. No, that's not putting it accurately

enough. They and my father and Demmy were astonished. There should have been no way that it could hap
pen. Cory simply couldn't have done it, any more than
the Dalai Lama could give up his religion and become
a rock star.

"Mrs. Gerber came to the house and had a fit over it,
that I do remember. Demmy was in a sort of quiet rage,
talking to my father in the den, with the door shut. I
think she threatened us with calamity for at least a generation. Next thing we knew, Jared came home alone
saying Cory had left him and run off somewhere. Mrs.
Gerber got the marriage annulled, and Cousin Demmy
went off looking for the girl."

"Did she find her?"

"I don't know. I only know what I overheard. At that
age, I wouldn't have been in on discussions of religious
matters. Even among adults, only the members of the
family who join the priestly caste would have been concerned, and even at twelve, I was considered not to qual-
ify. I was too talkative, too gregarious, not sincere
enough. My brother Tom did become part of the priestly
caste, the rest of us have gone into other professions."

"You're allowed to go into other professions?"

"Encouraged. Into the sciences, mostly. For the last
several decades the biological sciences have been very,
very big with our people. Some big project is no doubt
being planned, but though one brother is in on that, I'm
not. I'm an accountant."

"I'm sorry, I interrupted. You said you weren't in on
religious matters. . . ."

"I wasn't included in the talk about it. There were a
number of distractions, too, since that was about the time
the old farmhouse burned down. We weren't in it at the
time. Dad had taken all of us boys away for a camping
trip."

"What is this religion of yours called?"

He flushed slightly. "We usually just say, *our religion.*"

She turned her cup in the saucer, chasing elusive fragments of thought. "Nobody in your family was studying botany or anything like that, were they?"

He concentrated on replenishing his coffee. "They were, yes. And microbiology and molecular biology, and half a hundred other ologies, but if you're talking about the tree, the tree was just there. Whenever we see one like it, we know our people have lived there."

"But nobody knows what kind it is."

"I'm sure the Vorn do, but kids building tree houses don't care much what kind. I don't recall that anyone ever mentioned the species to me and I was never interested enough to ask."

"How well did you know Jared?"

He looked at her narrowly. "He was older than I was by five years. He was Tom's age. The only things I knew about him that were at all interesting were that he had been hit by lightning once and survived, and he was the only guy in high school who had a house of his own."

Dora set her own cup down, spilling a little into the saucer. "He owned the place then?"

"His mother bought that house for him when he was only thirteen or fourteen. For him to have when he got ready to have a place of his own."

"When he was thirteen?"

"Actually, that was very typical of her. She's a very consistent person, Mrs. Gerber. An abstemious, unemotional, inquisitive, thrifty kind of woman. I'm sure she never spends a dime without reasoning it out. I'm sure no day passed that she didn't tuck something away against a future need. She found a house that was rundown, going at a bargain price, and she bought the house in Jared's name. It was Jared's job to take care of it, right from the beginning. It was his place, and he did the work. Though my brothers said it was impossible, I suggested at the time that Jared's having the house was the reason Cory ran off with him. They would have had a place to live."

"I had no idea."

"Oh, yes. He was digging the foundations for the garage and patio, by hand, the summer he ran off with Cory."

"Have you seen the place lately?"

"Not lately, no. We moved, and good riddance according to my father and brothers." He summoned the waitperson and paid the bill, all in one quick motion, before she could offer to pay or share, then continued his account. "Sometimes I'd ride my bike over there, just to say hi. I saw Jared's place when he had it completed. I must say, he kept the place very neat."

"Too damn neat," she muttered, then, noticing his weighing look, "Jared, I mean." She shook her head. "Jared and his momma are very, very neat."

He stared at her, then smiled, suddenly and shockingly, like an unexpected sunrise. "You're fretting over Jared, aren't you? Maybe feeling responsible? You shouldn't. According to our religion, every man has a center of wildness in him, though in some it's vanishingly small. Maybe it was that kernel in Jared that made him take up with my cousin, but believe me, if so, he used it all up in the few frantic hours he spent with her. He had no idea what he was connecting to. By the time she ran off, there he was, poor fellow, already drained, lost, only a shell. Be glad you realized it in time."

"In time. . . ."

"For yourself. Every woman has that fount of wildness, too. I'd guess you haven't used yours. Civilization doesn't give us many safe outlets. Either we repress, or we find it easy to get sidetracked into something evil or destructive. That's why our people cling to our religion. It provides us a safe channel for the wildness in us all. With what's happening now, there may not be any other safe channels."

"What do you know about what's happening now?" she challenged him.

"Not a lot," he said, rising. "But I can see the forest for the trees. I can see that my people are concerned about what's going on. My father, who seldom says he was mistaken about anything, was worrying recently that some actions taken by the Vorn may have been mis-taken, because they didn't know this tree business was going to happen. It really worried him."

"Personally, I like the trees," she said stubbornly. "I like the birds. They're full of music."

He shook his head at her. "Well, maybe birds are the worst of it. I would hope they are. But from the comings and goings among my people, all the behind-closed-doors conferences, all the long faces, I'd say it's more than that. They're up to something, something big, and they have been for some little time now. I'm not privy to what it is, and even if I were, I couldn't tell you."

"That sounds unfriendly," she said.

"Which is one of the arguments I'm constantly having with my father," he said ruefully. "I don't go much for secrecy. But then, when you've lived with it for a few thousand years. . . ."

"That long?" she said, with a grin.

"So they say." He pressed her hand in his own, raised it in rueful salute, and was gone.

20

The Emperor, Faros VII

"The ersuniel tribes have always had a tendency toward isolation. Never a gregarious people, they have become known for long solitary wandering, for lonely practices of the management arts, ordinarily joining in company only for seasonal affairs such as the biennial mating rituals or the return of the piscidi. This eremitic tendency has, perhaps, contributed to their frequent selection as philosopher kings, as has their ability to see various points of view in any situation. As rulers over the multitudinous and not always cooperative affairs of earth's peoples, the ersuniel ability to enforce workable compromise provides a strong and stabilizing influence."

THE PEOPLES OF EARTH
HIS EXCELLENCY, EMPEROR FAROS VII

In a sumptuously furnished tower room high above the breakfasting travelers, the emperor set aside the manuscript he was working on and turned his attention to his solitary breakfast, taken upon a table set in a tall window looking out over the Crawling Sea. When he had opportunity, he preferred to eat with his fingers, alone and messily, rather than observe the mannerly behavior required in public. Eating with utensils was time consuming, one of those picky customs that set his teeth on edge, like wearing boots when he could walk better in soft slippers, or keeping his voice down when he wanted to roar at underlings for their continual stupidities. Nonetheless, for the most part, he did keep his voice down, he did eat with utensils, he did wear boots. He could not expect the peoples of his empire to stop frightening or disgusting one another if he did not take steps to do likewise. Eating like a barbarian was all right in private, but it wouldn't do at state banquets.

Which fact he had tried to explain to his nephew Fasahd on many occasions. Fasahd did not agree. Fasahd did not desire peace. Fasahd was going to make Faros break his oath to his sister, a sin which Faros regarded as only slightly less horrific than matricide.

"Sister," he said into the quiet room, "how could you have borne two such different sons as these, one all friendly good sense and the other all fangs and claws?" He was speaking metaphorically, of course. Fasahd was a good deal more than fangs and claws, which was what made him dangerous. How would Fasahd's mother have seen this current situation, if she had lived? Would she have taken Fasahd's part? Or Fasal Grun's? Or the emperor's?

The emperor rose from the table and went to the mirror, to remind himself, as he often said, who he was. He saw a body of size and bulk that, despite the slightly humped shoulders his family shared as a characteristic, was nonetheless quick and agile. He saw a certain controlled ferocity in the face, an alertness of eye, a keenness of senses. He reached out a hand to stroke that image, not out of self-love but out of need to verify what his eyes saw. Eyes could lie. Faces could smile while hiding villainy. His own must not. He could do and would do what his father and grandfather before him had done. He could do and would do what the future of the world demanded. He could and would carry out the plans arrived at with such effort and pain over so many generations.

And if, in order to achieve peace, he had to release himself from the oath he had sworn his sister, he would do so. Still, he hoped that would not be necessary.

He sat down at the table once again, reviewing the words he had just written, part of his work on the people of the earth.

"Long ago, so it is written, when great Korè walked openly in the lands of the people, none were so fair to her as the kapriel who accompanied her journeys, who went with her into the forests and plains, clearing the way before her, plucking up flowers which they put into her hands. The kapriel, so it is said, remember the ways of the wild, and as animal handlers they have made a place for themselves which cannot be filled by any other people."

He took up his pen, only to be interrupted by the sound of a person approaching his door. He anticipated the knock, which came softly.

"Enter."

The one who entered was a ponjic secretary, one who served as a kind of go-between whenever the emperor was away from his own court. The secretary bowed deeply, murmuring, "Your Excellency, I bring a message from the Prime Duke."

"And what does my nephew have to tell me today?"

"He wishes to advise the Great One, his uncle, that travelers have arrived telling of strange omens."

"Sorcery?" he demanded, with a curl of his lip.

"No, Your Effulgence. Omens, fortunes, predictions originating among the Seers of Sworp. An onchik with a geas dating back many years. A scuinan with a lost fortune. A ponja retelling a prophecy that is years old."

"Hah," he murmured. "Have they come to consult the seers?"

"It is said they are on their way to the Hospice of St. Weel."

The emperor looked up with slight impatience.

"One of them, the scuinic prince, much desires an audience with your Mightiness."

"Does he say why?"

"To bring greetings from his father, the sultan of Tavor."

The emperor waved this away, as unimportant.

"It might be very wise, however, for you to meet with the ponjic prince. He speaks of a danger that is coming. A horror that confronts the world. Something of that sort."

"Again! What in the name of Korè is going on?"

"I know no more than Your Excellency does."

"We've worked so hard. We've accomplished so much!"

"Certainly."

"By all the former gods, Zarl. By the ages and the sages—"

"Something else."

"And what might that be?"

"The ponjic prince. I heard him saying something to the other ponja, one dressed as a male but female for all that, though the prince is seemingly unaware of it. He was talking about certain trees they encountered during their journey and he used the phrase, 'natural selection.' "

"He what?"

"Your Excellency heard me the first time."

"He could have arrived at the phrase independently."

"Unlikely, sir."

"Do you suppose there's another . . . ?"

"Another library, sir?"

"Yes. I mean, we know there were others. Do you suppose others have survived?"

"Would you like to grant him an audience?"

"By all means," whispered Faros VII. Oh, yes, Zarl. By all means. With him alone."

21

Opalears: Account of an Audience

Prince Sahir was seriously annoyed.

"Why do you get a private audience?" he demanded. "Why not me?"

Izzy spoke between his teeth. "Did it ever occur to you I may be in serious trouble here?"

Sahir snorted. "Why?"

"Oh, my prince," I cried, greatly distraught, "you know why. Perhaps the emperor knows that Izzy used magic to save us from the Dire Duke."

Sahir fell silent. He had not considered that possibility. He lowered his eyes, though he did not go so far as to apologize. "Perhaps that is so. I forgive you."

"Kind of you," said Izzy. "If I end up sentenced to death, just remember your forgiveness. Use diplomacy. Tell the emperor you'll be his fast friend forever if he lets me go back to Palmia safely." He shuddered. He'd been shuddering ever since Faros VII had summoned him and asked that he come alone.

"I think that person is looking for you," I whispered,

indicating a liveried ponja standing in the doorway.

Izzy took a deep breath, rose, smoothed down his jacket and followed the ponja. Though I did not go with him, he told me all about it, later.

He followed for some little time, up flights of stairs and across open courtyards and down other flights of stairs, finally ascending what seemed to be the central tower.

"What's the protocol?" he murmured to his guide, when they stopped at last outside a gilded door.

"He's not much for head banging," murmured the other. "Bow on entering, speak when spoken to, bow before leaving, and that's about it." He turned to knock, then turned back. "Oh, yes. Don't use any words with bahs in them."

"Bahs?"

"The letter Bah, right." The secretary rapped, entered and summoned Izzy into the presence.

"Prince Izakar of Palmia," the secretary announced.

Izzy bowed.

"Come on over here," said a gruff voice.

Izzy looked up to confront an even larger version of Fasal Grun. This person was becoming grizzled with age, but his movements were agile as he beckoned to Izzy to come forward, to sit opposite him on one of the chairs set within the curve of an oriel window that looked out over the sea.

"Would you like some wine?" the emperor asked. "Cakes?"

"We have just had b—a meal, Your Majesty," said Izzy, carefully spelling each word to himself. The words, of necessity, were hesitant.

"Zarl's told me about your group," the emperor said, examining Izzy closely. "Some sort of a fortune lost? Some sort of prediction?"

Izzy took a deep breath. "Ah, Prince Sahir, of Tavor, was directed b—that is, received directions from a seer-ess to go to the Hospice at St. Weel, else some great disaster might bef—that is, happen. In my case, the prognostication came from the seeresses. I am to solve the Great Enigma or our posterity may b—that is, ah, is endangered." He fell silent, wiping his face with his pocket handkerchief.

The emperor gave him a sympathetic look, nodding. "You've been prince of Palmia for some time now."

"I have," Izzy responded.

"Nice old castle you have there. Palmody, isn't that the name of the town? Old town. Must go way, way, way back."

"Oh, it does, your Majesty. Way, way, way . . . in the past."

"Of course, your people don't believe anything went that far back, do they?"

Izzy took a deep breath. "No. No, they don't . . . accept any past that's very distant."

"I, on the other hand," mused the emperor, "and certain other people as well, do believe in a distant past."

"Do you, indeed?" said Izzy in his politest voice. "That's very interesting."

"We believe many things are left over from distant times," the emperor continued. "Ourselves, for example. Certain other creatures. Even some buildings. This one, for instance. I would say this building is at least a thousand years old."

"Amazing," murmured Izzy, wiping his face once more.

"And the building I occupy when I am at home . . . well, it's older yet. All of two thousand years. And what do you suppose exists beneath it?"

"Be—that is, under your castle, Your Majesty?"

"Exactly. What do you suppose?"

"A . . . cathedral?"

"What would that be?"

"I've heard . . . that some kind of religious build— that is, structures underlie current structures."

The emperor examined him narrowly. "Come, come, Prince Izakar. Our interests are not opposed. Isn't there something else that could underlie an old fortification?''

"Perhaps," Izzy said desperately, "Perhaps a . . . repository for, ah . . . manuscripts?''

"Why don't you say it? A library. A place for keeping books.''

"The words have bahs in them, Your Effulgence.''

"And so?''

"Your secretary told me. . . .''

"Zarl?'' Faros laughed, his humped shoulders shaking. "Up to his tricks again, is he. I despair.'' The emperor stretched his lips into a toothy grin and shook his head. "He does that. It amuses him. I should have known. Here I am, trying to find out what's going on, and here are you, busy spelling conversation to yourself. Now what is it that may lie beneath my old castle, Prince Izakar? That also, perhaps, lies beneath the castle in Palmody?''

Izzy took a deep breath and blurted, "A library, sir. A very ancient library. From times long gone.''

"Ahhhh.'' The emperor sat back in his chair, his head thrown back, his fingers gripping the arms. "So there is at least one other.''

"I thought mine was the only one,'' whispered Izzy.

"As I did mine, when I came to the throne,'' replied the emperor. "As did my father and grandfather before me. My researchers have told me there must be others.''

"I had no idea,'' murmured Izzy.

"Well, you should have had,'' grumped the emperor. "Here I am, trying to unify the world so that it won't go down the chutes again. I've been quite open about my motivation. Obviously, if I'm trying to prevent something that's happened before, I must have had knowledge of what it was that happened before. Hah?''

"I take Your Effulgence's point.'' Izzy nodded, wondering why it had escaped him until now.

"So does Fasal Grun. Good lad, Fasal Grun.'' He stared out the window for a long moment before continuing. "There's a prince with you, from Tavor. Do you trust him?

"He's been very generous during our travels, but I don't know enough about him to say one way or the other. My inclination would be to trust his companion, Nassif, more than I would him."

"She's ponjic, as you are. That would be your inclination."

"She?" Izzy gargled.

"She," said the emperor. "Dressed up like a boy, but then, that's for convenience sake, no doubt. I've heard the prince has an attendant with him, a big one?"

"Soaz? A mercenary, sir. A hireling. I would attest to his loyalty to the sultan of Tavor, but I know nothing about his sense of ethics."

"How about the countess? I've met her. She's always struck me as a practical person."

"I would say pragmatic, sir. She was very helpful on the way here."

"What about the armakfatid?"

"An enigma, Your Majesty."

"And the onchiki?"

"Well, Your Majesty, so long as something didn't come along to distract them, I'm sure they'd be quite trustworthy. If they remembered."

"My observations as well. Distractable. Charming, nonetheless. Like children."

"Exactly."

"Well, I'll leave it to you. Confide in whichever of them you choose, if you must. Otherwise, keep it to yourself." He gloomed out the window at the sun, sparkling on the sea, restlessly combing his hair with his long fingernails. A silent time went by.

Izzy shifted. "Keep what to myself, Your Majesty?"

"Ah? Oh. Yes. Well, my problem is that everything's falling apart."

"Everything?"

"Well, some things. Unexpected things. This business with Fasahd! He's always been belligerent, but he's also been loyal, up until recently. Now what do I hear? Cannibalism, that's what! You're not the first to tell me that!

Fasahd isn't bright, but he's certainly not hungry! He didn't think this up by himself. Someone has put him up to it. Then there's the trees. Why on earth should the trees be upset? We've gotten along famously for hundreds of years!

"All this distresses me, so I go to the Seeresses of Sworp, who are normally very reliable, and they tell me of dark influences, dire happenings, inimical forces. And you show up, bearing prophecies and predictions. Now I ask you! What inimical force? Eh? I'm the emperor. Who else is there?"

"Nothing untoward happening?"

"Nothing dark! Nothing dire! All these predictions, and nothing evident! How can all this tragedy be gathering without showing some sign? I have my agents out, here, there, busy as wasps on a jelly-muffin, gathering. All they hear are rumors. The destroyer is coming. The terminator has been put into action."

"What the trees call the 'walker on fire feet'?"

"I suppose. Now how do you know the trees call it that?"

"Someone mentioned it," mumbled Izzy, grasping for something to change the subject. "You think those . . . people at St. Weel could be involved?"

"Ah? It occurs to you too, does it? Process of elimination! Consider everyone else, and who's left? Hah? Those at St. Weel."

"Is Your Majesty considering conquering St. Weel?"

"No. Why would I? What's to conquer? It's a tiny little place, set high up on a cliff overlooking the sea. If those there are responsible for this disorder, I could blockade the place! Let no one in, no one out. That would stop the influence. But I'm not sure, don't you see? Maybe it's them, and maybe it's someone else."

"Your Mightiness wants me to find out which?"

"Exactly. Find out which."

"And Your Mightiness would rather not go yourself."

"Can't," brooded the emperor. "Simply can't. Whoever, whatever is prying and plotting, they'd like nothing better than for me to be off somewhere, out of touch, unable to control what's going on. No. You go. You and the Countess Elianne and the rest of you. Find out, and send me word."

"Your Mightiness . . ."

"Yes. What?"

"If . . . if I needed to use some method of which Your Mightiness would ordinarily disapprove. That is, those at St. Weel are reputed to be wizards. . . ."

"Magic? You want my permission to use magic?"

"I am merely seeking a sense of Your Greatness's wishes."

The emperor turned away, his great humped shoulders shaking. In a moment, Izzy realized he was laughing.

"By all means," the emperor said. "Use what you like. Just don't tell anyone I said so."

In the rose garden, the conversation that had taken place between Izzy and the emperor was quoted almost verbatim (so Izzy insisted) to me and the countess. We sat near an ornamental wall over which one could look over the city of Gulp to the surrounding hills or the sea. Before telling us anything, Izzy swore us to secrecy, and it was only after taking a really disgustingly terrible oath that the countess and I learned about libraries. And history. And cycles. And the fact that things in our world were much more complicated than either of us had ever known—or cared to know.

It was clear to me why Izzy had chosen the countess to hear this story. She was a very practical person who had studied the theory of government. She was, at least, able to follow what he was saying and make some sense of it. Why he had chosen me as a confidante, I had no idea. Perhaps it was merely that we were both ponjic. Though I eschew bigotry, similar racial backgrounds do count for something. I learned later he had found out I am female, and females have always been the confidantes of adventurers. It is called pillow talk—even when no pillows are involved—and it is very ancient.

"So the emperor will help us get to St. Weel?" asked the countess, cutting to the heart of the matter.

"He'll send imperial troops with us," Izzy confirmed. "There's a road from here, not a good one, but one that goes the whole way. He'll furnish wagons. We don't have to walk."

"And he postulates some inimical force?" she asked, raising her eyebrows.

"He does. And he has no more idea than we do who or what it might be. He has spies everywhere. Rumor is rampant and proof of anything disastrous is totally lacking."

"I simply can't imagine," the countess said, her brow wrinkled. "Fasahd is evil because he's envious, because he has a personality disorder. At least, that's what Blanche calls it. I've assumed it was just him, that he was the problem, so to speak, but you say the emperor believes it's someone or something else who's using Fasahd." She rotated her head upon her neck, as though working out kinks, or perhaps to make her brain work better. Her wig came a bit awry, and she straightened it, unconscious of what she was doing.

"I can't come up with a why! I am a member of the Council of Governments. Every few years we meet to discuss improving the lot of our people. I've met all the rulers, or their envoys, from Isfoin and Tavor, from Wycos and Palmia and the shore counties. By and large, all the peoples of the world—at least, as much of the world as I know about—are reasonably well housed and fed. We have sent a committee to investigate the Onchik-Dau for failure to maintain the crofts of the onchiki, but even there the evidence of misfeasance is slight. The Onchik-Dau have been heaving themselves around on the shores of the Crawling Sea, bellowing at one another for who knows how long, and we're not going to change them now! There have been no sicknesses for some time, none of those plagues we hear of in ancient tales. Festivals are frequent and well attended. Taxes are low.

Recompense is fair, and benefits for the orphaned or aged are adequate, due much, if I do say so myself, to my influence with the other rulers.

"During our next few sessions, I have hope that the various nations will see fit to offer benefits to those wanderers who contribute so much to our enjoyment: the players, the traveling musicians, the peddlers, the craftsmen, but even now, their lot is not a bad one. Conspiracy springs from disaffection, so I have been taught, and I simply cannot think of a disaffected class whose needs are not being addressed!"

"It might be something quite outside our usual sphere," commented Izzy. "Some magical or demonic force? Some invasion or subversion by foreign powers?"

The countess shook her head, as puzzled as I. "Foreign from where? Across the great ocean? No one crosses the great ocean! The transmontaine countries? Think how sparsely populated that area; think how rarely we see anyone from the transmontaine."

We are not to speak of this to the others?" I asked.

Izzy shook his head. "Countess Elianne may speak of it to her secretary, if her discretion is trusted. I would not tell anyone else among our party. At least, not yet."

"And why did you choose me to confide in?" the countess asked.

"Your attitude toward Fasahd," he murmured. "We have seen clearly that you are not allied with him. And as for you, Nassif, I chose you because I like you, though you misled me." He frowned at me sadly, shaking his head, and I knew he had at last penetrated my disguise. As I have said, Izzy is bright, but about some things he is impervious to the evidence of his senses.

He went on, "I have no reason to mistrust your Prince, but I have no reason to trust him, either. I would not confide in him yet."

I nodded in agreement. I was not sure that I trusted the Prince myself. From one day to the next, I was not sure what he was up to.

22

Incidents Leading to Liaisons

Dora came home from work to find Jared standing just outside her door, one white-knuckled hand clutching the door latch as though he had tried to get in and had forgotten to let go. He turned to stare at her, a strange, baffled look, as if he had expected someone else.

"What are you doing here, Jared?"

"I wanted to see where you're living," he said. His voice was distant, totally impersonal. "Momma gave me your address. It's very difficult to locate places now, Dora. It was very hard to find this place. I had to use the city maps and count the streets. All the street signs are overgrown." The words came in a tense monotone, each word of equal import and stretched to the breaking point.

"I'm sorry you went to all that trouble." She noticed that her voice did not quaver, though she felt it should. Jared was the last person she wanted on her doorstep, and she had no intention of letting him into her house.

"You might as well let go of the door. I'm not going to invite you in."

He merely stared with eyes that were sunken more deeply than she remembered. The lids were ringed with dark skin, almost like bruises. He had lost weight and looked haggard. Or hag ridden.

"I want you to come back to my place, Dora. I don't like living at the boardinghouse. Having ten people around. It's too . . . unsettling."

She moved uneasily, wondering whether she ought not to leave, pressing her arm against her holster to reassure herself that she was, after all, able to defend herself. "Move back into your house, Jared. It's still there. Ask your mother to find you a housekeeper."

"I don't like it there alone. I have to go in, to see to my . . . tools, but I hate all that . . . greenery. And I can't get rid of it." There was something plaintively demanding in his tone, like a whiny child. "If you come back, you can get rid of it."

"What on earth makes you think that?" she cried incredulously. "Even if I could do it, I wouldn't!"

"It tried to kill me," he said, explaining it to her in that same strained monotone, his head cocked, peering at her as though searching for something unobvious but known to be present. "I know that. And you didn't let it. So, you could make it . . . go away."

There was a question here. He was asking her something, trying to hint at something, with a threat implicit in his posture, in his tone.

She shook her head, frightened by the intensity of his expression. "Listen to what I'm telling you, Jared. I can't make it go away, I don't even want to make it go away. I like the stuff. I think it's great. If you don't want to be surrounded by greenery, move into town. There are apartment houses, hotels, lots of places the trees have left alone."

"I have to stay there where my work is," he said, stepping forward with frightening speed to fasten a hand into her hair, twisting, pulling, then dropping the hand onto her shoulder like a clamp, his thumb pressing deeply above her collarbone, his fingers making holes in her back. "And you have to help me with my work!"

"Let go of me, Jared."

He glared, his face inches from her own. "I won't. I have to stay there, in my place. All my equipment is there. And you can make the stuff go away. It didn't come until you were there."

Shuddering, she spoke between clenched teeth. "I had been there two years before it came, it came everywhere, and I had nothing to do with it. Move your tools, for God's sake!"

"No. That's where they belong. It's my place. It's where I mean to have them. . . ."

He dragged her back toward her doorway, reaching for the latch with his free hand, fingering it as though there were a combination, a special touch that would open it and let him drag her inside.

She stooped suddenly, coming away from his clamping hand and stepping back, putting distance between them. She put up a hand, rubbing at the place on her scalp where he had pulled her hair. It was tender. The air had become very still, with that dangerous hush she had learned to listen for.

"I'll make you come back," he said, craning his neck forward, showing his teeth. "It would be easier for you to just do it now, but I will use you to get rid of all this, all this stuff growing."

He made a gesture, an awkward motion, but so studied as to appear hieratic in its intention, then repeated it exactly, his eyes fixed burningly on her own. The air simmered and left her lungs in a rush. She felt dizzy, her eyes fogged, she tried to breathe and couldn't. The world began to darken.

Above Jared's head the leaflets on the weed turned in his direction, and several tendrils dropped suddenly across his face, scraping his eyelids, making him blink and push them away.

She gulped for air, suddenly released. The tendrils

were still there, fringing his face, and he batted at them, like a man fighting bees.

She gasped, "You won't make me do anything, Jared. I'm divorcing you." She put her hand on her gun but didn't pull it, preferring a weapon less dangerous, less fatal. "I . . . have a new boyfriend. He's a professor at the university. He likes trees. All this greenery doesn't bother him."

Jared's face, already gray, became ashen. "Do you . . . have you . . . does he come here?"

"Of course he comes here!"

"Does he sleep here?"

"Yes," she said, shouting the lie, making it more vehement. "He does. All the time."

He stepped away from her, mouth working as he mumbled: "That's it. You've spoiled it. Too late now. You can't do it now. I'll have to find someone else." He walked to the gate, opened it, stood for a moment framed by the side timbers, looking back at her over his shoulder. "I'll make you sorry for this, Dora. You shouldn't have moved out. You betrayed me. I needed you there and you betrayed me. You could have gone on living, but now you'll die with them. . . ."

The gate swung to behind him, closing with a solid clang. Behind her, a tree rustled, just one, then others, the movement extending from her little garden out into the woods and away west.

"What was all that?" she whispered. "What in the hell was all that?"

Was the man sane? Had he ever been sane? She stood shivering, her whole body shaking uncontrollably, hugging herself, holding herself together, shutting her eyes, taking deep breaths, trying to think of something, anything but Jared. Her scalp still hurt, and she rubbed it again. He'd pulled some hairs out, for sure. After a time she heard birdsong and realized it had been going on for a while, which meant he was gone. How she knew this was a mystery she did not want to bother to pursue.

She let herself in, carefully locking the door behind

her, stepping between boxes and over crates to be sure the large overhead garage doors were locked as well, thinking as she went up the stairs that no one could get through the bedroom or bathroom windows, overgrown as they were.

"Someone might put a ladder up against the big living room window," she told herself from the top of the stairs. "And break the glass." She stood in that window, looking out. This window was the weak point. Someone could get in that way. Not just someone, anyone, but Jared, who said he would kill her. And why in the name of heaven did he want to kill her? It was crazy!

She dropped into a chair beside the table, dug her notebook out of her purse, opened it to a clean page and wrote down everything she could remember of Jared's maundering. She had spoiled what? She couldn't do what? He would have to find what? Why? He'd fallen apart when she said she had a boyfriend. When she said the boyfriend slept over. At that point he'd stopped insisting she move back and instead he'd accused her of . . . whatever. Betrayal. Which meant . . . which meant that having a boyfriend somehow changed her own . . . status? Qualifications? For what?

He needs a virgin, an inner voice said. *Dora, he needs a virgin. He thinks a virgin can get rid of the greenery.*

She put her head into her hands as she heard her own voice making sounds, half giggle, half scream. She was imagining things. My God, what did she think he was going to do? Sacrifice her to the Tree? Use her blood as weedkiller? Jared needed a cook-housekeeper, that's all. It didn't matter who she was, so long as she kept everything clean, cooked that damned vague tomato food and kept her mouth shut.

She didn't like having made up the story she had. Lies could be dangerous. They could blow up in your face. Would he recognize the story for what it was? If he hung around out there, if he watched the house, and if he saw no one here. . . . He could lie in wait for her. Now that forest covered everything, there were so many hiding places. But . . . maybe . . . maybe she could arrange for it to be more than a mere story.

She went into the bedroom and pulled out the top bureau drawer, the little one, meant for keeping handkerchiefs or gloves, dumping it on the bureau top. She had put Abby McCord's card away among old receipts and odds and ends of makeup and a few bits of jewelry. She had promised to tell him about Harry Dionne, so she had a perfect excuse for calling him.

The phone rang six times before he answered. "McCord."

She cleared her throat. "Abby, it's Dora Henry. I told you I'd let you know when I spoke with Harry Dionne. I had breakfast with him recently. Would you like to come over for a drink? I'll tell you about it."

Long silence. "Can I get there? Can I find the place?"

"You can drive as far as the avenue. I'll meet you at the corner. It's only half a dozen blocks."

He wrote down the landmarks she gave him and told her he'd be there in thirty minutes. She took twenty of them to straighten up the place, check that there was beer in the fridge, and get out some chips and salsa. She had wine, too, if he'd rather. She'd bought herself half a dozen bottles as a housewarming gift. As she was about to leave, she turned back and got two steaks out of the freezer and put them in the microwave on thaw. Maybe he'd stay to dinner.

Wind chased her bicycle, scudding her like a leaf beneath the overhanging branches. She had thought she might be late, but it was almost twenty minutes more before Abby's little red car showed up, the convertible top raised against the threatening sky.

Dora motioned him to come over and park next to the tree that minded her bicycle for her. When he did so, she spoke to the tree, conscious of his eyes on her. "This is my friend, Abilene McCord. This is his car. Will you watch it for him, please, until he comes back?"

Branches lowered protectively. She turned to find him staring at her, brow furrowed in concentration. "It's all right,'' she said, fighting the laughter that threatened to erupt. "The tree won't let anyone fool with your car."

He backed away from the tree, watching, finally turning to walk beside her as she wheeled her bike down the curving path that had once been a quiet residential street.

"After what you showed me the other day, that shouldn't have surprised me, but it did. Why haven't the trees invaded the campus? They've let the campus mostly alone."

Dora nodded. "Also the football stadium, and the baseball park and the parking areas around them. They've left the city park fairly open, as well, though a lot of trees have come up in the zoo, in the enclosures and along the paths. Highways aren't bothered. Railways aren't bothered. The airport is still wide open. Downtown parking lots are open, just like the downtown streets. But the suburbs . . ." She shook her head.

"Doesn't it all imply motivation?"

She wiped a lone raindrop from her nose, squinting up at the lowering clouds. "I stopped by the library the other day to look up some articles I sort of half remembered. All over the world, cities and highways have been eating up the best land—I mean, the most fertile land, the best for growing things. Maybe the trees want to take it back."

"By making it difficult for suburban housing and streets? Why are they taking it easy on cities and public transportation?"

Dora grinned, remembering Grandma. "Maybe they don't want to kill us, just teach us a lesson."

He made a doubtful noise in his throat. "What did you find out from Harry Dionne?"

"Wait until we get to my place," she said. "Then I'll tell you all about it."

She put out beer, salsa and chips on the table by the window and pulled out the two leather chairs so they could look out at the grassy swale that led away to the clear line of sky between mountains and cloud. From long habit, she got out her notebook and went over the conversation she'd had with Harry Dionne, including the bits about Jared and the girl, but leaving out Harry's reference to women's "kernel of wildness." If she still had some wildness floating around, that was her business.

"Phil told me about your ex-husband," Abby remarked when she had finished. "Phil said he was a stick."

"In all the time I've known Jared, he's been almost completely unemotional," she admitted. "Though when he was here tonight—"

"Tonight?"

"He was waiting for me outside when I got home from work. He thought I would be able to remove the 'greenery' from around his house, the one we lived in."

"Why on earth . . . ?"

She shrugged, uncomfortably. "He got stung, and I guess I was responsible for saving his life. The only logical explanation I can come up with for his attitude is that he misinterpreted my saving him. It wasn't that I had any power over the growth, it's just that I knew CPR. And considering how he looked, I think the poison has affected his mind."

"Phil says he works for Pacific-Alaskan. If I were a tree, that would make him enemy number one. I'm not surprised he got stung."

She dipped a chip and munched it slowly. "You questioned motivation a few minutes ago. Are you now implying that the trees might know who Jared works for?"

"If they're aware enough to guard my car because you ask them to, or to provide me with a cutting because I ask them to, then, yes, they're aware enough to know what we do for a living. At least those of us who might prove to be threatening."

She mused. "I know Jared is a neatness freak, but I never thought of him as anti-tree, in a general way. Trees are his business. He talks a lot about sustainable yield . . ."

Abby snorted. "Sustainable yield means a single-species tree farm, which is about as far from a forest as you can get without paving it over. You know those ads Pacific-Alaskan runs on TV? The ones where the little girl asks if there will always be trees, and the company spokesman shows us his damn tree farm and says, Yes, Virginia, there really will be trees, as he walks down these endless beds of absolutely uniform seedlings. It's a case where you can't see the forest for the trees, because there is no forest! No birds, no wildflowers, no butterflies, no nothing but those rows and rows of absolutely uniform pines.

"One thing I notice about the woods out there—" he gestured toward the window "—I can count fifteen distinct species from here. That's just trees. Plus shrubs and grasses and various kinds of forbs. Harry Dionne was right to say other things than trees live in forests. I'd be amazed if there aren't all kinds of birds and insects and probably small mammals. . . ."

"Birds," she agreed. "The birdsong gets louder every day. I've given up using an alarm clock. I don't know about small mammals. I haven't really looked."

"Let's look," he said, rising, reaching out to take her by the hand. "Right now."

Bemusedly, she followed him down the stairs and out into the woods, through the narrow belt of trees beside the swale and then down the swale itself, away from the house. The last of the sun dropped beneath the blanket of muttering cloud to shine in their eyes. Looking back, Dora saw her window reflecting the sunset, shining like a golden mirror.

"There," he whispered. "Squirrel, up on that branch to your right."

She looked up to meet bright, black eyes peering down at her. The squirrel chattered and jerked his tail, making it flow in a sinuous curve. As he did so, something tiny and brown zipped across the grasses from behind one tree to another.

"Mouse?" she asked.

"Umm," he replied. "Or vole or ground squirrel. Whoa." He put his hand on her shoulder. "Look. Through the trees. There."

She followed his gaze to see a procession in black-and-white, a large skunk followed by four little ones, the five animals strung out like a child's pull toy, the line of them elongating, then clashing together, then stretching out again, tails waving, little feet trotting. The mother skunk took no notice of them as she crossed the swale and disappeared into the trees, her children following after.

"What else?" she whispered, enchanted.

"Oh, if we wanted to stay out, we'd probably see owls and maybe raccoons, and possibly coyotes. Some kind of cat, probably. Either a domestic cat gone wild or maybe a bobcat. It may be too soon for bobcat or deer to have invaded from the mountains, but I have no doubt they will. There! Look."

She saw a seemingly boneless form sliding up a slanting trunk. "What?"

"Weasel, I think. Too small to be anything else. Not close enough to water to be mink, not big enough for fisher. Since you have so many birds, I could have predicted some predator on eggs and baby birds." He stood staring into the treetops, ducking suddenly as a spate of huge raindrops splattered across his face. "I don't see a nest anywhere, and it's going to be too wet to look." He grabbed her arm and began to run. "Come on. Back to your house. If there's a restaurant within walking distance, I'll take you to dinner."

"There is, but I don't want to walk with it doing this! I've got steaks, and salad stuff. . . ."

He came inside after her, shutting the door behind them. "Isn't that a great idea! If I'd known, I'd have brought wine."

Wordlessly, she got out the wine. They had more beer while the steaks finished thawing, then wine with the steaks, drinking so thirstily that Dora opened a second bottle. They ate to the scent of wet leaves, the sound of rain, which kept falling with a hard, steady drumming on the roof. When the food was gone to the last shred, they put the dishes in the dishwasher and Dora got out a frozen dessert, pastry and ice cream, and they ate that as greedily, finishing the whole thing.

"It says serves six," she commented, looking ruefully at the empty package.

"Six midgets," he remarked comfortably, leaning back on the couch and placing his saucer on his flat stomach, holding it horizontal with a relaxed finger while the other hand plied the coffee cup. "Good food, good wine, good coffee."

"One of my few luxuries," she said. "Grandma always loved her coffee, and she always bought the beans and ground them fresh."

"And you eat," he remarked. "It's great to see a woman eat. I get so sick of that dieting talk." His eyes were fixed on her face, wholly approving.

"I'm lucky," she said, feeling his glance on her skin as though it reached through her clothes, like microwaves. "If I don't do this too often, my weight pretty well stays down. I burn calories. My friend Loulee, she's always dieting, but she doesn't eat anywhere near as much as I do. She's got fat genes. She can't help it." She flushed, aware she was babbling.

"Dora?"

"Ummm."

"You're as nervous as a cat! Are you worried that Jared might come back?" There was concern in his voice, almost tenderness.

Blankness. Here was a fork in the road. Did she take a step, or back off? Turn around, maybe, go somewhere else. Was she worried that Jared might come back? Well, wasn't that the reason she'd asked him to come over?

She swallowed and fought down the urge to run. "I guess. I mean, yes. Yes, of course. That was in my mind when I called you. I thought, if he came back, or if he hung around out there, he'd see I had company, and he'd go away."

"I can sleep on your couch. Quite frankly, I'd just as soon not go out in that downpour, if you don't mind."

She blushed, feeling the heat move from her throat onto her breast.

As though aware of her discomfort, he went to the window, turning his back to her, leaning against the glass and peering out at the downpour. "Do you realize it's been only a century that we've been able to go from house to car to office to car to wherever, with the heater on, and the defroster on, protected from the rain and the cold? It hasn't been much longer than that we've had lighting for streets. Think of all that darkness, all that world out there, all that mystery that we've turned into well-lighted concrete bunkers, safe and warm and dull."

She took a deep breath and got up to refill her coffee cup. Since she was on her feet, she went to stand beside him. It was almost totally dark. The woods could hide legions of shadowy attackers. The moon wouldn't rise until the early morning, if the sky cleared. It was raining hard. It wouldn't be polite to make Abby go out into the rain. . . .

"You can stay here, Abby. The couch is a sofa bed. It's more comfortable unfolded."

"Either way," he said from close beside her, his lips at her ear. "Folded or unfolded."

Her heart drummed, she felt the beginnings of panic. Leaning away from him she pushed the casements farther open, letting in the night. A heavy fragrance came on the moist air, flowery, musky, with something else in it, something she remembered from her breakfast with Harry Dionne. That strong, not unpleasant odor which she identified suddenly as a rain-on-the-garden smell: moist leaves, fecund soil. She took a deep breath, and another, as though she could not breathe deeply enough. When she turned he was close, and his arms went around her, pulling her against him until she felt the heat of his body through the light shirt he was wearing, felt the strength of his arms gathering her in.

Warm, and the smell of his skin, and the feel of his

arms. If she just let go, maybe there'd be trumpets. . . .
Oh, lord, she'd love some trumpets. Still . . . still!

"Abby . . ." she murmured. "Please. It's too . . .
quick."

He gave her a quick squeeze and released her. "It's
okay, delightful Dora. You don't need to worry about
me. An invitation to sleep on your couch is not an invitation to anything else. I know that."

He moved away, began gathering up the glasses, grinning at her, striking an elder-statesman pose, left hand
on chest, right hand raised as though taking an oath.
"Though my virtues have not been fully developed
without a good deal of effort, through long association
with a good wife who took great pains with my enlightenment, I have become one of those rare and wonderful
men who are able, with some degree of sincerity, to
pride themselves on being unmacho about sexual matters."

She felt the little laugh that bubbled up in her throat.
"Then you have lots of women friends, don't you?"

"The women I like well enough to get to know are
my friends, yes. How did you know?" He took the
glasses to the kitchen, rinsed them, glancing at her over
his shoulder. "You're thinking that we hardly know one
another."

She nodded. "We've met twice."

He grinned again. "You're perfectly right. We don't
know one another. But time will remedy that. I say this
merely to indicate that I'm willing to take time. Not an
eternity, of course, but a lengthy spell."

She fetched him a pillow, helped him find a book, put
out clean towels. She took herself off to bed and fell
asleep almost at once, surprisingly unworried, or maybe,
so she drowsily told herself, only rather drunk.

Sometime later, she thought she woke.

The world where she found herself was a rock-strewn
desert, with pillars of stone standing like chessmen on
calcined soil. She was walking toward one such pillar,
desirous of its shade, for the sun had burned her dry.

Her feet scuffed sand. Her breath rasped. The shade lay ahead of her, like a dark road, leading to the stone pillar itself. She came within the shadow and looked up to see an erose edge, the stone fanged with living things, angularly huddled shapes that looked down at her and cried out to one another in a strange tongue that she, nonetheless, understood: "See, there's one. There's one!"

She screamed and fled, out into the sands once more. . . . And woke, listening for the sound that had roused her.

There were wings outside, heavy wings, less crisp than the *snap, snap, snap* of a crow flight, far less silent than an owl. The roof creaked above the corner of the bedroom as though something weighty had just landed there, and through the window came the carrion smell of something long dead. The thing on the roof took a step, then another, coming across the roof toward the eave just above the window.

She came out of the bed in a flash, her hand going to the side of her head, where Jared had pulled those hairs loose. Momma had said it, Jared would have had her back by now, except she'd cleaned the house too well. She hadn't left any hair. No fingernail clippings. No sweat on the sheets. No flakes of skin in the carpet. . . .

Above her, the thing moved, another step toward the window.

The sofa springs creaked in the living room, once, then again. Abby said something to himself. There was a stumble, a muffled curse, and footsteps as he rose and went into the kitchen. Pipes banged, water ran and splashed. In a moment he went back to his bed.

When the silence returned, she listened for the heavy footsteps over her head, but they did not come again. She sniffed for the carrion smell, but it was gone.

Perhaps it had only come to learn if she'd been telling the truth.

Perhaps she had dreamed it. Perhaps.

*　　*　　*

When she arrived at work the following morning, Dora made a point of being very brisk and businesslike. She had the idea that anyone who looked at her could probably tell she'd spent the night with . . . well, something or somebody. Seeing herself in the mirror when she got up, she had thought it possible. She looked flustered. Definitely flustered, and it wasn't Abby's fault. He had gone early, before full light, refusing her company for the six-block walk to the avenue.

"Just tell the tree the car's yours," she'd remarked sleepily when he poked his head into the bedroom to say good-bye. "It'll probably remember, anyhow."

Then she was asleep again in the half light, until the birds woke her, caroling under a sky cleared by the night's rain. When she was brushing her teeth, she remembered the night visitation and stopped, mouth foaming, to stare at herself in the mirror. Had she dreamed that? Well, of course. She must have dreamed that.

Still, the sense of apprehension stayed with her, showing up as a pinched pallor around her mouth, a tendency to look over her shoulder. Phil didn't notice. He plumped himself down across from her in the office, already in full cry.

"Charlene is fit to be tied," he announced portentously.

"What's the matter with Charlene?"

"Well, hell, you know Charlene. Nothing stops her. She's like the postal service is supposed to be, not heat nor rain nor dark of night, you know. So she's got this listing on a house out on the edge of town, and even though you've got to walk most of half a mile to get there, she's been showing it right along, trees or no trees. So, yesterday afternoon she takes some people out there . . ."

"And?"

"And the house is gone."

"Gone?"

"Gone. I don't mean lost or strayed or stolen, I mean gone. The foundation is still there, most of the fence and the front gate, but the place is gone. Now there's just woods.''

"You think the trees ate it?"

"Who knows. This isn't all. Naturally, Charlene is some upset. She can't get a commission on a house that isn't there anymore. So she calls her boss, and they get to bitching about one thing and another, and her boss tells her about this house being listed by a young couple because he's been transferred to the coast, and it had two bedrooms, right, one for the young couple and one for the kids maybe someday. Only now it's only got one bedroom. The other bedroom got filled in.''

"Filled in?" she asked, hollowly. "You mean, trees growing in it?"

"I mean, the outside corner walls are gone and the roof over that corner of the house is gone, and the floor is gone and there's only one bedroom.''

"Unused space," she murmured, looking at the far wall as though consulting a crystal ball. "What about window screens? My trees made me window screens. And a hammock.''

"I didn't hear about window screens. I did hear about this place that had a leaky roof, only now there's new roof tiles made out of bark, and they don't leak.''

"The paper hasn't said a word about stuff like that.''

"Maybe the paper doesn't know. When Charlene talks about it, she whispers, like it was a secret. Like if she spoke out loud, something might come out of the woodwork and eat her.''

"I wonder if Abby McCord knows," she said. "Somebody ought to tell him.''

"So tell him," said Phil, shuffling his papers. "I called him last night, but he wasn't home.''

Her face went up in flames, but Phil didn't notice. He was busy hunting for something he couldn't find.

The captain came out of his office and leaned on the desk.

"You got some time?"

Phil said, "Sure. I mean, we're still working on the

Winston thing. Everybody loved the guy, so up till now we haven't found a motive, much less an idea who. We've got a—"

He'd been going to say that they had a new lead, but the captain interrupted. "Could you and Dora see this woman? The uniforms are two or three hours behind, responding to emergencies, people trapped or hurt or lost. Lots of people are lost. This woman has a baby gone. Disappeared."

"Kidnapped?" Dora asked.

"She just says gone. Go out there, will you?"

Dora grabbed the dogeared city map and they went. Phil drove and she counted streets. They stopped once or twice to pull growth away from street signs so they could read them, and they had to walk the last three blocks. Phil left the engine running and the lights on.

"You mean to do that?" she asked him.

"Guys downstairs say if you leave the engine on, the trees don't grow up around it," he said. "Firetrucks found that out. You leave something running, they leave it alone."

The woman was waiting for them on the front porch, largely pregnant, sitting among a cluster of shiny-faced children. Five, Dora counted, all under school age.

"You're Mrs. Holmes?"

The woman nodded, wiping her eyes with the hem of her dress. "Alesha's gone," she said. "I put her in her crib while she had her bottle. She usually plays there by her own self for a while, until Bobby and Francis get off to school and the others get fed. I went to get her and she's gone."

"Let us see the room," said Phil. "Where she was."

They went into the house, through a clean but cluttered living room and into a long hall with doors down both sides. The second door on the right was open, and they went in to see a crib and a double bed. "This is the girls' room," the woman said wearily. "We had more bedrooms, but the trees took the others. We didn't even have a chance to get the beds out."

"How many girls?" asked Dora, in a hushed voice.

"Four. The baby and these three," she said, indicating the three small children who had seated themselves on the bed. The fourth and fifth child stood in the door. "Four boys. Those two and Bobby and Francis. They've got one room, too. Jake wants us to have a football team, eleven boys, so we had six bedrooms and the sleeping porch out back, but that's all the trees left us—three bedrooms. One for the boys, one for the girls, and one for Jake and me."

Dora tried the windows, which were locked. She went down the hall, opening the other doors, finding forest outside three of them on the left, a bathroom and two other bedrooms on the right, forest outside the door at the end of the hall. Even though there were sizeable trees just outside the left-hand doors, there was enough space for a person to have come in between them and entered the house. Anyone could have. Dora didn't think anyone had.

"Jake says he'll nail them shut," said the woman from close behind her. "He just hasn't got to it yet."

Phil asked about the baby, age, weight, how dressed. Dora wrote it all down. She asked for a photograph and the woman came up with a fuzzy polaroid shot of a stout little pajamaed figure standing up in her crib, grinning toothlessly beneath a single upturned flip of light hair.

Then they hiked back to the car and sat in it, stunned.

"It's like Charlene's boss told her," said Phil, at last. "The woods just kind of ate parts of the house."

"It left them one bedroom for the boys, one for the girls, and one for the adults," said Dora. "Maybe that's all it figures people need."

"Some places in the world, a family'd live all in one room," Phil said. "You know. Like on the Discovery Channel. Or *National Geographic*. Those tribes along the Amazon. They don't even have beds, just hammocks. Or grass mats." He ran his fingers through his thinning hair. "Maybe this is just the first step."

"You and Charlene still have a guest room?"

"The dogs sleep in the guest room, and it was still there this morning when Charlene took them out for their walk."

"Let's get back to the office. I want to call Abby McCord."

She did call Abby, finding him in his own office. She'd planned to tell him about Charlene's experiences and the missing bedrooms and the missing baby, but first she found herself answering a lengthy interrogation about how she'd slept, and how she felt, and how much Abby had enjoyed the evening, and, and . . .

Finally he asked, "So, what's going on?"

Dora told him, then surprised herself by saying, "I think the trees decided that woman had enough children. They're not going to let her have any more."

"She has . . . what did you say? Eight left?"

"Today she does. Plus one in the oven. I have no idea how many she'll have tomorrow."

"You think the trees . . . what? Killed the baby? Ate it, like maybe it ate the cows?"

"Or relocated it. Lots of people want children who don't have them."

Long silence. Then a murmur, "Speaking of relocation, would you mind if I relocated to your place tonight? I'll bring supper."

Her ears turned warm. She started to say, no, not tonight, too soon, too much, too quick, but the words wouldn't come. Besides . . . besides, there were those bad dreams. That was a good enough reason. "I'd really appreciate the company," she murmured back, feeling the words like honey on her tongue. Oh, God, she was . . . she was, well, whatever she was!

"About seven," he almost whispered, over a voice husky with enjoyment. "I've got some stuff to take care of first."

She hung up and stared at the phone, looking up at last to see Phil staring at her.

"What would you appreciate?" he asked.

"Abby and I are having dinner together."

THE FAMILY TREE ℂ 265

"I told you!" he crowed. "Nice guy, isn't he?"

"He's very nice," she said, desperately trying to keep her face nice and neutral. "And you were very sweet to think of me, Phil. I take back anything I said to the contrary."

"Women," he snorted. "Don't even know what's good for you."

"No," she agreed. "We're just like men in that regard."

He grumbled his way off somewhere, leaving her wondering, what was good for her? She flushed, yet again. Tonight, suppose she said yes. Not that she planned to, but suppose she did. It would not be a good idea to go getting pregnant right off the bat. Getting pregnant would definitely not be a good thing right now.

When Phil went to the men's room, she called Dr. Silva and said it was an emergency. Her doctor said there'd been a lot of those recently and come over around four.

"What kind of emergencies were you talking about?" Dora asked as she put on her shoes after the exam. "You said you had a lot of them."

Dr. Rebecca Silva stripped off her gloves and wrote something on the chart in a minuscule hand. "False pregnancies. Women we thought were pregnant who aren't anymore," she said. "At last count, I had eleven of them."

Dora held up her hand like a traffic cop. "Let me see if I can guess. They all have other children, probably more than one."

Dr. Silva frowned. "Let me think. A couple of them are new patients, it'll be in their histories, but I don't remember off hand. The others, the old-timers, yes. I've delivered other children. I don't know, two or three, maybe, but certainly more than one. How did you know that?"

Dora rubbed her brow. "Let me tell you a story, and you tell me what you think. There are these trees, suddenly growing everywhere. At the edges of the town, any houses that're left vacant disappear. The trees eat them. Occupied houses, the trees eat any room that isn't used. In some occupied houses, where there are a lot of children, the trees eat all the bedrooms except three, one for boys, one for girls, one for the adults. I don't know about grandparents. Or aunts or uncles. Also, where there are large numbers of children, babies disappear . . ."

"Babies . . ."

"Disappear. This afternoon, Phil—Phil's my partner—and I went with a police dog team out to a house on Cayuga, pretty far out, and we had the dog sniff the crib where the baby had been, and then we went out looking for the baby. The dog smelled the trees and the grass and took a drink from the creek and chased a rabbit. This is one of the best tracking dogs known to the department. The guy who trains them, he and his dogs have found people in places you wouldn't believe, but today, nothing."

"Well, whoever took the baby probably carried it . . ."

"Right. And this dog should have been able to smell that. It was moist, but there wasn't any rain to wash it away, so the smell should have lingered on the air. He didn't smell anything. Which says to me, the baby didn't leave the house. Not as a baby."

"As what?"

"I think the trees ate it. Very gently and peacefully and without hurting it. The kid never yelled. I had eight brothers and sisters, so I figure if it had been hurt, it would have yelled. She would have."

Dr. Silva looked at her, appalled. "You're not serious."

"Right, I'm not serious. So, can I have the pills?"

"Here's the prescription. I'm still using a virgin spec on you, Dora, which is unusual in this day and at your age. I presume you intend to change your status. Please discuss sexual diseases with the intended. The pills are only for birth control; they won't protect you against the bad stuff. At this point in your cycle, you should be okay. Start the pills after your next period. If you don't get your period within the next week, come see me." She made a note. "You were just kidding about the baby, weren't you? I wouldn't recommend your telling that one where any media reporter can hear you."

"Right." Dora smiled again, feeling the falsity of it. A false smile moved your face differently. It felt stretched, as though it weren't participating. "And you were just kidding about those false pregnancies, weren't you?"

Dr. Silva's mouth opened, but nothing came out.

Opalears: From Seeresses to St. Weel

Prince Sahir was terribly annoyed. It was he who had wanted an audience with the emperor, but it was Prince Izakar who got it. It was Prince Sahir whose guards and handlers were so much in evidence, and it was Prince Izzy who was telling them when and where and what for. I could feel the explosion coming. I went in search of Soaz, finding him near the stables.

"Will you please go up there and talk to the two princes?" I begged him. "Prince Izakar is becoming all too authoritative, and Prince Sahir is resenting it. Something is going to blow up, and I can't imagine it would be wise to have the emperor angry at us just now."

Soaz made a troubled sound in his throat and went off to see to the two boys while I wandered around the stable yard, kicking bits of umminhi kibble that had been dropped by the grooms. Most of the mounts in the stable were horses, but people like the emperor preferred carriages or chariots, and the umminhi were evidently used to pull the imperial vehicle that stood in the nearby carriage house, large and golden and carved all over with mythical creatures.

When I thought it was safe, I went back up to the broad terrace outside the palace. Things were a bit quieter, though Sahir was still simmering. Prince Izakar was speaking to him in a conciliatory tone, while Soaz looked on benignly, his armored hand on Izzy's shoulder, one of the claws just tickling his neck. I wondered if the effect was calculated, deciding it was.

Izzy looked up at me and grinned. "The emperor is giving us two wagons. They'll be ready tomorrow, and I've asked for a meeting with the Seers of Sworp—"

"Thereby delaying us unnecessarily," said Sahir in his most annoying drawl. "I prefer to leave today. Soaz, will you see to it."

The air simmered again. Soaz took a deep breath. And then, from under the portico, came a languid voice. "Oh, Prince Sahir. And I was so looking forward to traveling with you."

"As you shall," said the prince, gallantly bowing in the countess's direction.

She was dressed all in pink, with ruffles that fluttered as she said, "Oh, I wish I could. Unfortunately, I've made plans here in Gulp for today. Will you let me join you tomorrow, Prince Izakar?"

Izzy looked at me, then at the countess, heaving a deep breath as he replied, "But of course, Countess Elianne. . . ."

"It doesn't really matter," grated Sahir in an ungraceful tone. "Tomorrow will do as well."

"Oh, good," she replied, giving him a melting glance. "We were such a congenial group. I did hate to see it broken up prematurely."

The countess smiled, Izzy smiled, even Sahir smiled, going to offer the countess his shoulder to lean upon. She twirled her parasol—which she did not need, it was quite cloudy—and she and Sahir wandered off in the direction, so I supposed, of the gardens.

Soaz sighed. "Sex," he growled.

"So I'm told," said Izzy.

"So I'm told, as well," I giggled, and the two of us went into a fit of laughter while Soaz stared at us out of his amber eyes. Fasal Grun came out of the residence accompanied by two guards, and we became at once serious, bowing to him as he approached. He was easy to respect. He had an almost awesome dignity, and Izzy said the emperor was even more impressive.

"Has it been settled that you leave tomorrow?" he asked in a quiet voice, with only a hint of a growl in it.

"It has, Your Excellency," said Soaz. "Prince Sahir agrees that the delay will not be inconvenient."

"Nice of him," said the viceroy. "Is it true that both he and you, Prince Izakar, were given warnings by the same seeress?"

"We have no way of knowing for sure," said Izakar. "A woman from Sworp made a prophecy at my birth. She subsequently went into the desert east of Isfoin, where a similar woman gave a reading of the bones to Prince Sahir's father. She could have been the same woman. That's one reason I want to meet with the Seeresses of Sworp, to see what they have to say. I don't know how it works. Do several of them have the same vision? Or do they have separate ones? Is there anything that the rest of them know that would explain about this Great Enigma business?"

"I have no idea," said Fasal Grun. "The emperor has let it be known that he prefers I not consult the society, but in view of your proposed trip to St. Weel, he has no objection to your doing so."

"I'm taking Nassif with me," said Izzy. "Just to make a record of the event."

Fasal Grun hunched his shoulders, stared at me for a moment, then waved a big hand as though shooing off flies. Evidently he cared not if I accompanied the prince.

Accordingly, we went. One of the palace servants led us to the place, not far from the residence, a shabby old building set in a kind of sculpture park where ornamental poultry stalked about and fountains either played or dribbled, depending upon their state of repair. We were met at the door by one of the seeresses, as we could tell by her dress. All of them wore high-necked gowns and tall forward curled hats with lappets down the sides. She led us into a central room, a kind of assembly hall, where the benches were arranged in circles, one within another. The central ones were crowded with the members of the society. We went down an aisle into the middle, where we were offered a bench of our own. I sat. Izzy stood, talking quietly with our guide about our reasons for coming.

When they had finished their conversation, the seeress told the others about our trip, why and how it was occasioned and what part the midwife-seeress had had in it, concluding with, "Prince Izakar of Palmia, Prince Sahir of Tavor, together with their companions, wish to consult our society for clarification of the purpose of their journey."

Silence. No one spoke. All the seeresses sat quietly, eyes closed, some of them rocking a little back and forth, some of them holding hands in pairs or trios, most of them so still it was hard to tell if they were alive. Their robes were all alike, their hats were all alike, even their faces were similar as they were all members of the ponjic tribe, though much leaner than Izzy or I, with more delicate chins and cheekbones.

Izzy came over and sat down beside me. "It may take a long while," he murmured. "Just relax."

"What are they doing?" I asked.

"Making their minds empty," he said. "Evidently these visions simply drop in, as you say the language of the onchiki dropped in, as Countess Elianne says the meaning of the armakfatidi drops in."

We sat. We waited. After a very long time, the seeress who had shown us in—I was fairly sure it was the same one—took us out into the hall and gave us some tea and biscuits and allowed us to visit the sanitary arrangement. When we had stretched and refreshed ourselves, we went back to our bench, and along about midafternoon the seeresses began to rouse, to stretch, to make casual remarks to one another, to get up and wander about.

I looked at Izzy, my eyebrows raised, and he returned the look. We had no idea if they had found out anything at all, and we were not enlightened until the group had first dispersed to the tea tables and then, after much drinking and discussion in corners, reassembled.

"There is a threat," their spokesperson told us. "The threat begins with some person having gone on a journey. This happened in the past, it is nothing that may be prevented, for it has already occurred. The result of this journey is a threat to all our lives, all the people of the world, every nation and every tribe. Various ones of us see this journey taking place, but we cannot understand what we see! There is something about the journey that is strange, weird, contrary to good sense. This may be why our sister called it the Great Enigma.

"We are agreed that the threat may be countered, though we do not know how. Our vision tells us that our sister was correct when she directed the sultan to St. Weel."

"What did they see?" I whispered to Izzy.

He shook his head at me, but one of the seeresses had heard me. "Child," she said, "at the end of our seeing we saw this world empty of intelligent life. We saw brute beasts and only they."

And that was all they told us. Izzy was somewhat downcast, and I didn't blame him. I put my arms around him and he leaned on my shoulder, cursing in a monotone, quite unlike his usually cheerful self.

I said, "Come, Prince Izakar! We are on an adventure! You must not give way like this. We must be indomitable, as all heroes are."

"I don't feel at all heroic," he said. "So far on this trip, I've mostly felt nauseated. Sometimes it's the magic and sometimes it's the food, but my stomach doesn't know the difference."

"You've been eating food prepared by Sahir's servants," I said. "It's too rich for our people. We need more fruit, more fiber. A bit of stewed kale would set you up. Come now. An upset tummy is no reason for giving way like this." I shook him a little, as I remembered my father shaking me when I was impossible.

It amused him. He smiled, though a wavering smile, and said, "Acquiring a taste for stewed kale is an enterprise surely to fail, for it's stuffed full of fiber like reeds on the Giber and tastes like they'd serve it in jail."

I laughed dutifully, for my father had had a taste both for kale and for the limeriki verse form, and so we walked back to the residence of the viceroy hand in hand, knowing little we had not known that morning. Someone had gone on a journey, and that fatal journey was a risk to us all. Who or why was as far as the stars, and St. Weel was not much closer.

Opalears: Incidents Leading to Liaisons

*"Long ago, so it is written, when great Korè walked
openly in the lands of the people, none were so fair to
her as the kapriel who accompanied her journeys, who
went with her into the forests and plains, clearing the
way before her, plucking up flowers which they put into
her hands. The kapriel, so it is said, remember the ways
of the wild, and as animal handlers they have made a
place for themselves which cannot be filled by any other
people.*

THE PEOPLES OF EARTH
HIS EXCELLENCY, EMPEROR FAROS VII

Our party, numbering fifteen persons and creatures
plus the imperial guards and a number of kapriel
handlers, to attend to the umminhi, set out on the following morning, two wagons pulled by teams of four
umminhi, full of us and our baggage, plus another
wagon for the veebles, plus a saddle umminhi for Prince
Izzy and a horse for Soaz. The emperor's ersuniel guards
walked beside the wagons, leading the teams that pulled

us. One of the guards, a grizzled oldster, knew the way to St. Weel, and he was our guide. Oyk ranged ahead along the road, while Irk brought up the rear.

Sahir and the countess did well enough in the wagon, with Dzilobommo and Blanche. The onchiki sometimes ran alongside, sometimes rode on the horse behind Soaz, sometimes climbed in the wagon with the veebles and went to sleep. When night came, we made camp with a good deal of ceremony. Tents were pitched, fires were lit, the umminhi were attached to picket lines downwind of us, six here, seven there. In the night I heard the umminhi crying from one line to the other, a strange, mournful sound. *Owaionglai. Owaionglai.* The guards stood watch, turn and turn about all night, calling the hours as though we had been in a city. I was bedded in a tent with the onchiki, which I was glad of, for they were warm companions, better than a blanket.

The nights became more chill, for we were climbing. There was no way along the shore, and even if there had been, we would have eschewed it, for it would have exposed us on the seaward side, where Fasahd was. In time, we would come over the high pass and descend again almost to the level of the Crawling Sea, for St. Weel was located on the sea cliffs.

On the fourth day, we began to encounter fields of flowers, clearings packed with riotous bloom in all shades of pink and red and purple, emitting a fragrance that was overwhelming. The gervatch flower, said the oldster who guided us. It bloomed in the lands around St. Weel and nowhere else, and we must not sleep among the flowers for at night their fragrance became chokingly dense. It was at night the nectar-bats came to fertilize the flowers. Seeing these fields had the effect of making us more eager, for, as Izzy reminded us, *them* trees had mentioned the gervatch flower.

On the fifth evening, we looked northward across a chasm and saw the walls of St. Weel growing from the top of the sea cliffs. The place was not particularly impressive, not so tall or broad as I had imagined.

"Most of it is hidden in the cliffs," said our guide. "All that whole rock wall is hollowed out. That bit showing there at the top is the tower, and the only way we can come at it is from below."

The next day was spent going down into the chasm by a breakneck road, which was narrow and quite frightening to the countess. She made little sounds of fear as she separated herself from the cliffside by judicious placement of her parasol, while Blanche made unkind remarks about 'fraidy cats—not apropos of the countess at all. When we reached the bottom of the chasm, we found that the road turned right, toward the sea, and by evening we had come out from the cliffs onto the shore. Above us, the tower of St. Weel burned in the evening sun, at the top of another winding road. It was late, and we were weary, so we postponed our approach to the height until the morrow.

It proved to be an unwise decision.

We made camp, or rather, the emperor's guards did. The umminhi were picketed back in a wooded cut in the shore cliffs, the veebles in another such, on long lines to allow them to graze. Dzilobommo oversaw preparation of an evening meal, created both from the stores we had brought from Gulp and things he had gathered along the trail: fish, for example, and the curly tops of ferns, and the roots of certain marsh plants. We let the fire go out and retired to bed. It was a clear night, and the moon was full, unfortunately, for its intrusive beams disclosed our tents to the ship which had evidently been sailing up and down the coast, looking for us.

The first we knew of it was when a guard, alerted by the sound of a keel rubbing the gravel of the shore, called out, "Ware," in a hysterical, just-alerted voice. Luckily, the boat had come ashore some distance down the beach, and the little time this provided was decisive.

Izzy shouted something at me about getting Blanche and the countess to safety, which I tried my best to do by dragging them both, still more than half asleep, into the trees at the mouth of the chasm where we had earlier tethered the veebles. We hid behind some convenient shrubbery from which we peeked out, trying to see what was happening.

The boat which had come ashore was a fairly small one, containing only eight or ten ruffians. I knew them for Fasahd's people, though the countess said none of them were large enough to be ersuniel. All we could see was shadowy forms and confused movement, and all we could hear were grunts and curses interspersed with yelps of pain. We were not outnumbered. Soaz, Izzy and Sahir had been trained to fight. Dzilobommo, said the countess, came from a warrior race. In addition, there were the onchiki who rushed among the attackers, cutting them about the legs and ankles, plus the ten guards the emperor had leant us, all of them well armed and armored.

I thought the battle had been decided in our favor, when Blanche suddenly whispered in my ear, pointing to our left. There three bulky shadows were slipping along the sea cliff, headed in our direction. Perhaps they had seen us run for cover, or perhaps they merely assumed that we would be out of the fray and the chasm was the only out available.

"Damn," said the countess, picking up her parasol and twisting the handle. A very sharp blade came out of it, one that glittered in the moonlight. I had a dagger at my belt, one I had spent a tiny gem on in Palmia, with no real intention of using it for anything but trimming my nails. Nonetheless, it was a real one, quite keen. Blanche slipped upward, into a nearby tree. I knew she planned to attack from above.

It seemed time for strategy. I whispered to the countess, and the two of us separated, each behind her own shrub. When the first of the attackers came sneaking by, we let him go between us, then both attacked from the rear, I at his hamstrings, she, pulling herself erect to strike upward at his heart. The countess was quicker with her blade than I with mine, but he fell with only a

Sheri S. Tepper

gurgle. Elianne withdrew her sword and wiped it fastidiously on the grass.

Meantime, Blanche had been making odd noises, gargles and curses, which drew the other two attackers in her direction. One stayed where he was while the other went forward, both of them facing away from us. We repeated our attack on the rearmost, with similar success, though not so silently. This one had time to roar before he fell.

Now we had a real attacker to deal with, for he spun about, saw us where we crouched, lifted his ax (the moonlight showed it quite clearly) and plunged toward us. As he came beneath the tree, Blanche came down on him, clutching him about the head, using her nails on his face, biting at him in an uncivilized frenzy. He could not strike at her without striking at himself. He dropped the ax and clawed at her, and as he did so, the countess leapt out and skewered him.

"Where did you learn to do that?" I asked, very impressed by her alacrity. This was not the person who had uttered little coos of dismay all day on the way down into the chasm.

She fluttered her eyelashes at me and straightened her wig, which had become disarranged in the battle. "My father had me working with fighters from the time I was a child," she whispered. "All rulers need to be able to protect themselves, as this attack makes clear. However, my dear Nassif, I would prefer that we say nothing at all about this to the gentlemen out there." And she gestured toward the shore, where the fight had petered out and our comrades were dragging bodies out of the camp. She looked at the bodies we had accounted for and sniffed. "I prefer a style of courtesy not usually offered to well-trained killers. We'll just leave them lie, shall we?"

Blanche was sitting on a stump, setting herself to rights, for she had become quite disheveled. I copied the countesses method of cleaning my blade, wiping it on the most recent corpse, and restored it to its sheath be-

fore assisting the countess in finding the other end of
her parasol. When Soaz came back to see if we were all
right, we were assembled near the veebles, our clothing
rearranged, looking properly apprehensive.

"Have there been wounds?" asked the countess, ever
practical.

"Izzy is dealing with them," said Soaz, sounding
rather surprised. "Evidently his training has included
medicine as well as magic. Your armakfatid is helping
him, as he helped us. I had never seen one of them fight
before."

"May we assume the attack is over?"

I started to say no, we couldn't, but Soaz beat me to
it. "I think not, Countess. We should not have camped
in this exposed location. Let us now get up the road, so
far as we may."

The umminhi were pulled from their pickets and re-
hitched. The wounded went into the wagons, including
Sahir, who'd been struck on the head. The rest of us
walked, Soaz and the unwounded guards before and after, the umminhi making their incomprehensible mutter,
the onchiki, uncharacteristically silent, leading the veebles. The tents we left on the shore, though we took time
to load all the supplies we could find in the dark. None
of us felt torches would be a good idea, not if Fasahd
was out there on his ship, awaiting the return of his men.
There had been eleven of them altogether. Eight had
attacked the camp, three had come after us, they were
all dead or as good as.

We went as quietly as possible. None of us felt like
talking. Above us, the tower crouched on its crag like a
bird of ill omen. It had two windows in which a dull
light gleamed, as they might have been eyes, watching
us. It occurred to me for the first time that St. Weel
might not welcome our visit, that its people might be
hostile toward us. If so, we were headed into danger
without way of escape, for Dzilobommo hissed from behind me, and I turned to see a web of moonlight on the

sea, with a black spider shape crawling on its oar-legs toward the shore. Another boat.

I passed on the word and we began to move more quickly. Unfortunately, the wagon harness was not silent; it jingled, though not loudly. In that stillness, even the slight sound echoed like a shout.

We went around a turn in the trail, and I heard a gasp from behind me. There, behind the guards who brought up the rear, was a rank of black-robed figures, following us. Even as I watched, stumbling along with my head turned over my shoulder, more figures came from the low growth at the side of the trail. They made no effort to move faster, or to attack us, but merely followed. They were large. As tall, almost, as Fasal Grun, though more slender.

We kept moving. After what seemed an appreciable fragment of forever, we came to the moat that separated the tower from the path, a deep rocky defile with straight sides, one we could neither leap across nor climb down into. We needed to do neither. The bridge came down soundlessly, though our wheels rumbled as we crossed it. The black clad figures came after us, most of them, at any rate, and as the last of them crossed, the bridge rose up again, like the shadow of a passing cloud. We came beneath the curtain wall, through the dark throat of the gate, and across a narrow sawdust-filled ditch into which the portcullis fell behind us with only a muffled whump. Whoever these people were, they were quiet about their business.

Now there were torches lit inside the walls, and we gathered uncertainly at the center of the courtyard.

"Have you wounded?" asked one of the black-robed persons. He spoke trade language, and we all understood him.

Izzy replied in the same language, and several of the black-robed ones helped him move the wounded into a long, low building at one side of the courtyard, one evidently used as a dormitory or infirmary, for there were rows of beds arranged along the walls. Next to this room was the stable, where the veebles, the thirteen umminhi and the one horse were taken, and next to that some sheds for wagons.

When all had been neatly disposed, one of the black-robes went down the line, examining the wounded guards and remarking to Izzy that he could see nothing more that needed doing except for an herb tea which would speed healing. For Sahir, he prescribed poultices and provided a draught against pain.

Izzy started to explain why we had come, but he was hushed immediately.

"Tomorrow," said the black-robed one. "Tonight, sleep. You are weary, and you are safe here."

Opalears: A Twist of Time

We slept in the same large room as the wounded, rousing at their moans of pain, hearing the recurrent chatter of the umminhi that came clearly through the wooden wall, turning restlessly upon our hard beds, then falling off into sleep again. The trip had been wearying, and all our bodies needed rest. When morning came, things seemed brighter. It was then we learned that the people of St. Weel had no intention of showing us their faces. They remained veiled from head to toe, gloved and booted as well, all in black, like the shadows they had seemed to be. They were all the same size, more or less, quite tall, and variously slender. They spoke trade language when with us, and when away from us—my ears have always been very good—a tongue I had never heard before.

I mentioned this to Izzy. He put himself where he could hear them apart from the others. Later he came to me, shrugging. Though some of the words seemed familiar, he could not tell what they were saying.

"Why do they hide themselves?" I asked.

He shrugged again. "They are known to be a stranger people," he said. "Some tribe unknown to us, perhaps from the transmontaine. They may prefer to appear mysterious rather than merely foreign. Being a stranger can be dangerous, but being mysterious is a kind of protection. Especially if they live in a fortress and are, seemingly, able to defend themselves. Think of ants. Or bees." He sighed. "Nassif. I feel a definite . . . malaise."

"You're depressed," I said. In the harim, we learned to recognize depression. There it was the result of too little to do, too much boredom and sameness, no challenges, no excitement. There one day was like another. The biggest event was the birth of a baby or the death of an aged inhabitant, either long expected. We had few surprises. Here, out in the world, depression came from moving in an unknown world, reacting rather than acting, from being constantly uncertain and alert to danger without being able to set a course that was more sure or less perilous. It came from this transient hesitation, this recurrent tension, this inability to stay focused on anything, including whether one could trust ones fellow travelers. I was not in charge, but I caught myself saying, "I should have done," or "Perhaps if I had," so I knew Izzy did it, too. I saw his face, thinking, telling over what he had decided last, wondering if it were right.

"Depressed," he repeated. "Perhaps."

"It will pass," I assured him. "Once we know what we are doing."

"Are we likely to find out here?" he asked angrily. "I have asked these people. They say wait. I am sick and tired of being told to wait."

"While you are waiting," I said, "you might see if you can figure out their language. You are the only one among us who is smart enough to do so, and it could be important." I thought if he occupied himself with some intellectual puzzle, he wouldn't have time to fret.

He gave me a long, level look, as though he were

284 ⬧ Sheri S. Tepper

going to snap at me, then grinned instead. "Very well, Nassif. I shall find out what I can."

The rest of us were content to rest, eat, sleep a little extra time, and eat again. It was late in the afternoon before the black-robed ones granted us an audience—us being Izakar, Sahir, and the countess, as persons of consequence, and myself, who was of no consequence. The others had come to accept me in the role Izzy had assigned me, that of recorder.

Our audience began with Izzy's recounting of what had brought us this far. He did not mention libraries. The countess was asked to explain Fasahd, which she did with a good deal of indignation. Sahir confirmed the reading of the bones, as quoted to him by his father.

Then we began to go astray. The blackrobes were, it seemed to me, unnecessarily interested in the talisman that had been given Sultan Tummyfat.

"He sent it to Soaz," said Sahir.

Nothing would do but we summon Soaz.

"I never got it," he said. "I heard from one of the chamber slaves that Great-tooth intercepted it. I accused him. He said Halfnose Nazir had taken it, and he executed him. Then Great-tooth died." His eyes glittered as he said this, and for the first time I had an inkling how it was that Great-tooth died. I felt a sudden fondness for Soaz.

"Was the talisman ever found?" they asked.

"No," said Sahir.

"Did it occur to anyone that perhaps Halfnose Nazir *had* taken it?" they asked.

I screamed a denial. Father would not steal anything.

"We did not say steal," they said patiently. "We said taken. If the talisman was intended for Soaz but was, instead, waylaid by the regent, could not Halfnose Nazir have taken it with the intent of giving it to Soaz?"

"Why would you think such a thing?" I cried.

"Because the talisman is here," they said. "We have a detector, and for several days the detector has said it was coming. Now it says it is here. It came with you."

"How could it be here?" I cried. "My father was executed. My mother died. I was enslaved. How could it be here?"

There, there, they said. Calm down. Did I have nothing with me that had belonged to my father?

I started to deny it, then remembered the few little books, the mantle, the little box. These were things my father had at least handled. I went to get them from our baggage, returning in mere moments.

They took the things from me and felt them. They opened the box and immediately found the secret drawer. The gems spilled out, were collected and restored, while I explained to Sahir that they had been given me to use for his benefit, by his mother. Thus far in the journey, I had not seen reason to mention them, which seemed to annoy him, though I didn't know why he should be annoyed. We had not suffered in want of anything.

One of the Weelians went on fiddling with the box. After a moment, he said, "Aha," in a pleased tone and pulled out another little panel, one I had not known was there. Inside was a folded bit of something. Parchment, I thought. It had a seal upon it.

"Unfold it," the discoverer told me, handing it to me with his gloved hand.

I did so. It was not folded into the likeness of a complicated animal or bird as onchiki fortunes were. It was simply folded around several layers of padding with something inside, then sealed with wax. When I had undone it, there was a device wrapped inside. It looked rather like a key, silvery and longer than it was wide, with both edges complicatedly wavy and oddly shaped holes down its middle.

"Ah," said the Weelians. "Here it is at last." There was something in their voices of both elation and dejection, an odd mixture, I thought. As though minds were gratified, though feelings were wounded.

"Here what is at last?" asked Izzy, irritated at them.

"I believe that's mine," said Sahir, reaching for it.

"No," replied one Weelian. "It was given to your father to bring here. It was taken from here thirty years ago, by one who rejected our way of life. . . ."

"Who went mad," said another.

"Who for whatever reason set out to do a dreadful and deadly thing," said the first firmly.

"Who?" I asked.

"A broken-hearted one," said one. "A traitor," said another. "One who wished you and all your peoples ill," said a third.

Their voices were very alike, as though they were, perhaps, of one family, but I thought they were all male voices. The first one spoke again. "After this was stolen from us, we sent word to the seers, asking that they search for it. Evidently one of them found it."

"What's it a key to?" I asked. "What does it open?"

The hooded heads turned this way and that, as though they shared glances, though I doubted they could do so through all that veiling.

"We have entirely too many secrets," I cried angrily. "Let us have done with secrets. If we are to accomplish anything, we must know what's going on!"

"It isn't that," said one of the Weelians, sounding rather petulant. "It's just that we have so much explaining to do, and we aren't sure where to begin."

"If it's about libraries," I snapped, "at least three of us know about them already."

Well, consternation and confusion! The Weelians acted as though I had made a naughty at the dinner table. When and where and how, they wanted to know, all at once. At which point Izakar yelled at them all to sit down and we would begin by telling them what some of us already knew.

They did, and we did. Soaz was glued to every word. I know Sahir was furious to have been kept in ignorance, but he was too intelligent to let that prevent his soaking up every bit of information Izzy mentioned. When he and the Weelians heard that the emperor had a library as well, they were all quite astounded, and when Izzy said that in his own library in Palmia there were actually Librarians, we could have felled them all with a breath, so astonished they were.

"The last cycle," one of the Weelians cried in an agonized voice. "Do you know what ended the last cycle?"

"A plague," said Izzy. "Some religionists declared a holy war and set loose a plague that killed virtually all the people."

The questioner took a deep breath. "Was there any mention of our various tribes during that cycle?"

"Oh, yes," Izzy told them. "Though not under the names we use, of course. Then they were called Frynch, Cherman, Zhapanees, Merican, ah, Stralian, Scandian, Joosh—very intelligent, the Joosh. I'm not sure which ones are which, I mean, among us, though I think the scuinic tribe may have been called Ahrabic."

"Pictures?" one of them asked. "Are there any pictures?"

Izzy shook his head. "Not in my Library, not in the emperor's. The Librarians says it's because of the graven image prohibition."

Immediately, the Weelians began to argue in their own language, using some trade language words. I heard the word "nuslik," which means "person." Several of those present threw up their arms and uttered cross-sounding words. If these were wizards, I thought, they certainly displayed gauche and unwizardly behavior. They were as uncertain as any gaggle of slaves in the harim, discussing how to go about cleaning out the fish pond.

"Hey," Izzy shouted into their turmoil. "Do you want to talk with us, or shall we go for a walk?"

"Oh, we'll talk," said one of them. I noticed for the first time that he had a fine red edge to his hood, and realized that many of the others also had color showing at the edge of their faces. This evidently expressed either their identities or their ranks, for this voice was the one that had done most of the talking up until now.

I said, "Do you have identities, or at least something we can call you? Can we call you Red?"

Laughter, low and somewhat embarrassed.

"By all means," he said, a catch in his voice. "Call me Red. Brother Red."

They sat us down. Someone went to fetch tea, which was very hot and aromatic and had something added to it with a very relaxing effect. Everywhere we went, people seemed to spend a lot of time drinking tea. I suppose it gave people something to do when they weren't sure what else to do or needed time to think. While we sat, and sipped, and shook our heads in amazement, they told us about St. Weel.

"Saint Wheel," Brother Red said. "Because down below is a thing that resembles a wheel. This part, up top, is fairly new. We—that is, our people—built part of it. The old part is buried in the mountain, deeper than you can imagine. It may have been a laboratory. Do you know that word? Laboratory? A place where experiments and investigations were done? Or it may have been part of a ship that crashed from some other world. There's much to be said for that opinion, and it happens to be the one I hold. Or it may have been some great wizardly center where a magic was done more marvelous than any today can imagine. Whichever of these it is, or something else entirely, its purpose has to do with the nature of time. Whoever made it or brought it or enchanted it into being is long gone. We do not know who they were.

"Our ancestors came upon this place centuries ago. Because of the mystery, and because it is a well-fortified place, able to be easily defended, some of us stayed here when the others went on, and then later, some of us were sent back, from time to time, to find out more about the place. We established a homeland west of here, called Chamony, but our people have been coming back and forth for a long time, learning what we can."

"Your tribe?" asked Izzy. "Is it numerous?"

"It is not," said Brother Red. "I would prefer that

you not tell the world that, since it would not help in our preservation, but we are very few. Fewer now than we were generations ago. Because we are so few, we keep ourselves separate to protect us. It is a very lonely life."

We nodded sympathetically. It would be hard, we agreed, to live all alone, with no other tribes about to lend a hand.

Brother Red heaved a deep breath. "We have known for several generations that our extinction was . . . probable. Some four decades ago, our researchers told us we had only a thirty percent chance of surviving the next century. Certain very stringent reproductive laws were put in place. The laws were upsetting for all of us, but most of us could . . . accept them. One of us, however, became obsessed with the probability of our extinction. I think he went a little mad—"

"A little!" blurted one of the others.

"Well, quite mad, then. He wanted to change the past. It was he who took the control to the Wheel, and he went back in time. . . ."

"In time?" Izzy asked indignantly. "Come now."

They nodded and murmured. Yes, it was ridiculous sounding. Yes, it seemed impossible, but that is what this place allowed. It allowed persons to go back.

Another of the brothers spoke angrily: "We do not call him our brother any longer. We call him Woput." (In Finialese, Woput means low-life or pond scum, with strong implications of depravity.) "This Woput stole the control and the key to the Wheel and he went back. After he had gone, we found the control, but we couldn't find the key. After he turned the thing on, he somehow got rid of the key. . . ."

"Tied it to a bird's leg, perhaps," said someone. "Threw it over the wall into the chasm, where a fish swallowed it. . . ."

Brother Red nodded. "The control relocks itself after use. It takes the key to turn it on. Woput didn't want us coming after him, and without the key, we couldn't. We had no idea how to make another key without taking the control apart. We were afraid to take the control apart. What if we couldn't put it together again?''

"How long ago?" asked the countess.

"Almost thirty years."

"What did he intend to do?"

It was Brother Red who answered. "We knew exactly what he intended to do, because he left a journal in which he had written all his thoughts, his doubts, his pain. He believed that we . . . our tribe was almost extinct because your people . . . your tribes had become so numerous. If you had died out long ago, our people would have survived. So, he went back in time to kill off the other tribes."

"How? How could he kill off the other tribes? One person?" I blurted.

Brother Red shrugged, his robed shoulders expressing both ignorance and despair. "We don't know, exactly. In his journal he said he would take 'direct action,' and he also said he would destroy the habitat of the lands where your peoples lived, killing the trees, the rivers—"

"You approved of this?" asked the countess.

He shook his head. There was a wave of general negation. "No." "Never." "He didn't tell us." "He may do more harm than good!" "He was always a hothead." "No, we didn't approve."

Izzy asked. "What did he mean by direct action?"

They shrugged, they shook their heads again. He, their colleague, had spent much time looking through old records. He evidently had found something there that made him believe he could succeed. Would he have gone, otherwise?

The countess said, "And you needed the key so you could go back to the time he got there and what? Stop him?"

Brother Red's voice was agitated. "He must be stopped, yes! If what you tell us about the seeresses is correct, if he isn't stopped, all intelligent life will end!

That's your Great Enigma. Stop the Woput then in order
to preserve life now. But we can't go back to the time
he arrived. The device doesn't work like that.''

"How does it work?" demanded Sahir.

One of the other brothers answered. "The device is
cyclical. This may be a design limitation, or it may be
that time itself is cyclical. We have argued both ways.
From the top, the device does look like a wheel, but
actually it's more helical than it is wheel-like. One cannot go back to just anytime. One cannot go back *along*
time at all, one can only cross one turn.''

"How long is one turn?" I asked.

"Three thousand years.''

"Let's see if I understand this," said Izzy. "If I were
to go back, or as you say, cross one turn, I would arrive
three thousand years ago, more or less, and thirty years
after your colleague had arrived.''

"Not more or less. Exactly three thousand years. And
he arrived about three thousand thirty years before now.
And we don't know what he's done, that is, nothing has
changed, here, so we believe he hasn't done anything
yet. That doesn't mean he won't.''

Izzy nodded. "And one or more of you intend to go
back—''

"No!" said one of the Weelians sharply. "No. Not
we. We are too few to risk any of us! Some of you.
There are lots of you.''

Soaz snarled, "It all sounds very sacrificial, Brothers.
There may be lots of us, but there is only one of me.
Also, the world is large. I've traveled over parts of it.
How on earth would we, any of us, find this colleague
of yours?''

"The control is still set as he left it. It couldn't have
been changed without the key. It is still set for the same
location he set it for. Whoever goes will go to that same
place.''

"Which place your colleague no doubt left some
thirty years ago," said Soaz. "It sounds unlikely of success, gentlemen.''

Izzy had been sitting silent with a very thoughtful expression. Now he said urgently, "Have you been talking a lot about this? Out here near the woods, for example? Did you discuss this business of the Woput killing trees and rivers and what not?"

Brother Red replied. "I suppose. We've had thirty years to discuss it, worry over it, try to figure out what to do. Why?"

"The trees have heard you. They're in revolt. They're frightened, and they don't know what they're frightened of. We ran into whole forests of them, upset and rebellious. They said they'd learned about the conspiracy from the place the gervatch flower blooms. That's here."

"Trees! The trees said!"

"The trees said," I confirmed in a loud voice. "I heard them. Izzy gave one of them a mouth, and they told us."

"Nassif," Izzy said sadly. "That might not have been a smart thing to tell them."

It seemed for a moment he was right. They were very quiet, all the hoods turned in our direction. "Sorcery?" asked Brother Red. "You can do sorcery?"

"Only a little," said Izzy, waving it away. The way his gesture told it, he did a few card tricks and perhaps a little amateur juggling.

This started another colloquy, nonetheless, much muttering and gesturing, while our group sat looking on, completely at sea.

"It shouldn't make any difference," said Brother Red, turning back to us. "At the end of the last cycle, there was lots of technology. I doubt sorcery will help you, but if it does, fine."

"Help us?" asked Sahir. "Why do you keep insisting it has to do with us?"

"You're here. You've brought the key. Two different prophecies have sent you all here, so it's evident the seeress knew you would come here. If you don't do this thing, we all die, so it's logical to assume you will do this thing. Someone has to. It's either that or sit back and wait for the end.''

We argued. Soaz threatened. We said we would take our guards and go, and the Weelians told us our guards, all those who could walk, had been sent back during our conference. They were already far past recall, on their way back to the emperor.

The countess interrupted. "Is it possible your traitor might have had an accomplice? Could that possibly have been the emperor's nephew, Fasahd?''

"We don't know what arrangements or alliances he made. We do know Woput was no Korèsan. It's possible that he spread lies among the Farsakians in order to undermine the Korèsans, and it's possible those lies have lived on, as lies tend to do. He could not, however, have made an ally of Fasahd, for Fasahd had not been born when Woput left.''

After a pause, Brother Red went on to say, "We know what books the Woput was reading before he left. Perhaps, if you were to read them, you would understand what he was up to. We can get those books from our library—''

"So you have one, too," snarled Soaz.

"Only our own. Since this place is secure, we have stored all our books and documents here, all those we have had from earliest times. It is not as large as the emperor's library, nor so well equipped as the one Prince Izakar describes, but it probably has documents in it that exist nowhere else.''

And that is where it stopped for the nonce. Izzy and Soaz and the countess spent the remainder of the day in the library. Sahir went in to chivvy them from time to time, but he had no stomach for helping them. I went in and out as well, sometimes listening to them mumble at one another. It was less amusing than helping Dzilobommo prepare food for us all or playing in the fountain with the onchiki. I told Lucy Low about everything, of course. I had meant it when I said we had entirely too many secrets.

Brother Red came upon the two of us where we were enjoying ourselves in the garden, though really it was only a paved terrace set about a fountain with some pots of flowers here and there against the walls.

"Oh, you are a strange and motley group to do what must be done," said Brother Red in his slightly nasal, slightly whining voice.

"We may be motley," I said indignantly, "but of us all, you and your ilk are the strangest."

"True." He seated himself on the curbing of the fountain and started to dip his fingers in the water, becoming aware, suddenly, of his gloves.

"You don't always wear those," I said.

He shook his head.

I pushed a little farther. "There are not any females here."

Having said which I waited, wanting him to make some comment, but he did not.

"Why?" I demanded.

"All our daughters and ladyfolk are far from here," he murmured. "A lifetime's journey, almost. I have not seen my love for ten long years."

"And why is that?"

He shuddered. I did not know if he was laughing or crying. "We are so few," he said at last. "We are inbred. We have known it for a long time. Our children are few, and often they do not live. They are born with hereditary diseases and conditions. . . . Our ancestors have much to answer for."

"Why? What did they do?"

He put a fingertip in the water, stirring it. "Long ago, they used machines and drugs to keep the unhealthy and unfit ones of us alive. In that past time it was believed that all persons must have children. It was a right deemed so precious that it was forced upon even those who did not value it or should not have had it. If one of our people became pregnant, our people used all their knowledge to assure the young would be born, no matter how sick or disabled. Then, if the young lived, they injected them and dosed them and radiated them and transfused and transplanted them, to keep them alive, and then, when they were grown, they used all their skills in assisting them to have children of their own.''

Lucy Low asked, "How did your people survive the plague?''

"We did not know about the plague until Izzy told us," said Brother Red. "We had no idea how our cycle ended. Our legends tell us our ancestors were part of the tribal government, and we were isolated in a protected place underground, a place with vast stores of food and water, a place of technology and laboratories and manufacture by machines. We lived in that place for a century before we emerged. By the time we did, our genetic weaknesses had permeated all our tribe and there were no other peoples to breed with. Only degenerate . . ." He fell silent, shaking his head.

"So sad," said Lucy Low.

"A tragedy," he agreed. "We carry that heritage. Our children still die, two out of every three.''

"Would you not do better breeding more frequently than every ten long years?" I asked, amazed.

He shrugged. "Our wise ones tell us we must breed more widely, not more frequently. Each female must have children by as many males as possible. Each male must impregnate as many different females as possible. If a child is born who is unhealthy, that child must not breed at all. I have fathered fifteen children there, where my dear love dwells, and she has had seven children, but only one of them is mine.''

"How many lived? Of yours?''

"Better than average. Of the fifteen, four are living and two are considered healthy. The others came feebly from the womb, struggled a time, then passed away, like flowers. Some of my colleagues can father no living children, no matter who the mother is.''

"So, when you have done fathering, you come here?''

"To avoid conflict among us, between our fatherings, we come here or to one of our other places, near the western sea, or far to the south, past Isfoin, to the jungles, where is another such place. And we dream of blessed Chamony of the Fountains, for there our hearts lie.''

"You love her still?'' asked Lucy Low.

He sighed dramatically. "I love, yes. We have always loved. And such a life as ours keeps love as pure as the dew upon the gervatch petal. We never have a chance to grow weary of one another.''

I heard him with distress, for his heart was on his tongue. "But if it helps your people to survive ...''

"Three chances out of ten we will survive. Our survival is only perhaps. And I think of what your friend said. What was it? 'While there are many of my people, there is only one of me.' So with us. While there are perhaps a thousand of our people, there is only one Beloved Maryam, there is only one me.''

Lucy Low said, "But if we go back in time ... perhaps we will change things.''

He laughed, a jeering sound. "That was the Woput's failing! Wanting to change things! How would you know you did not change them for the worse? The best we can ask is that you stop the Woput! That you prevent his interference! We don't expect you to do anything for us because we don't know what you could do.''

"You believe stopping him is a righteous thing for us to do?''

"Yes,'' he said, leaning wearily upon the curbing. "And who could argue against righteousness. I only wish righteousness could make us feel less lonely.''

"One's own extinction is a lonely business,'' said another of the Weelians, Brother Green, who came walking across the pavement, his hand outstretched. "But worse is to cause the extinction of another people. Our respected leader says that he who causes another's extinction will dwell forever in hell, an unforgiven executioner, to the end of time.''

"So he says,'' murmured Brother Red, staring at the wall of the terrace and beyond it, away north. I won-

dered where Chamony of the Fountains was. I wondered
if, when his Maryam was too old for childbearing,
Brother Red might be permitted to come home to her
once more. I did not ask, and they did not speak of it
further.

I could go on and on about the next two days. There
were a great many attacks (all verbal, of course) and
retreats. There were bargaining sessions. There were
threats and shouts and murmurings in corners and, I
should suppose from my own example, not a few tears.
None of us had set out on this journey with any sense
of personal commitment to fixing things. Well, Izakar,
perhaps, though nothing he said convinced me of his
dedication. We had all fallen into the journey, or gone
along, or been sent, and when all the complaints and
words were done, none of us were eager. We were
merely resigned to going forward. Or backward, as fate
would have it.

The trouble was that the Weelians were convincing
and the books were convincing. They told us things that
only Izzy had known about before, that three thousand
years before there had been more tribes than there were
today, each with its own nation or location, its own culture, language, cuisine, many of them with individual
styles of dress or a specific religion. They told us that
these peoples began to mix, just as we did in our own
time, and that some persons could not bear this! This
one would have only his own country and would kill to
maintain it; that one would have only his own language
and would kill for that; the next one would have only
his own religion and would kill for that; the final one
would have no other flag! So, the books said, some tribe
invoked its god and loosed a plague that destroyed almost everyone, including themselves.

According to Izzy, none of the gods of that time had
survived, except for Korè.

"It was Korè's people who fought for all the beings
of nature during a time when nature itself was threatened
with extinction. If this Woput wishes to change things,

he will try to eliminate Korè," Izzy told us.

"Did you find Korè in these books?" asked the countess.

"One of the books he was reading just before he left describes the rites of Korè," he said. "What is written is incomplete, but I can see how it might have tantalized him. Perhaps, in his madness, he extrapolated from these incomplete references . . ."

None of which was decisive. In the end, we knew only what we had been told at the beginning: this Woput, this low-life, had gone back to change things so that other tribes would die but not his own. In the end, after we had talked it to death, we agreed that someone had to go after him and put a stop to his . . . whatever.

"What does he look like?" demanded the countess. "How shall we recognize him?"

Much embarrassment among the Weelians. "He did not go bodily," they said. "He chose to take the body of someone living at that time, in order not to seem strange or out of place. That is why we still have the control, and now the key. Had he gone bodily, he could have taken them with him, as you will take them with you, so you can return. If he had had them, he could have returned, but he left them here, with his dead body, when he went."

This started the whole discussion over again, with a new set of information. I grew weary. The countess grew weary. We called an end to it and went to supper, where we told everyone about everything, much to the amazement of the onchiki and even of Dzilobommo, who evinced surprise by leaning back and staring at the ceiling without grummeling for a very long time. Soaz and Prince Sahir continued arguing in one corner, the countess seemed to be having a similar discussion with Blanche in another corner, the Weelians drifted about, making apocryphal noises. I told everyone I was going to bed, and this broke up the gathering.

I thought three thousand years was a very long time, but Izzy said it wasn't. He sat on the foot of my bed and whispered to me about time, and space and other worlds that revolved, perhaps, around the stars, and how it was all billions of years old. He told me about the Gyptians, whose culture had lasted for thousands of years but who had, in time, passed away, and of the Maya, who had built a great empire but had passed away, and the Gricks and the Perishans and the Rohmans and the Shinees, all passed away, then our peoples, too, all but the remnants of the Mercans and the Frynch and the Chermans and all who still lived in our tribes of the current age.

"The library says all those tribes used to fight among themselves. The emperor doesn't want civilization to fall apart again. He's trying so hard to prevent it," whispered Izzy, there in the dormitory, with the three wounded guards snoring in one corner and the umminhi muttering behind the wall. The onchiki were piled on the bed next to me, sleeping quietly, like children.

"Do you think it can be prevented?" I asked. "Is it what we were meant for?"

He threw up his hands. "I don't want to just sit here, waiting for the end."

"I will go with you, Prince Izakar," I said.

"And I," said Lucy Low, opening one eye from the bottom of the pile. "And Burrow and Mince will go, too."

"We all will," said the countess wearily from a distant bed. "If you young ones will please let us get some sleep. Three thousand years may not be forever, as you say, but it is a very long journey, and we should be well rested when we begin."

There were still fifteen of us when we were ready to depart. Three of the Weelians took us down into the place beneath the tower where their ancestors had found the thing. We saw the place for the first time, a circular platform made of something much like gray stone, only all of one piece, seamless, with great metal spokes running out from it into the mountain itself. This part did look rather like a wheel. Inside the circle was a great coil, like a gigantic worm or an enormous rope that wound down and down and down again into the very center of the earth. So we observed for ourselves when we walked out onto a kind of crane that extended over the middle. It was like looking down into a well, or into the coils of some unimaginably great black-speckled serpent. The Weelians lowered a light, and we could see that obdurate, terrible substance going around and around and around, forever. It had not been built, they told us, for even in the centuries since they had come here, it had grown, slowly turning its way into the world, like a great screw. They did not know if it was living or perhaps half living, or something else entirely.

Only the topmost coil was visible, and it was surrounded by a haze of violet light which, we were told, was impermeable. At the very end of the coil, however, was a thinning in the haze, an almost clear space, and the end of the coil itself had a gelatinous, almost transparent look.

"It isn't set yet," said Brother Red, commenting upon the gelatinous appearance of it. "Recent history takes a while to set. People really don't know what just happened. They only figure it out later."

Leading onto this clearing was a plank, as one might use to board a ship. The clear section was the present time, and there one could step upon the coil itself, a space large enough for several dozens to stand upon. Then, if the key were turned and the control were set, and if the traveler or travelers stood within the field it generated (so said the Weelians), they would sink down through the present time into the coil beneath.

The Woput, so they said, had put only his head into the field when he had gone without his body.

We were given the control, too. A simple device, the size of a book, in a red leather case. In one corner was a keyhole. In the opposite corner was a little window where a number showed, the number of times the control could be used. According to Brother Red, when the Woput left, the number had been "1," but we could all see it was now "3." Izzy thought it might vary with the amount of power available, perhaps recharging itself over time, though where the power might come from, he could not guess.

At the center of the control was one window of numbers which could be set for particular locations in past time, and a second window that could be set for the size and shape of the field. And, finally, at the bottom, an "On" button.

It had been agreed we would take some of our baggage, and the veebles, that we would go in our own bodies, taking the control and the key with us. I do not recall exactly the order of our going. I was very frightened. I do know that Izzy and I stepped onto the worm last, right after the onchiki. I remember that the countess and Sahir were very close together, the countess supporting Blanche. Dzilobommo and Soaz were warriors, of course. They did not need encouragement. When we all began to sink down, the veebles screamed, I do remember that. I felt I could not breathe, then everything went dark and I felt nothing at all but Izzy's hand, still holding mine.

26

A Return of Music

Dora dreamed of music: merry-go-round tootling, calliope *um-pah-pah*, amusement park and circus music, joyful faces and dancing feet. The dream music went on for what seemed a very long time, peaceful and delightful, fading and returning, as though blown by a variable wind. Though the music did not wake her, its cessation did, bringing her up into dark silence, the dream still in her mind, her self full of a lilting feeling that was wholly familiar. This was music she had often heard when she was a little girl. . . .

And it was that thought that brought her fully awake, that thought as much as the suddenly empty quiet.

She was alone in the place. Where was Abby?

Gone home, she reminded herself. He had an early class this morning. They had talked until late, until she heard and smelled the visitation, but when it had gone, she had yawningly bid Abby good-bye. Abby hadn't noticed the nightly visitor. Not yet.

She tried to remember the dream. She had dreamed

music like she had heard before the howlers drove it away. Why had they done that? The question was stupid, a thirty-year-old anger barely coalesced around a kernel of loss, and she pushed it away. Too late to wonder, too late to care, too late to do anything about it now. Now was only the darkness of her room, the wind moving the leaves against the big window, all senses extended, like tentacles, searching for the feeling she had dreamed.

"Music," she said aloud. "I heard it!" And with the words the music came again, bouncing on the wind through the open window of the outer room, a rollicking tune, but the same substance: simple, lively and compelling. She reached out with her bare feet for her sandals, legs pricking into gooseflesh in the chilly air, and fumbled for the throw that lay across the foot of the bed, drawing it around her naked shoulders and arms. She went out in search of the sound, finding it louder in the living room, louder yet at the foot of the stairs when she opened the door. She went as though irresistibly drawn, without considering the wisdom of it or wondering at the suddenness of it, through the opening where the gate had been and into the woods.

Late moonlight dripped through branches, making dim puddles of froggy light. Small warty things hopped heavily away from her. A drift of old silvery leaves marked a path down the swale, leaves that some fraction of her fussy mind cavilled at for their untimeliness. There'd been no time to accumulate old leaves, not in these new woods. A rivulet companioned her, the trickle of it caught up in the same music, not quite flute sounds, something shriller than a flute. Plucked strings, too, and a thumping of drums, growing louder the farther she went.

And then a flicker of amber light shining between the trees ahead of her, firelight in a clearing that silhouetted the trunks on the side toward her and silvered the white trunks and shining leaves on the far side. The clearing was where the music was.

Where they were.

She perceived them out of an implicit assumption that she was still dreaming. It would be quite all right to dream such a vision, quite acceptable in the night, in the world between realities. So she reassured herself as she tallied them:

An otter child, standing on its hind legs as it played a small harp. Three huge crouched rabbits, with packs on their backs, ears flat and noses wriggling, one of them eating a dandelion. Two more otters, one with a complicated sliding whistle, the other drumming on a cookpot with a wooden spoon. A large monkey strumming a mandolin. Another monkey, singing. A pig, a rather small one, bewigged and bejeweled, tapping time with a furled parasol as she watched. Beside her, a huge, white cockatoo. And two medium-sized brown, black-muzzled, curly-tailed dogs, heads cocked, gravely dancing to the rhythmic air.

A dream. Her dream. She stepped into the grove.

The singing monkey looked up and screamed. "Umminhi, juppy umminhi! Vaniscomai!"

The entire group vanished in an instant. Only the rabbits remained, crouched, their eyes shut.

"No," Dora cried, in the dream. "No, don't run away."

But they had gone. The fire was still there, reflecting from white-barked trees, from glittering leaves, from pairs of watchful eyes in the underbrush. "Please, don't go away," she begged.

"It talks," said another treble voice in heavily accented English. *"Iut towks lingooudj."*

"Well, of course I talk language," she cried. "Of course. Most people do."

"People?" someone said, another voice, a bit lower and growlsome.

"People," the treble voice answered.

"G'et damma 'people'?" growled another voice.

"People," the first voice repeated. "Ja Nuslik!"

"Gwaaan!" said the other, disbelieving. "Nuslik?"

One of the monkeys stepped out into the clearing, still

carrying his mandolin, his eyes very wide and his hands shaking slightly. He pointed to himself and said clearly and slowly, in strangely accented words, "I am nuslik, that is, person, named Izakar. Nassif is person. We are ponjic persons. Ah . . . countess is scuinan person. Blanche is sitid person. Others are onchiki persons. We have armakfatid and pheled also, but they go . . . exploring."

Dora made this out, though with some difficulty. It was, she thought, rather like watching a movie made in England or Australia, where one knew the language perfectly well, but it took a moment to twist one's ears to the less familiar accent and intonation. Still, she caught the sense of it, which she thought about for a while, quite patiently and cheerfully, enjoying the nonsense of it. "What are the rabbits?"

"Rabbits?" He looked confused.

"The ones with long ears." She pointed. The rabbits still had their eyes shut, as though what they could not see could not trouble them.

"Veebles!" he cried, with a grimace that might be intended as a smile. "Not people. Creatures. Now, what kind person you?"

"Human," she said.

"Ah." He frowned. "I not aware umminhi ever be . . . persons."

Ever be? The implications of that were . . . well, they were staggering. If this weren't a dream, she'd be staggered. As it was, she could take it as it came. So, where had these dream beings come from? Or was it . . . when?

"Are there no humans in your . . . world?" she asked carefully.

"Ah . . . umminhi. Pack creatures, yes. Riding creatures. Saddles, you know, and whips." He thought deeply of his reading in the library. "Run like the wind. Hi-ho Silver. Giddy-ap old chap."

"Really." She sat down on a convenient rock with a thump. "I suppose in your world the . . . umminhi don't talk."

"No. Sadly, no. They make muttering noises which

sometimes sound almost linguistic, but they do not talk.''

She nodded slowly, decoding the words one by one, absorbing it, speaking slowly when she replied. "Well, I guess that's only fair. In this place, now, monkeys like you don't talk. Or otters, or pigs, or cockatoos.''

The pig with the parasol came out from between the trees. Her wig was of dangling ringlets, through which her floppy ears were barely discernable. "Only . . . humans talk in this time?'' she asked in a high, slightly squealing voice with pauses between the words.

"Well, some people think dolphins can talk. And parrots, of course.''

"Parrots?''

"Feathers.'' She flapped her arms. "Wings. Ah, rather like the one with you, only without the crest.''

"Ah. Sitid nuslik,'' said the pig. "And what are dolphins?''

"Fish. No, not fish, mammals, but living in the ocean, like fish. They have a kind of whistle language, but we can't speak it.''

"I can,'' said Izzy. "Whistle language of sea people is well known in our . . . world. You called me monkey. Am I like your . . . monkeys?''

She looked at him more closely, slowly shaking her head. "No. I'd say you were a Japanese macaque, except you're better looking. Handsomer face. More brain space. In fact, you all have larger heads than . . . usual.''

This provoked a spate of conversation, even argument among the creatures. Their language—or languages, as the mandolin-playing monkey seemed to be an interpreter—sounded like nothing Dora had ever heard before. The interpreter turned to Dora and asked:

"Our history speaks of time when creatures, you would say animals, became less varied and persons became more varied. Fewer species of animals, more species of people. Is this so?''

"Fewer animals, yes. Not more kinds of people.''

Long silence while they looked at one another. "Do your trees talk? Or move about?"

She started to shake her head, then stopped. "Just now," she said, stunned. "New trees. They don't talk, but just recently they've begun to move about. The past few weeks."

"And is there someone . . . who attempts to . . . destroy trees?"

She started to say no, then shrugged. "Well, yes. My ex-husband would like nothing better. And there was something on TV tonight about new chemicals and a bunch of new biological treatments they've been making to destroy the new trees." The assortment huddled once more, shutting her out. She said, with some asperity, "Personally, I like the trees."

This brought them out of the huddle.

"You are sympathetic to . . . forests?" the monkey asked.

She chose not to answer his question. "My name is Dora. It would be polite of me to call you by name, also, but I'm afraid I didn't catch the names."

"I am Prince Izakar of Palmia," he said, pointing to himself. "And other ponji is Nassif. That is Countess Elianne of Estafan, and her secretary, Blanche. The littlest onchik is Lucy Low, the other two are Burrow and Mince."

"And they?" she asked, indicating the dogs.

"Oyk," he said. "And Irk."

"They don't talk?"

"Not much," said Oyk.

"Waste of time," said Irk.

"Unless necessary," said Oyk.

"The veebles don't talk," she said desperately.

"No," said Lucy Low in a whisper. "But I can read their minds."

Dora decided to risk it. If she was dreaming, let her wake. If she was merely crazy, let her find it out now.

"How is it I understand your speech?"

"It is trade language," said the monkey. "Trade language is based on ancient language of Inglitch, mostly. Inglitch is very old, but because it is trade language, it survives. We have other languages.''

''I, too, speak Inglit . . . English. And you've come from the future,'' she said.

Izzy spoke three words in another language. Long silence while they stared at her, rather fearfully.

''How did you guess that?'' Izzy asked, dumbfounded.

''Why does it bother you that I did guess it?''

The countess said carefuly, ''When you said 'future,' we thought for a moment maybe you are Woput we search for. I also want to know how you guessed.''

How had she? What was a Woput?

First things first. ''I am a . . . law enforcer. It is my job to look for clues in what people say, to guess at how things happen. I remember the questions you asked. Were there more animals? Were there talking trees? Was anyone trying to kill them? And you say English is very ancient, but modern English isn't all that ancient. A few hundred years, more or less. So, you must have come from the future.''

A very long pause full of angry whispers.

Dora asked, ''Why are there no speaking humans in your world?''

The pig in the wig went on, still softly, ''Izzy reads in library this age ends in religious war where disease is weapon. Izzy says plague is very terrible. If this is umminhi age, but future age is not, plague will kill almost all umminhi.'' She paused, adding thoughtfully, ''. . . and Weelians. Some few Weelians remain, still speaking. Many umminhi remain, but umminhi no longer intelligent or speaking.''

''Oh, my God. Humans are dead? Extinct?'' She felt a frisson of terror which she quickly suppressed. There was no immediate threat, obviously. ''There are diseases that affect only humans. Like AIDS. Or some kind of TB animals couldn't get.''

Prince Izakar said to the countess, ''But she recognizes our kinds, so our ancestors must be alive in this time. If this is umminhi age, and all umminhi die in plague, then our peoples took over.''

The countess nodded, thinking it out.

Dora mused, ''But you didn't know about humans until you saw me. . . .''

''We knew about *persons*,'' said Izzy. ''That is, I knew there was *civilization*. We knew we were *coming* to civilized world. But there were no pictures of people. I thought . . . assumed. . . .'' He took a deep breath. ''The Librarians told me about prior civilizations, and I assumed they were ours. In my library I read that this time, now, ends with a holy war. A plague. Many persons die, most persons die, but I did not think they meant umminhi! Even Librarians don't connect *persons* to umminhi. . . .''

''Your librarians are who?''

''Different peoples. Some ponji ones. Some pheled ones.''

''So, in your time, your kind of intelligent people are alive, but intelligent umminhi, that is humans, aren't. The plague killed them all, right? And the Weelians? Who are the Weelians?'' Without waiting for an answer, she plunged on. ''But now someone is trying to change history? He knows about this plague?''

Izzy cried, ''No! The Woput is Weelian, was Weelian. He doesn't know about the plague. The Weelians did not know of the plague until I told them. But yes, the Woput is trying to change history. To keep his people alive, whoever they are, by making sure that we die.''

''That is why wizards sent us,'' whispered Lucy Low. ''To find Woput. The wizards are very . . . larjh.''

''Wizards are as tall as you,'' said the countess, who seemed to be picking up Dora's accent or was, at least, becoming less difficult to understand. ''And bulkier. They wear long black robes and veils, and all we know about them is that they are very few and mysterious. Their kind, they say, is almost extinct.''

''Why have you come *here*?'' Dora asked, pointing

to the earth beneath their feet. "I mean to this exact place?"

"*Woput* came here," whispered Lucy Low. "To this very spot. So they say."

"What is a Woput?"

"Evil doer. Pond scum. The one who's doing it."

Dora thought about this for some time. "The Woput is a Weelian, right? The Weelian is a kind of person, right? The Weelians got mostly wiped out in the plague, right? And so did the, umm . . . humans." She clenched her hands tightly, wondering why she did not, at this juncture, wake up. "Do you particularly want to camp out here in the forest?"

The countess lifted her lip in a very tiny sneer. "Not particularly."

"My house is just through the trees. You can stay with me. It'll be a little crowded, but—"

"I can't leave the veebles," cried Lucy Low.

"Bring the rab—the veebles," said Dora. "They can sleep in the . . . the storage room. And the two . . . Oyk and Irk, they can keep guard, okay?"

"What is okay?" asked Izzy.

"It's a word that means . . . something is appropriate. Come on. We'll sort it out when we get there." And she watched as they gathered up their baggage, then led them back through the forest to the break in the trees that gave upon her yard, where they engaged in another of their disputatious colloquies. After a few moments of this, as he was helping unburden the veebles, Izzy advised her that the veebles would stay in the yard, guarded by Oyk and Irk, that the rest of them would go indoors with her, that when morning came, some attention must be paid to finding food for all of them. Lucy Low then removed the veeble harness and put it with the baggage, inside the door.

Dora found herself tallying, as she used to do when a little girl, how much food there was on hand. Fruit and nuts for the monkeys, something solid for the pig, rice, maybe, with flavorings of vegetable. She had canned salmon for the otters. Spinach and carrots for the veebles. Dog chow for Oyk and Irk. She'd have to borrow dog chow from the man next door. Even now she could hear her neighbor's Rottweiller barking, a challenging sound.

And what of the other ones? The ones that had gone hunting. "The other ones of you?" she asked Izzy, who was halfway up the stairs.

"Prince Sahir, his guard Soaz, and our cook. They'll find us by morning."

Their weariness was evident, and with little additional talk—to do mostly with oohing over the electric lights—the countess lay down upon the unfolded couch, on her side, her feet over the edge, head on pillow, her wig neatly arrayed on top of a nearby lamp. Lucy Low and her family curled up in a leather chair, all in a heap, like a fur stole. Izzy and Nassif were offered the other half of the couch, and they, too, curled up, one at the head, one at the foot, outer clothing neatly folded on a chair. Blanche perched on the back of Grandma's rocker, rocking it gently as she nestled her head down into her neck feathers, beak on chest.

Dora had left the door open downstairs, so the veebles and the dogs could get under cover if need be. Later, to the accompaniment of thunder and the patter of rain, she heard the dogs talking down below as they cleared a place for themselves. She thought she should have spread out her sleeping bag for them to lie on. Then she remembered, with faint dismay, that she had forgotten her sleeping bag. It was still hanging in the rafters of Jared's garage. The dismay faded into drowsiness. It was only a dream, after all. She didn't need a real sleeping bag. A dream one would suffice, and so convinced, she went away into quiet darkness and did not think of it at all.

She wakened in bright sunlight to confront Izzy, who was seated crosslegged on the other pillow, watching her face while combing his hair. He wore full trousers and a vest. He tied his long hair into a tassel at the back of his head. Nassif was watching him, rather enviously. Her hair—Dora knew she was a she—was short, hidden by the head cloth she wore.

"We found the sanitary facilities," said Izzy carefully.

"Bathroom," said Dora, only half awake, not yet realizing that she was awake at all.

"While Nassif and I have no trouble with . . . ah, latrine, neither countess nor onchiki can manage it. I have suggested they dig small place inside forest. Veebles will use forest, also."

"Very sensible," croaked Dora, sitting up. This wasn't a dream. She would never discuss latrines with a monkey in a dream. My God, it wasn't a dream. It was all true. Plague and all. She folded her arms across her chest, trying to stay calm.

"We would all like to use your . . . rainspout?"

This took a moment. "Shower?"

"Shower. Of course."

"Feel free." She fought down a hysterical giggle. "Hot is on the left, cold is on the right."

He looked puzzled for a moment, then his face cleared. "Temperatures of water. Of course. One mixes."

"Towels," she murmured, close to losing it. "In the cupboard."

Izzy and Nassif went away. She heard sounds from the bathroom, much splashing and high voices either exclaiming or complaining. Communal bathing was evidently in. Otters, monkeys, pig, cockatoo, all en famille. No modesty at all. So why did they wear clothing? She buried her face in the pillow. Japanese cultural style. Dress up in very fancy clothes, but bathe communally in the nude. By the time she had herself under control, the creatures—no, people, she reminded herself sternly, making her face solemn—the people were coming out of the bathroom, variously wrapped in towels or drying one another off or, as with Lucy Low and her brothers, with wet fur standing out in spikes around their necks, composing themselves before the window while they combed their fur with their clawed fingers and groomed themselves with their teeth. Blanche went back to her rocker, spread one wing to its fullest extent and began preening, feather by moist feather.

When Izzy was somewhat dried off and had resumed his clothing, he leapt upon the bed again, seated himself facing Dora and said, conversationally:

"I am interested to see latrine. I once drew up cistern plan to supply flush system, which I learned about in library, but when I put this meme before palace wizard, wizard put his hands over my mouth and said new ideas could get me decapitated as they did my father. Also he said actually doing something new would destroy faith of common people."

"Don't your people invent any new things?"

Izzy shook his head. "It is our religion. Not my religion, but official religion of my people. All is as is supposed to be, therefore, nothing changes. I could understand wizard's concern. When one's livelihood comes from confounding witches and undoing curses in order to cure inexplicable illnesses, it would be counterproductive to have people stay healthy through simple sanitation."

This was said in such a ponderous tone, Dora knew he was quoting someone. "Someone told you that."

"Old Mock. Librarian. Like father to me. He said it is same with religious leaders. When one's livelihood comes from issuing passports out of hell, it would be unprofitable to admit that no such place exists."

To hide her amusement, Dora rose and went to her living room window. It seemed important to assess what kind of day it was going to be. Rain would be a definite damper on things.

A sound came from below, Oyk's voice. "Here comes cook."

Waddling from the trees came a raccoon dressed in a starched though quite rumpled blue apron, paniers and a high puffy hat. He walked erect, then fell to all fours, dipping his nose to the ground, evidently following the trail they had left the night before, then stopped abruptly, rose to his hind legs and looked up at the window where she stood, his jaw dropping in surprise. Oyk strolled out to meet him. The raccoon spoke urgently. The dog scratched himself, as though to say, "So?" The raccoon shrugged, cast a covert glance upward, then followed Oyk back into the yard.

Dora went down to meet him.

"Dzilobommo," he tapped himself on the chest.

"Dora," she said, tapping herself likewise.

"Grummel, grummel, grummel."

"He says he's happy to meet you," said the countess, from behind her. "Armakfatidian language is not entirely oral. Their names are spoken, rest of it seems to be at least partially . . . extrasensory."

"Ah?" Dora responded.

"It tickles in your head," explained Lucy Low from halfway up the stairs. "If you hold your mind very still."

"I see," said Dora.

"Where are Sahir and Soaz?" the countess asked the raccoon.

"Grummel."

"They should be returning soon," said the countess, with a sideways glance at Dora. "You'll be . . . interested in meeting one another."

"No doubt," Dora replied, wondering if the others were sea monsters or dragons. Anything less could not be as interesting as those from the future she had already met. The future. Which was not, so she advised herself sternly, now! There would be time to panic later.

"I have to go to work," she said to the wall. "Either that or call in sick."

Izzy heard her, but didn't understand the idiom, and that took a few moments. They went back up the stairs to find the raccoon in the kitchen, high on Dora's step-stool, removing things from his basket. Mushrooms.

Roots. Greens, mostly dandelion greens. "Grummel," he told her gravely.

"He wants to know if you have grain of some kind," said the countess. "Rice or wheat or corn?"

Dora wordlessly provided a package of rice, the box of cornmeal, her flour cannister, and, after another grummel, eggs and fruit, which were handed back to her with a stern grummel which Nassif took to mean they were to be washed. Nassif leapt to the counter beside the sink and took care of that, while Dora went into her bedroom to get into her clothes. By the time she returned to the living room, the guests were seated variously while being served breakfast. With a flourish, the raccoon pulled out Dora's chair, handed her a napkin, and provided her with a coddled egg and some tart greens with grilled mushrooms as a garnish. The countess, newly bewigged, joined her at the table to be served the same, sitting on her haunches, one foreleg beside the plate, napkin tucked at neck, silverware clamped firmly in the split hoof of the other leg. Lucy Low's kindred dined upon fish and rice, eating directly from the bowl. Nassif, Izzy and Blanche concentrated upon the fruit. Oyk and Irk, so said Izzy, had gone hunting for themselves this morning, and the veebles were well content with the greens they could find in the woods.

They had almost finished when someone knocked at the door downstairs. Dora went down in a fatalistic mood, believing she might encounter almost anything, though the knock had not seemed in any way threatening.

"Abby!" she exclaimed. "What are you doing back here?"

"I forgot my briefcase. It's got the summer school exams I corrected last night, and I need them this—"

"Who is it?" called a voice from upstairs.

"Ah . . ." he said, fumbling for words. "If you have company, I'm, ah, that is . . ." He flushed.

He was interrupted by a volley of barks, and turned, surprised, as a large dog ran from the forest, skidded to a stop, pulled its ears and lips back and began growling at them. Dora recognized the Rottweiller that was usually confined to a run in the backyard next door.

Oyk and Irk came after him, walking very deliberately. One of them said, "Down, sir! I say, down!"

The Rottweiler sank to his haunches, whining.

"We apologize," said Oyk, with a sidewise glance at Abby. "We didn't realize he was not civilized when he invited us to share his food, so we left gate open. Should we take him back and reconfine him?"

Abby sagged against the wall. "Wha..." he murmured. "Gaa..."

"May I introduce Oyk and Irk," said Dora. "They're from the future."

Abby put his hand to his forehead.

"Why did you say, 'Down, sir'?" Dora asked.

"It is what one says to puppies who have no manners," said Oyk, seeming surprised at the question. "Such is our culture."

Abby shook his head, saying weakly, "Dora..."

"It's easier if you pretend you're dreaming," said Dora, turning back to Oyk and Irk. "If you would reconfine the, ah ... uncivilized creature, please."

"What's going on?" grated Abby.

"Upstairs there are two monkeys, and some otters, all of whom talk," she droned at him. "Oh, and a pig, cockatoo and raccoon."

He stared at her a long moment before smiling. "It makes jokes, so early in the morning? What is this, ventriloquism?"

"Come up," she said, offering him her hand. "I want you to meet them all." Come meet the in-laws, she said to herself. Come meet the family.

27

Opalears:
Explorations of a Previous Time

Dora, the talking female umminha, came up the stairs with a talking male umminha. I think until that moment we had all carried some suspicion that she might be singular, an exception to the general rule, but the one with her, the "man," as she said, was also a speaking creature, unmistakably a person. Since there were two of them of opposite sexes, we all had to believe there were probably more, even though umminhi breed as slowly as the proverbial elefant, taking years to reach reproductive age. One can ride a horse at the age of two, but umminhi cannot be burdened at all heavily until they are ten or twelve, and then only the larger ones. They are broken to the box-saddle and tump strap very early, learning to carry small things, then at sixteen or eighteen years of age they can be ridden.

This "man" was named Abby. Dora introduced him to all of us quite properly, the countess first, then Prince

Izakar. The "man" started to put out his hand to the countess, then stopped, obviously embarrassed. When it came time for him to be presented to me, I put out my own hand, clasping his, and allowing him to shake it gravely. This was obviously a present day custom among umminhi persons who walked on their hind legs, as Izzy and I usually did, as Dzilobommo could, when he wished. The others of us would be at a disadvantage if one hand were held. It could put one off balance, so to speak. Abby evidently realized this, for he simply bowed to the others, except for Blanche, who copied me in offering one hand.

"Our guests are from three millenia in the future," Dora said to the "man." She herself, I later learned, was not a "man." She was a womb-man. I thought this distinction interesting. She went on to tell him of our mission, all about the Woput, her words supplemented by lengthy explanations from Izzy and more cogent ones from the countess.

The man sat down, still staring at us as though he could not believe what he saw.

"Unfortunately," the countess said, "where we landed gives us no clue as to location of Woput. Sahir and Soaz went to reconnoiter, and they have not yet returned." She sounded rather worried.

"They would have found nothing much if they went west," Dora said. "The city is the other way. Still, it will be hard to find any clue to your Woput. Thirty years is a long time."

"Are we talking about out there?" asked Abby, gesturing toward the window. "Thirty years ago it was the air base. This end of it, as I recall, was pretty much left alone as grasslands. There were antelope out there, and small animals."

"How do you know?"

"The boy scouts used to camp there. Twenty years ago, I was a scout. It was a traditional campground, one the scouts had used at least since World War II."

Dora turned to Izzy. "When you say you came to the

same place, did you also come in the same season?"

Izzy shook his head, confused, looking to the others.

I said, "It was summer in the future when the Woput came. Two of the wizards were talking about him, and they said he picked a fine day to go back. It was one of the few summer days that year that there had been no rain."

"But was summer there also summer here?"

"I think it likely," said the countess. "The wizards said the end of the coil is current time, and one turn down is exactly three thousand real years."

"Real years?" asked Dora.

Abby nodded. "She probably means actual years, three hundred and sixty-five days plus a few hours."

"So," said Dora.

"So," said Abby eagerly, "thirty years ago, 1970, presumably in summer, somebody showed up out there on the air base. He may have been noticed."

"No," said Izzy. "Wizards say he did not come in his body. He used someone's body. Some person who was already there."

The man curled his lip, looking in that moment much like Soaz. I was glad to see this evidence of personhood in him. Summer after summer in my childhood I had ridden my umminha, Honey, and it was hard for me to reconcile her stupidity and wilfulness with this um-minha's ability to display real thought and motivation. I had never believed umminhi could think. It was hard to admit that these two were thinking, but I made myself accept it by thinking of them as ponjic persons in um-minhi masks.

"Well," the man said, "we can find out who was there. Maybe."

Dora frowned. "Scout records?"

"And base records. Maybe even newspaper clippings. If a guy had his body taken over, maybe there was a story about it. I imagine he'd yell a little, or keel over, or something."

He looked quite excited at the prospect, and I was

annoyed to see that my comrades did not appreciate what this man was suggesting.

"He's going to help us find the Woput!" I told them. "We should say thank you."

Izzy raised his brows at me and shook his head slightly.

Dora saw this. I thought under the circumstances that she was quite calm about it when she said, "You have just realized that your wizards of St. Weel are probably human."

"I suspected it last night," said the countess. "When we met you. When you said this is age of umminhi. Weelians were of the government of this age. They survived because they were in a deep, protected place. That would make them umminhi, is it not so?"

"What?" asked the man. "What's going on?"

"Their Woput was human," said Dora. "That's why he came back! He felt his people, the human race, should have survived instead of these . . . people. He came back to our time in an attempt to change history. Now these people are wondering why we should want to help them, because we could conceivably be on opposing sides in the matter."

"I don't see that at all," said Abby. "There are far too many people. I mean, human people."

"I find it odd that you should think so," said Prince Izakar rather stiffly. "I have never heard one of my people say there were too many of us."

"Perhaps there aren't too many of you," Abby said rather loudly. "There are too many of us. My God, even the trees know it! They're pushing us around, compressing us, nibbling off our houses, maybe making off with babies."

Dora held up her hand. "Please. Prince Izakar, in our time, now, there are human people who are tree-huggers, animal lovers, ecologists, environmentalists. They have few children, for they know man is endangering the earth. They tend to be obsessive recyclers, and they worry about the future of the world a lot. Among that group, you will find allies. There are, however, other humans who would not care if every tree in the world were cut down."

"Now, Dora," said Abby somewhat angrily.

"Well, there are," she said stiffly. "Their prime motivation is money, or jobs—for humans, of course—because money and jobs buy votes or power. If wiping out forests means jobs and room for more people, they will wipe out the forests. If killing animals means jobs and more room for people, they will drive the animals to extinction. Animals and forests do not vote. These destroyers care only that more room and more jobs be made available to accommodate the ever increasing number of people they encourage to be born, because an ever increasing population fuels our economic system."

The countess said, "But can't they see what is happening to the world? Don't they worry about it?"

Dora snorted. "They worry only that they be allowed to live out their own lives in power and comfort. They buy the kind of lives they are destroying for others. They live in gated communities or in mansions on stretches of untouched land or perhaps in twelve-room apartments at the tops of very tall, exclusive buildings. As for the poor, as for the animals, as for the trees, let them die."

"She's talking politics," Abby explained to us, patting her on the shoulder.

I had already decided that! The countess, when she discusses Fasal Grun versus Fasahd, uses many of the same ideas Dora was using. Fasahd is a cannibal, without doubt, but the humans Dora spoke of sounded very person-eating to me.

"I'm sorry," Dora said. "I shouldn't rant on and on like that, but hearing that all of us, or most of us, are to be wiped out shortly makes me so . . . I have nephews, and nieces, and I love them. I have sisters and brothers. . . . I don't know whether to be angry or glad! I've thought of it, God knows, but even though we deserve it, I've always believed—always prayed that it would get just bad enough that *everyone* would admit it, and then we could fix it before it was too late.''

The man put his arms around her, very tenderly, I thought. When he looked at her, he looked rather like Izzy looking at me, and I found the idea surprising. I had thought Izzy's regard was mere . . . fellow-tribe feeling, but perhaps it was more than that. I turned away, and there was Izzy, looking at me in that exact same way. I averted my eyes, feeling very strange inside.

Dora leaned her cheek against the man's for a moment before pushing herself away from him. ''We must think,'' she said. ''We must all think, very clearly. I believe we are all allies here, but we must be sure what is involved.''

The countess drew herself up and nodded. ''You are wise to suggest this, person. I fear thus far, none of us have had time to think at all.''

Both Dora and Abby ''called in sick,'' which seemed to be something one could do in their world, providing one did not do it very frequently. It seemed that ''sick of the routine,'' or ''sick of life in general'' qualified one to take advantage of the opportunity. I thought how nice that would be for a slave in the harim. If I didn't want to wash vegetables, I would just call in sick. The idea was amusing, and when I told Lucy Low, she too was amused.

''If I don't want to swim out in the icy water and catch salmon in my teeth, I'll just call in sick,'' she said. Then she and her brothers and I all lost ourselves in giggles, they at the thought of sickness being an excuse, I at the thought of Lucy Low with a salmon in her teeth. Though they were, come to think of it, extremely sharp teeth.

Dora said the first order of business ought to be to guarantee the safety of us new arrivals. Her announcement of this priority started a general discussion.

''Look,'' she said, when we had gone astray from the subject several times. ''I'm trying to explain why you are not safe here, in this time. You are less safe as speaking, dressed-up people than you are as plain animals.

While you do look slightly different from the animals I'm familiar with, it's a difference that most people won't notice, because most humans don't really look at animals provided they're not wearing clothing and commenting on the weather! Those who do really look at animals would probably be your friends, but there are the exceptions—the media people, for instance—''

We were unfamiliar with the word, so we interrupted her and she stopped to tell us about media people. "They are really cannibals," she concluded. "They eat people three meals a day plus snacks!"

"Are you saying we dare not carry out our mission?" the countess asked.

"She's saying that if you're going to survive in order to carry out your mission, anyplace you go, anything you do has to be carefully thought out," Abby replied. "In the forest, you're probably fairly safe. Here, in Dora's house, you're okay. Half a dozen blocks that way is an avenue where there is no forest. As you approach the city, there are fewer and fewer trees. If you go to the city, asking to look at records, you'll be mobbed within minutes."

"Killed?" asked Lucy Low, her eyes very wide.

"Locked up in a cage," said Dora. "In a zoo, or worse, in a laboratory. Where people would take samples of your blood and your bone and your brains." She sighed. "Where they'd probably vivisect you to find out what made you tick and then *tsk tsk* when you died. You'll have to trust us to do part of your mission for you. We can bring you the documents, so you can see them for yourself. . . ."

"If there are any." Abby frowned, staring out the window at the morning forest. "It's like a needle in a haystack."

Dzilobommo interrupted with a lengthy grummel.

Blanche persisted. "Dzilobommo wants to know why you are helping us? What is your advantage?"

Dora cried, "I'm not sure we have one. Knowing what you have told me, of course I'll try to survive. I may not make it. The human race may not make it, but if humans die, does intelligence have to die as well? Earth includes its creatures, and that means you! Why shouldn't we want to help you?"

"But other umminhi . . . persons will not think the same?" Blanche persisted.

"A lot of human beings don't think at all," Dora said in a weary voice. "So long as they have their flowerpot on the windowsill and their canary in a cage, they will live forever in concrete without realizing they are in prison."

"If they do not know, what difference does it make?" I asked.

Abby shook his head at me. "To them, none. To you? Perhaps everything. Aren't we allowed to choose sides?"

Another long silence during which we looked at one another. I believed the umminhi. I think Izzy believed them. I wasn't sure about the others. The countess rose, saying our group would go into the forest, for private consultation, leaving the umminhi to talk together. We trooped away down the stairs, all of us, and from the window Dora watched us wander off among the trees, all but the veebles, who were sprawled against the sunny wall of the house, half asleep.

A little way into the woods we met Sahir and Soaz, who looked very tired and dirty, and while they rested we told them our news.

28

Criminal Connections

"They don't trust us," Dora said, as the visitors disappeared into the woods.

"They have good reason not to," said Abby.

"Maybe more than you know," she said, dryly. "I've just realized this may be why Winston was killed, and Martin Chamberlain, and maybe the other scientist. They were all working in genetics. I wouldn't be surprised to find that the animals out at Randall Pharmaceuticals are the ancestors of our guests."

"Do the animals at the pharmaceutical company talk?"

"According to Joe Penton, they had a dog that did."

"Take our guests out there and have them wander around and find out."

"Have them talk to the animals?"

"If they can communicate, they're not animals, are they, Dora?"

"I've never thought so, no. Intelligent creatures are as human as most of us."

"Scientists argue about that."

"Scientists!" She made a spitting motion. "Back in the 1850s, scientists wrote that blacks were not human, that it was perfectly proper to enslave them. In the early 1900s, scientists said that women benefitted from clitorectomies, because it stopped their infantalism and allowed them to mature, though they were still too fragile to work outside the home. Right up until the 1990s, scientists could explain why gays were abnormal and perverted and needed to be cured or imprisoned. Research is often slanted by conviction, and you know it, Abby. If there's power or reputation to be made, you can find some scientist who will say most anything."

"My God," he said. "What debate club did you graduate from?"

She flushed. "Grandma and I used to talk about it. We read a lot."

"I love nature, too, dear one, but I'm not sure your guests are natural creatures."

"So we're not sure of that," she said angrily. "So what? Even if they resulted from experimentation, who's to say that same experimentation wouldn't have occurred in nature, given enough time? We're the result of nature's constant reshuffling, aren't we?" She turned away, shaking her head. "If a man and woman use their sex organs to make a baby, the baby's natural and human. If a human being uses his brain to make a reasoning creature, is that less natural or human? Natural or not, it would be wrong not to help them."

"I'd like to put Dzilobommo in my car and take him to visit a friend of mine who has a pet raccoon. I'd like to know if Dzilobommo can talk to him."

"You'd have to take Lucy Low along, or the countess, as translator."

"I can't imagine the countess being willing to go without her clothes."

"Well, Lucy doesn't wear any. Her head is oddly shaped for an otter, though. And she's big."

"Maybe a cross between the giant otters of South America and a North American species?"

"More likely sea otter," she said. "Though her feet aren't entirely webbed, particularly the front ones. She's only about two and a half feet tall when she stands on her hind legs."

"Izzy and Nassif?"

"Japanese macaques. They're the ones with stubby tails. The heads are different, though. I'm surprised they're monkeys, not apes. Maybe there are apes, in their world."

"Dora, I'm amazed at you. You seem very little surprised by any of this!"

She shook her head. "Oh, hell, Abby, I've always thought of animals as people. Many of them, at any rate. Not sheep. Not cows, much. But goats, yeah, and dogs and cats, sure, and monkeys, of course. And apes. Elephants. Dolphins. Whales. Some kinds of birds."

"Cockroaches?"

"No. Not any kind of insect, except maybe a whole hive, as a kind of . . . what? Corporate personality?"

"You really meant all that stuff you were spouting while they were here, it wasn't just fluff? For their benefit?"

"Did you think it was fluff?" she asked angrily, then gulped at being angry. Not with Abby. Why not? Well, because . . . Because he had suddenly become very important to her. Did she dare be angry with Abby? Would he let her be angry sometimes?

Evidently he would, for he said:

"Don't get in an uproar, love. Just being sure. If we're going to do something affecting the entire human race, here, I want to be sure I understand what the ground rules are."

She thought about it as she moved about, clearing the dishes, stacking them in the dishwasher, putting away the items Dzilobommo had used. "I like our guests. I don't want to see them wiped out. I like a lot of humans. I don't want to see us wiped out, either. I don't want to die of a plague. I don't want my brothers and sisters to die in one. If this Woput from the future succeeds in stopping the animal research, it will destroy our guests, but it won't do anything to stop the plague. The Woput doesn't even know about the plague. He doesn't know the real reason humans get wiped out. His people, the so-called Weelians, didn't know until Izzy told them."

"You feel if the holy war can't be stopped, better for our guests' races to survive than for none of us to do so."

"Well, yes, don't you?" She examined his face closely, fighting down the urge to lean against him, let him put his arms protectively around her. She gritted her teeth and told herself to behave. "If creation has a purpose intelligible to us, then the development of intelligence may be it. Better intelligent pigs and dogs and monkeys than no intelligence at all!"

"You realize we may already be too late," he said.

"How do you mean?"

"If the animals are the result of the experimentation at Randall Pharmaceuticals, the scientist has been killed. We're too late to do anything about that. . . ."

She shook her head. "Maybe not. The experimental animals may still be alive. And I've got a pile of papers in the bedroom with bibliographies referring to dozens of other scientists. There are a lot more than three people working on this, though the Woput may have targeted them all!"

"Where do the trees fit in?"

"Fit into what?"

"Why did the trees start doing what they're doing? Is that research that got out of hand? Is it an invasion? Is it a weapon that got loose? What's going on with the trees?"

"I don't know," she said, plopping herself down on the couch. "Abby, I honest to God don't have a clue about the trees, and seemingly neither do my guests, but I know somebody who might."

He waited, head cocked.

"Harry Dionne," she said. "Or maybe his father."

He laughed. "What do you think? It's an angelic visitation?"

"Harry talked about religion, but he didn't say a word about angels." She gave him a reproving look and went to the phone to call Harry Dionne.

29

Opalears: The Disbelievers

Out in the woods we were having a conversation about one thing and another. We told Soaz and Prince Sahir all about Dora and her man Abby, but we couldn't convince them the womb-man was actually intelligent.

"All you're saying is she *sounds* intelligent," said Sahir. "But it could just as well be instinctive behavior, copying responses she has heard in response to certain cue words. We all know that umminha simply are not intelligent."

"Even in our time, they use tools," said the countess.

"Tools!" Soaz snarled. "They will pull a board loose and use it to level a sleeping place. That's not tool-using."

"They put things around themselves to keep themselves warm," I offered. "And around the bottoms of their young."

"As does any veeble, making a nest for its sucklings."

330

"They understand commands," said Lucy Low.

"So do veebles," growled Soaz. "And we all know umminhi make sounds like talk, but it has no sense in it."

"It could be a language we simply don't understand," I offered.

Izzy shook his head. "It isn't. I read an account in my library, some ponjic scrivener in Isfoin wrote a paper on it. The sounds umminhi make are not recognizable in any known language."

"Of our time," I persisted. "But what about this time? There may be languages spoken now that we know nothing of."

Izzy shook his head. "My library records history for over seven thousand years. It begins with the Gyptian era, and every language spoken from that time to our time is in my library."

"But the paper was written in Isfoin," I shouted. "Where they don't *have* your library! That author could only compare it to known languages *there*."

"Hush," said the countess. "All this talk is to no purpose. The umminha is intelligent. Her responses are not instinctive. Only your prejudice could make you believe so, Prince Sahir. We have for so long rejoiced in being intelligent, in pointing to the poor beasts who are not and comparing ourselves to them, that it is hard for us to relinquish our position of superiority. No matter what the umminhi of our age are like, this one here, now, is intelligent. And so is the man."

"Well, I don't believe it," said Prince Sahir. "I believe when we move out into the world, we will find we have landed in some kind of zoo. We will find our people out there, and we will find the umminhi in stables, where they belong."

"If the umminhi are correct, we would be mistaken to move into the world at all."

"They're lying," said Sahir.

"Come now," said the countess angrily, rising to her full height. "A creature without intelligence cannot lie.

You can't have it both ways, Prince Sahir. If the creature is lying, she is intelligent. If she's telling us the truth about the danger we're in, she is intelligent."

"You yourself say 'creature,' " said Soaz, sulkily.

"Habit," she said. "Nonetheless, I believe her."

So did I. So did the onchiki. Blanche offered no opinion, one way or the other. Dzilobommo felt she was probably intelligent, because of the ingredients he found in her kitchen. Cuisine, he grummeled, was equivalent to intelligence. Only Sahir and Soaz believed, or claimed to believe, that Dora and her mate were merely animals who uttered previously learned phrases when cued by conversation, and who had also, possibly, taken over a dwelling built by ponjic people.

Of course, Sahir and Soaz had not seen Dora and her mate, a fact Izzy reminded me of. "My library is full of people asserting natural law on the basis of behavior that has never been observed in nature," he whispered, before turning toward the prince. "Will you proceed on your beliefs?" he asked. "Will you leave the rest of us to go out in the city?"

"What city?" growled Soaz. "We have only the words of umminhi to tell us there is a city."

"Very well," said the countess in a tone I had not heard her use before, a very regal tone, one that held anger, but anger strictly controlled. "If you do not distrust Blanche's eyes or ears or voice, I suggest we attempt to verify what Dora told us. The city, so says Dora, is beyond, in that direction," and she pointed toward the house. "According to Abby, there is an avenue in that direction." She pointed again, perpendicular to the first line. "I suggest Blanche fly, very quietly, to that avenue, then along that avenue until she can see the city. When she has seen it, when she can either verify or has disproved what we have been told, let her return to us here."

"Blanche and I," said Sahir. "We will both go to this avenue and see what we shall see."

The countess seemed mindful to disagree with him,

but she had been put out of temper. She merely turned away from him, suggesting to the rest of us that we return to the house. No matter whether occupied by persons or by creatures, she said, the house at least seemed safe.

We politely hailed Dora from the foot of the stairs. When we came into the room, Soaz making his leather trousers creak with tension as he stared around himself with slitted eyes, I went forward to make the introduction.

"We met others of us in forest," I said. "Prince Sahir has gone with Blanche to explore, and this is the eunuch, Soaz."

"I'm sorry," said Dora. "We do it to cats in our time, too."

"Do what?" Izzy asked.

"Neuter them. Cut off their . . . well, you know. So they can't make kittens."

Izzy said something to Soaz, who screamed in rage, his fangs gleaming and the fur on his tail standing out.

Izzy said nervously, "In our . . . society it doesn't mean that. Eunuch. It simply means he guarded females of another tribe, ah, species. Soaz wishes me to tell you he can make kittens, cubs, whenever he feels like it."

Dora swallowed deeply, and I saw her struggling not to laugh. Abby said something loud and hearty to turn attention away, and we assembled ourselves comfortably in the room while Dora and Abby went to the kitchen area to get food for Soaz, politely refusing Dzilobommo's offer of assistance.

I heard Soaz say to Izzy, "You see! You call that intelligence?"

Quickly, I followed the umminhi, staying out of sight beside the cold box as they whispered to one another.

"Now what's he!" demanded Abby.

"I don't know. He's got kind of a Persian look to him, but he's bigger than any domestic cat I ever saw. What do you think? Forty, fifty pounds?"

"He's spotted."

"Well, not really. It's kind of an interrupted tabby. Grandma had a mama cat like that. It looks like spots, but it's really interrupted stripes—"

"What's the difference?" he hissed. "He's spotted, he's striped, he's Persian, he's a mutated cheetah. That doesn't matter. What matters is, he talks!"

"If it weren't for that rather fluffy fur, his head shape would be more evident. It's big. Room enough in there for vocal chords, a bigger brain . . ."

I looked at Soaz with new eyes. He did, indeed, have a very large head. But then, so did I. Compared to the umminhi, that is. But then, they were taller.

"Sahir doesn't think you are intelligent," I said, coming out from behind the cold box, speaking quite loudly, so the others could hear me.

"We haven't had the pleasure of meeting Sahir," said Abby.

"He says you just make noises. They don't mean anything."

"Well, if that were so, conversation would be difficult, wouldn't it?" he said.

"Oh, Abby," Dora said. "I don't blame him. Think of all those people who've worked with apes. The ape learns hundreds of signs or symbols, and the ape learns to ask for things and comment on things, and then some linguist pops up and says it isn't language at all, it's just labeling or recitation of nouns or the researcher misinterpreted, or the standards weren't rigorous, because the grammar isn't there. Think of that gray parrot that can identify colors and shapes and materials. Not language, they say. They assume speech isn't speech without grammar, and they assume human grammar is the only kind there is."

"Well, if it isn't the only kind of speech, why do *we* speak it?" I asked.

Dora sighed. I had heard the countess sigh in just such a fashion. Of these small things are similarities drawn.

"My guess," she said. "My guess is that a scientist we know of, a Dr. Edgar Winston, or perhaps one of his colleagues, did some gene mixing and came up with animals who had some humanish interpolations in their brains plus a more or less parrot or human voice box and tongue muscles. I say muscles, because Soaz's tongue is not manlike, but his words are.''

Prince Izakar said, in a voice of dawning awareness, ''You're saying that there is in this . . . world . . . science of . . . ummm . . . changing creatures? Changing their shape? Their nature? Their, ah . . . characteristics?''

''Genetics,'' she said. ''Playing with DNA. Putting one creature's gene's in another creature's body, or mind. Yes. Up until recently it was mostly vegetables, but they are recombining human and animal DNA. The man who was foremost in the research was murdered recently.''

More conversation, even more intense.

Then Izzy said incredulously, ''You are saying, we are not people who have evolved but are . . . creations of your people?''

Dora looked at Abby, shrugging. We read what she meant, though she did not want to say it.

''In light of what we find here, one would almost think it possible,'' said the countess at last, her solemn voice giving the words an ominous weight. ''If you are only . . . speaking species in this time, we would have to consider . . . if your people could have created us.''

Soaz screamed. ''No. Impossible! We were not created by umminhi!''

Silently, Dora crossed the room to a long, low bookcase that separated the room from the stair. She took from it a book, and she placed the book on the low table beside the couch. Izzy leapt upon the table, and so did I. We looked at the cover. It said:

The Audubon Society
ENCYCLOPEDIA OF
ANIMAL LIFE

Beneath the words was a picture of a regal person, his hair radiating from his forehead, his sideburns and beard smooth and well groomed, his eyes very wise, his expression one of kindly tolerance.

"The emperor!" cried Izzy. "A picture of the emperor!"

The countess came to look. "It is! How can you have a picture of Emperor Faros VII?"

Abby said very quietly: "It is a picture of a grizzly bear."

We stared at the two umminhi, our mouths open. Dora's expression was sympathetic to our confusion. "Look at the book," she said. "Look at the book."

Oh, we looked at the book. We found many ponji people in it. Lemurs and vervets and orangutans and chimpanzees and there, on page 39, a picture that could almost have been of Izzy. Macaque, it said. He was standing naked in a forest. The kasturic people, who do so much of our building, were there. Beavers, they were called. The sea people were there, and the Onchik-Dau, what are called sea lions. There were many pheleds. Soaz looked at those pictures long and hard. He was most like the lynx, I thought, looking from him to picture and back to him again. The kannic people were there, foxes and coyotes—almost like Oyk and Irk—and wolves. Dzilobommo's people were there, on the same page as a mythical creature all our children knew, the panda. Who has not received a little stuffed panda doll as a child? I had one. I used to sleep with it.

There was the legendary elefant, huge and horrid, and there were the horses and burros, in many kinds. One was even striped. There were creatures we had never heard of: the rhinoceros and the tapir—relatives of the scuinic people, said the book—and the giraffe. There was only one, very unflattering picture of a scuinic person, and it was labeled "wild boar." There were pictures of bison and deer—Soaz said they still existed, far to the south of Isfoin. There were also goats, much like our kapriel people. Then there were the birds, with a beautiful picture of one of Blanche's kin, the Hyacinthine Macaw. And then the serpents and the fishes. Our mammalian peoples were all spoken of in the first few pages of the book. We were not many compared to all the swimming and squirming creatures of the world.

None of the peoples or creatures in the book wore clothing.

"Prince Sahir should have taken off his clothing," I cried. "If a human sees him, he will be in danger."

I had no sooner uttered the words than we heard Blanche, screaming at us from below. We could not make out her words until she arrived at the top of the stairs, where she flapped her wings in a frenzy and screamed:

"The prince has been captured; Prince Sahir has been captured. The umminhi have taken him away."

Meeting Prince Sahir

Dora knotted her hands into fists and hit the wall. "Damn," she said. "He should have been warned. . . ."

"We never had the chance to warn him," said Abby. "The thing is, how are we going to get him back?"

"Describe the happening, Blanche!" demanded the countess. "Who was it took the prince?"

"Umminhi . . ."

"We know that, dear. Calm down. Describe them. Perhaps Dora can tell something from their clothing, or their size or something."

Blanche fluttered for a few moments more, eventually calming down enough to say, "They came in a vehicle. It had a room in the front for the umminhi, and rooms along the sides with doors. The umminhi had caught a kannic person who looked rather like Oyk, and they were putting him into one of the little rooms along the side. The prince saw this, and he stepped out of the trees and demanded to know what they were doing.

"One of the men had a long pole in his hand. He reached out with it before the prince could move, and swooped him up. It was a net on the pole, I think. The umminhi laughed very loudly and they put the prince into another of the little rooms, then they stood looking at him for a long time, shaking their heads, then they got in the front room of the vehicle and it moved away. I followed, among the trees, calling the prince's name, and he screamed at me to get help." She moaned. "I should have told him to be more careful!"

"Which direction did the vehicle go?" demanded Dora.

Blanche shivered. "I was on the near side of the avenue, and it went to my left."

"Toward town," said Dora. "Were there words on the side of the vehicle?"

"Yes. I did not read them. They were in a circle around some kind of emblem. . . ."

"Animal control truck," said Abby. "Has to be."

"We'll go in your car," said Dora. "We'll need to get to the pound as soon as possible."

"Why?" demanded the countess. "Why such a hurry?"

"He might be . . . injured," said Dora. "He was wearing clothing, and he probably doesn't have the sense to keep his mouth shut. The animal control officers are going to tell everyone they've caught a talking pig, and it won't be an hour before the media find out, plus maybe the people at Randall Pharmaceuticals. Edgar Winston may have been their chief genius, but other people out there are working on the same thing!"

"I will go with you," the countess announced.

"With all due respect," said Dora. "We will be better able to save the prince if we go alone. I am a law enforcement officer. That is my job. I have identification that entitles me to go into places and ask questions. It would be better if I could do that without people wondering why I have animals with me."

"She's right," said Izzy. "We will be safer staying here."

"We are not accomplishing our mission here," said Soaz.

"No," agreed Abby. "But, as we've said before, you're going to have to trust us to help you accomplish your mission. Your job is to find your Woput, ours, as I see it, is to help you, but first, presumably, you want Prince Sahir saved."

The visitors could only agree.

"I wish one of us could go along. Even Blanche . . . ," said the countess.

"The safest ones to go along would be Oyk and Irk," said Dora. "They're laconic anyhow, and lots of people ride around with dogs in the car. We'll take them, if you like."

Dora brushed her hair, got into her jacket, and was met at the foot of the stairs by Oyk and Irk, both of whom announced their readiness to go along.

"Do you know the command, *heel*?" asked Dora.

"It is one we use with puppies," admitted Oyk in a grudging growl.

"Well, it's one that will keep you safe," said Dora. "One of you heel to me, and the other one to Abby, left side, close, and you'll be almost as safe as if you were on the leash. And for heaven's sake, don't say anything!"

They jogged down the street to the avenue, where Abby's car was parked, top down, beside the custodial tree. Oyk and Irk got in the back. As soon as they started to move, the two kannids put their front feet on the window and stuck their heads out into the windstream.

"Why do you do that?" Dora asked.

"Oh, the smells," said Oyk. "The wonderful smells, going by so fast, it's like . . . oh, it's like . . ."

"Music," said Irk. "It feels exactly as I have heard Prince Izakar describe music. Crescendos. Diminuendos. Arpeggios. Harmonies. Melodies. Ahhhh." He took a deep breath, nostrils quivering, then let it out again with a sigh.

Dora and Abby exchanged glances. "Well," said Dora, "haven't you wondered?"

"Not really," he said. "I always figured they liked the smells."

"Musically?"

He shrugged. "It's probably the only analogy he could come up with. I think taste would be closer, personally. A meal created by a master chef, complete with wines. . . ." He licked his lips. "Where is the pound, by the way?"

She gave him directions. It was past noon when they arrived at the hill overlooking the city. Oyk and Irk stopped smelling the wind and sat quite erect on the rear seat, taking it all in.

"It's a lot bigger than Palmody," said Oyk.

"It's a lot bigger than anything," Irk agreed.

"It's too big, and that's what we meant when we said there are too many of us," remarked Abby, making a left turn onto a cross street busy with pedestrians.

"Umminhi," said Oyk gravely, as though his worst fears had been realized. "Ganchi umminhi."

A few more turns, a bumpy crossing over railroad tracks, and they came to the long, low building that housed the pound.

"I want you to understand the dangers and communicate them to your colleagues," said Dora in a low voice. "So I'm going to try to get you in there. Heel, just like before, and if the guy in charge says you have to leave, you wait until Abby takes you out, understand?"

"We would be perfectly capable of coming out by ourselves," said Oyk.

"Not unless you understood human speech," growled Dora. "Which you must not let on that you do!"

The two subsided, putting themselves in close heel position and staying there as Abby and Dora negotiated the doors. The desk inside was empty. Dora pushed a brightly labeled button, and they sat down to wait.

"What's our story?" asked Abby.

"You're my neighbor, you lost your pig, I've brought you down to see if they have it."

"And if the pig has been talking?"

"I'll think of something," muttered Dora.

There was noise beyond the double doors, shouting and laughter.

"Dora," whispered Irk. "I hear Prince Sahir."

She stared down at him. "You can hear him?"

"My ears are very good. He's talking. He's yelling, in fact. He's calling them sons of menstruating mares. That is very dirty talk."

"Oh, Lord," said Abby.

"All right," Dora mused. "We say he isn't a talking pig, he swallowed a microphone."

"I'll try," said Abby.

They got up from the bench and pushed their way through the double doors. Beyond a file room and office was another door, this one opening on a long aisle between cages. The people at the end of the aisle were conducting an excited conversation, above the sound of which rose a frenzied voice.

"You let me out at once, you hear, you beasts, you creatures, fit for nothing but riding on, you evil-doers . . ."

Abby began laughing loudly. This attracted the attention of the people at the end of the aisle, who turned and moved toward them as Abby shouted, "You've got my pig! Good, I thought I'd lost him."

Abby was at once surrounded. He began a long, complicated story about the pig and the microphone, while Oyk and Irk slipped around the group and trotted down to the end of the aisle. Inside the cage raged a furious Sahir, his clothing torn, one ear crumpled. He opened his mouth to scream at the sight of Oyk and Irk.

"Don't say a word," whispered Oyk. "Not another word."

Prince Sahir subsided, seething.

"Dora and Abby are trying to get you out. Don't say a word more to any umminha, not any. If Dora and Abby can't get you out, remain silent. The more you talk, the more they will be determined to keep you. You must make them think you are a creature! If it were me, I'd get those clothes off."

"Hey," came a shout from down the aisle. "What're those dogs doing there?"

"They're mine," said Dora in a firm, no nonsense voice. "Come, Irk. Come, Oyk."

Obediently, with a last warning look at Sahir, the kanni turned and trotted back up the aisle.

"Heel," said Dora.

A belligerent man in a brown shirt was saying, "Swallowed a microphone, eh? So how come he seemed to be answering questions we asked?"

"Well, it's got a receiver and transmitter," Abby said. "My brother's at the other end, listening and answering. He's a practical joker, and he's the one who dressed up the pig and put the mike in his food trough, then the pig swallowed the microphone and got out of the yard. . . . Well, you know the rest."

"And you can prove this is your pig?"

Dora knelt down and patted Oyk, whispering urgently, "What was he wearing?"

"Trousers, robe, headcloth, all white cotton," muttered Oyk.

"He was wearing trousers, a robe, and a headcloth, all white cotton," said Dora.

"I guess that's your pig, all right," said the brown-shirted man. "Well, I'll tell the lab people when they come that he's yours, and you can get him from them."

"What lab people?" asked Abby.

"People from Randall Pharmaceuticals," said the brownshirt. "Ramon, there, he used to work for Randall. He called them as soon as the pig got here, figured it was one of their animals. They said they were missing a talking pig, but they didn't know what he was wearing. You know what he's wearing, but you say he don't really talk. So, I figure, you work it out between you.''

Dora thought of using her badge, then discarded the idea. Actually having Sahir at Randall might get them some information they needed.

''Well, then, Abby and I'll just go down and see Piggy,'' she said.

They were not allowed to go alone. When they arrived outside the pen, they found Sahir, naked as a sausage, lying sprawled on the ragged remnants of his clothing.

''Poor Piggy,'' said Dora in a cooing voice. ''We're going to get issums home just as soon as we can, but issums has to go to Randall Pharmaceuticals first, because they thought issums was a talky pig. They cut up talky pigs to see what makes them talk. That's all right. Dora and Abby will go to Randall Pharmaceuticals and bring issums home, very soon.''

The cage's occupant glared at her from piggy eyes in which all sign of intelligence had been overlaid by anger and shame.

''Squee-uink,'' said Prince Sahir.

At Randall Pharmaceuticals

When the Randall Pharmaceutical truck showed up half an hour later, complete with animal cage in the back, Dora and Abby waited until Sahir had been loaded—silently—then followed the truck to the lab. Just inside the gate it turned to the right and drove down the lane that led past the animal pens. Using her badge to get past the gate, Dora directed Abby to follow them. Beside the last pens she saw the driver leaning out of his window, talking to Joe Penton.

"Oyk and Irk," she said softly. "When we get down there, you see if you can wander around the pens very quietly and assess what's going on. Do any of those animals talk? Are they intelligent? The men seem to be putting the prince in with the other pigs. Let's hope he makes friends easily."

Abby parked between the truck and the pens. Dora got out on the side nearest the men while the dogs left quietly on the other side and trotted away. Abby got out to lean nonchalantly against the car while Dora strolled over to join Joe and the driver.

"Joe," she said, raising a hand. "How's things?"

"Hi, Sergeant," he said. "You still working on this case?"

"Still am. Actually, it's my day off, but my friend over there lost his pet pig, and when we found it at the pound, the guy there said Randall had claimed it. You know anything about that?"

Joe shook his head in disgust. "It's Bill, you know, Bill Twenzel? He gets this call, and he thinks it's some kinda practical joke, so he plays along, he says sure, if it talks, it's our pig. Then it turned out it wasn't a joke, they really had a pig that talked, so by this time one of the muckety-muck lab guys here, Marsh McGovern— who's a VIP, Very Idiotic Pain in the Ass—he hears this conversation about a talking pig. So this guy, Marsh, he sends the truck, and here we are with one of the bosses innerested in this pig." He unlatched the gate of the pen and held it open while the driver manhandled Sahir through it, then shut and latched it once more. The driver raised a hand in farewell, then took himself and truck back the way he had come.

Dora persisted, "So you're saying even though he belongs to a friend of mine, you can't let us have him?"

"I'm sorry, Sergeant, but you know, orders is orders. I can't let him go, not until Marsh sees him. Prob'ly tomorrow. I'll explain it and the guy'll let me turn him over to you."

"Well, it was a joke, sort of," said Dora, quite loudly, hoping Sahir would pay attention. "He swallowed a microphone, like in a cordless phone, you know, so he must have sounded like he was talking."

"I be damned. Marsh McGovern, he'll probably want to X-ray him."

"Today?" asked Dora, trying not to betray the panic this announcement provoked.

"Nah. He's all tied up today. Tomorrow, like I say. He'll see the mike on the film, and he'll know it was a false alarm. Ordinarily, it wouldn'a happened, but Marsh's got this wild hair, you know. He's just sure one of these days, some animal is going to mutate and start talking. The other lab people, they laugh at him, but I guess he's smart enough, except for believing in UFOs.''

"Why UFOs?'' drawled Abby, who had walked over to the pigpen and was reaching his hands through the wire to scratch the backs of two friendly inhabitants. Prince Sahir sat in one corner, naked, morose and scowling. "What have UFOs got to do with animal mutations?''

"Well, he figures that's where the mutation will come from, you know? He's positive men didn't evolve here by themselves. He thinks ETs came, millions of years ago, and they mutated an ape so we'd evolve. And now it's time for some other animal to make a great leap forward, that's how he talks.''

"Well, I guess tomorrow is good enough. One day away from home won't kill him.'' Dora dug the side of her shoe into the soil. "Say, Joe, my friend has to run an errand. Is it okay if I stay here and look at the animals until he gets back?''

Joe shrugged, cast a quick look up the hill, and said, "I don't guess anybody'll mind. If they do, just say you're still investigating, you know.''

He wandered on about his duties. Dora and Abby had a whispered conversation, after which Abby took off in his car, stopping at the gate to explain he'd be returning. Dora, meantime, wandered among the pens, looking for Oyk and Irk.

She found them outside a cage housing a small black bear and two cubs. Both kanni looked up alertly when Dora came around the corner, and Oyk—who was slightly larger and had a curlier tail—came trotting over.

"She talks,'' he said. "Six kanni talk. The scuinans in with the prince talk. That's all so far.''

"My God,'' whispered Dora.

"Who is your god?'' asked Oyk. "You speak of it often.''

Dora gritted her teeth. "Another time, Oyk. Right now I've got to figure out . . . do the people here know that the animals . . . that is, the . . . ah, other tribes can talk?"

"They say their protector knew. They called him Daddy Eddy. But he taught them not to talk to anyone but him."

"What other creat—that is, people might be here? Raccoon, ah . . . armakfatidi?"

"There is one, but she grummels."

"From something Dr. Winston did?"

"No. I think all armakfatidi grummel, always have grummeled. Just, no one could hear them before our time."

"Onchiki?"

"The scuinans say the onchiki were taken inside."

Oyk watched her fixedly while she frowned at her feet, murmuring, "We'll have to get them out of here somehow. They're not safe here, not in the long run, not with Edgar Winston dead."

They started down the next line of cages, Oyk trotting ahead and eyeing the inhabitants of each pen with interest. He went around a corner, was out of sight for a few moments, then came speeding back. "Pheleda," he said, turning once more and looking over his shoulder at Dora. "Wants to talk to you."

She hurried, stopping short as she rounded the corner and confronted the large cat who awaited her. Lynx, she said to herself. Not quite that large, but otherwise, much like. So like Soaz as to be his sister. Oyk murmured to the big cat, and she came close to the fence. "Is it true you have a male with you?" she purred, rubbing herself against the wire. "The dog says you do."

"Yes," whispered Dora.

"I'd like to meet him. It's very lonely here. I'm all by myself."

She went back to her sheltered bed and lay down, fixing Dora with wide, golden eyes. "Tell him," she called.

Dora moved away, shaking her head, trying to get her tumbling thoughts into an order that made sense. Edgar Winston had done whatever he had done, had created whatever he had created, and then the Woput killed him. But the Woput didn't kill the creations. So, possibly, the Woput didn't know Winston had yet succeeded. And he mustn't know!

Oyk came to walk beside her, then Irk. They did not talk. The three of them strolled, trying to appear casual, stopping outside each cage to inspect the inhabitants, whispering to them, but receiving no further response. It was impossible to know whether the animals could not or would not talk, and Dora felt her frustration growing.

It was Irk who heard Abby returning. They met him at the corner, where he sat in the car, making a great crumple of a paper bag and a small box.

"You got one," said Dora.

"I got one," he confirmed, displaying the small battery powered receiver-transmitter assembly. "It's the smallest one they had. A pig might be able to swallow it."

Dora took it from him and went to the corner pen, where seven pairs of eyes watched her curiously. "This device," she said, displaying it, "should be found in your pen. It should look chewed, and it should be found in your . . . droppings. It will explain how one of you seemed to be talking when, in fact, we all know you can't."

She reached through the wire and laid the device on the ground. One of the pigs, not Sahir, came to pick it up and carry it to the back of the pen. Several pairs of eyes looked it over carefully before returning to Dora.

"Thank you," she said.

"Thank you," said someone. It was the same voice she had heard earlier in the summer saying, "Poor guy."

"We'll be back," she remarked. "We think it would be a good idea to get you out of here."

"We can dig out anytime. Any of us," said the same voice. "We can even hide the holes."

"Why haven't you?" she asked, carefully not looking at the pen.

"Nowhere to go," said the voice. "We figure, we'd have to have someplace to go. Daddy Eddy said it isn't safe out there."

Dora nodded, then raised her voice and called, "Joe?"

His voice came from up the hill. "Over here. You need something?"

She walked toward the voice. "Just saying good-bye. Hey, this is really a marvelous collection of animals. Almost a zoo."

Joe emerged from behind a feeder and leaned against a post, becoming expansive as he gestured widely at the pens. "This's only part of it, Sergeant. Dr. Winston, when he finished with some of his experiments, he used to give some of the animals to friends of his, like pets, you know? Even with all these here, I bet he gave twice that many away."

Dora kept her face carefully neutral, clenching her hands into fists to hide the fact that they trembled. "What kind of animals, Joe?"

"Oh, he had some bears, bigger ones than here, you know. Here you can't keep anything really big. They was just cubs, but they was getting big. He has friends with a place in Alaska, and they took the bears up there. Then he had some goats, and some beavers, oh, a whole bunch of different ones. He'd been doing this research for a long time, started when he was just a young man. He was retirement age, you know, almost seventy. They let him stay on."

Dora said, "Well, don't let anybody do anything to Abby's pig, okay? Call us first."

"What's your number?"

She wrote it down for him, home and precinct. "Maybe I can save you a call? What time tomorrow you think I could see this guy Marsh?"

Joe didn't know. Joe would find out. Joe would call her.

"I guess this is the best we can do right now," said Abby as they headed out the gate. "It's after twelve. You want to have lunch?"

"I've got information for the whole family, and they'll all be hungry," she said, with a glance at the two dogs. "Let's stop at the market, instead."

Opalears: Korè Speaks

While the umminhi were gone, I groomed the veebles and gave them apples I found in the cold
box. Veebles will do almost anything for an apple. Dzilobommo and Blanche went out into the woods for, so
they said, some peace and quiet. Soaz prowled from
room to room, looking in closets and drawers and under
furniture. Finally, he must have decided it was safe
enough in the place, for he curled up on Dora's bed and
went to sleep. Izzy and the countess were having a long,
long talk, and the onchiki had found they could apply
soap to the bathing place and make a slide of it. I decided to sneak about a little in the trees, and I went as
far as the avenue Dora had described before losing my
courage and returning home. I said "home" to myself,
for though Dora's house was not my home, it had a very
homely feel.

The onchiki had finished their play when I arrived,
and I told them they must clean up the soap, or someone
might slip and break a bone. They did so, with much

babble and splashing, then they all piled onto the bed and fell asleep beside Soaz. We were all napping by the time Dora and Abby and Oyk and Irk returned, without the prince. At the first sound of their arrival, Soaz woke and came into the outer room, glaring about himself in a threatening way, his tail thrashing. Only when he saw it was Dora did he sit and groom himself, pretending he hadn't been startled at all.

"All of you sit down," said Dora. "And I'll tell you what's happened."

We sat. She and Abby told us what they had done; Oyk and Irk confirmed where they had gone, what they had seen, what they had talked of with the animals at the place where Prince Sahir was now. When Dora told us what the man had said about many of the speaking peoples being already gone, the countess exclaimed; Soaz growled; Prince Izakar asked many questions, some of them not at all pertinent; and at the end of an hour we were all sitting glumly, wondering what to do next.

Dora said, "Obviously, some of Dr. Winston's, ah . . . people are already out in the world, presumably provided for by humans he trusted. However, if your peoples are to be sure of survival, I think we must plan to get all of them away from the laboratory. It won't do just to get them out. They themselves know they have to have a refuge, someplace they can be safe."

"Is anyplace safer than this?" asked the countess, waving a hand at the forest outside the window. "Ersuns live in such places. Scuini live in such places. The only problem I can think of is finding enough food. . . ."

"The sultana gave me gems," I reminded them. "Even in this age, they could buy food for a long time."

"I have another concern," said Dora. "You have spoken several times of cannibals in your time, that is, an intelligent animal who eats another intelligent animal? Am I right? What will the mother bear at Randall Pharmaceuticals do if we bring her to our forest and she encounters a . . . scuinic mother, with babies? Will she eat the babies?''

''If you mean the one in the pen, she might,'' said Oyk. ''She talks, but I don't know if anybody has taught her anything like religion.''

''The same may be true of your . . . fellow tribespeople?''

Oyk looked at Irk, who licked his nose and said, ''They probably don't have any religion, either.''

''I'd never thought of that,'' said Izzy, wide-eyed.

Abby sat back, his legs crossed as I have seen Izzy sometimes sit, looking very personlike. ''Dora's right, I'm afraid. There's more to this than just letting some of your people out of the labs. If these are your ancestors, they must be fed and protected and taught to respect one another, or the big ones will eat the little ones and that will be that. None of them have learned survival skills, which means men would probably dispose of all those not lost to the wild. Or, after men are gone, as you tell us we will be gone, in the absence of an ethical framework the future will be all lions and tigers and bears, and no scuini or onchiki.''

We got the book out again and looked at pictures of lions and tigers, though we were already familiar with bears. Every time I opened the book, I still thought the picture on the front was of Faros VII.

During all this, Soaz had been ominously quiet. Now he spoke:

''Perhaps it would be better to let people do as they like. Let only the strong survive.'' He smiled, letting his fangs show.

''If you don't care what you eat,'' said Izzy in a lazy voice. ''If you want to live in cave instead of house. If you want to be hot in summer, cold in the winter, and walk instead of ride. Don't forget, Soaz, it is ponjic people who do most of the construction, and it is kasturic people who cut our timber and grow our vegetables and cut wood to keep us warm in winter. It is kapriel people who tend our livestock. It is armakfatidi who do our cooking.''

Soaz lifted his hand in front of his face and stared at it, his nose wrinkling. "Why didn't Winston give us all fingers?''

Dora said quietly, "Because he was interested in language. As I understand evolution, it's a random algorithmic process, and it doesn't produce every useful thing in every organism. I've always wondered why *our* evolutionary process didn't give us better sense.''

Another long silence.

The countess cleared her throat. "We should postpone the matter of philosophy. It is too confusing for us to consider at a time when we must focus on survival. Dora and Abby remind us what Izzy told us earlier: Woput believes that his people, the umminhi, did not survive because our peoples took over in some way; he believes this because he does not know about the plague that comes. Dora and Abby say—unselfishly, in my opinion—that better some intelligence survives than that none survives. Since I am an intelligent person from the future, I agree, quite selfishly, that some intelligence should survive. In order for this to happen, we must free all our people Winston was working with and they must not eat one another. Let us talk only of how to do that.''

"Some of Winston's, ah . . . subjects are inside the building," said Dora. "The onchiki, for instance. I don't know how many others, or of what kind. There may be other intelligent ones outside, too, who simply wouldn't talk to Oyk or Irk.''

"Some kapris, I think," said Irk. "One of them gave me very strange look.''

A bell sounded, then, loudly and vehemently, a kind of rattling ring. The phone, Abby said it was, as Dora went to talk to it. It had not made that noise when she spoke to it before, but Abby explained that it rang to tell her someone was talking to her. I thought, not for the first time, that civilization—if this was what we were in—had some bad points. That noise, for one, and the smell on the avenue for another.

She spoke for some time to someone called Mr. Dionne. Dzilobommo and Blanche returned just as she was finishing her conversation.

"This man I spoke to," she said in that way she had of saying important things as though they were nothing at all, as a child does, perhaps, wishing to express urgencies but either shy or afraid of drawing attention. "This man's name is Harry Dionne, and he belongs to a numerous family that I believe has some connection with the trees that are taking us over. I have no proof of that. I have no explanation, but I think the Dionnes are involved. Harry's father is a priest of their religion, and I have asked Harry to get him to come here, if he will. His name is Vorn, and he lives some distance away, so it will take a day or so, even if he catches a flight here as soon as possible."

"A flight?" asked Soaz.

This started yet another discussion, with more books pulled from the shelves, this time with pictures of airplanes. Izzy had seen such pictures before, but I must confess I was not greatly interested in airplanes, for they probably smell even worse than the vehicles on the avenue and are noisier than the telephone. What I was interested in was getting away from the awful thoughts I was having, all about our people maybe dying or never having existed in the first place! Or our letting the speaking creatures loose, then the Woput finding them anyway. I imagined the Woput killing me, killing Izzy. I wanted to go into the forest with Izzy and hear him tell me what he thought about all this. Or maybe hear him tell me something else, and maybe look at me in that way he sometimes did, or even pat my shoulder and tell me it would be all right.

It was not to be. No one cared for my feelings, as was probably quite proper. After all, we were on a quest to save the world—who cared for one adolescent being's feelings? Why then, did I feel so slighted? I did feel so.

Peevish and a little angry and left out of things. It has been my experience that when one feels this way, one usually does the most illogical thing possible, which is to go off and be even lonelier. I went out into the woods to the place the veebles were grazing, and I sat there under a tree.

It was late in the afternoon. The sunlight came low among the boughs, making a splendor of gold and green. The woods had been there, so Dora said, only a little time, and yet the moss beneath me was as deep and soft as the moss beneath the trees on the way to Isher. The resilient green grew over and around many tiny twigs that littered the forest floor, and all this made a cushioned brittleness, with the twigs snapping like little bones when I walked on them. The roots of the trees snaked out and down in coils of brown and gray and lichened green; the low turf was scattered with pink stars; and when I bent down, I smelled thyme and saw the dark leaves twining among the feathered grasses. So beautiful, the feel, the smell.

Across the clearing tall spikes of open flowers bloomed white and red against a golden willow. I had seen them in my own time, along the fences at the farm. We called them Towering Tess, and we made dolls of the blooms and buds, putting them together with bits of wood. They were not a forest flower, but then, this was a new forest.

The trees, so Dora had said, didn't fit. The books the Weelians had showed us did not speak of this uprising of trees. In this time it seemed no one had planted them, no one claimed responsibility for them, they had come as if by their own volition, all at once, out of nothing. One could not ask the trees, for trees told no history. They did not speak of pasts. Even in our time, my time, trees told no tales of glory or triumph. They existed, mighty and lasting things, outliving us by hundreds of times our short lives, seeing springs and falls as we saw dawns and dusks, knowing the great wheel of the seasons as we knew the wheel of stars in a single night.

Trees had no spoken language. What Izzy had given them, there on the road to Fan-Kyu Cyndly, had been no tree tongue. That had been people voices, sorcerously grafted as orchard men may graft dubious scions upon durable roots. So our unworthy words issued from that bark tongue, telling us of a distress older than time.

We die, the trees cried. *We die!*

But it was not *then* they died. The dying that distressed them was the dying talked of by the wizards at St. Weel, and it happened not then, but now. I had taken books from Dora's shelves. I had read what was happening in this time! Though this new forest grew mightily, elsewhere the mighty jungles fell. Elsewhere the coastal rain forests that furred the body of the world were torn and riven. Elsewhere the last of the old growth, the last of the world's own garments were ripped away. It was in this time, now, that the mother of us all was stripped naked and left to die in shame of her children, she who had been robed in glory like this, adorned like this. I bent my head upon the roots and wept, sorrowing for the trees.

"Nassifeh," said a voice. I thought for a moment it was my mother's voice. "Nassifeh, do not weep."

"Who is it?" I asked. "Who speaks?"

"Korè," said the voice. "Korè speaks for the trees. From the place she was entombed, she speaks. From the place she was hidden, under stone. Even there in dry darkness, roots can grow and stone will split. So Korè is grown out of her tomb into the open air. From the place she is now, she speaks, raising up the trees to heal her wounds and to take vengeance. Rejoice, Nassifeh."

"Korè, eaua Korè," I cried, the words wrenched up from deep in me. I got to my feet, looking around me, seeing no one. No face. No lips to speak. Where did the words come from?

They came from everywhere, all around me, whispering. "The one you seek is still here, in this time. He sought to kill me and failed. He may not fail to kill you.

Tell Dora that even now he dwells in the shade of the tree. I will lead you to him. Tell the sorcerer.''

Came a little wind, then, fluttering the leaves, and the presence was gone. I ran screaming for the house.

33

The Roots of the Tree

Dora could not at first make out what Nassif was saying. Then she thought it mere hysteria, though only for a moment, for the others in the room took it more than seriously.

"Korè?" cried Soaz. "Korè spoke to you?"

"Cory?" Dora asked. "Cory who?"

"She is speaking of the goddess," said Izzy. "The incarnation of life. Maid, mother and sage, the tripartite goddess: birth and growth, maturity and reproduction, age and death. Korè is the eidolon of fecundation. Most of the people in our time worship her, if only secretly. I am a Korèsan. Faros VII is a Korèsan. . . ."

"Most of us are, at least philosophically," snapped the countess. "Nassif, please, child, settle down and tell us more simply. . . ."

Nassif repeated herself several times, while the assembled group evinced various degrees of astonishment.

"I was to tell Dora," she concluded. "And the sorcerer."

"Well what does 'the shade of the tree' mean to you, Dora?" asked the countess.

Dora shook her head, trying to think. "It reminds me of what I was saying earlier. The Dionnes have a tree. They call it a family tree, one they plant everywhere they go. I don't know what kind it is. Harry Dionne doesn't know, either, but he told me his father probably knows. That tree casts a very great shade, so I suppose anyone who lives in that neighborhood is in the shade of that tree."

"But," said Abby in a contentious tone, "since they planted the same tree everywhere they went, it could be one of the others, somewhere else."

Dora moved about fretfully. "Vorn Dionne is coming here. Can't this wait until he arrives? I'm more worried about the, ah . . . people still left at the lab, to tell the truth. That's what we have to do first, get the animals out of those pens. They're sitting ducks if we leave them there."

"But Korè said tell the sorcerer," complained Nassif. "There must be reason for that. . . ."

"To find out about the trees, of course," said Izzy. "Since no one knows where they came from or why, that fact is evidently important."

"Possibly important, yes," Dora agreed reluctantly. "But not first priority right now!"

"Since you already know where one of these trees is," persisted the countess, "and since Korè sent her message to you, Dora, isn't it reasonable to suppose the shade she mentions is of the tree you already know? Any other interpretation would be unnecessarily complicated!" She glared at Abby as she said this, tossing her head.

Abby grinned and said admiringly, "Well reasoned. I'll stop arguing. Do you want to see the tree? It's quite something."

They were all eager to do so, except for Dora, who was inexplicably reluctant.

"You don't want to go near Jared's place," said Abby.

"That's true," she cried, with a little laugh that threatened to turn into hysteria. "I'm afraid he's got the vulture there. If that's what it is."

"Vulture?" he asked, taking her shoulders in his hands to stop her shaking. "Dora, what vulture?"

Tears welled in the corner of her eyes, and she put her hand to her face, almost shamedly. "When he came here, he jerked out some of my hair. And that night, a thing came. It stank. It landed on the roof. . . ."

Izzy put down the book he was looking at and came over to her, pulling on her hand until she sat down beside him. He asked her what the thing had felt like, smelled like, sounded like.

"Has it come here more than once?" he asked.

"Yes. But when it hears Abby, it goes away. . . ."

Abby cried, "Why didn't you tell me?"

"It was crazy," she said. "It was . . . crazy."

"No," said Izzy. "Not crazy. It is sorcery. In our time, there is sorcery. A sorcerer from our time came here. Now here there is sorcery. So, we must ask, what person do you believe is troubling you?"

Dora found words tumbling as she told him all about Jared and herself, about not knowing why she'd married him, about cleaning the house when she left him, concluding, ". . . and aside from having a cook and housekeeper, I never knew why he'd married me, either."

"It is clear why he married you," said Izzy, patting her hand and speaking very solemnly. "If he is a maker of evil magic, you were a necessary ingredient. Some powerful magic requires a vir—" He stopped, frowned, cast a sideways glance at Abby. "A female person, the presence of, the blood of, sometimes, with evil magic, the life of. He is not a person you would ordinarily be attracted to, so I have no doubt he put an enchantment on you to get you to marry him."

Abby said, "Come on! Could he do that?"

Izzy nodded. "It was only a superficial relationship,

and it is easy to bring about small changes. From what Dora says, her life changed but little, her routine scarcely at all. I could have done such an enchantment, even though we are of different tribes.'' He laughed at the expression on Dora's face. ''I would not do it, but I could. Your false mate wanted you for something, Dora. It would be interesting to know what. Perhaps we will find out, even though you have escaped him.''

''But why this . . . thing?'' Abby demanded.

''He's angry,'' replied Izzy. ''So he persecutes her.''

''You can't be talking about Jared?'' Dora said. ''He's such an . . . ordinary man! He's an engineer. He designs machines. He . . . how did he learn to do sorcery?''

Izzy gave her a slanted look. ''I thought you understood what I was saying. He is the Woput! He must be!''

''Jared!'' She shook her head, disbelieving. ''Jared?''

He reached out to pat her. ''Listen to yourself talk. You say he is an angry man. The Weelians said the Woput was an angry person. Jared took your hair. What would he use it for but sorcery? The Weelians told us the Woput did sorcery. And most of all, we find contiguity: Jared is here, in this place, where the Woput also came.''

''If he put a spell on her, how did she escape him?'' asked Abby, with a troubled look at Dora.

Izzy shrugged. ''It was a habit spell, and such are easily broken. Any real break in Dora's routine would weaken it. Any cluster of small, noncustomary happenings.''

''Like his being poisoned,'' Abby offered.

''Yes. His being poisoned, or removed from the house, or anything like that. Dora, you should—Dora!''

She wasn't listening, was lost, mouth open, totally unable to believe what she was hearing. It was bad enough to have married a Jared, but to have been married to a Woput? It was either horribly awful or terribly funny. One or the other. She couldn't decide which. Izzy shook her by the shoulder and she gave him a dazed look.

Izzy spoke firmly. "You should have told me about this stink sending. I can put protections on this place, and you do not need to be afraid to go to Woput's place. The stink sending has no reality between manifestations. It is made to come here, only, not to dwell in any other place."

Reluctantly, though still rather dazed and disbelieving, she agreed to go with them to Jared's place. Abby's little car would not hold them all, and Dora's was still tightly wedged in by trees, so in the end they decided that Izzy, Elianne, Soaz and Nassif would go along. It was getting dark, too dark for anyone to see and wonder overmuch at a large feline, two monkeys and a pig in the car. Blanche was left in charge of the onchiki and the establishment. Dzilobommo grummeled he would prepare an evening meal for their return.

While the visitors walked toward the avenue through the woods, Dora and Abby stopped momentarily at Dora's car to pick up the key to Jared's place along with the flashlight she had always kept in the trunk.

"I left my sleeping bag in his garage," she said. "With all the . . . guests, there's barely room for us all to sleep, and if we have more visitors, I'm going to need extra. Since we're going over there, we can pick it up." She was angry at herself for being frightened. She was even angrier for giving in and going where she felt danger waited. Dumb. Cops learned not to be dumb like that, not when they could help it.

Abby put his arm around her, pulling her close. "I'll bring mine over, too," he said in a troubled voice. "Things seemed pretty crowded, but I think I'll stay from now on, no matter how crowded they get!"

Abby put the top up on his car. The drive was uneventful, virtually silent, and it was almost dark when they arrived. Jared's place was unlighted, though some of the houses on the block showed an amber glow at the windows. They parked as near one side of the curving lane as possible, leaving the lights on. Woods had taken over all the open space on the street and around the houses, and the six of them stumbled their way among smaller trees toward the great one that loomed in its own deep shadow.

Izzy and the countess leaned against it, Izzy muttering repetitive phrases the countess recognized as enchantments. Ignoring these attempts at sorcery, Soaz climbed into the tree, out onto its largest branch, high above the earth, smelling it, rubbing his face against it. Nassif merely stared at the tree, the hairs on the back of her neck erect, as though she felt a chill.

"Somebody," she said. "Somebody here."

"Who, Nassif?" asked Izzy, who was having no luck eliciting information by magic.

She whispered, "It's like the voice in the forest, only bigger, stronger."

When they had looked at the tree long enough to realize it was not going to explain things, they wandered down what had been the alley to Jared's garage. Dora's key let her in, and she flashed her light upward into the rafters. Her sleeping bag still hung there, a dusty bundle, but as she moved toward it she tripped and fell forward onto a row of storage cartons. The lowered light disclosed thick concrete slabs that had been tilted and thrust up from below, the floor of the garage riven and overgrown with roots that coiled up from the soil like great serpents, seeming almost to move in that wavering light.

Nassif shivered, now feeling the presence all around her, touching her. The words came back to her, unbidden, and she spoke them again: " 'Korè speaks for the trees. From the place she was entombed, she speaks. From the place she was hidden, under stone . . . ' "

"Cory!" exclaimed Dora. "Cory was the girl Jared married. The girl who ran off somewhere. . . ." She fell silent, remembering what Harry Dionne had said. "Jared was digging the foundations for this garage when he met Cory. . . ."

"Tell us," said the countess. "Tell us this story."

Dora waved her away. "Not here. Please. In the car. I don't want to stick around here."

Izzy murmured, "She's right. There is something going on here that we should be careful of."

Abby retrieved the sleeping bag, and they went back to the car where, during the drive home, Dora told the story, first the way Jared's mother had told it, then the way Harry Dionne had told it. "Harry said Jared had no idea what he'd connected to. . . ."

"But perhaps the Woput did!" the countess whispered. "What if he came here, knowing Korè would be here, on this street? There are Korèsans in our time. There are records, a priesthood, temples, one great one, the Reedbed Temple, beside the locks at Giber in Isfoin. . . ."

"Why would Woput care about the Korèsans?" asked Abby. "Did he believe the Korèsans had something to do with human extinction?"

Izzy said, "The Korèsans have to do with the preservation of nature, and that's what our tribes once lived on. We weren't always city dwellers. We couldn't have lived without woods and rivers and plains. Woput knew that."

"So," said the countess, "what if the Woput found an ancient record concerning the Korèsans, and he picked a person from the same neighborhood to put himself into—"

"How would he know?" Soaz objected. "From three thousand years, how would he know what neighborhood? Did you find some record he might have read, back at St. Weel?"

"No," said Izzy. "There are no ancient records of the Korèsans. Not in the library of St. Weel, not in my library, either. They were . . . are a secretive people. But, as Dora has reminded us, the Weelians are wizards. Woput could have used magic to locate his quarry."

"Would magic work at St. Weel?" asked Soaz. "With that huge time spiral so close?"

"If it was created through technology, possibly not.

If it is a natural thing, probably so. Either way, the Wo-put could have wandered out into wildlands, and there he could have used sorcery to look into time, to find a person in this time whose life would intersect that of Korè. . . .''

''What kind of sorcery?'' Abby asked.

''Any one of various kinds,'' said Izzy. ''I was taught several enchantments to uncover connections: linkage chants for persons, simultaneity chants for events, cross-over chants for places. . . .''

''But I thought you'd told us the Woput came where you all came, in the woods west of Dora's house!'' said Abby.

''He did,'' cried the countess. ''But it is not logical to assume he went into that lonely place by pure chance! We must assume he chose it for a reason. Izzy, wouldn't it be easier to get into a specific target the fewer other people there were around?''

Izzy nodded. ''Never having done it, I can't say for sure, but certainly it makes sense. If the Woput was pre-pared to make his attempt at a moment's notice, if he kept constant sorcerous surveillance on his quarry, then when that quarry went into a lonely place, the Woput had only to set the control for that same place and enter the wheel.''

''Jared?'' Dora cried, her voice breaking. ''We're still talking about Jared, aren't we?''

''I speak of Woput,'' said Izzy. ''Who is also Jared.''

She said, ''And I speak of Jared who married Cory. His mother says he married her, only I don't think he really did. Because Jared was pouring concrete, here, at the time, and Nassif hears Korè—Cory say she was en-tombed. It has to be him. . . .''

''Do not go so fast,'' said the countess. ''Let us not chase this idea, perhaps losing our way in the process. First, we need proof. . . .''

''Like?'' Dora demanded.

Abby nodded, tallying points on his fingers. ''We

need to know if Jared was there. We need to know if he was . . . changed about that time.''

"I don't know if he was changed, but I know he was there!" cried Dora. "His mother said he was there with a group from school, and he was hit by lightning."

Izzy nodded, grinning madly. Everything was falling together nicely, making what seemed to him the very best sort of sense. Dora, on the other hand, thought she might come unglued at any moment, and Abby was pre-occupied with Dora's state of mind as betrayed by her lips, by her face disclosed by the streetlights, by her eyes, by the tension in her body.

They drove the rest of the way in virtual silence, with Soaz growling and Izzy gloating and the countess calming them all by saying that morning was almost sure to come again because it always had before.

Opalears: Nassif Reflects

It took me a while to sort out what we had found out, or thought we had. Jared was the umminhi who had been mated to Dora, only not really. More like enslaved, I thought. She was mated to him as I was to Sultan Tummyfat: as cook, washer-up, mender. Only she did it of her own will, it was not done to her, only perhaps it was, for the Woput might have enchanted her.

As we ate the late supper Dzilobommo had prepared, Izzy and I spoke of what it might feel like, having Woput enter into one. Dora said Jared had been hit by lightning, and Woput might feel like that. Dora wondered out loud whether Jared remained after Woput came, or whether the person was all Woput now? Did Woput know what Jared knew? Izzy and Soaz joined this discussion, which was to no purpose for nobody knew any answers. Dora said she would find out, she wanted to know, she would ask Jared's mother.

The talk went on, but the countess did not join in. She left the table and went into the sleeping room. Also, I did not feel like arguing. I was tired. The onchiki had been playing with the soap again, and they were tired. Blanche and Dzilobommo had been arguing about food. They were tired. When we had eaten, we weary ones went into the other room and almost closed the door. We could still hear Izzy and Soaz and the humans, but it was less noisy.

For some reason I started thinking about technology. Izzy said magic wouldn't work where there was technology. On Dora's bed was a wonderful mattress. Soft, but resilient, like moss in the woods, but without twigs. Was this mattress technology? I would like to have this mattress, even if I couldn't do magic on it. Except a certain kind, maybe.

"Stop giggling," said Lucy Low, sticking her nose in my neck and curling tightly against me.

In the big room, the voices stopped. Outside, trees moved and night birds called. In this strange world, in this strange time, trying to do strange things no one had done before, I was at home among friends upon a lovely mattress. I thought to myself that there are worse things than comfort. At that moment, everything else could wait.

35

Saving Sahir, et al.

While the guests settled themselves, Dora and Abby poured themselves each a drink and sat sipping at them while the place grew quiet. After a peek into her bedroom, they decided not to disturb the people piled on her bed. Instead, they held a whispered conference, set the alarm for five thirty, then unfolded the couch in the living room and lay down upon it, still fully dressed. When the clock rang, Dora made coffee, Abby shook the sleep from his eyes and announced his intention of going home to pack some clothes and toiletries and pick up his own sleeping bag and air mattress. Dora surprised herself by kissing him good-bye, then surprised herself even more by doing it again.

"Hey, Dora," he murmured into her ear. "You could come with me. Help me pack."

She sagged against him, tempted, then drew resolutely away. "We already assigned me a duty this morning, McCord. Don't throw us off course."

"I'm not being irresistible. You are."

371

She giggled. "It's all my fault, right, my hair all which away, and sleep in my eyes and my mouth tastes like the bottom of a birdcage, no offence to Blanche. It'll keep, Abby. Won't it?"

He answered her with an incendiary look, hugged her again and was gone. Dora breathed heavily for a few moments, then washed her face, called a cab, and wakened Oyk and took him with her to the avenue to meet it.

"I don't carry no dogs," the driver said belligerently.

"This is a police dog," said Dora, showing her badge and trying to ignore Oyk's expression, which was one of disdain.

"That's no police dog. Police dogs don't have tails like that."

"I didn't say a German Shepherd, I said a police dog. He's a tracking dog. I lost a notebook on an investigation yesterday, and I brought the dog to help me find it."

"So how come you don't got a police car."

"Because I'd just as soon the lieutenant doesn't know I lost my case notes, you mind?"

Still belligerently, the cabby took them to Randall Pharmaceuticals, where Dora had him wait while she and Oyk went down along the outside of the fence into the woods at the bottom of the hill. There Dora fished a dog-eared notebook from her pocket and leaned against a tree while Oyk slipped under the fence and up the hill to the pens. He returned shortly, then he and Dora came back to the cab, she triumphantly waving the notebook.

Home again, she carried the phone into the bathroom and called Abby's pager. When he called back, she said:

"Oyk told all of them to get ready for a jailbreak tonight. Oyk and I figured if he could get under the fence, everybody else could get under it, or over it, and all of them can dig out of their pens and hide the holes. All we have to do is transport them here for the time being. I figured we'll rent two vans, one for the predators and one for the prey, just in case. Then when we get them here, Soaz and Izzy can keep them separated.''

"That doesn't take care of the ones inside," Abby argued. "The fence isn't electrified, but I know damned well the building has all kinds of security."

"One thing at a time." Dora said, feeling slightly annoyed with him. "We can't do everything at once! If the pens are easier for us, they'd be easier for the Woput, too."

She did not say Jared. She was ninety percent sure Jared was the Woput, but she did not say Jared. She felt saying his name might invoke his attention. She didn't want to see him, or confront him, or accuse him. She wanted to ask his mama one last question, then she wanted quietly to dispose of him, once and for all, decisively, without anyone's noticing. It was like having stepped into dog shit. One did not display it. One did not say, out loud, "dog shit." One wiped one's foot and tried to ignore the smell.

, "You're going to see your ex-ma-in-law?" Abby asked, reading her mind.

"This morning. Phil and I'll make time to drive over there. I just want one answer from her."

"Last night I got to thinking. If he killed Winston, maybe you could prove it."

She choked and had some trouble clearing her throat. "I thought of that myself, Abby. It was one of the first things I thought of last night when Jared popped up as a suspect, but I have a little trouble coming up with probable cause for an investigation. If I tell the lieutenant that a bunch of otters and cats and pigs and dogs and monkeys told me that somebody came from three thousand years in the future and invaded the body of my ex-husband in order to kill off a bunch of scientists and talking animals and so forth . . ." Her voice trailed off into hiccoughing self-mockery.

"All right," he said grudgingly. "I get the picture."

"What is probable cause?" asked Izzy, when she had hung up.

"You're awake," she said unnecessarily.

"I woke up when you went out. I have been considering protective magic for this place. What is probable cause?"

"It's a protection for citizens. It says that police people cannot just stop you or harass you or invade your house or place of employment, or your car or your boat or whatever, unless there is probable cause to think you committed a crime."

Izzy frowned. "Does this apply only to your people or to . . . no. In this time, others are not people, so of course it applies only to your people. If an . . . animal kills someone, what happens?"

"Well, people get killed by animals every year. Campers or hikers provoke bears, or run afoul of bull elk. Swimmers get eaten by sharks. If the animal can be caught, we usually kill it. Usually. Of course, if the animal is smart enough to get away, nothing happens. It wouldn't be investigated like a homicide."

"So, if 'bear' or 'cat' killed Woput, you would not have to investigate," he said thoughtfully.

"It wouldn't be required by my job, no," she said, searching his face, which was enigmatic.

"And would you yourself require it?"

"I wouldn't look very hard," she said after a moment's thought. "Ah, given the circumstances, I might not look at all."

He blinked at her. She busied herself, carrying the phone back to the kitchen and saying to the group at large:

"Listen, will you all be okay here today? I mean, you've got to stay out of sight. Does everyone accept that? If you go out, do it without clothes, please. Don't talk to people. And by the way, Lucy Low, you and Mince and Burrow stay out of the soap. I noticed last night your fur is getting all tangled and messed up. I'll try to remember to bring home some conditioner."

"They get bored," said Izzy. "So do I. Even in Palmia, with the aunts, I have seldom been so bored."

"Watch television. Listen to music." She showed him how to work the TV, radio and CD player. "What might be really helpful would be for you to go out in the woods and see how much magic you can do. You said there were constraints last night. It might be a good idea to know where they are, because we may need to fight fire with fire, so to speak.

"By the way, Abby and I brought lots of food yesterday. There's stuff in the refrigerator and the cupboards for Oyk and Irk and the veebles, too. By tonight, we should have a lot of information we don't have now."

And she was out, away, leaving Izzy to crouch by the window and peer out at the morning forest.

"This isn't how quests are supposed to go," said the countess from behind him. "We're supposed to be engaged in acts of derring-do. We should be rescuing Prince Sahir."

"Dora has that in hand," said Oyk. "We went out there very early this morning."

"How was he?" asked the countess.

"Very angry," replied Oyk. "The others in his pen do not respect princes, particularly. They told him to shut up and await events. He had several new bruises and at least one tusk puncture."

"Do you realize that Dora and Abby are cannibals?" the countess sniffed, angered on behalf of the absent prince. "They have meat in their cold box."

"They aren't cannibals," said Izzy. "They do not eat intelligent creatures. Difficult though it may be for us to keep in mind, our people in this time are not intelligent. Umminhi in this time eat scuinan flesh, but pigs can't talk. But then, in our time, scuinans eat umminhi flesh, and humans can't talk."

The countess flushed. It was true. Old umminhi, or those unsuited to carrying burdens, were routinely slaughtered. Their meat, called veel, was ground for the making of veeliki-bana, a kind of stuffed pastry that was served with chile sauce. The meat of the very young ones, which were slaughtered only after a lengthy fattening, was considered a delicacy for the gourmet trade.

"Dora and Abby are as ethical as you and I," said Izzy. "Hard to believe, but true."

"The Zhapanees eat sea people," said Soaz. "And the sea people are speaking people in this time, too. There's a book about it here."

"Abby says Zhapanees live in such crowded conditions, many of them don't think of their own women as people, much less other tribes," said Izzy patiently. "Also, that book concerns attempts by nature lovers to make Zhapanees stop eating sea people. It is as Dora says: some umminhi in this time are good; some are bad. Some are smart, some are stupid. Even among our peoples, this is so."

"Where are Zhapanees?" asked Lucy Low. "Near or far?"

This led to the bookshelf again, and the book of maps Dora had already shown them. Zhapan, or Japan, or Nippon, was very far, across a great ocean.

"Where is Crawling Sea?" Lucy demanded. They looked. Dora had shown them where they were, and there was no Crawling Sea. No Sharbak Range. No Big or Little Stonies.

"It could be on other side of world," said the countess. "Some far place from this. Or, nearby, but perhaps a great upheaval happened, an earthquake or volcano."

"Maybe we have come to another world," said Lucy Low.

Izzy shrugged. "No. If we had much time and little to do, we could find Crawling Sea and mountains and all. I would rather watch TV." Privately, he had decided to do what Dora suggested: go out in the woods and see how much magic was possible.

Dora, meantime, had arrived at the precinct, apologized to Phil for missing work the previous day, explained she'd had a bad day. "I thought maybe you and

I could run over and find out from Mrs. Winston if she knows of any friends her husband had up in Alaska.''

"Alaska?''

"The guy out at Randall Pharmaceuticals, he mentioned Dr. Winston had some friends in Alaska. They might have a lead for us, and maybe his wife knows who they are, or, maybe they'll be in Winston's address book.''

They phoned. Mrs. Winston was at work. They phoned her at work. Mrs. Winston knew exactly where her late husband's address book was. She would call the housekeeper and Phil could pick it up anytime this morning. Fine. Yes. She was glad to know they were still working on it. She had thought she'd be over her grief by now, but the longer she was without her husband, the more she missed him.

"I don't know about this case,'' Phil said, hanging up the phone. "Everything seems to be getting more and more tangled up.''

"Cases get that way sometimes,'' she opined. "Then they straighten out. Come on, Phil. Let's go pick the thing up. And on the way, let me stop at the boarding-house for a minute. I want to ask my former mother-in-law something.''

Mrs. Gerber had aged in recent weeks, Dora thought. She had new lines around her mouth and eyes.

"Jared isn't well,'' she confided in a whisper. "Dora, you shouldn't have left him. He was fine when he had you to take care of him. These days, it's hard for him to get up and go to work.''

"Well, he wasn't fine when we lived together, Momma Gerber. He got that poisoning, you know. I think it may have long-term effects. Or it could be an effect of that time he got hit by lightning, when he was a boy. . . .''

"He got over that completely.''

"I wanted to ask you about that. Did he seem different to you, after that happened?''

"Well, of course he did, Dora. You couldn't have

something like that happen and not feel different! He had trouble pronouncing his words, and he kind of had to think what he was going to say, and for a while he was real slow remembering people's names and how to get places. Why, right there at first, he didn't even know who I was.''

"Did he get all his memory back?''

Mrs. Gerber flushed. "No. He used to have this sweet little thing he'd say to me at night, even when he was a big boy, and after he got hit by lightning, he never said it again. Like it just went out of his head.''

Dora shook her head, speaking without thinking. "I can't figure out why he ever married me. . . .'' He, meaning the Woput.

"Well, I know why,'' said the older woman, pinching her lips together. "Those girls at his office, chasing him all the time, inviting him to dinner, all that, drove him out of his mind. Jared does not like being bothered! He picked you, Dora. A nice, quiet girl, accommodating, not demanding, someone who'd be grateful for a quiet home. He asked me if you kept your room neat, and I said, like a pin. He wanted someone he could have around without being bothered all the time.''

For a moment Dora couldn't speak. "Not exactly fair to me, was it?''

Momma Gerber pinched her lips again, even more tightly. "I don't know why not. A good home. Good food. There's many a woman would consider that a bargain. And you had your own work, too. It wasn't as though you sat around there all day.''

Dora stood up. "It grieves me to admit that some women would have settled for that. I'm no longer one of them.'' She took a deep breath, patted Mama Gerber on the shoulder and went back out to the car.

"You're looking all nervy,'' said Phil. "Like Charlene before she goes to the beauty parlor.''

"Yeah, well, we women get that way. We get this longing for the hair dryer, Phil.''

He didn't hear the sarcasm. "Hair dryer?''

"The sound it makes, and the fact it surrounds your whole brain in warm air. You sit there on that worn mother-of-pearl leatherette and your thoughts kind of evaporate. You find yourself reading about Michael Jackson or Elizabeth Taylor for the thirtieth time as though you actually cared. You become for a time what women are supposed to be, totally vacuous and compliant. . . ."

He finally caught on. "You're on the prod! So, what's with Jared and his mama?"

"I don't much care," she lied.

Together they drove to the house in the country club, where Phil fetched the address book and turned it over to Dora. She went through it, finding to her enormous satisfaction that there were at least three addresses in Alaska, plus others in remoter parts of Montana, Washington, and Michigan. Beneath some of the addresses were tiny notations in black ink. 2gb,mf. 1gb,f. 5p,3m2f. 4o,2&2. 6m,3&3. A dozen others.

Two grizzly bears, male and female. One grizzly bear, female. Given her guests' identification of the cover of the animal encyclopedia, she'd been expecting grizzlies. Five . . . pigs, three male, two female. Four otters, two and two. Or could be ocelots? Six monkeys . . . or macaques, three and three. Or could it be mink? Or macaw, mongoose, magpie. . . . Whichever, Winston had already dispersed them into the wild. And he'd done it secretly; it had never appeared in the press, so there had been no record of it for the Woput to find.

Maybe. On the other hand, in the non-Woput world, Winston had not been murdered but had lived, perhaps to be quite old. In his golden years, he might have written a memoir which had survived at St. Weel. He might have mentioned in that book every person who had protected his creations. Even now, the Woput might be searching for them.

Back at the station, Dora dug out the stack of scientific papers she'd been given and spent the afternoon locating and calling those scientists across the country who seemed to be involved in similar research to that done by Edgar Winston. Many other people were working on pieces of the genetic puzzle, they said, but no one else was doing what Winnie had done. Of those who had contributed most to the basic research, several mentioned Martin Chamberlain and Jennifer Williams.

Dora forbore mentioning that both of them were dead, though several of her informants had already learned of it.

"You finding anything?" Phil asked, about three in the afternoon, dropping by her desk with a fresh cup of coffee.

"It's mostly what I don't find," she told him. "I don't find anyone else that this Wo—that is, murderer is likely to go after. The three victims here in this city seemed to be the people most involved in a particular kind of research."

"So if the research is the common factor, what the hell's the motive?"

Dora had been considering the need for an acceptable motive. "There's animal rights groups, right?"

"Sure. But Winston wasn't doing anything bad. I mean, he wasn't cutting up the animals, or torturing them or anything."

Dora agreed. "But some of these groups, they might not care what was really going on, right? Anybody experimenting on animals, he was a bad guy, so wipe him out."

"You think that's what happened?"

"Could be. We ought to look at animal rights groups next. If that doesn't give us anything, go at it from the other side. There's farm and ranch groups who're anti-animal rights. The American Farm Bureau, for instance—it fights animal rights legislation. . . ."

"How'd you know that?"

"I lived on Grandma's farm until just a couple of years ago, Phil. She had Farm Bureau Insurance, and I saw the mailings. Anyhow, so maybe some *anti*-animal rights group figures out Winnie was proving animals were smarter than we think or something. Like, let's say Winnie could prove a pig could think almost like a person. That'd stir up the hog farmers, wouldn't it? That'd make the anti-animal rights people pretty mad." She waved an inclusive hand, trying to obscure the problems with this spontaneous persiflage.

"That's sounds kinda complicated to me, Dora. I like the other idea better."

"Well, so did I. That's why I said we should do it first. I've started a list. You want to take the first five?"

That took care of Phil for an hour or two. Dora called to arrange the rental of two vans, having checked with Abby to be sure he'd be available as driver. Then she got a call from Harry Dionne, saying his father would be in the following afternoon.

"I think I'd better mention he's now the archpriest," Harry said in a slightly concerned voice, evincing more emotion than Dora had yet known him to show.

"That would mean what?" she asked.

"Beard, oak-leaf wreath, robes, staff, all that. A year or so ago, Dad ascended to the . . . well, it'd be like the papacy if we had one. Or like archbishop of Canterbury? At any rate, he rarely goes out in ordinary clothes anymore, and if we go out anywhere, the local group will probably insist on a procession. I just didn't want you to be surprised."

"It takes rather a lot to surprise me these days," she replied. "Ah . . . do you suppose you could get your father to come over to my place? I have some . . . important things that I think he should see."

"Things?"

"Tell him things relating to Cory's disappearance."

"That happened almost thirty years ago."

"Nonetheless. Tell him I know she was never found and I know why."

"I'll see what I can do."

She spent the rest of the afternoon typing up a report for the lieutenant, taking it in to him and waiting while he read through it.

"Sounds good, Henry," he said. "I'm not sure you're getting anywhere, but I can't fault the work."

"It's slow," she admitted. "How have things been with the trees lately? We still getting as many calls?"

"Things have settled some," he admitted. "Mayor's task force reports that every apartment in the city is now rented, including those in buildings that were almost vacant a few months ago. That big new apartment-condo complex out southeast, it's fully leased even though it's not half finished."

"Did we ever get anywhere with that baby that disappeared?"

"Those babies. Kind of hard to focus on one when there've been a few dozen. Ran them through the computer looking for common factors, they're all third living children or lower birth order. It's happening other places, too. One guy called it kind of arboreal birth control."

"My God, I'd think we'd be having riots!"

"No riots. A lot of hysterical mommies and daddies, but not much else. They don't know what's happened to the kids and neither do we. We do know we're getting compressed, moved in tighter and tighter. My wife, she yelled at me for five years, I had to move us out in the country near where her friends lived. Now, every day it's move back in the city, back in the city. My kids, Livia's fourteen, Brian's sixteen, they've done a hundred eighty from where they were a few months ago. They were both cutting school, Livia was sneaking cigarettes, both of them with a mouth on them you wouldn't believe. Now all the kids out there have started this Cory group—"

"Cory group!"

"That's what they call it, don't ask me why. They leave the house on Friday night, don't come back until Sunday. I ask them what they're doing, they say they're talking to the trees. I thought it was a lot of bull, so I went out there with them. That's what they do, sit around cross-legged and talk to trees. And the smoking's stopped. Whatever this Cory thing is, it isn't . . . harmful. Not that I can see."

"Not a problem, then."

"Well, yeah, a problem, or half of one. My wife, she wants to move back into town; the kids they want to stay where they are. Either way, I'm the villain."

"Maybe your wife will get used to it."

"Not my wife. She sees a squirrel, she has hysterics because it's planning to bite her. She sees a garter snake, she falls apart in little pieces. Not my wife she won't get used to it. She wants the whole world paved and air-conditioned, then she'll be happy."

He laughed. Dora smiled weakly, waving the report at him. "You want me to go on with this, then?"

"Sure. You might get somewhere. Maybe the address book will give you a lead."

The address book already had, but she didn't mention that. As soon as the clock would allow, she left the office, went to the car rental place and shuttled the two vans to a public parking lot, taking time with the second one to make a side trip to a pet store for several sacks of cedar shavings and some alfalfa-based feed pellets. While the veebles —and presumably the goats, if there were any talking goats—could graze quite nicely in the woods, if they had to hide out, they'd need food already prepared and she didn't have time to drive to a feed store for hay.

Finally, all preparations made, she took the bus home, arriving about ten minutes before Abby did. She was greeted by a group in full babble, wanting to tell her about Izzy's attempts at magic in the forest.

"Stop," Dora begged. "Listen, I can only deal with one thing at a time. I want to tell you the plan, while it's still clear in my mind! Izzy and Soaz and Oyk and Irk will go with Abby and me to pick up the vans, as soon as it's dark enough. Because we don't know how the . . . people in the pens will react to one another, I thought we'd put—I'll use my own words for them— the bear and the cat and the dogs into one van with Oyk and Soaz, the pigs and the goats and whatever else in the other one with Izzy and Irk.''

"Where will everyone sleep?" asked the countess. "We are already crowded.''

"This isn't crowded,'' said Lucy Low. "Why at home—''

Dora interrupted firmly. "We'll clear a space downstairs for anyone who needs shelter. I've got some sacks of bedding material in the van. I wanted straw, but none of the feed stores were close. Maybe I can pick up some tomorrow. And hay.''

"Someone's knocking. . . .'' said Mince.

"It's Abby. Please let him in.'' Dora went over her plans, ticking off the points. "When we've dropped off our new visitors, Abby and I will take the vans back downtown. We don't want them seen here.''

Abby came puffing up the stairs. "I brought more groceries,'' he said. "I thought we might be running low.''

Dzilobommo and Nassif went to help him dispose of the vegetables and packaged goods he had brought, and Abby left them to it while he went to move his car back to the avenue before it was treed. Dzilobommo had already prepared food for the evening meal, and he began setting it out while Dora finished her explanation.

". . . then tomorrow, Abby and I'll take the vans to the carwash, then back to the rental place. There should be nothing to link us to the disappearance. Once the people are here, we can call the people in Winston's address book—the local ones—and make arrangements for housing them.''

"It sounds well thought out,'' said the countess in her soothing voice. "You sound as though the day has been stressful.''

"It was,'' said Dora, her voice breaking. "I verified that Woput is definitely Jared, or the other way round. After Jared got hit by lightning, he didn't remember who he was. He had to learn all over again.''

"So he's not even partly Jared?''

Dora shook her head. "His mother says he never re-membered really private things, so I think we have to believe he's all Woput. She should have known he was different, changed, but she's not a very perceptive woman, and he's all she had in the way of family. Per-haps she didn't want to see that he wasn't really her son. And I feel a fool, of course. Why didn't I see that he wasn't really a . . . well, whatever."

"You are distressed," the countess said. "I know. But think, this is good knowledge, for now we know where he is, who he is. Now we can take proper steps to confound him. Sit down. Nassif, bring Dora a cup of tea."

Dora was brought a cup of tea, and some savory bits that Dzilobommo had baked, and she ate and sipped qui-etly while Izzy explained what he had learned from the trees.

When he had finished, she rubbed her head fretfully. "I'll have to think about it later, certainly we need to talk of it before Vorn Dionne arrives. Right now, I feel like my mind is about to explode."

They ate their dinner while Blanche told them a story of the stolen eggs of Kumper-Kraw, a very funny story at which the onchiki laughed immoderately. This was followed by a rendition of certain folk tunes by the on-chiki themselves, and the recitation of a Farakiel love poem as translated into fractured Inglitch by Izzy. When Dora finished her supper, she was amazed to find the sky already darkening, and she realized the diversion had been planned, probably by the countess, in order to give her, Dora, some moments of relaxation.

"Thank you," she said. "Keep your fingers crossed."

It proved an inappropriate idiom, which both Blanche and the onchiki found offensive, as they could not com-ply with the direction. The figure of speech had to be explained before Abby and Dora could leave on their night's work, their four chosen companions with them.

36

A Gathering of Tribes

At Randall Pharmaceuticals, Dora and Abby found the gates shut and the guardhouse untenanted. They turned down the slope along the outside of the fence toward the line of trees that marked the lower boundary, and there they waited in fidgety silence while their companions went under the fence and up among the pens.

The pigs were to be brought out first. Dora listened for Sahir, whose loud complaints she thought she would hear long before she saw him, but the night was utterly quiet. After what seemed far too long a time, they heard scuffling noises by the fence and Soaz came darting up to them, the shadowy bulk of a bear behind him.

"I thought you were going to bring the pigs first?" said Dora.

"Gone," breathed Soaz. "The Woput got them."

"He got Sahir?"

"All of them."

"All of the animals but the bear?"

"No. All the pigs. Others are still here. We're bringing them."

Oyk came through the fringe of trees, four dogs trotting quietly at his heels. Soaz darted away again, leaving the bear and her cubs standing quietly beside the van.

"How do you do," said Dora. "I'm sorry, I don't know your names."

"Rosa," said the bear, in a breathy contralto. "I have not named the children yet."

Irk came out of the trees, followed by a medium-sized raccoon and by the lovely female cat Dora had seen previously. Soaz came bounding forward. "Sheba," he said, making introductions. "Dora. Abby."

Oyk and Irk trotted back the way they had come, returning in a moment. Oyk said in an annoyed voice, "Dora, we are sure the goats can talk, but they won't. All the buck does is fart at us and look the other way."

"Did that raccoon talk?"

"The raccoon grummels."

"That's right. You said that before. Damn, damn, damn!" She screwed up her face, trying to think. "We don't dare leave any creature here that the Woput can come after. Go back in there, go to every pen and tell the creatures in it that this is their last chance at safety, and if you think they can talk but won't, bring them anyhow! We can't wait forever, so make it fast."

She put her head in her hands and growled, not quite silently, "I should have been quicker! When did he come?"

The bear rose on her hind legs, sniffing the air, one foreleg resting on the head of each cub. "After the humans left the big building. When it was almost dark. He came in a big car and opened the gate. I was watching. He had a net. The new pig, he was in a panic. He got in front of the hole, and the others couldn't escape, so the man got them all."

"Did he say anything?"

"Just that he was taking them to his place, that they would be the first race of inferiors destroyed."

"Did they talk?"

"We all warned them not to. I don't think he cared if they talked or not."

Dora drew herself up. "Would you agree to assist in a rescue mission?"

The bear showed her teeth. "If you will help me find the male I mated with, wherever Daddy Eddy took him, I will help you rescue the pigs. That is, if the children are kept safe."

"You're fond of him," said Dora. "The male."

"Not particularly, no," said Rosa in a thoughtful voice. "He is no more than competent at what I need him for, but these two are almost two years old. It is time for me to mate again, and I prefer a male who talks! Don't you?" She glanced meaningfully at Abby.

Dora flushed, started to speak, and was interrupted by Oyk, who called, "The buck has his horns caught in the wire."

Abby said, "I thought that might happen. I brought wire cutters."

He went into the trees, returning in a few moments followed by four goats, one buck with long, curly horns, and three spike-horned does. The buck snorted and made a farting noise. The does murmured a chorus of nervous thank-yous that only expectation made intelligible. Everyone hurried; no one talked; and as soon as they were loaded, Dora announced they were going to attempt rescuing Sahir and the scuini.

"Do you think that's wise?" Abby whispered.

"Abby, I can't just leave them there. It could be the whole scuinic race. And Sahir, we know Sahir. He's our friend."

"He's a snotty little git," said Abby. "But I suppose if you're a sultan's son you get like that. Lord, this is turning into a cross between Indiana Jones and the San Diego Zoo."

They drove almost furtively, slowing well in advance of every cross street, keeping exactly to the center of their lanes, attracting no attention whatsoever. They turned off the avenue at the boardinghouse corner and crept down the swerving alley that had been left by the trees. A large, dark car was parked in front of Jared's place, blocking the way. They parked the vans some little distance behind it.

Dora had been thinking about the situation during the drive, and she had her strategy firmly in mind.

"Rosa, if you'll go back to the garage and make sure no one's in it, then you can come to the back door. Abby and I'll meet you there. I've still got a key. Your children can stay locked in the van where they'll be safe. Oyk, can the new dogs . . . kanni help? All right, two of you on each side and two in front, just in case somebody comes bursting out of the house and tries to get away. Soaz, if you and Sheba can guard that car and the vans to be sure no one gets away or gets hurt. The others can help best by staying quiet."

Rosa vanished into the darkness; the dogs scattered in various directions; Sheba made an impressive, almost slow-motion leap from the van. Dora took her gun from her holster, then dug into the bottom of her purse for the other one she always carried, just in case. After giving her troops a few moments to get into place, she beckoned to Abby and headed for the back door.

Rosa emerged from the dark. "Nobody in garage," she said. "Very old, strong smell there, but no person."

"Okay, so they're in the house," Dora whispered, putting her key in the lock while giving silent thanks that she was still wearing the trousers with the key in the pocket. The door opened into the kitchen, which was in darkness except for a thin line of light showing at the edge of the basement door.

"Wait," Dora directed. "I need to be sure they aren't up here somewhere." She handed the extra gun to Abby. "You know how to use this?"

"You point it and pull the trigger," he replied. "Oh, you have to get a bullet into the what-you-call-it first."

Dora took it from him, jacked a shell into the chamber and then sneaked off, checking the dining room and living room. A thick blanket of dust lay over everything, on the hall floor, on the stairs. No one had come into these rooms for weeks.

She arrived back at the basement door at the same moment a squealing scream tore the quiet to shreds. She ripped open the door and plunged down the stairs, halting at their foot to see Jared poised in the cone of light below a shaded bulb, Sahir's wriggling figure beneath his foot, both hands on the haft of a wide, double-edged blade that glittered in the light. He was dressed for the sacrificial rite, wearing a long black robe like those the countess had described the Weelians wearing, though his face was bare.

"Jared," Dora said very softly, in the wifely voice she had perfected while living with him. "What are you doing?"

He looked up, mouth open, squinting into the shadows, able to see her only vaguely in the darkness. "Dora? Why are you here?" His voice cracked, his hand shook.

"I had the report of a theft, Jared. Some valuable animals were stolen from Randall Pharmaceuticals. Someone followed your car here."

"Not stolen," he grunted, still squinting, trying to see who was behind her. "Mine. I bought them. I paid the man at the lab a lot of money for them. They're mine."

"No, Jared. They belong to Mrs. Winston. No one at the lab had any right to sell them. They really are stolen property. I have to take them back."

"Mine!" he screamed at her. "Dirty, filthy, mudeaters, shit-wallowers, don't deserve to . . ."

"To what, Jared?"

"To . . . to . . . take up space."

"You bought them just to kill them?"

"I can. If I want. They're mine. I can kill them if I want to. I can *eat* them if I want to."

"But what a strange way to do it, Jared. People might misunderstand."

"Who cares. There's no law against it. You've got no right to interfere!"

Abby stumbled on the step behind her. Jared leaned forward, peering. "Who's that?"

"Just a friend," said Abby, moving down beside Dora.

Jared sneered. "The boyfriend? Not your cop friend, Phil? So it's not really police business, Dora?" He said her name as though he were spitting an obscenity.

Dora let her hand move into the light, the gun glinting dully. "Put that blade down, Jared."

"Put the knife down, Jared," said the pig, unwisely.

Sahir was, as Abby had said, a snotty little git who didn't know when to keep his stupid mouth shut. Dora saw the Jared facade become Woput, saw him possessed of an ancient, cold fury, eyes slitted, neck swollen.

"They're mine," he screamed, leaping at Dora with the blade extended, slashing with it, making a lethal circle of gleaming light and razor steel. It wasn't a knife. It was a part of some machine. Others like it were ranked along one wall, the light glinting from their faceted surfaces.

Dora stumbled away from him, her foot catching the edge of the step. She fell heavily to one side, taking Abby down with her. Sahir squirmed away and ran for the stairs, pursued by Jared, who seized his hind leg in one hand and jerked him upward triumphantly, turning his back to the stairs as he held the wriggling Sahir aloft.

"Mine," he repeated, putting the glittering edge to Sahir's throat. "I didn't need you after all! I found someone else to use! I found them without you. . . ."

Huge paws reached around his arms, pulling them back. Claws dug deeply into his flesh. Sahir dropped, squealing in fear and surprise. The blade fell from Jared's hand as he shouted incoherently, his eyes very wide. Rosa pushed him facedown and stood on him, leaning her head forward to put her jaws delicately at either side of his neck.

"Who?" cried Jared. "What?"

Dora was struggling to get her feet under her, trying to decide what she would do when she got up, but Rosa didn't wait for instructions. She simply hunched her shoulders and bit down. There was a cracking sound. Jared's body twitched, then spasmed, arms and legs flailing as though from an electrical shock, the whole body twisting and shaking. The bear leapt aside. The spasms continued interminably, like a fit of grand mal, until the body went limp all at once. From somewhere outside came a pained and horrified screech, or a scream, or a howl, or all three, the sound going on and on, diminishing so slowly into silence they could not feel it had ceased, but rather that it had moved away, past hearing.

Then there was only the sound of Rosa's deep breathing and a murmuring of pigs from the corner.

Dora grasped the stair railing and pulled herself off the floor, turning to give Abby her shaking hand. He rose, cursing, white-faced. "God! Did she kill him?"

Dora nodded, "I think so."

She knelt by the body, felt of the neck. Nothing. No pulse, no breath. "Now what?" she mumbled to herself. "Now what the hell? I didn't plan . . ." She felt nothing, she realized. Shock, yes, but no sympathy, no pain. She looked up at Abby's troubled face. "He's dead. The Woput's dead."

Abby absentmindedly brushed the dust from his clothes.

Rosa said, "Good. He is better dead."

Dora tried to speak and could not, cleared her throat and tried again.

"Abby. Can you get that net off the other pigs over there in the corner? Take that knife thing. The net'll probably have to be cut." She panted for a moment. "Damn, that's the wrong thing to do."

"I've already done it," said Abby, cutting the last few meshes and freeing the six terrified pigs who had been huddled inside the net.

"Well, wipe the blade and put it back in Jared's hand. Get his fingerprints all over it, including the sharp part.

It's wide and doubled-edged, so it's probably the same thing he used to kill Winston and the others. Rosa, this house is thick in dust and I left my footprints all over upstairs. Go upstairs, wherever I walked, and put your footprints on top of mine. Be sure there are no shoe prints left up there. Get Oyk and Irk to help you. Then you all come down here and do the same thing. Be sure there are no pig prints or shoe prints left, only bear and dog feet. Abby, take the net out and put it in the van.

"You people." She gestured at the pigs. "Come with me. Quickly, silently, and if anyone's out there on the street, stay out of sight."

Sahir opened his mouth, but she glared at him, hissing a threat to finish what Jared had started if he didn't obey. When she tried to get up, she couldn't. She was dizzy. It took a moment for the wave of dizziness to subside enough that she could climb the stairs. At the back door she found Soaz waiting with Sheba.

"Put the scuini in the van with the goats," she directed, turning back to wait for those still inside. "And keep Sahir quiet."

In a few moments, Oyk and Irk came out, followed by Rosa, who announced, "The light is still on down there."

"Leave it. We'll leave this back door open, too."

"You want it to seem he was killed by a forest being?"

"As I've explained to our people, Rosa, if he's killed by a forest person, a non-human person, what we would call a beast, the police won't investigate in the same way they would if they thought he was killed by another human. So long as you aren't found, and we have no intention you should be, we don't need to explain anything."

The bear nodded, licking her jaws as she led the way back to the van.

Abby drove away. Dora watched him go, unable to get her own vehicle in motion. She was shaking too hard. Finally, seeing the red brake lights at the end of the block, waiting there, she turned the key and let the van roll silently away. She made the rest of the distance in a fog, as in a dream. During the drive there was barely a sound from the rescued peoples except for an outraged monologue from Sahir, muttered rather than shrieked. When it had gone on for some time, it was interrupted.

"Why don't you shut up," said one of the new pigs.

"Why should I?" demanded Sahir.

"Because if you'd listened to us instead of telling us how important you were, you'd have known about the tunnel. If it hadn't been for you, we could have gotten away, you idiot."

After which there was silence. When they arrived at the street before Dora's place, the new acquisitions slipped out of the vans, a few at a time, and were directed where to go by Soaz or Izzy.

Abby came to find Dora still behind the wheel, still shaking.

"Are you all right?"

"Yes. No. I don't know. I can't seem to stop . . ."

"It wasn't Jared, Dora. There was no Jared!"

"I know. I just . . . can't quite accept it yet."

Abby carried the bedding material back to the garage. Dora fetched a broom, and they swept the vans as clean as possible. Nassif appeared with a cup of something hot and reviving, and when she and Abby started for the public lot downtown, Dora was in control of herself.

It was almost midnight before they returned, walking the few blocks from the avenue with their heads down, plodding, inexpressibly weary.

Izzy met them at the gate. "Is everything taken care of?"

Dora went over what she'd done, tallying each point. "I called nine-one-one from a public phone downtown. I said I was walking on that street, that I heard a terrible scream, that I saw an open door and a large shape disappearing in the trees. I did not give them a name." She put her arms around herself, quelling her internal tremors.

Abby replaced them with his own, hugging her close. "Where is everyone?"

"The kapris are in the garage. They ate a few mouthfuls, just enough to settle them. The buck has finally said a word or two, not including 'thank you.' Oyk and Irk have taken their tribesmen into the woods. Irk found a den there yesterday, under a rocky place, and they would rather live in the open. The new armakfatid is upstairs with Dzilobommo, as is Sheba with Soaz, and Rosa with her children. Rosa says they will sleep outside, however, as your place is getting very crowded."

"The pigs?"

"Sahir is upstairs. He's in a rage, of course, but Nassif got him quiet, finally. The others prefer a place with the kapris and the veebles. They are not accustomed to clothing or to being, what would one say, sanitary minded? They can be, it is merely a matter of turning their attention to the matter, but for now . . ."

"I understand," said Dora, gratefully. She'd fleetingly wondered about that while they were making rescue plans. When she'd seen the condition of the pens at Randall Pharmaceuticals, it hadn't indicated housetraining. "What about Sheba and Rosa?"

"Cats are naturally fastidious," Izzy remarked. "They always attend, so it is no trouble. Rosa is keeping an eye on her children."

"Is there room for me up there?" asked Abby in a weary voice.

"We have all made places for ourselves in the outer room," said Izzy, carefully looking elsewhere. "The inner room is vacant, awaiting you and Dora. We thought, after your labors . . ."

"Izzy, you're sweet," said Dora, leaning forward and kissing him, surprising both herself and him.

Opalears: Rehearsals

Dora and Abby left the new people with us and took the vans back to the city, and Dzilobommo began a list. Hay, he wrote. And more grain of all kinds. And many more apples and carrots and other root vegetables. The new armakfatid stood very near him, as though she had been lonely for so long she could not believe she had a fellow person to grummel with. Dzilobommo looked at her kindly, put his nose in her ear and licked her face.

Sahir went into the bathroom and got into the shower, yelling at me to come turn on the water. I left, but he stayed in there. After a long time, I went to the doorway and asked him how he felt.

"Dirty," he snarled. "I stink of barbarians."

I knew what was bothering him. "Prince Sahir," I whispered. "No one saw anything but seven naked animals. In this time, all the animals go naked. There is no shame to it."

It wasn't precisely true, for Soaz had seen. Izzy had

396

seen, and from what Izzy said, Sahir had behaved stupidly, and Sahir knew it. He would not be comforted. I scrubbed his back, thinking of his mother, the sultana, and how she had foreseen this time. He had a tusk wound on his rump, and I put medicine on it from Dora's cabinet. I brought him clean clothing. When he came into the room where the rest of us were, he wore clean trousers and shirt, and his headcloth was white as the snow on the peaks of the Sharbak Mountains.

"You look rested," said the countess soothingly, forebearing to ask him questions. She knew he had been greatly shamed and wished to put it out of his mind.

It was then Izzy suggested we leave the sleeping room for Dora and Abby, when they returned. They would be very weary, Izzy said, and a little privacy would be welcome to them. It was the least we could do, and we arranged ourselves as comfortably as possible and were mostly asleep when they returned. I was awake enough, however, to hear that Dora and Abby fell onto the bed and into sleep without any sweet words or romancing.

I had thought that Dora and Abby were mates, but the more I saw them together, the more I thought not. Not yet, at any rate. Sometimes in her face I saw confusion, flicking like fish behind her eyes: "What is this? What am I feeling? What can I do about it?" I saw him looking at her with an expression much less equivocal. If she would, he certainly would. I thought she cared for him, but worried at the feeling, as a kanna worries at a bone, not content until he has shattered it.

In the morning, Abby left early, and when Dora came sleepily from her room, she greeted us all, and bowed to the new armakfatid and to Sheba, who had spent the night curled up next to Soaz. While she was having her coffee, the phone rang, and she answered it, once again speaking to the Dionne person. When she put the instrument away, she said, "He'll be bringing the archpriest here, tonight around suppertime. The archpriest will have to be told everything. Could one of you tell the story, so he has it from the horse's mouth?"

Then, seeing our expressions, she said, "No, not from the horse's mouth, forget I said that, from one of you."

"Nassif will do it," said Sahir. "She tells stories well."

I opened my mouth to object, but then closed it again. It was what I did well, so why should I not do it? Izzy would talk forever and would say everything except the story itself; the countess would be too diplomatic; Blanche too dry; Soaz too disapproving. I could be a horse-mouth if one was wanted.

"Also," said Dora, "since you are worshipers of Cory—"

"Korè," said Izzy, correcting her pronunciation. "Kohr-RAY."

"Since you are worshipers," she went on, "is there some prayer or ritual you could do to convince this man you are . . . coreligionists?"

Izzy said he would think of something. Dora had a bite of breakfast, took the list Dzilobommo had prepared and shook her head. "We're feeding an army." She sounded depressed. Or perhaps she was just very tired.

I went to remind her. "Please, take some of the gems to pay for our food."

"I won't have time to market jewels today, Nassif. Maybe tomorrow. Before I leave, let's see if the news is reporting on what happened last night."

She turned on the TV and found the story we all had expected: the death of a man, killed by a big animal or animals in the basement of his home, where, seemingly, he had not lived for some time. Police, so the teller said, had searched the woods around the house but had found nothing.

Dora turned it off and sat for a moment with her head down.

Anything else?" asked Izzy.

"I was just thinking what we have to do before I can . . . take a rest."

"Perhaps we could help you more?"

"No. I'll manage." She gave a short, almost mirthless laugh.

"What?" asked Izzy.

"I was thinking about the archpriest, when you tell him you made a tree talk," she answered with a fierce grin. "Be ready to show off, Izzy. Before we're through, I've got a hunch you'll have to prove it."

And then she was gone, out and away, catching the bus to town, where she would return the vans and shop for foodstuffs, which she said she would bring early in the day, if she could. I kept forgetting that Dora had a job, that she was not free to go and do as she liked. In Tavor, not many people had jobs. People had businesses or they worked on farms or they made things, like pottery or cloth, but few of them had jobs that began at one hour and ended at another hour, during which time one's life was not one's own. If one wanted a person like that, one had a slave.

I rallied our people and the guests, and we cleaned the house. As a former slave, I knew more about this than the others did, so I found myself directing matters. Dora had explained the machine which cleaned the floor, though it did not do it as well as I could do it on hands and knees in not much more time. Another machine washed the dishes, and another the clothes. We washed everything, the sheets, the blankets, all the plates. We put everything back as it had been when we arrived, including the scattered books onto the shelves. Dzilobommo, with the new armakfatid watching him from a high stool, set about preparing a luncheon, and I cleaned up after him, as I had done in the kitchens in the palace.

After lunch, Soaz and Sheba went out into the woods to find Oyk and Irk and their friends, and the onchiki went downstairs to meet the new people they had not met last night. Rosa had made herself a place in the corner of the garage downstairs. She had put Dora's sleeping bag in it, and several large cartons on top, so it was like a cave. If winter came, she said, it would serve as a place for hibernation. I felt she and her children should be far away by the time for hibernation. The kapris had gone out into the woods to browse, leaving the lower door open and staying within sight of the house, so they could take cover at need. With the three ersuns, the pheledas, the six new scuini, the four new kanni, an equal number of kapris and the one armakfatid, there were nineteen new people plus the twelve of us, plus three veebles: thirty-six counting Abby and Dora. We were indeed feeding an army.

The problem we had feared, that the bear and the big cat would eat the others, was unfounded. If they were not hungry, they said, they would not kill. If they had a choice, they would never kill speaking people. If they were starving, they could not say what they would do. Well. Neither could I.

We spent some time rehearsing what we would do when the priest of Korè came. In Tavor, the Korèsans worshiped openly, and both Sahir and Soaz could describe the rites. Izzy taught us a hymn as it was sung at the Temple of Korè near Giber. He had not been there. Obviously, a Bubblian prince could not travel to Giber, but he had learned the hymn from non-Bubblians who had been there. I rehearsed my story. The countess told us how we were to arrange ourselves in accordance with protocol.

Midafternoon, Izzy shouted a warning, and we all hid, for a vehicle had come to the street. It was only Dora, who had borrowed Phil's car to bring the hay and other things. She went away again, saying she would return in a few hours.

Late in the afternoon, we turned on the TV and heard once again that Jared Gerber had been killed by a large animal in the basement of his home. Persons were warned not to leave their doors open. Also, said the speaker, evidence had been found linking Jared Gerber to the murders of scientists earlier in the year.

"I am pleased I killed him," said Rosa, licking her jaws.

"You didn't kill him," said Izzy in the strained voice

he had been using all day. 'All you did was make his body unsuitable for habitation. The Woput is not dead.''

This stopped us for a time, and we all looked at one another fearfully while Izzy explained the Woput had simply moved on. ''It must have something to do with the way he came here in the first place. He's able to exist, at least momentarily, in a disembodied state.''

''Why didn't you say so before?'' demanded the countess.

''I thought Dora needed a respite,'' he said. ''She's looking terribly tired. I was going to tell her later.''

''Well, if he's moved into some other body, he doesn't know where we are,'' said Sahir sulkily. ''So we're safe for the time being.''

''Of course he knows where we are,'' said Izzy. ''Or he knows how to find out. He saw Dora; he called her by name; he has been here; he has sent a visitation here, night after night. He knows that she knows where we are. The fact he is in a new body now will not stop him for long.'' Izzy stopped for a moment, as though wanting to say something more, but evidently changed his mind. All he said was, ''Next time he comes, it will be with something more lethal than a blade.''

Though Izzy and Soaz had told us all the events of the evening, we had not thought of the implications. Even the countess had not understood what the death of Jared Gerber meant. Not for the first time, I thought Izzy might be smarter than the rest of us.

After that, it seemed wisest to stay close to the house.

38

The Pretender

Dora started the day pretending surprise at the news of Jared's death and feigning concern about his being killed by a beast.

Phil was put in charge of collecting evidence at Jared's place, without Dora, who might presumably have a conflict of interest. Dora told Phil that Jared had often said some weird things about scientists, that since he worked at the same place as the victim, Williams, perhaps Phil should keep his eyes open for any connection to the three deaths, including any weapon that might have been used. He gave her a funny look when he left, and an even funnier one when he came back with the blades and some notebooks.

At which point, Dora continued her pretence by feigning shock when Phil told her Jared did seem to be implicated in Winston's murder, and Chamberlain's, and maybe others as well. Finally, she spent some time counterfeiting sadness to Mrs. Gerber, whom she phoned to offer condolences. The only feeling which actually

touched her was her own weariness and sorrow for
Momma Gerber. It was sad to think the woman had not
had a son for almost thirty years and had not had the
wit to know the difference. Motherhood, so Grandma
used to say, can be both blind and stupid. But then,
wifehood could be the same.

The lieutenant conferred with someone higher up
about tracking the beast responsible for Jared's death,
but the matter ended up referred to the animal control
officers, who recognized bear footprints well enough,
but were unable to track that same bear—understanda-
ble, since it had departed in a van. Dora took part in the
intermittent discussions that went on, shaking her head,
foreseeing dire consequences, and being reminded of
other, irrelevant cases by her colleagues. She did not
have to pretend to weariness and depression, which
those who did not know her well read as grief.

Midafternoon, Dora borrowed Phil's car and made a
hurried three-point shopping trip. The house was impec-
cably clean when she arrived home with the supplies.
Even the garage had been swept and neatened, with cartons and tools piled neatly to make individual spaces for
each tribal group. When everything had been unloaded,
she went back to the car, pursued by Nassif.

"Dora, you need to know," she whispered.

"What do I need to know, Nassif?"

"The Woput isn't dead. The Jared body is dead, but
the Woput's still alive. And Izzy says he knows where
we all are."

Dora was staggered. Despite her absolute certainty
that Izzy was right, the *all right, of course, what else*
clarity of the notion, it had not crossed her mind until
that moment that the being who had occupied Jared Gerber could still be alive.

"Izzy says when Woput comes, he'll have something
worse than a knife," Nassif murmured.

"He can't get it from Jared's place," Dora whispered.
"There've been cops and reporters all over the place
since early this morning. He'll have to take some time

to find out whose body he's in. I imagine it happened more or less at random, so that body may not have access to the things Woput might need." She stopped. Something she had just said bothered her, but she couldn't focus on it. There were other things to do at the moment. "I thought we had a little time. We don't. We have no time at all. As soon as we talk to Harry Dionne's father, we have to start finding places for all of you!"

Rubbing her forehead fretfully, she took herself away once more, returning about six by her regular bus-bike route. Abby showed up half an hour later to be given the news.

"There's no end to this, is there? How do we kill the damn thing?"

"Drive a stake through its heart," Dora said, half hysterically. "Shoot it with a silver bullet."

"I'm thinking about it," said Izzy. "I will think of something."

"Think of it in a hurry," snarled the countess. "I, like Dora, am growing impatient with these troubles. They swarm around us, like gnats!"

It was beginning to get dark before they heard the distant clamor that became decipherable as it neared: Drums. Panpipes. Lyres.

"Places everyone," said the countess in an imperious voice as Dora went down the stairs and out the driveway, Abby close behind.

Music trickled at them as they stood at the curb. "I remember this," said Dora, almost fretfully.

"What do you remember, Dora?"

"The music. Lately, everything's been punctuated by music. Do you know that Kurasawa film, the one about dreams?"

"I've seen it. Short episodes, isn't it?"

"One of them is about a village of watermills. And at the end there's a procession, actually it's a funeral procession, and it has this same kind of music. Solemn-joyous, all at once.'' She hummed, rising and falling on her toes.

He took her hand. "Shhh. I see them.''

A dozen robed figures: slender women lifting sistra to make a soft jangle, then pause, then jangle; others tootling on pan pipes, breathy, repetitive phrases. The musicians wore white; they were crowned with flowers. Then came a dozen young men, carrying torches that flared fitfully in the dusk, the flames seeming to rise and fall to the sound of the pipes. Smoke rose from swinging censers, blowing toward them in aromatic clouds to the *tap tap* of tambours. In the midst of this noise and array walked the archpriest, just as Harry had described him, bearded, robed, crowned in oak leaves and holding a scepter of holly. Beside him, his face frozen into imperturbability, walked Harry himself.

With sudden insight, Dora realized that facial expression had been hard won. Poor Harry. Think of all the explanations he would have had to make when he was a kid. And since. Think of the family gatherings. With an apologetic glance in his direction, Dora bowed, not so deeply as to seem overawed, but deeply enough to be polite.

"Dora Henry,'' said Harry. "His Worthiness, the Archpriest Vorn Dionne.''

"Sir,'' said Dora, bowing slightly again. "If you and your son would be so kind as to accompany me to my house, just a few feet, your entourage can await you here.''

"Our business cannot be done here?'' murmured the archpriest, in a basso so deep it made the air tremble.

"We have things to show Your . . . Excellency. They are private things, matters to do with Korè, for your eyes and those of your son.''

"If they are to do with Korè, they are not for this son,'' said Vorn, making a small, dismissive wave at Harry. "He is not of priestly caste.''

"As Your Excellency wishes.'' Dora threw another apologetic glance at Harry, receiving a shrug in return.

"So what," it said. "I'm used to it. I'll wait."

Dora led the way. Vorn followed without enthusiasm, his very gait expressing doubt. I am here, his footsteps said, but I do not believe you know anything worthy of my notice. They went through the gate and shut it behind them. Assembled outside the door to Dora's house were Rosa and her cubs, the kapris, the kanni, plus Sheba and Soaz.

"His Worthiness, Archpriest of Korè," said Dora in a ringing tone, feeling herself rise to the occasion.

"Worthiness," said the assembled multitude, bowing. "Hail Korè. Korè Eaeü."

The archpriest staggered. Abby caught him, offering an arm. Vorn drew himself up and away from Dora.

"What is this? Trickery?"

"No trickery," said Dora, giving him a direct look. "Please, come in."

The others were assembled upstairs, the scuini, the armakfatidi, the onchiki, Blanche, Izzy and Nassif. They began singing when the downstairs door opened, accompanying themselves as when Dora had heard them first, on the mandolin and harp, on the slide whistle and the drum. It was a hymn to Korè they sang, one Izzy had set to a tune they already knew.

One of the leather chairs had been moved near the top of the stairs and the archpriest sank dazedly onto it. The song ended. Lucy Low put down her harp, Izzy his mandolin, and they and Vorn stared at one another.

"Well?" Vorn said at last in a voice that trembled only slightly. "Will someone explain—"

"I will," said Nassif, standing forth. "Once upon a time . . ."

Opalears: Among the Korèsans

"**O**nce upon a time," I said, "a time far away, but in this same world, there will be a remnant of humans at a place called St. Weel...."

I told what I had been rehearsing on and off all day, in between worries, and the story flowed out, all this I have been telling, plus Dora's story as I knew it from her, and Izzy's, and the story he learned from his library as well as the stories learned from the libraries of the emperor and at St. Weel. I told of the creation of our peoples in this time by Dr. Edgar Winston—at which the Vorn showed surprise, even dismay—and of the plague that would come, of the death of almost all the humans, at which the Vorn frowned and shook his head. I told of our survival—the forest people, the river people, the desert people, pheled and scuinan, ponji and armakfatidi, onchiki and kanni, ersuns and kapris and sitidas.

I told of the Woput, and of his travel into his past, this time, how he sought out the embodiment of Korè and murdered her. I told how the Woput even now endangered us. I told how Korè herself had sent the ucor to wreak vengeance, and at this his dismay increased.

"How do you know this?" he demanded, this old, bearded man. "How can you possibly know this?"

"I talked to the trees," said Izzy.

"Talked?" scoffed the archpriest. "I suppose you're a magician!"

Izzy drew himself up. "Why is that so difficult for religious people to understand? Your people do magic here, every generation or so, when you embody Korè in a human form. You do not call it magic; you call it religion. It doesn't matter what you call it: Korè is an elemental, more powerful than storm, more marvelous than ocean, more potent than volcano. You draw on this power, this marvel, this potency, and you embody it in a virgin girl and you control it, carefully and reverently. Then when Korè is symbolically mated with her people in the person of a priestly son, the power is naturally released. It is poured out, into your people and into the world, for the preservation of life. Isn't this true?"

The archpriest glowered. "Where have you learned of this? These are sacred things, secret things. . . ."

Izzy went on: "In this time, yes. You are a tiny minority in this time. In our time these matters are still held sacred, but they are not held secret from the worshipers of Korè, who are many. It is, you might say, our state religion. Even I, reared in another tradition, am philosophically a Korèsan. Also, I am a good wizard, and I had a good library.

"The Woput, however, was no Korèsan, he is a bad wizard, and his library was not as good as mine. His sources spoke of the ritual I have described, but only in a general way. They did not explain what really happens. He thought if he killed the girl, the embodiment, he would kill Korè. He assumed if he killed Korè, he would kill the forests and the seas, and the other tribes would die. So he killed the girl, which only angered Korè, greatly angered Her. Then he buried the girl under the floor of Jared's garage, along with all the unexpended power she had been given. He succeeded in confining that power—though only that—but while confined, it grew and fulminated, and when the tomb was broken, all that force was ready to come out. As it has come out."

"This is why the trees have come? They told you this?"

"Korè told me this, through the trees. The Woput was in Jared Gerber. He took the girl, killed the girl, and buried her where he did because that place was convenient. Korè, however, was in the great tree, sacred to her, as she is to lesser extent in all living things, and from the great tree roots went out to break the slab around the girl. When the accumulated power burst out, the forests began to grow. They are an expression of Korè's anger, at the Woput and at those who are like him."

"Wouldn't he have known about these forests? Wouldn't there have been records, in his time?" Vorn looked from person to person, his nostrils flared, his eyes angry and, I thought, a bit frightened.

It was the countess who answered. "The records the Woput knew of, in his time, were written before he returned here. The forests are a result of his coming here; they were not here before he came. When we go back, if we are able to go back, the records may *then* speak of forests, but the records did not mention them before."

The old man shook his head. "I am astonished at the trees. I am astonished by all of you. Our prophecies speak of other peoples emerging from the womb of earth, but we had not known you were already . . . here. In our councils, in our decisions, your existence and the existence of these new forests are things we had not . . . had not considered. Had not counted on."

"A wild factor," said Abby, watching him closely.

"I recognize your confusion," said Dora. "It's like a dream. I've been living in it for weeks."

The old man combed his beard with his fingers, adjusted his leafy crown, then heaved himself to his feet.

His face was lined and his eyes were sunken as he said:

"There is more, much more we must talk of, but now is not the time. The people with me are from our local chapter. They enjoy the music and the incense, the marching about. They do me honor, but they are merely believers, not elders, and it is the elders who must consider this. They will have to come here. There is no other choice. I will stay at my son's home, awaiting them."

He looked down, slightly flushing. "I owe him an apology. Though my affection for him made me respond to his plea, I frankly thought . . . well, I thought he was being foolishly deluded."

"He was courageous to brave your disbelief," I said.

"This is not something I can consider alone. . . ."

"What will you consider?" asked the countess, one eyebrow rising in slight suspicion. "Whether we are worthy of your help?"

He turned on her in astonishment. "Of course you are worthy of our help! Everything we have done, everything we have decided has always been to make the way clear for Korè, in all her diversity. That means you, all of you. We thought to make a place for you when you came, but you are already here. We will protect you and your people as best we can. Korè would have us do no less. But there are other matters to consider. . . ."

He thought for a moment, then continued. "There is perhaps something we can do immediately. Many Korèsans live in this area, some of them out among the forests. You say the Woput endangers you. Perhaps you would be safer with my people, Korè's people, than with Winston's people. If I understand you correctly, in that future time, the Woput may have seen records made by Winston, records that say where his . . . creations were sent, who kept them, who protected them. My people, on the other hand, do not leave records. When we act for the good of the earth, we do so secretly. Secrecy has become a way of life for us."

He took a small book from his pocket, and he, Dora

and Abby conferred for a time. Evidently the book was in code, for he dictated numbers and code words to Dora by which she could get in touch with the Korèsans. I hoped Dora did not intend to separate those of us who had come so far together. When she turned and smiled at me, I knew the hope was not needed. It was a familial look that said she had no intention of sending us away with the new people.

While Dora and Abby escorted the archpriest back to his entourage, we relaxed, sighing. Izzy began to laugh, and the countess asked him why.

"I always wanted to hear the hymn of Korè sung before the archpriest, but I never thought the archpriest would be an umminhi."

We all laughed, but softly, so Abby and Dora would not hear. They had been kind to us, they had protected us, they had faced danger for us. We did not want to hurt their feelings.

40

Diaspora

The next day was Saturday, a day of farewells. In the morning, early, while Abby made coffee and neatened up the beds, Dora made phone calls, referred to code words, gave her phone number and received phone calls from others. The people who called did not mention where they lived, or what their names were, and Dora didn't ask. Rosa and her children went away first, taken by a quiet couple who drove a Range Rover with curtained windows. Their home was in the mountains, and they had the means to be sure that Rosa and her family had a safe place to live, people to talk with, and adequate food to eat.

Also, they said, they would see if they could find out where Rosa's mate had been taken if Dora could give them some leads. After warning them not to give their true name or location, and not to call from a phone which could be used to locate them—warnings they considered unnecessary—Dora went through Winston's address book to pull out the possibles: 1bb m, and 4b 2&2,

and a couple of other enigmatic entries that might mean almost anything. As Dora herself said, it could be black bear, but it could also be bald buffalo or barefoot beaver.

The goats went next, in a horse trailer drawn behind a faded red pickup driven by a laconic, denim-clad couple with one equally laconic teenaged son. The six new pigs were picked up shortly thereafter by two gray-haired sisters in a station wagon, and two of the dogs, male and female, went in the same vehicle, the other pair waiting for a battered jeep driven by a dark-skinned woman with long, braided black hair. All of these vehicles had been traveling muddy roads, for their license plates were unreadable.

Soaz would not be separated from Sheba and the female armakfatid would not leave Dzilobommo. Her name, he said, was Dzilalu.

Not necessary, said Dora. Dzilalu and Sheba might stay.

Izzy disagreed. "It may be necessary. How do we know what people are needed here and now to create our tribes a thousand years from now? Maybe Dzilalu and Sheba should be taken away from here."

"If she stays here," said Soaz, "I stay here. Otherwise, where she goes, I go." Soaz, so they all said, was smitten.

Izzy grumbled, but he did not argue further.

Dora, listening to Soaz and Sheba murmuring together, sought to satisfy her curiosity about Winston's creations. "Sheba," she said. "You and the others lived right out there in public, in pens. Winston must have had other people working with him, plus the lab people and the animal keepers. How was it that none of them knew you could talk? Joe and Bill didn't know. At least they didn't say anything to me."

Sheba stretched, a languorous stretch that seemed to double the length of her body. "Daddy Eddy had a place in the mountains where we were born," she purred. "We stayed there until we learned to be careful. Sometimes his woman came to see us, but we never let her know, either.''

"Why did he take you to the lab at all?"

"Oh, to do tests, and X-rays, and things like that. We never had to stay long. He moved us back and forth a lot. It was kind of a game. We all knew we'd go somewhere else as soon as he had all the information he needed. We trusted him.''

"It would seem to me someone would forget and babble. Rosa's babies, for instance.''

"It's only been a little while we've had second generation," said Sheba, a troubled expression on her face. "Rosa's babies were over a year old before any of us saw them. The pigs are second generation, and the four dogs. And there are still people at the mountain place. I just thought of that.''

"They could be hungry," cried Dora.

"No, no," said Sheba. "There are humans there to take care, and they know what to do if Daddy Eddy does not return. He told us all what to do.''

"But there are still some of you inside the lab." Dora stared at her feet. "And he was taking you all back and forth all the time, which he could do, from the lab's point of view, because they belonged to him. What I said to Jared was right. In a legal sense, you belong to Mrs. Winston, because if you were Winston's property, she inherited!''

Izzy looked up alertly. "You think she could get them out of there?"

"I think it's a tactic we'd better explore, and as soon as possible.''

Abby yawned. "I foresee a chauffeuring session.''

Mrs. Winston, reached by phone, was home and willing to see them. It was late afternoon. They were offered drinks. Dora accepted a glass of wine, Abby a scotch. Dora had introduced Abby as Professor Abilene McCord, a biologist from the university.

"We've grown to respect your husband," Dora said carefully. She sipped her wine, thinking how to make the case as tactfully as possible. "His colleagues think so highly of him. His treatment of the animals was so generous and highly ethical. We . . . we've become concerned about the animals left there at the lab. It was evidently Dr. Winston's practice to place most of his animals with people he knew would care for them. We found the addresses in his address book. Those animals are now your property . . ."

"And you want me to get them?"

"It isn't what we want that's terribly important, but if you don't take charge of them, something might happen to them that your husband would have greatly regretted," said Abby.

"I have to leave town tomorrow," she said. "I'll be gone for a week, but when I get back the following Sunday—"

"That may be too late," said Dora desperately. "If they are let go by the lab, they may be used in medical tests. They may be dead by the time you return. Or infected with AIDS. I'd be happy to contact Mr. Winston's friends, if you'll give me the authority. . . ."

Mrs. Winston stared at them both for a long time, a very strange expression on her face. "Winnie succeeded, didn't he?"

Dora kept her own face perfectly blank.

The woman smiled. "He succeeded. He did what he tried to do. And now you want to save his . . . his children."

"You knew what he was trying to do?" asked Abby.

"We used to talk about it. Long ago. We could never have children, he and I. Winnie had had many pets when he was a child, and he often spoke of their intelligence. He often spoke of his lab children, though he stopped talking about what he was trying to do some years ago. I thought . . . well, I thought it had just been a dream, that it had been impossible, a lovely fantasy. Why didn't he tell me?"

"Perhaps he didn't want to endanger you," whispered Dora. "What he was doing got him killed."

"They'd have killed me, too?"

"Perhaps. Whoever they are."

She sat staring into an unseen distance for a long time, then shook herself, rose and went to her desk where she took out a sheet of stationery. She wrote briefly, then ran the note through a copier and signed both copies. "I've put Mr. McCord's name on it," she said. "As a cop, you shouldn't be involved, should you? You might be suspected of . . . oh, extorting this from me."

Dora smiled, touched. "You're right. I didn't think of that. What is this?"

"A bill of sale. I've sold the animals to Mr. Abilene McCord, in return for which he agrees to see that they are given to good homes. Isn't that the phrase? Make the arrangements. I'll be at this number in San Francisco, if needed." She jotted it down, then turned away, dabbing at her eyes. "I don't want to endanger you or them with delay. But later on, if there's opportunity . . . I'd like to meet them."

It was late on Saturday. Still, on the off chance that someone was there, Abby drove them to Randall Pharmaceuticals. The building was closed, but the enclosure bristled with security men and with a large crew busy installing new fences. Abby and Dora observed this from the car with both disappointment and satisfaction. They couldn't get the animals today, but then, no one else was likely to, either.

On Sunday, Vorn Dionne returned to Dora's place together with his dozen elders—a mixed bunch as to sex and race, though all with seven or more decades behind them. To Dora's relief, they all, including the archpriest, were dressed in ordinary clothing and without additional entourage. It was also a relief that they chose to hold their meeting out in the woods, with guards well out to be sure they were not interrupted. Dora and Izzy and Nassif and the countess attended, by invitation. Abby was also invited, but he'd said he had to take the day to catch up with his life, particularly his laundry and his bills.

Amid the circle of old people, Nassif told the story of the Great Enigma once again, and Izzy explained how he had talked to the trees, demonstrating the process to the edification of those assembled, who, when the tree opened its mouth and howled with rage, were more than slightly impressed. Dora, looking around at the wrinkled faces, saw many emotions there: interest and amusement and vindication, none of which were unlikely for Korèsans. Less accountable was the pain she saw in some of their faces, controlled pain, as she had noticed sometimes in victims of chronic illness, pain so customary that it was merely accepted rather than regarded.

Well, she told herself, they are elderly. Pain comes to the elderly, as Grandma had often said, and sorrow, also, over loved ones departed, both pain and sorrow no doubt sent by nature to make death seem more attractive. Grandma had said it with a wink. These people did not look up to winking. Whatever their agony or sorrow might be, it had evidently been with them for some time.

"You see that I was not deluded," said the archpriest, when the tree had been released into its natural silence and all the murmuring was done. "When I came here yesterday, I was surprised. No, stunned. This was the last thing I suspected, but here is the truth, in front of us. Our prophets were correct to say the family tree has many branches. Korè's other children have come among us already."

The elders shared significant glances, veiled looks, full of intention. Dora frowned slightly, made wary by these looks, and the countess shifted uncomfortably, also, feeling those glances like touches, each one freighted with a heaviness, a burden weighty beyond bearing.

One white-haired, olive-skinned woman broke the silence by asking in a gentle, almost whispering voice, "In that future time, is it known who brought this plague among mankind?"

Izzy could only shake his head and tell them that the person or tribe or country was not named in the sources he had read. The attack was biological and it was religiously motivated, that's all he could tell them.

"Have you thought about it?" the old woman asked, looking around the circle, her gaze settling upon Dora.

Dora nodded. "Of course. I have wondered."

"Who do you think?"

Dora shrugged, making a rueful face. "The Catholics in Northern Ireland? Or the Protestants? Or are they both peaceable for the moment? The Shiites in Iran or Iraq or Libya? Or Farrakan, who shares their views? Any side at all in Bosnia? The Self Righteous-Right in Israel? Or the even more Self-Righteous Right in America? Maybe the Hindus in India? Or the Tamils in Sri Lanka? The nihilists in Japan? Any day I read the paper there would be candidates mentioned."

"So many possibilities," the old woman said, staring intently around herself. "So very many."

"The books said only that it was religious, not political," said Izzy.

Someone chuckled, one of the elders, a slender black man, who said, "Oh, son, when folks get to the point they're voting their religion and worshiping their politics, you think there's any line between them?"

"Well, you're not political," said Izzy.

Several of the elders smiled, though ruefully. One said, "Korè is the embodiment of life in its splendid variety. So long as her people were weak, a minority, widespread, we were protected from corruption and our worship remained pure. We always asked ourselves, if power were put into our hands, would we use it wisely? Would we choose to do what should be done? For all Korè's children?"

They all looked at one another, and again Dora saw that sadness, that sorrow. Well, why shouldn't they be sorrowful? They had just been told they were all to die. Presumably they had children, and grandchildren. The thought would be a sorrowful one.

The old woman said in a strong, no-nonsense voice, "Let us choose to believe that not all of us will die.

Perhaps the plague is not to kill us all, but to teach us something.''

Dora was startled into speech. ''My grandmother used to say that about bindweed in the garden, that she wasn't trying to kill it, just teach it some manners.''

The old woman nodded. There were murmurs. The archpriest said, ''Yes, Dora. That is a good thought.''

The other elders said nothing, merely stared into their laps or into the woods, lost in a private vision.

Still, Dora thought, the old woman was right. The plague wouldn't kill all humans. The Weelians would survive it. Three thousand years was not a bad record of survival, even though they were now losing the battle. Not *now*, of course, but *then*, which seemed like now when Izzy spoke of it.

''In the meantime,'' the archpriest said, ''do you need our help with your Woput? If he knows where you are, you must leave. You must go somewhere else.''

''I've been thinking and thinking about it,'' said Dora. ''Seemingly, we can't kill him. This morning, Izzy told me he thought we'd better try to find him and send him back into his own time while keeping the control here. There he will be impotent to do much harm, and so long as the control is here, he can't come back.''

Izzy sighed deeply. ''Respected Elders, Dora, I haven't mentioned it until now, but we can't ignore reality any longer. I think we may have a serious problem with our Woput. When the body of Jared died, there in the basement, I heard a scream from somewhere outside. . . .''

''So did we all,'' said the countess.

''My point is, it was from somewhere nearby. After I heard that howl, I kept wondering what a suddenly disembodied intelligence might do. Wouldn't it search for . . . for something, anything familiar? He was only a block or so from a place he knew well, a place inhabited by people he knew well. . . .''

''The boardinghouse?'' Dora cried. ''You mean the boardinghouse?''

"People, living close together? How many?" asked one of the elders, a quiet one with an eye patch, who had thus far taken it all in without comment.

"Oh, nine or ten," said Dora. "Counting Jared's mother. Normally there'd be three or four more, but Mrs. Gerber was doing some repainting so some of the rooms are vacant. You're thinking he ended up in one of them. . . ."

"It would mean he could be back in action quickly," said one of the female elders. "Since it was a place he knew, people he knew, there might have been no period of extreme confusion. No aphasia or amnesia. It is possible nothing happened to make anyone suspicious. . . ."

"How will we find out?" the archpriest asked.

"By asking about things the Woput does not know?" suggested Izzy.

"But Jared—that is, the Woput had been living there recently," she cried. "He knew them all. He could copy their habits, their personalities. If he wanted to."

"Would he want to, necessarily?" the old woman asked.

Izzy replied. "He might not bother. He might be preoccupied with other things. Tell us about the boarders, Dora."

Dora composed herself, half shut her eyes and concentrated. "If it's the Woput, and if he is not pretending to be someone else, he or she will show no sign of libido. He will be preoccupied with neatness and order. He will have no pets and tolerate none. Now, Mr. Calclough is a notable fanny pincher, and he used to talk about his girlfriend, a meter maid. Mr. Fries is a health nut. He does martial arts exercises in his room every morning, and it makes the whole house shake, and Momma Gerber complains about his leaving his towels and socks all over the floor.

"Mr. Singley has fish, tropical fish, in a tank, the kind with the little diver and the air bubbles, you know. Mrs. Sohn had a very old canary, but it's dead, so that may not help. If Woput got into Ms. Michaelson, you probably'd never know it from how she acts. She's neat as a pin and sexless as—'' She'd been going to say, ''As I am.''

She took a deep breath. ''However, she has no brakes on her mouth and no traffic signals in her head. The verbiage comes at you nonstop from all directions.''

''That's very helpful. Unless the Woput knows them well enough to pretend.''

Doggedly, Dora went on: ''He does. But as Izzy says, he may not bother. Momma . . . well, Momma Gerber is a stiff, rather impersonal woman, polite enough but not warm. The one thing I know about her that the Woput doesn't is that Jared used to say something sweet to her at bedtime, before he got hit by lightning. Afterward, he didn't remember, but Momma did. If she doesn't remember anything about it now . . .'' She subsided, fighting down the urge to scream, then went on:

''One thing in our favor: even though I was there when the Jared body died, the Woput doesn't know that I know who he really is or why he came. I called him Jared. I accused him of stealing the pigs. I didn't mention his killing Winston or coming from the future or anything. So, he doesn't know about the people who came from the future, or the fact the control is here.''

''Unless Sahir told him,'' said Izzy.

Dora's mouth dropped open in dismay. Of course. Sahir could have told him.

Several of the elders had been taking notes, including the man with the eye patch, who now asked, ''If he has seen television, he knows his Jared body was killed by an animal. Did he see the animal?''

''I don't think so, no. Rosa came from behind him.''

''And did you say anything to . . . Rosa?''

''No,'' she said. ''Though Prince Sahir spoke in my hearing, and the Woput might remember that.''

The archpriest asked Izzy, ''How does the control work, Prince Izakar? You plan to use it to return to your own time?''

Izzy nodded, though he wore a troubled frown on his

face. "The Weelians showed it to us when we came. It's very simple. The key is turned on, then the coordinates of the physical destination are entered—if you're going back. If you're going forward, you can only end up at the hospice, that's the only place it goes. Then there are keys that set the size of the field, and there's a little light to tell you if the control is inside the field or out of it. Then a button is pushed, and the field moves you up either back one turn to the now, or forward one turn into the then, where you step off."

"A reversible field?"

Izzy shook his head. "If you're now, you go then. If you're then, you come now. It's a closed loop."

"One can't leave now and go back to 1000 B.C.?"

"B.C.?" said Izzy.

"Three thousand years ago," said Dora.

"They told me you can go one turn from the end of the loop and that's all. One of the Weelians speculated to me that the thing is growing, and it hardens as it grows. Three thousand years ago is the last place soft enough to penetrate."

"How strange," murmured Vorn.

Izzy went on. "If the control field contains your body, your body goes back. If the field surrounds only your head, only your mind goes back—which is what the Woput did. And if the control isn't inside the field when it turns on, it stays where it is. Simple-minded, really."

"Who made this thing?" the archpriest murmured in a fretful tone. "This timeworm. It seems a pointless invention."

Izzy smiled ruefully. "The Weelians don't know who made it or where it came from. No one in our time knows. The seeress referred to a Great Enigma, and maybe that's why. It may be a magical creation, and one of the Weelians suggested it was a natural phenomenon. That seems unlikely to me, for when the Weelians found it, the control was there, and the control is obviously a manufactured thing. I myself believe it was created by another race, come to our world from out of space."

"Um," said the elder with the eye patch, turning to the white-haired, olive-skinned woman. "Better one or two of us investigate this boardinghouse. You and I, Benedeta? An elderly couple looking for temporary housing? Leaving Dora completely out of it?"

It was agreed. Dora told them what she had planned for the next day, and the elders agreed to assist her and Abby by providing vehicles and drivers to pick up the animals from the Randall Building. When the group left, sans sistra or incense, nothing about them would have drawn any attention to them at all.

41

Opalears: Sahir Sulks

When the religious people were gone, the countess
went back to the house and tried to find out from
Sahir if he had told the Woput anything at all, but he
made a cutting, unpleasant remark, then walked off into
the woods. Soaz went after him. Oyk and Irk went out
with the onchiki, while the rest of us gathered in Dora's
house. We made tea. She had some interesting kinds.
The armakfatidi were in the kitchen, inventing something delicious. Sheba curled up on the bed in the sleeping room. Blanche perched on the stair rail. The rest of
us sat around the table.

"The Korèsans are very pleasant persons," said the
countess, lowering her lips to her cup, as she did when
she was being informal. "Though something is going on
with them they did not tell us about. Did you feel it?"

"I felt something," Dora confessed. "Secret societies
are probably like that, don't you think? Passwords and
secret signs. I think they are allies of yours. I said there
would be allies."

"I know. But we did not expect Korèsans in this time. We did not expect talking umminhi in this time. We did not expect our Woput to become someone else. Most of all, we did not expect to find friends. There is little doubt these Korèsans are our friends. Are they yours, do you think?"

Dora flushed, smiling a little. "If you mean their judgmental attitude toward people, I'd say they're clannish. They may be more accepting of you all than they would be of another human who doesn't accept their way of life."

The countess nodded. "Non-humans are by no means perfect. One of us scuini has been very stupid, I'm afraid. Sahir won't tell me what he said to the Woput, but I fear he told about our coming from a future time."

Izzy looked around as though tallying those of us present. Dora, the countess, Blanche, me and him. The armakfatidi were not listening to us. Sheba was asleep. Only the five of us could hear. He whispered:

"If the Woput knows we came from the future, then the Woput knows the control is probably here. Maybe we'd better hide the control and the key. We wouldn't want something to happen we weren't all agreed on."

The countess nodded. The five of us went downstairs. The control was in a red leather case about the size of a book, and the case was in one of our packs. Izzy took the control out of the case and returned the case to the pack, then we went out of the house and hid the control very well. As for the key, Izzy put that on a thong around his neck, under his clothes, after which we returned to our teacups.

"Let's remember that we're not sure Sahir said anything," Dora reminded us. "We must consider him innocent, not prejudge him."

The countess smiled at her. "You are quick to defend him. Just as you were very quick to befriend us."

Dora laughed weakly. "Oh, not prejudging people is just part of my job, but befriending you . . . If you only knew how long you had been my friends. People like you, I mean. When I was a child . . .'' Her voice trailed away.

"What?'' the countess urged. "Tell me!''

"Oh, when I was a little child I talked to people like you all the time: four-legged people, winged people, furred people, feathered people, all the time. Grandma said it was the same for her. She said she knew others who had been the same, children who reached out instinctively to anything that shared life with them, who talked with other creatures and heard—I believe this—heard them talk back.

"Adults say it is fantasy, of course. Perhaps it is real, but temporary, then we grow older and the music stops and our friends are no longer our friends. When you came . . .''

There was silence. "I think that's remarkable,'' said the countess at last. "I have no experience like it.''

"But you do,'' cried Dora. "You live in a world like it.''

Blanche said, "Our world is not that perfect, Dora. We have our struggles and our conflicts, too. I know what you mean, however. When I was very little, I used to hear music, also. Mine was bird music, but it had the same feeling you describe.''

"Perhaps the reason is simple,'' Izzy commented. "Perhaps when we are very young, we can hear Korè speaking through all life.''

"While we're still part of everything,'' mused Dora. "Before we grow up and learn to believe we're something separate.''

"Dora, you have interesting thoughts,'' said the countess.

"Kind of you to say so,'' said Dora, sighing. "But I know I've never been very interesting.''

I had been only half listening, until then. I looked up, hearing something in her voice that resonated in mine. I started to ask her a question, but Izzy beat me to it.

"Why do you say that?''

She flushed, as though aware only then of what she

had said. "I never . . . never had a chance to be, maybe. No. I think . . . girls have a hard time being interesting. It's actually easier to be famous, or notorious, than it is to be interesting. In our world, girls climb very well until they hit puberty—sexual maturity—and then they begin to fall out of the tree. They start role-playing instead of thinking, flirting instead of learning. They start admiring how smart the boys are—or how athletic or how handsome—instead of concentrating on their own intelligence."

"Aren't they educated as well?" asked Izzy.

She shook her head. "It's not that, not exactly. Women fought very hard for equality in education, and now it turns out women do better if they go to all-female schools. Most of the women who have high positions in government and business graduated from women's schools. In girls' schools, they can concentrate on the reality of intelligence; if they're with males, biology takes over. It's no one's fault. It just happens."

"Aaah," said Izzy. "And you do not trust males."

She flushed. "Men are biological. Women are biological. We pretend our minds are in control, but that's a very tenuous control at best, and a civilized society can't be built on uncontrolled biology. I see it in my work: intelligence betrayed by lust, by jealousy, by macho ownership; otherwise trustworthy men who can't be trusted at all around women, or vice versa. Hell, look at Congress. Well-intentioned, progressive, admired lawmakers who end up losing it all because they can't control how they react to women! And I certainly don't trust how most women are around men. We get stupid!"

"That's why you and Abby are not lovers," I said, unthinking.

Dora turned very red, turned and fled into the bathroom, from which we soon heard sounds of water running very hard.

"That was not tactful," said the countess in an admonishing voice.

I grew somewhat annoyed at this. Why did I always

have to be tactful? Sahir was not tactful. Izzy was not tactful. Soaz was not tactful. Only the countess and Blanche and I were expected to be tactful. I said as much, and this time it was the countess who turned rather pink.

We simmered for a moment until Blanche murmured, "She is pretty for an umminhi. I have been watching the television. She compares well with those considered attractive. Less thin than some, but healthier looking."

We thought about this for a time. I offered, "Abby is also attractive of his kind."

Izzy nodded. "He has a foxy face, but his eyes are clear, his teeth are very white; I like the look of him. Of course, I am not an umminhi female. . . ." He looked at me and winked. I was glad he was not an umminhi female.

"What a pity if all her life the only man she should have known was a Woput," said the countess. "It would be good if she could learn that Abby is trustworthy, and that one can love without turning into a slooge."

"Slooge?" asked Izzy.

"It is what we scuini call the occasional female among us who has a litter and from that moment on is interested only in suckling, mating, suckling, mating. She becomes a slooge. We educated females feel that one carefully planned litter in a lifetime is enough; life has so many challenges. The slooge, however, must continually be bearing. Her litters are a burden on her people and the world, many of them run away and get eaten, and when she is too old to bear any longer, she is useless for anything."

"Some of the sultanas must be slooges," I said, without thinking. "Of course, they're not allowed to be anything else!" I popped my hand in front of my mouth. "Ooh, don't tell Sahir I said that."

The bathroom door opened and Dora came out, her face wet but calm. She gritted her teeth and announced, "Nassif, you may be quite correct as to the reason Abby and I aren't lovers."

The countess nodded. "It's all right, dear. Nassif and I understand completely."

"I heard what you've been saying," said Dora from between her teeth. "My mother was evidently what you call a slooge. I do not want to be a slooge. It's a risk I've been unwilling to take. It's kind of you to interest yourself in my personal life, kind of you to think me attractive, but it's really none of your business, and I would just as soon not talk about it anymore."

Across the room, the armakfatidi looked up alertly, then went ostentatiously back to their cookery. The countess was momentarily astonished, but in a moment she returned to her tea, for all the world as though no one had said anything. I wanted to argue with Dora, to make her like Abby better, but I knew it wouldn't do any good. She still looked distressed and annoyed, either with us, or herself, or both. Whichever, further conversation would only make her angry.

Izzy, for a wonder, kept his mouth shut, and after a moment, Dora sat down with us once more.

When the others returned to the house shortly thereafter, Sheba emerged from the bedroom, and we were family again. As family, we spent the evening discussing the following day's expedition to rescue the last of Daddy Eddy's children from the lab.

42

Daddy Eddy's Children

Dora took the day off, riding with Abby as he led the procession of three vans to Randall Pharmaceuticals. This time the vans had been rented by Harry Dionne, who had also provided the other two drivers, local Korèsans who waited outside while Abby and Dora went into the lab. The new lab director, whom Abby had talked to earlier by phone, was waiting for them, a person they had already heard of: Dr. Marsh McGovern, white-faced and petulant, with a shiny little mustache and an air of affected self-importance.

"McCord, McCord? Don't I know that name?"

"You had a pig of mine. A case of mistaken identity."

"Oh. Right. The one with the microphone. Well, I did think at the time it was too good to be true. You see, I have this theory about the extraterrestrial inception of evolution on earth. . . ."

"I'd love to hear about it, but not today. We need to get the animals loaded."

"I was *quite* certain the animals belonged to the lab," he said in a grating whine. "You're saying none of them do?"

"None at all," said Abby pleasantly. "Dr. Winston had some moral and ethical problems with animal experimentation. The only way he could justify it to himself was if he provided good homes for his subjects when he had learned what he set out to learn."

"When I was promoted to head of lab, they did not inform me, and I'm far from learning everything *I* want to know."

"Then you'll have to obtain subjects of your own," Abby replied, still pleasantly.

"I really think it will be necessary to appeal this. Get a court order or something. . . ."

Dora put on her gravely concerned face. "Mrs. Winston would be very distressed. She might bring suit against the lab. At that juncture, the lab might feel you had made a very expensive choice. You must be very secure in your position here."

"Oh," he fretted. "Oh, well. Perhaps I can arrange to keep the beavers, at least. And the parrots. I do want to do some more work with the parrots—"

Dora nodded. "And very brave. Not many people would take that kind of risk with their reputations, particularly not people new to their jobs."

"All the animals belong to Mrs. Winston?"

"Each and every mouse—"

"We don't have mice—"

"Each and every beaver. Each and every parrot. How many?"

"Six of each."

"What else do you have?"

"There are five otters, not that there was any earthly reason for Winston to work with otters. Some of the things that man did. Quite insane. We have monkeys, of course. Ten of those, not counting the babies."

"Babies?"

"Five babies. Oh, well, I don't suppose you brought cages."

"We did, yes," said Abby. "There are three vans downstairs. We brought enough cages for all the animals."

"Where are they going?"

"Right now into a large truck that will transport them elsewhere." This was specious, but everyone had agreed that the fewer people who knew where the animals were, the better. Abby smiled, putting his hand on the man's shoulder and urging him through the door into the large, bare room where Winston had worked. All surfaces were hard and neutrally colored; even the light falling through the tall windows seemed denatured, and the sky seen through the tinted glass had no color at all. The cages were ranged along one wall, clean, but too small, each holding one or more huddled, depressed-looking creatures who glanced up briefly, then turned away, intent on their own misery. Dora took this in and said in a bright, imperative tone:

"Dr. McGovern, will you go down with Mr. McCord, please, and see that the vans are conveniently located, that the cages are brought up, and that dollies are provided." She nodded significantly at Abby, and he took the man by the arm, leading him away.

She went to the cage nearest. "My name is Dora," she said softly. "My friend is Abby, and there are some other friends with us. Daddy Eddy's wife has sent us. I'm sorry you've been here so long, but we're taking you to safety. Please, help us by coming as quietly as you can."

She went down the line, repeating this message.

A small gray parrot squawked, "Pretty Polly? Grawk. Rosa's in the pen, grawk. Sheba's in the pen."

"You can knock off the grawks," said Dora in her most patient voice. "Rosa was in the pen, but she's been rescued. All the ones outside have been rescued. Rosa is with us, and Sheba, and six pigs and four dogs and the goats. I understand there are others, in the mountains and with Daddy Eddy's friends.''

The beavers were in the bottom cages. One of them craned forward, looking up at her. "Thith ith for real?"

"As real as I can make it, friend."

"I am tho thick of wire . . .'' said someone else.

Muttered conversation ran down the lines of cages, growing gradually louder, culminating in the unmistakable merriment of onchiki speech.

"Hush," Dora commanded. "They're coming back."

There was silence. Dora moved out to the middle of the room, where she was ostentatiously examining her nails when the double doors crashed open to the thrust of a long, low, cage-laden, powered truck driven by her old friend Joe.

"Hey, Sergeant Henry," he said, grinning at her. "How come you're here?"

"Mrs. Winston asked me to come along," she said. "I met her when we were investigating . . . you know."

"Hey, what's this I heard? Some nutcase named Gerber? Lived with his ma? Went crazy, killed a whole pile of Ph.D.s?"

Dora looked at him closely. He was without guile and obviously didn't know anything about her having been married to the nutcase.

She murmured, "That's what I hear, too."

"So, this guy McCord's going to take the animals, huh? McGovern's having a fit. Tell you the truth, I'll miss them, but they'll be better off. Dr. Winston, he never left them in these little cages this long."

"Dr. McGovern will, when he gets others."

Joe looked over his shoulder, hunching toward her in conspiratorial pose. "Tell the truth, Sergeant, he's no good. If that guy ever had an idea, he'd faint from the shock." He took a cage and positioned it next to a door where a beaver waited, suspiciously eager to depart.

"How come Mr. McCord's taking them?" Joe asked.

"Well, Dr. Winston's wife didn't want his animals misused or hurt."

"Who would?" he remarked, heaving a thirty-pound beaver onto the truck. Dora positioned another cage. Even Joe looked slightly surprised at how amenable the animals were. They seemed almost to leap into the cages. When the truck was loaded, Joe drove it out, saying he'd be back. It took three trips, the last two assisted by Abby, who returned sans McGovern.

"He's in somebody's office having a fit," Abby murmured. "I didn't get the feeling anyone was paying much attention."

"This is the guy who believes in UFOs," said Dora. "We should be more sympathetic."

"Why? All that superstition—"

"In the same category as talking animals and time travel and that stuff, right?"

His lips twisted, acknowledging the jab. "That was the last load."

"Did they all fit in the vans?"

"So far we've got them all into two vans. We got some of them to share cages. If it wouldn't have attracted too much attention, we'd have done without the cages entirely. Anyhow, the two vans can go directly to the distribution point they set up without having to sort the critters out."

"That's probably safer," agreed Dora. She was rather sorry about it, actually. She had wanted to talk to the beavers. She fidgeted. "Did the otters manage to keep quiet?"

"One boss beaver had to tell them to shut up."

"Before the van leaves, Abby, ask the creatures again if there are any other speaking critters out in the pens. I keep having this horrible feeling we've missed somebody."

"Will do." He departed, leaving Dora with one lone parrot, the small gray one who had mentioned Rosa.

"I can ride on your shoulder," offered the parrot. "I don't need a cage."

Dora opened the cage door and offered an arm, which the parrot walked sideways along, ending on the shoulder. "I won't poop on you," it said. "Daddy Eddy taught us that isn't polite."

"Thank you," murmured Dora. "Well, farewell to the old homestead, and all that."

"I could do a verse of 'Home Sweet Home,' " the parrot offered. "My name's Francis, by the way."

"You all have people names," she commented as they went out the door and down the corridor.

"Daddy Eddy thought it was smarter. It's less suspicious to be overheard talking to someone named Francis than to someone named Spot or Fluffy. Most of us named ourselves. I rather like Francis. Of course, I found out later it could be either male or female."

"Hush," breathed Dora, alert to several curious faces looking their way.

"Cracker," said Francis loudly. "Polly wants a cracker, awk."

The persons turned away, no longer interested.

"Put a cork in it," squawked Francis, feelingly. "Polly put a cork in it."

"Probably best," murmured Dora, as several someones looked up from their desks, smiled and went back to business. "Definitely best."

When they came out of the building, the second van was already halfway to the gate.

"You've missed your ride," Dora said. "You'll have to come with me." They got into the third van, where Francis moved onto the back of the seat and teetered there, peering alternately through the windshield and side windows at Abby, who was signing some kind of paperwork on the dock. He lifted a hand in farewell and trotted over to the van.

"Abby, this is Francis," said Dora, as Abby slid behind the wheel. "Did we get them all?"

Abby nodded, starting the van and driving slowly away from the dock. "According to the monkeys, yes. The only reason they'd been brought to the lab at all was to do some genetic tests on the babies."

"I was so afraid we'd miss somebody." She heaved

a deep sigh as they approached the gate, where a large panel truck was stopped, the driver arguing with the gate guard. Abby didn't turn his head, but Dora, glancing sideways, recognized the driver.

"That's Mr. Calclough," she breathed. "Abby. That's one of the boarders!"

"You want me to stop?"

"Not where he'll see us, no. Park somewhere we can see the truck. We'll wait until he leaves the gate."

"Who is Mr. Calclough?" asked Francis.

"Well, he may be the current Woput," said Dora. "I can't imagine why else he'd be here!"

"Woput?"

"The bad guy. The one who's trying to do you in."

"Somebody's trying to do us in? You mean, as in dead?"

"Francis, it's a long story, one I'll let Blanche tell you when we get home. Right now I need to concentrate, so be very quiet, will you?"

They parked around the nearest corner, the truck still in sight. After some time, it backed up to make the turn, then went off down the street. Dora got out and walked back to the gate.

"The guy who was just here," she said, showing her badge. "The one in the panel truck. What did he want?"

"Said he was here to pick up some animals. He had a letter from Mrs. Winston, but I told him it was a mistake, Mrs. Winston's animals were already gone."

Dora nodded thanks and jogged back the way she had come. "Winston's place," she said to Abby. "Quick as we can. When was Mrs. Winston leaving town?"

"Yesterday, wasn't it?"

"I thought that's what she said. We need to check."

"What's going on?"

"The guy had a letter purportedly from Mrs. Winston," Dora answered. "I'm afraid he may have gotten it by . . . violence, maybe. She could be hurt."

"Damn, this gets worse and worse," murmured Abby. "She could be dead."

Mrs. Winston, according to the housekeeper, was neither hurt nor dead, but had departed in a taxi the previous afternoon, on her way to the airport. The housekeeper had seen her go, had locked up the house and departed, returning this morning to pick up some dry cleaning. She had found the french doors onto the back terrace broken open, the desk in disorder, and Mrs. Winston's stationery thrown around.

"I just got here a few minutes ago," the housekeeper cried. "I didn't even see that someone had broken in until just before you came."

Dora asked her to call the police and report the incident, then returned to the car where Francis still teetered, singing softly to himself. "Mid pleasures and palaces . . ."

He interrupted his song as Abby got behind the wheel once more, "Now where?"

"Home," Dora said. "My home. The others went other places, because, unfortunately, the bad guy knows where I live."

"Into the jaws of death flew the six hundred," caroled Francis. "Nice of you to include me."

"You'll be company for Blanche."

"Blanche is?"

"A cockatoo."

"Not exactly my class," said Francis. "Cockatoos are too, too, don't you know. They consider us common."

Abby interrupted. "Where did you all learn so much language? You have better vocabularies than nine-tenths of my college students!"

"Books on tape, mostly," said Francis. "British and Canadian films. Audio-visual courses. Daddy Eddy was determined we should have the best, and when we were at the cabin, we had lots of time to play Scrabble."

"Do you know where the others are, the ones he gave away?" Dora asked.

"Placed," said Francis stiffly, with a definite sniff. "He didn't *give* us away, he placed us. Yes, I do know. Several of us know. It's our job to know, so when we need to, we can get in touch with one another. We are, so to speak, psittaci-memoranda.''

"Can you remember an additional phone number?" Dora asked, repeating it twice.

"Can I remember my own name?" the parrot remarked, rather snippily, repeating the number back to her "What's this number for?"

"Sheba and Dzilula are still with us, but the others who were in the pens outside have been placed among the local Korèsans. Rosa and her cubs. The pigs. The dogs. The goats. I'm sorry, I never learned their names; we were in too much of a hurry. That phone number can be used to get in touch with one of the Korèsans, who will get in touch with others. The code word is *Niagara Falls McCord.*''

"Niagara . . . ?" Francis cocked his head, questioningly.

"Private joke," said Abby. "Just remember it."

"And Korèsans are who?"

Abby replied. "A local religious group who believe in the diversity of life. Friends. Allies. Headed by a man named Vorn Dionne.''

Dora looked out the window for a moment, fretfully. "Actually, I'll have to get in touch with Dionne. I've got to tell him we saw Calclough at the lab.''

"Quit simmering," Abby advised her, with a fond though slightly apprehensive glance. "We'll be home in five minutes.''

They turned down the swerving lane that led past Dora's house, down the aisle of trees where leaves danced in the sun, past hillocks of greenery marking the presence of houses, through white-trunked groves, then green-trunked ones, through glades of flowers. They drove. They drove further. The lane turned. They drove through more groves and more glades and were back on the avenue.

"What?" asked Francis.

"That's what I'd like to know," Dora muttered. "Try it again, Abby.''

They tried it again, with the same result. The road did not lead where it was supposed to lead.

Abby parked under the usual tree. "Do you suppose if we walked . . . ?"

Dora shook her head. "Phone."

"You don't have a cellular phone."

"Too expensive. There's one at the drugstore on the corner."

She stood in the booth, nervously shifting from foot to foot, listening to the repetitive ringing. At last the machine picked up, and she said loudly, "This is Dora. Someone please pick up the phone! This is Dora, I need to speak to someone. Please pick up the phone. Come on, somebody . . ."

"Dora?" It wasn't a voice she recognized.

"May I speak with Izakar, please?" she asked.

"Dora, are you alone?"

"Abby's here."

"Is everything all right?"

"Pretty much, yes. Blanche?"

"Yes. Izzy's outside holding an enchantment on the woods to keep something nasty out. The nasty has been trying to get in here ever since you left."

"Can Izzy let us through?"

"Just you and Abby?"

"And a small, gray parrot. His name is Francis."

The phone thunked hollowly as Blanche set it down. Dora heard voices, the clatter of hooves on the stairs. After a time, a returning clatter, then a rustle. "Dora. Izzy says look at your watch, then walk down the lane for as many minutes as it usually takes you, then stop and watch the time. Exactly fifteen minutes from now, he'll drop the spell for just a moment. You should be able to see your car. Use that as a landmark and come to the house, or where it ought to be. He'll let you through."

"Fifteen minutes from now," said Dora. "Are you looking at a clock?"

"Now," said Blanche, and hung up.

Dora stopped at the van to collect Francis, then she and Abby walked down the lane. "How long does it usually take us?" she wondered, looking at her watch.

"It takes me about ten minutes," said Abby. "When I don't hurry."

"Well, let's not hurry."

They walked for ten minutes, seeing nothing that looked at all familiar. They stopped.

"Five minutes to wait," Dora remarked.

"Something stinks," said Abby. "Like something dead."

She looked up. The thing had never come in daylight, but the smell was unmistakable. She handed Francis to Abby and took her gun from its holster.

"You always carry that?" Abby asked.

"Well, I'm supposed to," she said. "And lately, I've considered it sensible."

There was something up there in the trees. She could feel it. So could Francis, for he was looking where she was looking.

"It's up there," the parrot whispered. "I can see it against the light. Like a shadow."

"How big?" asked Dora.

"Too damned big," said Francis feelingly. "I should have stayed in the lab."

"Calclough hasn't had time to do this," whispered Abby. "We didn't take more than twenty minutes detouring to Mrs. Winston's place."

Dora shook her head. "It isn't Calclough. This has been going on all morning."

"A car has just appeared," muttered Francis. "Behind you."

There was a car, Dora's, facing the other way. They darted toward it, turned right and raced into absolutely uncharted territory. A hole opened. They plunged through in a cloud of nauseating stench, feeling the hole close around them. Something huge and terrible tried to come after them and hit an invisible barrier, screaming in rage.

They were standing just outside Dora's gate. Inside, Izzy was busy with three fires and three candles marking a six-pointed star, with lines and signs laid out on the ground, with the pouring and mixing of ingredients as he kept up a chanted though breathless encouragement of whatever power he had summoned. They didn't interrupt him.

The countess was waiting, and she led the way past the veebles and up the stairs to the living room, where Nassif and Blanche awaited them.

Dora took time only to introduce Francis to Blanche, then went directly to the phone and called Harry Dionne. "Is your dad there, Harry?"

"The archpriest is present, yes." Harry was miffed about something. He and his father had probably been at it again.

"Archpriest, whatever, tell him we're under siege here. I need to talk to him." She put her hand over the phone and asked, "Did Izzy say anything about where this is coming from or who's doing it?"

"The person, whoever, has to be close," offered Nassif. "Since the nasty is in the direction of the street, Izzy thinks it's out that way."

"Then we need to go out the back door, don't we? Through the woods. Hello, Your Worthiness? Listen . . ."

Across the room, Abby murmured, "What happened, exactly?"

Nassif answered. "You had only been gone a little while when Izzy got very restless. He said he smelled trouble. Then we all smelled it, getting stronger and stronger. Izzy grabbed his kit and went outside. I helped him. We got the fires lit and he was making a barrier against the smelly thing when we heard it."

"Heard it?" asked Dora, turning from the phone. "On the roof?"

"No. Heard it screaming. Should it have been on the roof?"

"That's where it's been before." She turned back to her conversation with the archpriest.

"So you heard it screaming, like what?" asked Abby.

"Like a huge bird. So then Izzy sent the onchiki and the armakfatidi out into the trees, to get wood, to keep the fires going. They've been going back and forth ever since."

"Why do the fires have to keep going?"

"To keep the kettles steaming, because that's what keeps the spell going."

"Why doesn't he put it on the stove?" asked Abby.

"Too techno," said the countess. "Too many high-tech parts."

"Where's Sahir?"

"He went out, early, before this happened. Soaz and Sheba and Oyk and Irk are looking for him. Inside the barrier, needless to say."

"How big is this barrier?"

"Izzy says he's got it out about a quarter mile."

"Can he take a break? I need to talk to him," said Dora, hanging up. "Vorn Dionne is willing to help, but we'll have to tell him what kind of help we need."

They clattered downstairs, where Izzy beckoned to Abby, showing him what to do, telling him what to say, then staggered over to Dora, shaking his head. "I told Lucy Low and Dzilobommo to find the others and bring them in. We'll have to make a break for it pretty soon. I can't keep this up."

"We may not have to. Can the person who's doing this, that is, the Woput, can he be located? Is there some way that Vorn Dionne and his people can find him, and stop him, while he's concentrated on us, here?"

"Killing him won't help."

"I know that. Vorn knows that. But maybe he can tie him up, or gag him or something."

"Well, the sorcerer is nearby, I'm sure of that. So, tell Vorn to bring enough people to do a search, have them start down at the avenue, where you always park, then come this way, well spread out. They'll be looking for someone more or less out in the open. He'll have a fire, too. In this kind of spell, fire is always the enabler. He . . . or, I suppose, she will obviously be doing something strange. Gestures, powders, invocations. Sneak up on him or her, get a bag over his head and gag him. Don't let him, or her, keep the use of eyes or tongue. Oh, and put out the fire. That's important, put out the fire."

Dora retreated upstairs to the phone. Abby, between gestures, remarked, "Dora says this thing has been on the roof before."

"Not this thing hasn't," muttered Izzy, returning to his task. "A little one, maybe, but not this thing."

They kept up the fires. The onchiki and armakfatidi returned to be introduced to Francis. After a time Sheba and Soaz, Oyk and Irk returned, but there was no sign of Sahir.

Opalears: A General Culmination

Sahir had spoken to me before he went away that morning. He had said he needed to be by himself, "to think." I probably should have talked him out of it, but at the time, Sahir's doing some thinking seemed a good idea. We were all, to use Dora's words, rather pissed with Sahir.

The nasty thing came not long after, and we spent the next few hours scurrying about, some of us helping Izzy while others searched for Sahir. At one point, the phone rang. We didn't answer it, of course, but the machine did, so we heard the message. It was the elder with the eye patch, the one who had said he would go to the boardinghouse. He said the Woput had gone into either Ms. Michaelson—because they'd been introduced to that reputedly talkative woman and she hadn't said a word—or Mr. Fries, the messy one—because they'd noticed him neatening up the dining room. I wrote this down, to tell Dora.

Then it was just more of the same until the phone

rang again, and we heard Dora's voice, then she and Abby and the new psitid arrived. Dora talked to the priest, but nothing changed for what seemed like forever. Poor Izzy was so tired and sick, I worried about him, and then about four o'clock in the afternoon, the nasty thing went away, bang, just like that.

Izzy almost fell down, he was so exhausted. Abby carried him upstairs and Dzilobommo made something restorative. Dora and I went out looking for whoever or whatever. We found Vorn Dionne out in the street with several other people, mostly young and mostly rather husky, and in the midst of them all, tied up and gagged and blindfolded, was a woman.

"Is that Momma Gerber?" said Dora, disbelieving. "Momma Gerber!"

It was Momma Gerber, kicking and struggling like someone a lot younger and stronger than she looked. The archpriest's men carried her back to the house. Abby took one look and told us to put the tied-up woman somewhere where she couldn't hear us. He and quite a group of Vorn's people took her out in the woods and tied her to a tree, very tightly. A couple of young men stayed there to guard her, and when the others returned, Vorn picked two—both elders— to stay with him while the rest of his people went back to wait at their vehicles.

Abby dropped into a chair, rubbing at his head with both hands, as though he had a pain. "We saw Mr. Calclough at the lab. There's a message on the machine from your colleagues who went to the boardinghouse. They think it's either Ms. Michaelson or Mr. Fries. Now, you've got Momma Gerber."

"I was afraid of this," said Izzy in a faint, pained voice. "After Rosa killed Jared, when we heard that howl, it sounded like more than one voice. Then when we spoke of the boardinghouse and I realized Woput-Jared had known all the occupants, I thought he might have occupied more than one of them. I'm afraid we've got a hive of Woputs by now."

"All of them sorcerers?" asked Vorn, with a significant glance at his colleagues, then answered himself disgustedly, "Of course."

"As I see it," Izzy went on, pulling himself up on the pillow, "the longer we wait, the worse it will get. If we move immediately, we may have the advantage of surprise. Right now they think Momma-Woput has us pinned down. At this point, the other Woputs don't know that we know who or where they are. Mr. Calclough didn't see Dora or Abby at the lab. The Korèsan couple who inquired at the boardinghouse did so anonymously."

"But if Momma knows," asked Dora, "won't the others know, too?"

Izzy shook his head. "The Woput had one personality up until he split," said Izzy. "But the minute he split, he was in separate bodies that were receiving separate sensory information. At that point, he started diverging. All of them know everything the Woput knew up until he took over their bodies, but from that point on, each of them began to differentiate. They're doing what they're doing by agreement, not by mind reading."

"You're sure?" asked Vorn.

"I'm almost absolutely sure," said Izzy. "I sensed only one normally powerful mind out there. If they could link minds, I think I'd have noticed more oomph to it somehow."

"So the others don't know we've got Momma," Abby muttered. "They don't know we know where they are. Which may mean they haven't laid on any protection."

"Why this all-out assault?" Dora wanted to know. "Momma-Woput didn't know the animals were gone from the lab. Only Calclough-Woput knew that."

"I think Sahir talked," I said sadly. "I think he told Jared-Woput we were from the future. The Woputs don't only want to kill the people from the lab, they also want to kill us."

"Did Sahir tell you that?" asked the countess.

I shook my head, ashamed of my prince. "No. But that's the only way I can explain how he's been acting."

"He has been acting oddly," said the countess. "But he is outside our consideration right now. If he's out there in the woods somewhere, he'll come back, or he won't. If that thing got him, he won't, and that's all there is to it."

"My point is," said Izzy, "we can't afford to wait here for him. We've done everything here that we can do. If we're to surprise anyone, we have to go to the boardinghouse now. We have to take the time control. Once they're all in the house, we can set the field so it catches them all, us all. Except Abby and Dora and the Korèsans, of course. Once we're back where we started from, even a whole hive of Woputs can't do much damage."

"You should warn the Weelians they'll be coming," said the archpriest, looking at his two friends, who nodded, yes, they should be warned. "If that's possible."

"We can send a message through," mused Izzy. "The control can be adjusted to a larger or smaller field. But there are only two uses of the control left. If we send a message, that will leave us with only one use, and a large number of us to move."

"Well then, send some of us with the message," said Blanche. "Get those of us who would be less useful in the business out of the way. Then the final use won't need to be so . . . powerful."

This idea met general agreement. Logistically, it made sense. The onchiki could go back, and Blanche, and Sheba, and the armakfatidi. The countess insisted upon staying, "seeing it through," as she said. We all agreed we might need Soaz, but Soaz wanted Sheba to be safe.

"But we'll take the veebles now," cried Lucy Low.

"And me," said Francis, turning to Blanche for confirmation. "I'd consider it an adventure." The two of them had been huddled for the last several hours, getting to know one another.

We counted: this would leave six, or seven, if Sahir

showed up. Plus Abby and Dora and the Korèsans.
Enough to regroup and replan if we had to, as Izzy remarked.

The countess, Dora, Soaz and I went to get the control, Soaz taking the lead, as usual, and going directly
to the pack where the control had been. He dumped the
pack's contents on the ground and rummaged through
them looking for the red leather case, which was not
there.

"Ah," said the countess. "Well, well."

"It's gone!" screamed Soaz. "We're trapped here."

The countess soothed. "Only the case is gone, Soaz.
I think we have to accept that Sahir took it. I think he
probably wanted to go back by himself."

"But why?" Soaz yowled.

"So he could tell everyone how brave he'd been," I
said bitterly. "So he could tell them how he'd fought
heroically for us, but we'd all died."

"But if we don't stop the Woput," said Dora, "his
people will perish. He knows we need the control for
that."

The countess shrugged. "I think to Sahir, the future
of his people or any people is peripheral to his picture
of himself. Is it not so with people now? You and we
are not very different, Dora. Looking beyond one's own
lifetime is very difficult. Only highly evolved creatures
can do it, and none of us, perhaps, are evolved that far."

She sounded more sad than angry. I was angry. Sahir
hadn't gotten away with the control, of course, because
we'd hidden it, but I was still angry!

"You moved it!" Soaz accused us.

"We were concerned," the countess replied. "Let us
say, we were not sure all was well with Prince Sahir."

When we retrieved the control, we took it back upstairs and told everyone what had happened. Izzy was
sitting up, less pale, a little recovered. Nothing was to
be gained by waiting, so we all agreed. Izzy checked the
little window, to be sure how many uses we had left,
and it still showed the number two, two uses only until

it recharged itself or did whatever else it was supposed to do.

People mumbled to one another, saying half-hearted good-byes. We trooped downstairs, rather disheartened. Parting is never easy, particularly when things are so uncertain. Those who were to make the journey assembled outside the door to Dora's place: Lucy Low, Mince and Burrow; the veebles; Dzilobommo and Dzilula; Blanche and Francis; and Sheba—reluctantly. She didn't want to leave Soaz, but he insisted. Dora knelt beside the onchiki and hugged them, stroked the veebles, bowed to the armakfatidi and the others.

Izzy took the key from around his neck, turned on the control, fiddled with the setting, getting it just right, then backed off until the little green light went on to tell him he was out of the field. He lifted one hand in farewell as he pressed the button. They went, all at once. I was looking very closely, and I saw them rise like smoke, like smoke vanishing in a wind.

The archpriest had stood at Izzy's shoulder, following every step of the procedure with total concentration. Now he and his two friends came with us as we, much sobered, returned upstairs. Dora stroked the chair where Lucy Low and her brothers had been lying. "I will miss them."

"There are others, here," said the archpriest, examining her face with that same intent look he had displayed downstairs, as though he was memorizing her. "Perhaps you will make their protection your lifework."

"I'd like that," Dora said, smiling at him. "It would be like a return to paradise."

"In recognition of that intent, I have a present for you," said Vorn. He fished in a pocket and took out a pendant that hung from a slender chain. "Silver and malachite," he said. "The colors and symbol of Korè."

He held it out where we could see it. The polished green stone was mounted in silver and inlaid with a silver tree, each twig perfect and distinct.

"When you see someone wearing this sign, you will

know you are seeing one of Korè's people." Vorn put his hand on her shoulder, smiled at her, patted her in a fatherly fashion, and she leaned forward to hug him. I think she was as surprised as he was. When he put the chain around her neck, she had tears in her eyes.

Vorn turned to Abby, to present him with another, similar jewel, this one on a bracelet. Abby didn't weep, but he did seem properly solemn when he held out his wrist and let Vorn fasten it there. I thought it was nice of Vorn to have made the gesture. Abby and Dora had done so much for us, and we really had no way to repay them.

Vorn's people fetched the several cars and vans they had arrived in so we could load everyone aboard, including the Woput woman, now with a bag over her head. We were careful to say nothing at all in her hearing, just in case Izzy was wrong about the new Woputs being separate creatures.

We parked in front of Jared's old place, broke open the back door and went in, taking Momma-Woput with us and putting her in the basement. We all felt it likely that the Woputs would either be at the boardinghouse, or gather there to await a report from Momma. Dora knew the place well, and at her direction Oyk and Irk went on reconnaissance, anonymous as any two small dogs, peeking through windows to see who was where, while some of the Korèsans helped by walking by on the sidewalk to see what cars were there. The rest of us waited as patiently as possible.

Only five persons were there when they first looked. They went back and forth over the next hour or so, telling us who had come, who was there. We talked some about Sahir. The countess and Soaz were both worried about him. Vorn Dionne said he would provide a sanctuary for Sahir, if and when he showed up, and that solved that problem. I confess to being relieved. Sahir had behaved very badly indeed, but I had hated the thought of his being left behind, with no friends to care for him.

By sunset, Oyk and Irk had counted all the five people Dora had identified, plus four others. With Momma, that made ten.

"Jared said there were ten," Dora commented. "That must be all of them."

According to Oyk and Irk, the ten were busily engaged in preparing for something that looked sorcerous. Sending the nasty back to Dora's place, possibly. Well, nasty though they might, it would do them no good. Nobody was home at Dora's place, and by the time she got back, the Woputs would be gone.

By this time darkness was well advanced, so we got Momma-Woput out of the basement and carried her through the trees, slipping across the vacant lanes left for cars, and arriving at last at the rear of the house. Dora said that in ordinary times this would have been impossible, but now the trees gave us excellent cover. The plan was that we would assemble in the paved area at the rear of the house, along the alley. The control would be set to make a large field, including both the area and the house itself, so we could all go through at the same time on the single charge remaining in the control. Vorn Dionne would take charge of using the control, and afterward he would hide it and the key where it would never be found. At first we had thought Abby and Dora would do this, but the archpriest convinced us he was better qualified for this task, since secrecy was his business. His custody of the control would keep any future Woput from coming back and meddling.

So Abby and Dora were left with no role beyond waving us good-bye and letting us say one last time how grateful we all were. We had kept everything very simple. We had gone over it a dozen times without thinking of anything that might go wrong with it.

Of course, we'd ignored one element.

We assembled in back of the house, taking roll, as it were, to be sure we were all present and accounted for. Momma Woput was laid against the building, still tied. Izzy took charge of setting the control properly, double-checking, before turning the device over to Vorn. At that point Vorn's people, who had surrounded the house to keep anyone from leaving, went away from the boardinghouse, back into the trees, well out of the way. Oyk and Irk made a final circuit and came to tell us everyone was inside. They joined the rest of us at the rear of the house.

Abby and Dora backed off until Vorn said they were out of the field, though they were still quite close enough to say good-bye. I could see tears on Dora's cheeks. Vorn called to her, asking if she had her pendant, and she said yes.

"Hold it, my dear. It will comfort you in the separation," he said. "And hold on to Abby, as well."

Vorn's people waved from the woods. Vorn himself moved his finger toward the button . . .

And Sahir came screaming out of the woods like a comet, yelling no, no, no, they couldn't do that to him, they'd lied to him, the control wasn't in the case. We turned, appalled, just in time to see him hit Dora's legs, to see her grab for Abby, to see them both go tumbling, just as Vorn's finger came down . . .

And we all went somewhere else.

44

Opalears: On a Certain Future Day

The transit, returning, was no more pleasant than the transit going. Momma Gerber came with us, and Mrs. Sohn, Ms. Michaelson, Mr. Calclough, Mr. Fries, Mr. Singley, and four unnamed but irate individuals we had never seen before. Evidently they hadn't been holding any of their sorcerous materials when the button got pushed, for whatever enchantments they had been up to did not survive the trip. Dora and Abby arrived with us. The control stayed in the past, as had been intended.

Sahir was with us, needless to say, still in a rage, screaming and frothing at the mouth. Soaz took it for about a split second, then hit him a blow that carried him all the way off the timeworm and onto the platform. Soaz was very seriously annoyed.

Brother Red was there, with others. "Which ones?" he demanded of Izzy, who wordlessly pointed out all of the Woputs.

"Them?" asked Brother Red, pointing to Abby and Dora.

453

"Friends," said Izzy. "Let them alone. They weren't supposed to have come."

The brothers couldn't take their eyes from Dora. They helped her off the Wheel, paying more attention to her than they did to the ten Woputs, who were only belatedly manhandled into a kind of vault at one side of the area, stripped to rid them of any sorcerous materials they might have about them, and the door locked upon them.

"What are you going to do with them?" asked Dora. "And why don't you take those silly hoods off? We know what you are."

Brother Red fumbled with his veils, removing them slowly. I thought him a not unpleasant looking human (as I was being careful to call them for Dora's sake), though rather sickly, no worse than some we had seen in the past.

"What are you going to do with them?" Dora repeated.

Brother Red shook his head slowly. "When Blanche came and told us about them, we hoped they might be of fertile or childbearing age, but we're afraid they're too old. So . . . we could kill them. Or we could turn them loose. Or, we could turn them over to Faros VII. He would probably appreciate that."

She held out her hand. "I'm Dora. And you are?"

He took her hand and didn't let it go. "I know." He stared at her, eating her with his eyes, ignoring Abby who stood next to her. "You might as well just call me Brother . . . Red."

Sheba had been waiting for Soaz, and he went to her, rubbing her face with his own. Looking over their heads, I saw the others waiting on the balcony: the onchiki, the armakfatidi, Francis and Blanche.

Brother Red finally tore himself away from Dora. "Did you succeed?" he asked Izzy. "Did you save your tribes?"

"Probably," said Izzy in a very weary voice.

The countess nodded. "Probably," she confirmed, more firmly. "Yes, very likely."

Brother Red fixed his eyes on Dora once again. "Then perhaps we can concentrate on saving ours. . . ."

Over the next hour or so, every Weelian in the place had a few suggestive words with Dora who, obviously, did not know what the Weelians were hinting at. We did not enlighten her, for though Dora was going through the motions of good sense, it was all on the surface. Both she and Abby were in a state of shock. They kept going over it and over it. "Vorn should have had us stand farther back. I thought we were too close. Maybe he didn't read the field properly." And so on. Then, when they'd said it once, they said it over again.

The countess sympathized. I sympathized. No matter how much we felt for them, the control was still back in the twenty-first century, and neither Dora nor Abby could accept the implications of that even though they knew it to be true. They couldn't go back. Until or unless the Korèsans figured out how the thing worked and either sent it or brought it into the future, where we were. When we were. Which could not be until, unless, the thing recharged to the point that was possible. If the Korèsans decided it was a good idea. Which they might not.

They were both full of comments and questions about what had happened, but they were too shaken even to formulate them sensibly. Each of them would start to say something, then grimace, as though the words caught in their throats. I noticed how the two of them clung together, just as Vorn had told them to do, he wearing his bracelet, she her pendant, almost as though they'd been going-away gifts.

We all were ushered up out of that gloomy place into the courtyard where I had played with the onchiki what seemed a lifetime ago. I realized how short a time it had actually been when I saw one of the imperial guards lounging against the wall in the sun, obviously just now recovering from the wounds he had received during the battle on the shore. He saw Brother Red's unveiled face, and there was a moment's tension, which was immediately soothed by the countess. The tension passed. Luckily, the guard was phlegmatic and not very bright.

We hadn't eaten in hours, and we were voraciously hungry, a condition which Dzilobommo's ministrations greatly eased. After the meal, we went to the dormitory, each of us taking possession of a bed, a place, leaving a corner for Dora and Abby to be together. They could not seem to get out of touching distance, one of the other. I could understand that. They were the only familiar beings to one another. The rest of us, well-intentioned though we might be, were still strangers.

The imperial umminhi were still in the stable, awaiting our return, and when Dora and Abby questioned the strange chattering they heard from the adjoining building, I personally took them to see the creatures.

"My God," said Dora. "They look like Olympic athletes."

Now that I had seen *humans*, I knew what she meant. Indeed, the umminhi were very lean and muscular. Their teeth and bones were good, important in a beast of burden, and their hair was glossy. These creatures had been recently groomed and oiled, so their skins were glossy also, set off by the silver collars and breeders' tags all umminhi wore. Seen like this, more than a dozen of them, they were almost frightening.

Abby said, "They have to be healthy, of course. No breeder would keep unhealthy ones alive to breed from."

The umminhi stared at Dora and Abby. Their nostrils flared. Three of them, a gelding and two stallions, came closer to the gate, eyes flashing.

"Tohwnawaitohwnawaitownahwaeeee," the gelding muttered. Another umminha replied with a mutter of its own.

"What's that?" Dora asked, glancing at Abby. He raised his eyebrows at her, then looked back at the umminhi.

"Oh, Dora, they just do it," I said. "It doesn't mean

anything. They make that kind of chattering, over and over. My little mare, Honey, made the same noises."

"Ohaeaitgreoraike, owheyonglai," chattered one of the stallions.

"Owheyonglai, owheyonglai," the gelding repeated, coming to the barred stable door, where he and the stallions pressed tightly against the barrier, their collars gleaming between the bars, their eyes fixed on Dora and Abby.

Dora actually reached out a hand to touch their collars. I grabbed her wrist and snatched it back. "Careful!"

"There's no need for this," Dora said in a half hysterical voice. "If there ever was."

"There is a need!" I said. "They have to be kept locked up. Sometimes they attack people."

Dora turned away with a stunned, frantic look on her face. "Really? Have you ever known one to?"

I tried to think. I hadn't actually known of a case, but I'd heard stories.

"Yswaiaimte," the stallion whickered. "Aiiii?"

To me the call was unmistakably sexual, and I flushed. Dora, however, turned around and looked at the beast, a long, long look, turning away again with a troubled face. Well, I knew that trouble. I had felt the same when I saw on the television how ponjic people were treated by the humans in Dora's time. And sea people. And even Onchik-Dau, in circuses. It is sad to put bars around any creature, truly, but the umminhi could not live long if they were not kept. They are too stupid to survive in the wild.

We went back to the dormitory for a few hours sleep. Then we had another meal and drank some of the brothers' ale, after which Abby and Dora wandered back to the stables again, where I heard their voices and those of the umminhi, almost a conversation. Honey and I used to sound like that, when I was a child. I used to have conversations with her, me talking, her chattering. I could understand Dora and Abby. They thought the umminhi were like themselves. It would take time before they could accept that they were not.

Finally, in the early evening, we met in the courtyard, to tell the assembled brothers about the Great Enigma, about the Korèsans, the trees, everything that had happened. When we came to the end of our story, they had questions to ask of Sahir, who sat against the wall, refusing to say anything except, "Ask Soaz." He had talked to Soaz, for Soaz had threatened to castrate him if he didn't.

Yes, Soaz said, Sahir had taken the red leather box without ever looking inside it. He had eavesdropped on our plans, then he'd hidden in one of the vans at Dora's house, intending to go to the boardinghouse and move the Woputs himself, thereby erasing the many stains to his honor.

"And would you have come back with the Woputs, Prince Sahir?" Brother Red asked him. "And if so, would you have left the control for your friends? Or would you have abandoned them where they were to return to your own time alone? To tell whatever story you would."

Sahir looked at the sky and did not answer, which led us to believe we already knew the answer.

The countess was much saddened by all this. I knew she had liked Sahir. But then, some males are pleasant in a sexual way when they have nothing else at all to recommend them. I suppose the same is true of females. The following morning, after many surprises, the countess remarked as much to me, over tea.

During all this, I continued to notice the regard which the brothers gave to our *human* travelers, to Dora particularly. They were so intent upon her that it made her nervous. "It's like walking through a prison," she whispered to us. "All those men, eating you up with their eyes!"

"Perhaps it is somewhat similar," said the countess. "They have been here, without female companionship, for a very long time. And, as I have heard Abby remark, you are very attractive, Dora.''

By this time, the reality of the situation was beginning to sink in on both the humans, and their initial confusion was giving way to a kind of despair. They understood that all of us had lives to go back to or forward to, except themselves. When this was finally said, openly, by Dora herself, Brother Red contradicted her. There was a place for her, he said. She could live among her kind at Chamony.

''At Chamony?''

They described it, the orchards, the fountains, the pleasant leas, the little houses, so cozy. The children . . .

''Abby and I could go there?''

No, said the brothers, Abby could not be allowed to stay with her there.

She demanded explanation, of course, which was forthcoming. The brothers explained fully what they had only hinted at previously, in great detail with many statistics and talk of genetics, and how she was still young enough to have ten or twelve children, or even more. During this lecture, Dora fell into a long, twitchy silence which I thought betokened dismay but instead erupted in a seething ire that escalated into pure rage.

''So you'd have me be a slooge!'' she screamed at Brother Red. ''A brood mare, a bitch dropping a litter, a breeding sow!''

The countess cringed, for this was very dirty language.

Dora plunged on: ''Well let me tell you this, you male chauvinist . . . person! I would rather die!''

''I'm sorry you feel that way,'' said Brother Red in a tight, angry voice. ''We did prefer that you help us voluntarily.''

Abby turned quite red. ''Do you mean to tell me you'll make her go there whether she wants to or not? Make her . . . breed? Whether she wants to or not?''

''We have no choice.''

''But that's quite immoral,'' said the countess. ''Quite

improper. After all she has done for us—''

''For you!'' cried Brother Red. ''Yes, for you! Not for us! Not for humanity! I'm sorry, but we've voted on it. Abby may do as he likes, but Dora must go to Chamony.''

She rose, pale as ashes. ''I'll leave here now.''

''You can't. The road is guarded. The cliffs are impassible.''

She looked around at the Weelians. So did the rest of us. They all had that peculiar expression, a kind of sickly lustful determination, like a child stealing candy and quite determined to be as bad and make itself as miserable as possible. Even if they were sickly, however, there were too many of them for us to fight. And they probably had weapons, which we had not. After a moment, without a word, Dora and Abby went out of the courtyard in the direction of the stables.

Brother Red was looking at his shoes, his mouth pursed up.

''If Korè rules this world,'' said Izzy, ''I see why she chooses to let you Weelians go extinct. You're not fit to live.''

''We have as much right to survive as you do,'' said the Weelian stubbornly.

''Survival schmurvival,'' Izzy snarled. ''Who says you need to survive? Leave it to the rest of us tribes, we're doing all right. By and large we show more tolerance and acceptance and good sense than *humans* like you! We don't force our females to have babies. Go extinct! I quite frankly don't care! Faros VII will probably do far better with the world than you ever did!''

''Haven't we suffered enough?'' cried Brother Red. ''Don't we deserve a chance?''

''As Korè wills,'' cried the countess. ''You claim to be Korèsans. Why don't you put yourself in Her hands and let it be. As Korè wills!'' Her voice reverberated in the walled courtyard, sending echoes across the mountain. She had spoken very, very loudly, and from her mouth the name of the goddess seemed to take on a resonance of its own, coming back at us from a great distance. "Korè . . . ay . . . ay . . . ay."

From outside the courtyard someone else cried that name as well. "Korè . . . ay . . . ay . . . ay." It must have been an echo, but it silenced us. Or perhaps it was the countess who had silenced us.

After a time, the Weelians left us alone, and we began to talk of helping Dora escape. Or sending a mission to Chamony to rescue her after she'd been taken there. Or getting Faros to send an army to Chamony to conquer it. Or, or, or. Before we knew it, it was night, and we all retreated to the dormitory to whisper to Abby and Dora what we'd been talking of.

"I won't go to Chamony," said Dora.

"They'll force you," I said.

"I won't go," said Dora. "Don't worry about it."

I told the countess I was afraid Dora was going to harm herself, so the countess went to talk with her. All she would do was repeat that she wasn't going to Chamony, and that made us more worried than if she'd cried and yelled. She sounded so very grim and determined.

Most of us went to sleep, but I couldn't. When Abby and Dora went outside into the night, I sneaked after them, just to be sure nothing bad happened to them.

"I never could have imagined this, not in a thousand years," said Abby. He put his arms around her tenderly, and she laid her head on his shoulder.

A lantern hung in the gateway, and I could see the tears on her face reflecting its light, threads of gold spun out across her cheeks. She rubbed at them with the backs of her hands.

"I wish I hadn't said no that night," she said. "I thought I'd have all the time in the world to get to know you. But after that we were never really alone, and now . . ."

"Now we can't let it happen," he said desperately. "There has to be a way out of this. . . ."

They murmured, then, and I crept away, back to my bed. It wasn't fair to eavesdrop on them. Eventually, I fell asleep. Later in the night I woke to find them gone.

I went out into the night. Afar, up the cliff on the other side of the chasm, there were torches. I heard shouts, a scream. It was Dora's voice. That roused us all, and we were sitting angrily on the sides of our beds when a group of the Weelians came into the dormitory with Dora and Abby held fast among them. They had tried to climb the chasm and had been caught.

The countess went to them. I heard them murmuring together. After the countess went back to bed, I heard Dora and Abby sneak out once more. I started to go after them, thinking they were going to try another escape, but then I heard their voices in the stable, next door, and realized they only wanted to be alone.

The next morning, Brother Red announced that he was sending Dora away that morning.

"No, you will not," she cried. Her face looked carved from stone. "You will do nothing of the kind. You will accept your fate as Korè has determined it, and you will stop perpetuating your sickly selves on the face of this earth."

We had never seen a human in what the countess called a righteous rage. It was very impressive.

"Come," said Brother Red. "Tie her up."

Two of the Weelians came from the stable carrying straps with buckles, and I realized they were going to put her in umminhi harness. She began to laugh, chokingly, and Abby picked up a rock from the ground and held it, poised. The rest of us were petrified, unable to think what we could do or say. We didn't have a chance to decide, for there came a loud shattering sound at the stable, then the *shoof shoof* of shod feet, then the creak of the gate at the entrance to the courtyard.

There the biggest umminhi stallion stood, with glaring eyes and flowing hair, his teeth bared, mouth open, nostrils flared angrily, completely loose, no bridle, no bit, no hobbles, those deadly forelegs clenched in our direction. Behind him were the other umminhi, a full dozen of them, all their eyes wild as they looked about at the

Weelians, their gaze coming at last to rest on Dora. . . .

We were afraid to move.

"Dora," the stallion said. "Abby. You were right. The time has come. You in the black skirt! Put down that harness or I'll make you eat it!"

45

Opalears: A Twig on the Tree

Of all those assembled in the courtyard, it was probably the brothers who were most distressed, disturbed, driven out of countenance and out of control. They screamed and shook, a few tried to fight and several of them peed themselves, but the umminhi simply rushed into the courtyard, knocked some of them down, pushed some others over, took the harness away from the brother who was holding it, then herded all the brothers into the wagon barn and shut the door on them. One of the umminhi stayed there on guard, and when the others left, Abby and Dora rose without a word to any of us and went out to the stable with them. Dora was in tears but seemed very little surprised. Those of us left behind were in a state very much like hysteria.

Even the countess was out of herself. And Sahir? Well, if anyone could have been more upset than the brothers, it was Sahir, who came unhinged and began bouncing off the walls, shrieking at the top of his lungs. I imagine he would have felt less threatened if a veeble had stood upon its hind legs and hit him in the face.

Even though, remembering Honey, I may have felt slightly more kindly toward umminhi than the others did, I knew how they felt. All people in our time felt the same way. Umminhi were dirty. They were treacherous. They were sexually depraved, mating constantly, in any season. They smelled. They were said to attack female riders, or sometimes male ones. They were expensive to breed, expensive to maintain, hard to train.

And they were stupid. So we all said. So we all had said, for generations. Whenever we felt insecure about ourselves, we could look at the difference between ourselves and umminhi and know we were blessed. We, the tribes, were the end result of evolution, but they, the umminhi were merely creatures, prunable twigs from the family tree. Perhaps that is why we kept them, just so we could feel our own superiority.

And now a dozen umminhi were down by the gate, talking to Dora and Abby like ... people! Lucy Low sneaked down where they were, hid herself and listened. When she returned, she was bubbling with what she'd overheard. It seemed the umminhi had always been able to talk, she said. All of them could talk, not just these.

"Then why didn't they?" cried the countess.

Lucy Low said, "The big umminha said that long ago, when our people came into being, when the plague came that killed most humans, some 'human' survivors took a vow of silence, a vow to atone to the creatures of the world by serving and assisting them. They set up libraries to preserve knowledge. They took an oath to protect diversity, to go naked and silent, to be beasts of burden, to suffer what creatures had suffered at human hands in order to atone. ..."

"So that's how the libraries survived," cried Izzy. "And they must be the ones who weeded out all the pictures, who broke history in half so we wouldn't know their past wasn't ours!"

"Yes," breathed Lucy Low. "They did it."

''What are these Weelians?'' Soaz demanded. ''Are these vow-breakers?''

Lucy cried, ''No. The umminhi had nothing to do with the Weelians. The Weelians are a separate bunch. They already told us how they survived.''

''How did Dora know they could talk?'' I asked Lucy. ''How did she find out?''

Lucy said, ''That language the umminhi spoke, Dora knew it.''

''Umminhi have no known language!'' Izzy cried.

''It was 'pig latin,' '' said Lucy Low. ''That's what Dora called it.''

''What is pig latin?'' asked the countess, very offended at this dirty language. ''I've never heard of it.''

None of us had.

When Dora returned, we regarded her almost with awe. For a long time no one said anything to her, but then I asked, ''When I took you to the stable that first time, did they say something to you?''

She gave me a long, blind look, as though she saw beyond me to something else entirely. ''Yes, Nassif. Though it took me some time to realize what it was they had said. They said 'Atone, atone, atone. Oh, great Korè, how long.' And then one of them asked if it was time.''

''Time for what?'' the countess demanded.

''Evidently it was prophesied that a speaking human would come, wearing the sign of Korè, and that would be a sign that the penitence was done.'' She lifted the pendant. ''Understandably enough, they wear the same sign.'' She looked around at us, shaking her head at our stupidity. ''They are Korèsans! They are descendents of Vorn Dionne and all his great family.''

In the instant I realized how often I had seen that sign. In my childhood. And since. The design of the silver tree was on the breeders' tags that all umminhi wore. We shook our heads, amazed at our own blindness. For a time, we could not speak.

''It seems extreme,'' the countess said. ''Their atonement. Granted, in your time, Dora, creatures were sometimes treated badly, and granted that humans misbehaved toward the earth, but still . . . three thousand years!''

''It seems extreme to me, too, but they think not.'' Dora shrugged. ''I don't understand all of it. They're reluctant to talk about it . . . to talk about anything. They've been almost silent for three thousand years! Teaching the little ones to talk in secret, talking among themselves only rarely, on ritual occasions. They weren't ready to break silence even after I spoke to them, not until they talked with some of the others. It was the sight of the Weelians getting that harness that decided them. If I was the holy messenger, they weren't going to have me defiled.'' She laughed, a little hysterically. ''Thank . . . whoever.''

''What did you say to them, to get them to talk?'' the countess asked.

''I told them in the name of the archpriest Vorn that three thousand years was long enough. That was evidently what they'd been waiting for.''

His Excellency, Faros VII

The word went out from St. Weel: *The sign has come. Three thousand years is long enough.* There were many who carried that word. Wherever the message arrived, the umminhi took off their harnesses, bid their handlers good day, and walked away.

The ten Woputs remained at St. Weel, awaiting the arrival of cages in which they might be transported and a detachment of imperial guards to escort them, but those who had come from Gulp to St. Weel set out on the journey to Gulp once more. The group now included the one imperial guard who had been left over, Dora and Abby, Francis and Sheba and Dzilula and all thirteen of the imperial umminhi—now clad in loin cloths and mantles, their hair braided, their fetters removed. Sahir was also part of the group, though reluctantly. He had agreed to go only after Soaz told him his behavior would not be reported to Sultan Tummyfat. This had been enough to somewhat restore Sahir's volatile spirits. It was enough, Soaz said, that Sahir had gone, as the seeress directed. The seeress had not required him to be decent.

As the procession wended its way across the gervatch fields and into the mountain passes, it began to pick up additional umminhi, some sent as messengers, some coming out of nowhere, saying they had received the word. Several of these newcomers volunteered as runners to go on ahead, carrying a message from Izzy to the emperor that announced their imminent arrival.

Three days out, just a few hours from Gulp, the caravan was met by an advance party of imperial servants bearing tents and mattresses and all manner of luxuries to make the final stage of their journey more pleasant. When the servants pitched the tents, Nassif told them they needed only one for Abby and Dora, with the beds laid side by side. Later, Nassif herself showed Abby and Dora into the extravagant pavilion, though she didn't stick around, so she told Izzy, to see if they took the hint. Instead, she sat with Izzy by the fire, watching the tent flap to see what happened.

"Do we know each other well enough, do you think?" Abby asked, staring at the silken coverlets and piled cushions.

"If we don't now, likely we never will," she replied. "Oh, Abby, if we become lovers, will it just be because we have no one else?"

He gave her a serious look. "Usually when people become lovers it's because they *feel* they have no one else and want no one else. I'll grant you, there are exceptions, but I, at least," and here he paused to cast a significant glance at her, "feel unexceptional."

She laughed, somewhat ruefully. "Well, you did give up the world for me. I know lovers are always saying they'd do that, but you're the only one I know who ever actually did."

"I did, didn't I? Oh, my, what you got me into, lady."

"Are you sorry?" she asked, examining his face closely for signs of regret.

"Well, I'm confused," he answered. "I wake up in the morning expecting to teach a class at the university.

Instead, I find myself talking with a very charming pig, or perhaps sharing breakfast with several otters. I still can't figure out how it happened.''

"Oh, I think that's perfectly clear," she said. "I think Vorn wanted us to come with the others. You and me. I think he purposely included us in the field.''

He looked at her dumbfounded. "Why? For our benefit? There was no plague yet. It might not have happened for decades, not for centuries. . . .''

"Maybe he thought it would come sooner than that. I don't know. But I do know he planned that we would be in that field.''

"Then I can't blame you for it, can I?''

"Were you planning to?''

He thought about it, throwing himself down on the soft bedding and pulling her down to sit beside him. "I think not. I confess, in between spasms of outrage and fear and half a dozen other emotions I've been feeling over the past few days, I keep encountering these little bursts of pure elation. They scare me far more than the actual reality does! They're seductive. I get this little rush, this heightened sense of importance. I mean, it's an adventure! How many of us get to have adventures?''

"I certainly never planned on one.'' She nestled into his shoulder, then, catching sight of Nassif and Izzy, who were paying suspiciously too much attention to the tent flap, she rose, and fastened the flap tight, making sure it was quite securely tied before returning to Abby's side. He had, in the meantime, found a carafe of wine and had poured them each a generous glass.

"Do you think they have birth control in this day and age?'' she asked after a time.

"You could ask the countess.''

"I'd hate to end up being a slooge after all that screaming I was doing.''

"Ah,'' he said, putting his wineglass in a safe place. "Were you thinking of risking slooge-hood?''

"It's not too great a risk tonight, or tomorrow night, or this week—only they probably don't have weeks in this time—and yes, I was thinking that grieving for home is silly when maybe this is paradise, though I'd like to find out for sure.''

She turned to him, awkwardly opening her arms, wineglass tilting. He took it from her, put it aside, then drew her down beside him on the piled mattresses, soft as down, running his hands along her arms, softer yet, letting his lips find the curve of her throat. "How would you know if it were paradise?''

She murmured, "Oh, I'd hear trumpets. The horns of elfland. Faintly blowing. Grandma assured me—''

He closed her mouth with a kiss, and then another, and then lost track of the kisses in the counting of buttons, then lost track of the buttons in the clothing that wasn't needed anymore, in the sound of the wind on the tent and the crickets outside and voices calling, all going away into a long, languorous candle-lit quiet, where she flushed like a rose in his arms, rose to him like a wave, melted into his own wave that broke on an uncharted shore to the sound of glorious, glorious trumpets. . . .

"I hear them," she whispered in amazement. "I mean, I really hear them.''

And so did he.

They slept late in the morning. When Dora came out of the pavilion, she found Nassif and Izzy by the fire still, as though they had not moved.

"You must have been tired," said Nassif in an all too careful voice, which only resolution kept from being overly cheerful.

"I was," Dora replied in a satisfied tone, with a tiny smirk. "The trumpets kept me awake.''

"Not very polite of them," agreed Izzy. "But when the emperor sends his own troops to escort us into the city, I guess the trumpeters feel they have to arrive in full fanfare.''

"The emperor . . ." she said. "The trumpeters . . ."
She looked across Izzy's shoulder to the line of liveried trumpeters assembling for the march, their tabards shin-

ing, their long, brass instruments gleaming in the morning sun. "The trumpeters!"

"They came shortly after dark last night," said Izzy, puzzled at her. "I thought you said you heard them?"

"Oh, yes."

And she laughed, so chokingly that Nassif had to pound her on the back.

When they came down the hill into Gulp, later that day, there were over a hundred umminhi with the travelers, male and female, including some with children. Dora commented on this fact to Nassif, who walked beside her.

"Foals, I would have once called them," said Nassif, in a strange, tight voice.

"Does it bother you, their being here?" Dora asked.

"It did. It was very disturbing. I was very upset until . . . until I saw one of the mares . . . females lean down, pick up Lucy Low, and deposit her in the basket—saddle I would have said once—that rests on her own shoulders. It seemed an un-umminhi thing to do. And yet, it is the kind of thing you would do, which calls my own judgment into question."

Dora looked in the direction Nassif pointed out. There in the shoulder basket, the onchik rode, quite relaxed, playing upon her harp. It was not long until that sound was joined by voices and other instruments, and they went down the last hill on a tuneful wave that rippled around them all the way into the city.

The city, which was swarming with folk. The emperor was at the residence of his nephew, Fasal Grun, and all the travelers, including the umminhi, were escorted there, the crowds pressing after them, some curious, some wide-eyed and amazed, some muttering about the end of the world. All and all, thought Dora, a crowd like any crowd. All of the travelers were shown into the audience hall, though they could barely fit, where Faros VII sat on the chair of state, a green mantle flowing from his shoulders to the floor, his hand holding the orb of the ruler, his head crowned with ivy and oak, the symbols, so the butler said, of Faros's reign.

"Korèsan symbols," whispered Izzy, nodding wisely to himself.

"So you have returned," the emperor said, including all of the troupe in his benevolent gaze.

"In a manner of speaking," said Izzy. "May I introduce the two friends from the past who assisted us there and have, accidentally, attended us here as well."

"I have been informed," said the emperor, holding out his hand. "Dora. Abby."

Not paw, thought Dora, moving to bend over it. Hand. Not Bear. Emperor. She took a deep breath. "Your Excellency."

Abby was beside her, bowing in his turn. "Your Excellency."

They retreated. Sheba was introduced, and Dzilula, and Francis. Then it was time for the umminhi, who named themselves in a long and solemn roll call. They all had names. Those who were present had titles, as well, from that secret umminhi world of elders and priests and messengers. The one who had first spoken to Dora was chief among them. His name was Vorn.

When the introductions had been completed, the emperor leaned forward a little, fixing Vorn with his eyes. "Since I was told of this great event, I have been considering how you and your people will live. There is a land in the transmontaine. It is a good land, so I am told, largely unpopulated, with pastures and arable fields and many natural resources."

"We know of it," said Vorn. "Some of our people have been there."

"I would grant that land in perpetuity to the umminhi," said the emperor, speaking slowly and carefully, as though afraid he might be misunderstood. "If they would take it, and care for it."

"The umminhi would accept it, with gratitude. We would care for it as a parent her children."

The emperor nodded, satisfied thus far. He went on:

"I would grant the umminhi free passage through all my lands, if they would come and go peaceably."

"As we pledge ourselves to do," said Vorn.

"Ah." The emperor smiled. "Then today we have done well."

The crowd relaxed. People murmured to one another. The emperor nodded to himself, speaking quietly to his ponjic secretary, who came among the travelers and asked if the ones who had come from St. Weel would join the emperor for light refreshment in the adjoining chamber.

This place was smaller, and quieter, a room opening through tall windows onto a wide balcony. It held comfortable chairs and small tables, plus another great chair for the emperor, who could scarcely have sat in anything smaller. They were served with food and drink. The emperor ate a portion of grilled fish with every evidence of enjoyment, using a fork especially made to fit between his fingers. He wiped his muzzle with a napkin, which he set aside when he was finished, clasping his huge hands across his belly. At his side, his ponjic secretary stood, bearing a notepad, which he presented for the emperor's perusal.

"I have an announcement," Faros said, when the others had finished their food and were lingering over the teacups. "It concerns my nephew, Fasahd." A strange expression crossed his face, only momentarily, as though he had a sudden pain. "I wish to assure Countess Elianne of Estafan that Fasahd will no longer be a trouble to her. He has seen the error of his ways."

They did not ask how, or why. It was obvious that Faros VII did not wish to discuss it. Without giving them time to speculate, he glanced at the pad held by his secretary and continued:

"Prince Izakar, is this timeworm something I need to worry over?"

Izzy bowed. "The timeworm, Your Excellency, is useless without the control. The control stayed in the past. I don't know what Vorn Dionne did with it. Perhaps he secreted it somewhere where it would be safe for three thousand years, but who would know? The seers, perhaps? My own counsel would be to alert the seers to keep an eye out for it, and otherwise to leave the timeworm alone.''

"And what of the Weelians?''

"They will probably all die out, Your Excellency.''

"Is this true?'' the emperor asked Vorn. "You will not breed with them, to save their line?''

"Their line is sickly, Your Excellency. Even their newborn babies need drugs in order to live. They cannot breed without the intervention of laboratories, and all their energies for generations have gone into those laboratories. We have already suggested to them that they give up their breeding program, which makes them all miserable, and allow themselves to live out their lives in whatever happiness they can find.''

"A tragic people,'' remarked Faros. "Truly, a tragic people. When you told me they were once of a ruling caste, I looked them up in my library. Their ancient home was called Wahsinton.''

Another glance at the notepad. "Now, will we have any more trouble with the trees?''

Izzy replied, "I think the word is getting around, Your Excellency. The original rumor started at St. Weel, but we've been talking about the matter loudly while on the trail. No danger to the trees, we've said, over and over. No one is going to chop down the trees. The trees are fine. They needn't be concerned.''

The emperor fixed Vorn with his brown eyes and said, "And is that true? The umminhi are determined upon that? They will not cut down whole forests, as once they did, in the long ago?''

Vorn bowed. "Some humans may have done so, Your Excellency. Our people never did. We Korèsans, of whatever tribe, are stewards of the earth, not despoilers.''

Faros gave him a regal nod, reached out a hand for the pad, and ran a great claw down the line of notes.

"Nextly, I am concerned about our good friends, you, Dora and Abby. Izakar has spoken your praises constantly, as has the countess Elianne. Being thus thrust into a world not your own must seem an uncertain reward for such kindness. What will you do now? You would be welcome to live in the palace, as my guests."

"Your Excellency is most kind," Dora said. "And your gift to the umminhi is a measure of your great generosity. Abby and I have just been speaking together, and we would like to join the umminhi in the transmontaine."

Abby added, "If they will have us. Building a new country is an exciting prospect."

The emperor nodded benevolently. "I see. I think that is a good choice. If, however, you should ever have needs that cannot be met in the transmontaine, feel free to call upon me." He gestured the secretary away and sat back, seeming almost to forget they were there for a little time. They began to chat together, falling silent when they became aware he was looking at Dora, his hand beckoning.

Dora went over to him. "Your Excellency?"

"I feel very foolish, but I do not understand this business of the atonement. Do you?"

Dora shook her head. "I assumed it was atonement for the way in which humans treated other creatures, Your Excellency. But there does seem to be something more to it than that."

"Will he talk to me, do you think? Vorn? I do not wish to pry, or frighten him, but I am very interested in finding out about it."

"Oh, yes, Your Excellency. I know you're accustomed to thinking of the umminhi as uncivilized, but they're really very . . . well mannered. Let me bring him over."

Which she did, along with Izzy, and the four of them wandered out onto a balcony that looked down onto the gardens and over the garden wall into the streets of Gulp, where the people moved about in all their variety.

Faros, however, did not broach the question of the atonement, instead he led Izzy and Vorn into a deep and complicated discussion about city management, and after a time Dora slipped along the balcony to the place where Abby stood, looking out over the city. They leaned on the railing together, arm in arm, while Faros VII led the conversation on into various channels, his furry voice bumbling along, poking its nose into subject after subject, with Vorn and Izzy following after like two cubs. Dora listened with amusement and respect. Faros was being disarming. He would get to the subject in his own good time.

Finally the emperor moved one great arm, flinging wide his green velvet cape, letting it fall into watery folds around his soft boots. "A thing I've wondered about over and over, Prince Izakar. Did you ever find out who it was who started the great plague, all those thousands of years ago?"

Izzy bowed slightly. "I didn't, Your Excellency."

Vorn hummed in his throat, a troubled sound.

Faros VII nodded ponderously. "Ah. I was thinking about it today. Actually, Vorn, it was you made me think of it."

"Really, Your Excellency." His face was very pale and strained.

"Yes, yes. It was this umminhi atonement that made me think of it. You might be interested in my thoughts?"

Vorn looked down, without replying.

"Of course, Your Excellency," said Izzy, with a puzzled glance at Vorn. "Very interested."

"My thoughts had to do with guilt. I am interested in guilt. I have had a recent experience with guilt. My nephew had to be . . . disciplined. No. Let us not use polite words for unpleasant reality. He felt it was more important to be true to his nature than to create a peaceful world. His nature was a violent one, which wished to rule at all costs. There was only one way to stop him eating people, which was to kill him. I feel very guilty about it, even though it had to be done. He was not merely a person who had gone wrong. He was family. I feel that I must atone—to my sister's memory, perhaps.

"Now, if I had had to kill a few pheledas, or perhaps some scuini, I would feel sad and guilty, yes. I would feel I had fallen short of my own ideals and should resolve to do better, but I would not feel this same great sorrow. You follow me?"

Vorn made a sound, a painful grating in his throat.

Faros went on. "Atonement is a remedy for sorrow for one's behavior, sorrow over something deeper than mere shortcoming. A great atonement, three millennia of atonement, must be based on a very great sorrow. Wouldn't you say so, Vorn?"

Vorn nodded reluctantly.

Faros echoed the nod. "So I questioned, what great guilt could have been incurred by the umminhi? More than mere unconscionable behavior to—well, animals? Something they would feel was greater, far greater than that?"

From the place down the balcony where they had been listening, Dora and Abby, suddenly alert, turned and moved toward the others.

The emperor laid one hand on Vorn's shoulder, lifting his face with the other hand. "The plague was already well advanced by the time Izzy and the others went back, wasn't it? If Dora and Abby had stayed, they would have died of it, would they not?"

Vorn bowed his head, saying in a strained voice, "Yes. Our people got the idea from another plague that happened about that same time, one that lay hidden for decades before the dying began. The one my people designed was, indeed, underway. So our teachings say. Dora and Abby would have died."

"Your forefathers, the Korèsans, made sure that Dora and Abby came to this time. It wasn't accident, was it? They were saved, because of the great help they had given?"

"Yes."

"What?" cried Abby, lost.

"Was the plague the only way?" asked Faros, very gently. "Are you sure it was the only way?"

Vorn made a dry, gulping sound, a swallowed sob. "Oh, Your Excellency, don't you think I've asked that? Don't you think all of us have asked that, century after century! The trees fighting back, Korè rising up like that . . . we hadn't counted on that! Would that have worked? We don't know, for by the time the trees rose up, we had already acted and there was no way to undo it! Was there any other way? We'd already tried every other way. . . ."

Dora came to him, put her arms around him. "Shhh," she said. "Oh, Vorn, don't weep! You've atoned enough!" She looked into the emperor's face. "Of course *their* people tried every other way. But there were more of the other people! The ones who didn't care!"

"You're sure?" Faros persisted.

"I was there!" she cried. "Abby was there! Nobody listened. The human babies kept coming. The forests kept burning. The oceans were fished dry. The whales and the cheetahs and the pandas kept going extinct! Ask Abby! Nobody listened."

Abby said, "Dora. What are you talking about?" He pulled her away from Vorn and held her tightly, looking almost angrily at the emperor, who stood there, shaking his huge head, sympathy in his eyes.

Dora cried, "It was the only way, Abby. It really was. I don't blame Vorn Dionne for doing it. People would have figured out how to kill the new trees. They were already working on it. . . ."

The emperor put his hand on Vorn's shoulder and patted it, staggering the man with its weight. From inside the room, several umminhi came to lead Vorn away, murmuring to him in brokenhearted voices.

In the circle of Abby's arms, Dora muttered, "There's the garden, Abby. And there's the bindweed. And unless you're ruthless, the bindweed always wins!"

"By Korè," whispered Izzy. "By Korè!"

"Remarkable," said the emperor in a tone of enormous satisfaction. "Quite remarkable."

"Among all the peoples of our world, possibly the most mysterious are the umminhi. Long maligned, long misunderstood, long thought to be stubborn and stupid and unsanitary, only their stubbornness remains unchallenged. What other tribe would have killed off all but a tiny few of its own people in order to save the other tribes and their habitat, and would then have spent three millennia atoning for that deed. . . .

"One can only say, of the umminhi, they are a very mannerly people."

THE PEOPLES OF EARTH
HIS EXCELLENCY, EMPEROR FAROS VII

On a mudworld named "Swampsix," Questioner II sat in a reed hut near the shuttleport, so called though it was only a badly mown clearing amid endless stretches of deadly guillotine grass, its razor leaves snicking together with every breeze. The place was clamorous with frogbirds, soggy from the usual afternoon downpour—the livid skies still drooling, though the suns had gone down some time since—and totally lacking in amenities, a condition which the Questioner refused to notice.

She could feel comfort, she could perceive beauty, she could appreciate music, she had pleasure receptors for tastes, smells, and touches, but when duty took her to worlds where comfort, beauty and pleasure were absent, she turned her receptors off. Questioner's review of Swampsix had consisted of an instantaneous recognition of ugly realities requiring no prolonged verification.

She had come quite far, she had seen quite enough, but her ship was not scheduled to return for two days. She had been passing the time playing cards, a complicated kind of solitaire that took her mind off her recurrent feelings of amorphous and aimless sadness. Or maybe anger. Or maybe sheer peevishness. She had no explanation for these emotions, which seemed to rise like smoke whenever she was unoccupied, but she knew from long experience they would be less intrusive if she was distracted.

Additional distraction presented itself in the form of a small shuttle that plunged from the zenith and settled onto the mown area to emit a stooped and stuttering Flagian, a trader from his dress, who came tottering unerringly toward her. Questioner rose and awaited him, the cards scattered on the equipment box that served her as a table. He was an aged and floppy-fleshed fellow, one of those whose forefathers had survived the Flagian Miscalculation by virtue of being several systems removed at the time it occurred.

"Questioner?" he asked, with a certain diffidence, peering shortsightedly through the tinted glasses that protected his pink eyes. "I am Ybor Transit."

"We have met before," she said. "You sold me that information about the indigenous dancers on Newholme."

"Aha," he murmured. "You do remember. I have been searching for you because I have something else you may find interesting. Is it true you are a collector of information on non-mankind races?"

"More or less," she said coolly.

"I have in my possession an actual sensory recording of a Quaggian event." He paused, adding, in a hushed and mysterious voice, "A ritual event."

"Wouldn't it be unintelligible to me?" she asked in the uninterested tone she reserved for traders, politicians, and members of her politically appointed entourage. "The Quaggi do not talk with us at all."

"May I sit down, ma'am? Thank you kindly." He lowered himself onto one of the smaller equipment cases. "The Quaggi do talk to traders, ma'am. There are certain botanical substances which they require, and they are sufficiently interested in obtaining these to answer a few questions now and again. As a matter of fact, the BIT, that's the Brotherhood of Interstellar Trade, ma'am, has circulated a list of questions so that each trader calling upon the Quaggi can ask one or more of them. Thus we fill in our knowledge in an orderly fashion.''

"Remarkable," said the Questioner, seating herself across from him. "I had no idea you were so well organized."

"We aren't, in many manners." The old Flagian gave her a gap-toothed grin. He went on, "We are curious, however, and there's no denying that the more one knows about a client, the better it is for trade."

"Are the Quaggi bi-sexual, as we've been told."

"They say so."

"Why have we never seen a female?"

"They say members of their opposite sex are mindless and incompetent, useful only for breeding and therefore confined to planetary life. We've never seen any, so I assume we haven't found the planet where they're kept, yet. We have learned this much through the use of translator devices."

"Is there a translator built into the thing you're trying to sell me?"

"In this case, it doesn't matter," muttered the Flagian, fingering a scar that cast a fuchsia shadow across the rose-pink expanse of his furrowed forehead. "This is an all emissions record that needs no language. In expert opinion it dates some million standard years ago."

"Ah, now. Come, come."

"Madam, I guarantee your satisfaction." He fretted through several pockets, plucking and sorting. "Here, my location code. Here, my bonding agency. Here, my registered genetic identity. I will refund if you are not fascinated."

Questioner found herself liking him. "You've seen the Quaggi?"

He shook his head, jowls flapping. "I have, yes. They look like large piles of rock with huge compound eyes and some manipulating palps in front. They sit in monumental circles on carefully leveled plains on otherwise lifeless planets. They barely move as they commune, who knows with whom or what. In payment for the botanicals we offer, they extrude small chips of gold, platinum or other precious metals. Other than that, they do nothing. Some of their circles are millennia, perhaps even aeons old. . . .''

The trader stared aloft and shrugged, both face and gesture conveying his awe at the inscrutability of the universe. ''When I was last there, I witnessed an outsider Quaggi come before one of these circles. It offered a recording, similar to the one I'm offering you. The recording was passed around the circle, after which the newcomer tore off its wings and antennae and joined the circle. The record was thrown aside, as on a trash heap. When I stopped by the trash heap, I found this one unbroken recording.''

''What do you want for it?''

He named a figure. She laughed and named another. When they agreed, he handed over a peculiarly shaped and stoppered flask that contained, so far as she could tell, several large handfuls of coarse gray gravel.

''And what is this?''

''The recording. The Quaggi applicant brings this container, the members of the circle in turn swallow the crystals and excrete them back into the container. Evidently they read it internally. However, you can pour the stuff into a hopper, and read the same thing the Quaggi do.''

''What hopper?''

''The hopper of an EQUASER, an electronic Quaggi sensory reconstructor, made by the Korm as part of a communications system for their ships.''

''Aha!'' She grinned at him, all her teeth showing. ''How remarkable. And I suppose you just happen to have at least one such device for sale!''

''Only because it is useless to me without the recording. . . .''

''Useless, but, one presumes, not valueless?''

''Oh, no, ma'am.'' He echoed her grin with a gummy one of his own. ''Not at all valueless.'' He saw the annoyance on her face and took a deep breath. "Questioner, I would rather have you as a friend than an enemy. The BIT has always felt so. You have paid us well for the reports we bring you, those little things we see that local governments won't tell you."

"That's true," she murmured. "The BIT finds the truth of many things that governments deny."

"So, I make an offer. You tell me a few things about yourself, I give you the Korm device for nothing."

"You traders have a list of questions about me, too?"

"It isn't a long list," he said apologetically. "It would take you little time to respond perhaps to one or two little queries."

She grinned, suddenly diverted. "Ask away."

"We want to know . . . what are you like? How would you describe your personality?"

She stared at him. It was the last question she would have expected and one of the few for which she had no ready answer. "Let me see," she said at last. "I suppose I am task driven. My stimulus comes from duty. I am singleminded, stubborn, terrier-like in my approach to whatever job is before me. Human people who work with me say that I am a stern taskmaster, and this is true, though I do have a sense of humor. Haraldson said no entities could do this job unless they had a sense of the ridiculous, and I am frequently amused, even at myself. While I have the senses needed for enjoyment, it is difficult for me to enjoy because I can not forget the amount of work that is awaiting me, and there never seems to be enough time to do it all."

"Too strong a conscience!" he opined. "Perhaps a little wine would help? Or a euphoric capsule?"

"They can affect me, of course, but I distrust them. I am too likely, afterward, to judge myself harshly. I was designed to be a judge, and I do not withhold judgment from myself." She paused a moment, then murmured, "Least of all from myself."

"Is it fair to say you are relentless, unforgiving, capable of very stern action?"

She said, "It is fair, yes. I can do good only by doing my job relentlessly. If my judgments could be escaped or modified, the edicts would become mere suggestions rather than what they were intended to be: a framework by which mankind can turn himself into something better than he is."

He frowned, forehead deeply furrowed. "Tell me, truly, when you make these terrible judgments, or at any other time, do you feel anything?"

She was taken aback. Still, they had a bargain. It was incumbent upon her to answer as honestly as possible. "When I make a judgment, I always feel I am doing right," she replied. "If I do not feel it is right, I cannot do it.

"At other times, however, I have other kinds of feelings and I do not know why, or how, or from what source the feelings come. When I am intent upon my work, I am largely unaware of existing as an entity separate from the task. When there is a pause in my duties, however, sometimes I feel sadness or fear or longing for things I have never had, or cannot define. Sometimes I know things, and I cannot find the source of knowing anywhere in my files or my perception systems. I have thought, perhaps, that these feelings come from the human brains that were incorporated into me, but I cannot tell for sure."

"Ah," murmured the trader. "What brains were they?"

She shook her head. "I don't know. I wasn't informed."

"Would you like to know?"

She felt the mental equivalent of a gasp, a brief cessation of sense, a network-wide shock. "The HoTA designs and systems for the Questioners are top secret. I incorporate certain technical achievements which have a likelihood of misuse, and COW believes them better kept under lock and key."

"True. We know when you were made, however, and we know that the HoTA ships went here and there at that time. HoTA ships are quite easily recognizable, and the BIT keeps track of where ships go, and when. If brains were taken from persons who were dying at the time, it could not have been done in total secrecy. Linkages would have been necessary, and there are records . . ."

"If you could learn who . . . when, why, I would be prepared to reward you very well," said Questioner, surprising herself with the sudden spate of interest she felt.

"Your regard would be reward enough." The Flagian bowed respectfully, took his payment for the recording in Council of Worlds monetary units, repeated his compliments, and departed, staying well away from the snicking grasses and not without a backward glance. Each time he met the Questioner he was surprised that she did not seem more exotic.

The Questioner knew perfectly well what he was thinking. To outward appearance, she was simply a stout woman of indeterminate age with a rather large head covered with iron gray hair worn in a bun. She was, however, a good deal more than that. She was enormously strong; she could swim, dive, fly, brachiate, crawl, or climb mountains. She could provide emergency medical assistance and do quick field repairs on a great variety of complicated equipment. She could cook, sing quite well, and compose fairly literary poetry in several languages. She supposed she could fall in love, though she had never done so. Though the senses were there, the stimulus was not.

When the Trader's shuttle took off in a fountain of flung clods and crushed grasses, she set aside all thoughts of him and of herself and settled into a stable position. With the flask of gravel-data, the newly acquired hopper device and the probability of two uninterrupted days before her own ship arrived, she could look forward to a period of peace. Her so-called aides were aboard the ship, where they were no doubt plotting to kill one another. Let the idiot captain deal with them. Better there than here.

With a satisfied hum, she poured the gravel—crystals of uniform color and size—into the funnel-shaped port atop the device she had just bartered for. As instructed by the trader, she put the flask into a receptacle at the bottom of the device, moved one of the bars to the right, another to the left, and pushed a button. . . .

And was in a darkness of space, confronting a new, young planetary system. Her viewpoint shifted erratically, as though the recording device was being moved or anchored. Abruptly, the viewpoint settled, only to be interrupted by the edge of an enormous . . . well, it looked rather like a membrane of some kind. A wing, perhaps. Whatever it was, it receded off one side of the view, never allowing Questioner to see what kind of creature it was part of.

She returned her attention to the sun, around which three young planets whirled in fiery rings. The recording system obviously compressed the action. Mechanical time lapse equipment, perhaps. Or, considering that the Quaggi exchanged information through these crystals, an organic system which secreted memories: information pearls, secreted over time by Quaggian oysters. In any case, the recording device was also orbiting the sun, allowing a good view of a nearby planet with eight moons, three in one orbital plane, three smaller ones, no doubt captured asteroids, with orbits at considerable angles to the other three, and two tiny orbiting rocks, close to the planet, moving very fast.

Her view could be extended in every direction. When she turned slowly to look away from the sun, she saw two gas giants and then, after careful search, the shadow arcs of several smaller, colder worlds farther out. Beyond them was a circling field of galactic flotsam and jetsam, a cometary collection, perhaps remnants of some larger and older thing, and beyond that the darkness of space sequined by a far off scatter of fully formed stars and galaxies.

She returned her attention to the nearest planet where thin plates of surface rock were thrust across great furnaces of the deep to be suddenly pimpled with a rash of baby volcanoes, each vent a basaltic core that hardened inside its ashen cone into a cyclopean crystalline pillar. Echoes from within the planet allowed her to perceive a spongy crust built up by recurrent layers of lava tubes superimposed on sedimentary structures. She could detect great caverns held aloft by basaltic pillars, one atop another, some created by fire, some by water, some by both together, some mere bubbles with a pillar or two, others measureless caverns with forests of columns.

Here and there chasms split through the layers, bringing light to the inner world. Those deepest down had been invaded by the abyssal oceans where scalding vents spewed black smoke while complicated molecules rocked in the steaming waters at the edge of the white-hot magma, spinning in the heat, accumulating and replicating themselves, adhering, separating, drifting away on the currents of the sea.

She turned her gaze outward, and this time saw in the far dark of the cometary field a thing that raised itself upon wide, pale wings and moved inward to roost upon a tiny moon of a cold planet. The Questioner watched the planet as it passed behind the sun, emerged, then arced toward her once more. As it swung by she received the fleeting impression of a wing of pale fire unfolding across the stars.

Something living sat on that cold rock, something from outside. Something akin to time; certainly something accustomed to waiting; a bat the size of a mountain range, perhaps? Or something like an octopus, with membranes stretched between its tentacles to make a winglike structure? Something very large, certainly, and something very old.

Her concentration was interrupted by a vast mooing or bellowing of radio waves coming from somewhere in the system, spreading outward in all directions, a message repeating over and over. *Come. Come. Here is a new planet, still warm. Here are fires, still burning. I await. I await.*

The message was in no words she knew, no language she had ever heard, and yet it was unmistakable in intent. It was a summons, and something within her responded to it, something she had not known was there. For the time, that was the only response. She could detect no other.

She turned to watch life erupting on the nearest planet. She could feel its burgeoning, though most of it was below the surface. It grew everywhere through the spongified outer layer of the planet, invading tubes and tunnels, caverns and caves, bubbles and blast holes, vents and veins. All spaces were room for it, all interconnected, one draining into another, some floored in fertile soil, some hollow and echoing, some running out beneath the sea where the dry stone corridors shushed to the sound of outer waters, like great ears alive to the sound of their own blood, and all of them seething with life.

Questioner could feel that life; she could sense its manifestations and varieties. She was not surprised. Life always happened. It might survive an hour, or a year, or a millennium. It might kill itself after a billion years or be killed in half a million, but on this kind of planet and on a dozen or a hundred other kinds of planets, some kind of life always happened.

All this time, the great mooing had gone on in the background and was now answered by another voice, another call coming from the outer dark, faintly and far away. Questioner increased her visual acuity to detect a point of light moving slowly toward the system. When she looked back at the planet, she saw that life had emerged upon its surface. The planetary life forms were less interesting, however, than the interlopers from afar: the one who summoned; the other who came in response, now near enough to take form, a creature sailing with fiery wings upon the solar winds.

At the edge of the cometary field the wings lifted above the plane of that field to fly across it toward the inner planets. It approached the young sun slowly, reluctantly, draggingly, ever slower the nearer it came.

And there, from near the farthest, coldest world, tentacles of cold fire reached out to catch and hold the newcomer fast. The captor transmitted a howl of triumph. The captive screamed in a blast of waveforms. The Questioner understood both howl and scream, the one of triumph, the other of terror and pain. She knew that pain would gain the victim nothing. Her, the Questioner told herself, assigning roles to this drama. The victim would be female. The attacker would be male. It was *his* tentacles that held *her* fast.

There were flares of energy and agonized shrieks of radiation as the far planet swung slowly to the left, behind the sun. When it emerged once more, one set of wings rose above it and flew directly toward the Questioner. On that far surface of cold stone and gelid gas, across half the icy sphere, the newer arrival sprawled silent and motionless amid a charred wreckage of broken wings. Probably she was dead. At this distance, Questioner could not clearly make out her shape or configuration. She strained to see, but the approaching wings filled her view, a smell of fire and sulphur, a sound of hissing, an overwhelming darkness, and the representation came to an end in a sputter of smells and electronic noise, a clutter of meaningless wave forms and chemical spewings. Beside her on the soggy soil, the device clicked and turned itself off. The data gravel had run through into its flask once more.

Had the participants in the record been Quaggi? Neither creature had looked like the Quaggi she had seen pictured or heard the Flagian describe. But then, butterflies did not look like caterpillars, either. Or vice versa.

While the record was still quite fresh in her memory, she ran the solar system through her planetary catalogue, and came up with a match. The system was numbered ARZ97405. The moonlet where the interstellar being had been assaulted and killed was so unimportant that it was not even listed, but the planet she had watched most closely was now a mankind occupied world called Newholme. Newholme. Well, now. Wasn't that coincidental. She had witnessed the birth of a planet that was on her list of planets to be visited! A planet the Flagian Trader had already sold her information about! She was moved to put Newholme upon her ASAP list, particularly since the Council of Worlds had received disturbing reports of its own. Human rights violations. The possibility of another large scale "miscalculation." Planetary instability.

The enigmatic record she had just seen tipped the scale. She would move the visit to Newholme forward in her itinerary. She would recruit some appropriate assistants and schedule the visit within the next cycle. And, when she was in the vicinity, she would stop at that far out moonlet and see just what it was that had died there. Perhaps the Brotherhood of Interstellar Traders would offer her something for that information. Unless the BIT had been there before her!

Questioner sighed, a very human sigh. She had not moved or eaten or drunk for some time, and she was experiencing that slight disorientation and fuddlement that a human might notice as weariness and discomfort. A cracking sound made her look upward, to see her own ship settling toward the soggy arena of the shuttleport. In two real time days, she had seen a million years of planetary history. Remarkable.

Steam rose. Mud splattered. The landing was sloppy, which meant the captain had taken the helm. He was also a political appointee, one who had graduated eight hundred and ninety-fifth out of a class of nine hundred at the academy. If it weren't for the professionals on board, most of them Gablians, the ship would never arrive anywhere. Dutifully, though in considerable annoyance, the Questioner rose and made her ponderous way toward the ship.

THE FAMILY TREE

Sheri Stewart Tepper was born in Colorado, where she lived until recently. For many years she worked for various non-profit-making organizations, and was a writer of children's stories. She has two grown children of her own, and one grandchild. She sold her first adult novel in 1982. As well as science fiction and fantasy novels, Sheri Tepper has written crime and horror novels under her own name and various pseudonyms. She now lives in New Mexico. Her fantasy novel *Beauty* was voted best novel of the year by readers of *Locus*, and her recent science fiction novel, *Gibbon's Decline and Fall*, was short-listed for the Arthur C. Clarke Award, as was *The Family Tree* itself.